Desert Deception

SUSANNE MATTHEWS

While some of the locations used in this novel are actual places, all characters, events and the main setting of Fortune, Arizona are fictitious. Any resemblance to actual persons living or dead, places, or actual events is strictly coincidental.

Copyright Susanne Matthews 2016
ISBN: 978-0-9948983-1-9

PUBLISHER
MHSLM Publishing

COVER ART
Danielle Doolittle

DEDICATION

TO MISTY CAIL
THIS STORY WAS BORN IN AN IDEA WE SHARED.
NEVER GIVE UP YOUR DREAMS.

.

CONTENTS

ACKNOWLEDGMENTS

As always, I want to thank my husband and my family for the patience they show when I lose myself in creating a book. Without their support I couldn't do this.

To the Scribbler Sisters, you know who you are, thank you for your encouragement and ideas. You help me through the black moments, always reminding me of the light at the end of the tunnel.

"A mine is a simple hole in the ground owned by a liar."

Mark Twain

CHAPTER ONE

Casey Stevens turned off the Apache Trail, also known as Highway 88, onto the Skansen Mine Road and headed into Fortune, slowing her hot pink and black Harley-Davidson motorcycle, careful to stay under the speed limit. Back in the day, there'd always been a deputy, hiding just up ahead behind the billboard or one of the abandoned buildings, waiting to nail some unsuspecting tourist who'd failed to slow down to the town's ridiculously low speed limit. This might be her new toy's first major road trip, but that didn't mean she wanted a ticket as a souvenir.

The joys of the open road had stopped her from dwelling on her cases, but nothing could ease the disquiet she felt about returning to the town and the memories she'd avoided for fifteen years, and the closer she got to home, the more unsettled she became. Coming back to the scene of the crime, as it were, was a mistake, and she knew it. Nothing good would come of this, but Mom had insisted, and here she was.

The Bluetooth attached to her helmet buzzed startling her out of her reverie, providing further proof that leaving Santa Fe now had been a colossal error. Ken, the second chair on her current case, had called four times since she'd left her apartment this morning. Considering it was only a seven-hour-drive, that was three times too many.

Knowing she needed to answer the call, not wanting to ride while she was distracted, especially if they argued as they had two hours ago, Casey cautiously steered the bike onto the unpaved shoulder and stopped less than ten feet from the sign in front of her. *Welcome to Fortune. Population: 26,847*

"What are they counting, jackalopes?" she mumbled aloud. When she'd left, there hadn't been fifteen thousand people in town. That had to be one hell of a population explosion.

The Bluetooth sounded again. Dismounting, she pulled off her helmet, shaking her head, sending her ponytail swaying back and forth. Pulling the smartphone out of the zippered pocket of her leather jacket, she answered the call. "Don't worry about anything. I'm heading back. I'll be there as soon as I can."

"Hello to you, too, Red," a man said and chuckled. "Someone rattling your chain?"

Closing her eyes, she smothered a groan. "Hi, Ryan," she said, recognizing the voice. "Sorry about that. I thought you were his highness calling again."

Ryan chuckled. "Baby Boss giving you a hard time?"

"You could say that. He can't seem to find anything. I swear he would lose his head if it wasn't attached." Pulling a bottle out of the insulated pouch on her tank bag, she squirted cold water into her mouth.

"Probably, but someone's always picking up after him, so he's never had to stand on his own two feet before. Now, where is it you're headed back to on this lovely Friday afternoon?"

"Santa Fe," she said huffing out the word. "This was a mistake. I don't know what made me think that incompetent ass could manage anything as complicated as filing papers on his own."

Ryan's laughter filled her ears. "I can believe that, but you aren't coming back here until your vacation is over."

"I have to. I've worked too hard to see it all go down the toilet." She wanted to stomp her foot, but what good would it do? Pacing up and down the soft shoulder, she fought to contain her annoyance.

"Listen, Cassandra," Ryan said, using her full name, knowing it would irritate her.

"Bite me."

"Love to, babe, but it didn't work when we tried it before, and Sally would have my nuts for breakfast. Call Wanda. Wonder Woman can babysit Baby Boss for a few days. If you don't want to stay the two weeks you'd planned, fine, but the woman I know is no coward."

"But—"

"No buts," he interrupted. "If I find you back in Santa Fe before Labor Day, I'll personally drag you and your cute, little ass back to your mother's house. And you know you can't hide from me. I'm the best gumshoe in the business."

"Damn you. Fine, but if I lose my job because of this, you'll be supporting me."

He chuckled. "I could start my own harem. Listen, before we get completely off-track, I called to tell you I found the guy who filled the order for the building supplies."

"Get out of here! So is he going to help us or not?"

"Help, big time."

"Where was he?"

"Someone paid him to take an overseas vacation, but his mother and the fear of God convinced him to tell the truth."

"And you didn't help persuade him?" she asked, knowing he had probably scared the dickens out of the young man in question.

"Let's just say I showed him the error of his ways, and before you ask, I didn't lay a finger on him." He laughed. "I didn't have to. My bark is worse than my bite."

"When you put it that way, this should be all we need to get the case thrown out. How can I ever thank you?"

"By enjoying your time with your family. Hell, go hiking in those spooky mountains of yours … who knows you might stumble on that missing gold mine."

Casey laughed. "Like that's ever going to happen. If no one's found the Lost Dutchman by now, it doesn't exist."

"Well, the legend says the man had gold under his bed when he died."

"Right, and the Apache claim the doorway to hell is there, too, but so far, no one's found that either."

"You know what they say: where there's smoke, there's fire. Call me if things live down to your lowest expectations, and you need a laugh. Otherwise, I'll see you in a couple of weeks."

"I will, and thanks, Ryan. You always come through, don't you?"

"What can I say? I'm gifted."

Ending the call, she finished the water, returned the empty bottle to the bag, pulled on her helmet, and mounted the bike. A motorcycle wasn't as comforting as living, breathing horseflesh beneath her, but the engine's vibrations soothed her frazzled nerves. Easing her Harley back onto the road, she left the town sign behind her. She'd do her best to enjoy her time with family—she just wished they were meeting anywhere but here.

Located fifty miles southeast of Phoenix, on the edge of the Superstition Mountains in the Tonto National Forest, Fortune had become a boom town when Hezekiah Skansen struck gold in 1841. In its heyday, the family had owned and operated more than ten mines in the area, but like so many other pits, the gold vein broke, and one by one, the mines closed, leaving ghost towns filled with lost dreams in their wake.

But Fortune fared better than most. The ranchers who'd grazed cattle and horses on their land thanks to irrigation from creeks fed by the Salt River had stayed, but what had kept the town alive had been the creation of the Tonto National Monument in 1907, followed by the building of the Roosevelt Dam in 1911, creating six lakes that had turned a reasonably the barren section of desert into an excellent recreational area. The region attracted all kinds of people from amateur archeologists and paleontologists to hardened prospectors searching for gold. Northern residents, seeking heat in the dead of winter, not wanting the overcrowding of the larger cities like Phoenix and

Scottsdale, flocked to the area as did avid naturalists attracted by the beauty of the Sonoran Desert.

At the insistence of the Skansen family, who'd owned just about all of the town by 1910, downtown Fortune had retained its Wild West façade, and over the years had served as a backdrop for countless B movie westerns. Since one of the Skansen mines still put out gold, it provided some employment, but the town's real income continued to be tourism.

"For me, it was hell, plain and simple, and here I am walking right back into it," she fumed, knowing the next fourteen days would be challenging at best.

Within minutes, she entered the town, noting the way it had dressed itself up for the celebration. The boardwalks had been swept clean, weak boards replaced by new ones that hadn't yet faded to dull gray. The last thing anyone wanted was for an unsuspecting tourist to twist an ankle crashing through a rotten board. It wouldn't take much to imagine the sheriff and his deputy coming down the street on horseback rather than in a modern-day squad car. Time stood still in Fortune.

Driving along Main Street, she passed *Johnson's Livery Stable* advertising horses and mules for rent. *Juan's Barber Shop* offered a shave or haircut … ten dollars instead of ten cents. A sign in the window of *The Fortune Savings and Loan* proclaimed an interest rate of only two percent on new mortgages. The only thing missing was the wooden Indian in front of *Bailey's Sweet Shop*—formerly *Bailey's Cigar Store*—no doubt a necessary concession to the times.

Older shops and stores, some of them rubbing elbows with new businesses housed in heritage buildings, were festooned in red, white, and blue bunting. While some of the original adobe facades might boast a new coat of whitewash, for the most part it looked as if time had crept backwards. She shook her head. Fortune survived as it always had, making the best of what it had, and shaking a stubborn fist to the sky.

Two doors down from *Barclay's Bar and Grill*, renamed the *Golden Nugget Saloon* for Gold Rush Days, stood her sister's bakery and coffee shop, *Cookies and Cream*. Business was brisk judging by the steady stream of people moving in and out of the place. To afford the costs associated with opening her own business, Randy and her four-year-old son, Jaxon, had moved in with her parents, something Casey considered a fate worse than death.

The only store that had ever interested her was *Walker's Emporium*, a fancy name for what had been the town's first general store. It had been her favorite haunt as a teenager. Mr. Walker had always stocked a large number of books, and there she could escape to new worlds and enjoy wonderful adventures. Overweight, bullied, a misfit in her own town, reading had been the only thing to get her through those awkward, unhappy teen years.

After easing her modern-day horse into one of the parking spots across the street from the shop and turning off the engine, she removed her helmet, yanked the elastic out of her hair, shook her head side to side in imitation of a model in some shampoo commercial, and ran her fingers through her tangled curls. In concession to the heat of late-August, and the bright sun, she lowered the zipper on the black leather jacket she wore, removed her mirrored sunglasses from her tank bag, and put them on.

While most of the people parading along the boardwalk appeared to be tourists, she noticed a few older faces she recognized. More than one person passing by took a second look at the woman in skin-tight, black leather. She felt their gazes following her as she sauntered over to Walker's, helmet hanging casually from her hand the way another woman's purse might. Smiling, proud of the way she'd transformed herself over the years, she wondered if anyone realized who she was.

Casey stood on the sidewalk admiring her old hangout, letting the past claim her before pushing the brass handle to open the door. The antique bell tinkled, announcing her arrival just as it had years ago. Memories of the time spent in this place washed over her. The familiar aroma of coffee beans, exotic spices, candle wax, and old books surrounded her. Ceiling fans spun lazily—more for show than for cooling since the store was air conditioned. Eagerly, she stepped forward, anxious to see Mr. Walker again. They'd spent hours together going over maps and encyclopedias, examining the latest edition of *National Geographic*, discussing the wonderful places they would visit if they could.

While the front of the store looked just as it had with its mixture of real and reproduction Indian artifacts, crystals, polished petrified wood, and other memorabilia from the area, sadness filled her. No matter what he'd been doing, Mr. Walker had always come at the sound of the bell. Perhaps he didn't own the store anymore. It was common practice for new owners to keep a business's original name. Goodwill was a marketable commodity these days, and nowhere more so than in Fortune.

"Hello, is anyone here?" Her voice echoed in the emptiness of the shop.

A touch nervous—the insecurity of the past catching up with her—she moved through the archway into the addition that housed the bulk of the store's retail items, passing by computer terminals and shelves heaped with books, candles, pottery, glassware, and native jewelry along with bags of fake gold dust and gold-plated nuggets. The walls boasted several decorative mirrors and watercolors of the mountains and the desert, as well as other wall hangings made of iron, wood, or some combination. She started when a man cleared his throat.

Looking in the direction of the sound, she was pleasantly surprised when a stranger stepped out from between two rows of shelves. The man was most definitely not the one she'd expected.

Tall, well over six feet, with broad shoulders and a narrow waist, he wore jeans that hugged him in all the right places and a tight-fitting green T-shirt with Walker's Emporium emblazoned in bright, yellow letters on his chest under the outline of Superstition Mountain. Clean shaven, with warm brown eyes peering at her from behind large black framed glasses, the arms of which disappeared into hair, the color of rich, dark chocolate, a touch too long and yet, just right on him, he was quite possibly one of the most attractive men she'd seen in a long time. His bronzed complexion testified to his Spanish ancestry and time outdoors, and from the biceps revealed by his shirt sleeves, he was no ordinary shopkeeper. Her mouth watered.

This man, familiar and yet not, drew her as none had ever done. He could have been a conquistador, one who'd been left behind when Coronado had abandoned his search for *Cibola,* the fabled seven cities of gold, the blood of his ancestors thick in his veins. As he approached, the scent of his sandalwood cologne tantalized her.

"Can I help you?" he asked, stopping next to the cash register a few feet away from her, his whiskey-smooth voice caressing her as did his bold gaze.

She cleared her throat, her tongue darting out to lick her dry lips. Calling on the persona she used in court, she smiled. "I was looking for Mr. Walker. Is he around?" Her heart pounded loudly in her ears. Could he hear it?

"I'm Cole Walker, but you must mean my dad, Senior. I'm sorry, but he isn't here right now. Is there something I can do for you?"

This god is Cole Walker Junior? her brain screamed, as raging hormones threatened to take over and destroy what little common sense she'd managed to find.

"I … I didn't recognize you," she said haltingly, wondering whose husky voice that was.

She'd always liked Cole, the quiet, smart guy who'd smiled at her once in a while—the boy who'd kept to himself, carried books around, and wanted to learn things the way she had. At one time, she'd fantasized an entire relationship with him, one that had ended with a "happily ever after." Mesmerized, her gaze searched his puzzled face, eventually finding the teenager she remembered in the chiseled features of the man before her. Like her, Cole had undergone massive physical changes. Even taller than he'd been, gone was his acne and hundred-pound weakling scrawny frame. Instead, she stared at perfection.

"I'm sorry I missed him. Where is he?" Not that it was any of her business.

"My parents are visiting my sister in Florida," he answered easily, that downhome country friendliness in his voice, but his eyes betrayed his curiosity. "They travel a lot these days."

"That's great." Her brain functioned again, albeit slowly. "I'll bet he's having a wonderful time. He always wanted to travel. We used to talk about all the places in the world we would visit—"

"You know my father?" The confusion in his voice matched his furrowed brow.

"I do." Casey smiled. "When I was growing up in Fortune, this place was like my second home."

He stared at her, making her feel a trifle uncomfortable. When she removed her sunglasses, the shock of recognition was enough to make her laugh.

"I don't believe it. Cassandra Stevens? That can't be you."

The look on his face was one of stunned approval. Surprised he remembered her name, even if it was the one she despised, associating it with the bullied girl she'd been, she nodded. "In the flesh, but people call me Casey now."

"I heard you were coming home for Gold Rush Days. Your mother talks about you all the time. So, you're a big-city attorney. I'm impressed." He looked her up and down again, the appreciative gleam in his eye hard to miss. "You're a hell of an improvement over Mr. Stone."

Horace Stone had been practicing law in Fortune for as long as she could remember. In fact, he'd been the one to trigger her interest in the career she'd chosen.

"Thanks. I guess Mom still feels the need to feed the gossip mill." Her voice was laced with sarcasm. Some things hadn't changed.

"Did you want something? Or did you stop by just to see my father?"

9

"Actually, I did, but since I'm here, I might as well pick up a new novel to read while I'm home."

His gaze raked her once more, and Casey fought to maintain her casual stance. She wasn't the fat girl, with thick glasses, who'd walked through her teen years with her nose in a book, praying no one would notice her and would leave her alone. The carrot hair she'd hated had darkened to copper, and while it was still unmanageable at times, she'd learned to tame it when she had to. Her leather outfit hugged her curves, and although she was beginning to feel uncomfortably warm, she wasn't sure if the cause was her clothing or the man standing in front of her.

Needing to cool off, she slowly unzipped her jacket the rest of the way, revealing the skin-tight, low cut tank top beneath. His eyes followed the gaping zipper teeth as they opened, the gesture making her feel even warmer.

"I can help you with that." His voice was husky, his eyes fixed on her cleavage.

"Help me with what?" Her voice was breathy and so unlike hers she barely recognized it.

Images of the way he might help her ran through her mind, doing nothing to cool her overheated libido.

"You wanted a book, remember? I've moved things around, but I can help you find one."

Casey felt her cheeks heat anew, embarrassed he might see how much he affected her. Ignoring her discomfort, she smiled, hoping she appeared cool and confident.

"No, that's okay. I'll just browse the shelves on my own. I'm sure I'll find something in here I like."

"Go right ahead. If you need anything, just holler."

She sauntered away from the cash register, feeling his eyes on her, the sway in her hip more pronounced because of her heeled boots. If she played her cards right, maybe they could spend some time together getting reacquainted, not that they'd actually been friends back then. Hell, they'd exchanged more words just now than they ever had.

Turning to look over her shoulder, she grinned, her fingers itching to follow his as he ran them nervously through his hair. She'd definitely had an effect on him—she hoped it was as strong as the one he'd had on her.

* * * *

Cole straightened the magazines and newspapers, trying to look busy while Casey browsed the bookshelves, unable to do anything but think about the woman a mere twenty feet away. Only two years older than she was, he remembered her—at least he recalled the girl she'd been—and the woman standing ten feet away from him had certainly changed.

She still had the peaches and cream complexion associated with her Irish ancestors, skin that could burn in the shade as he recalled, but her freckles weren't as pronounced as they'd been. She'd dropped at least fifty pounds, and that carrot top she'd worn in tight braids against her head was now a fiery crown of flames. Her soda bottle bottom glasses were gone, no doubt replaced by laser eye surgery or contacts, but her expressive eyes, sometimes blue, sometimes green, but always with a touch of gold in them, were as familiar as ever. That was how he'd recognized her. Once he'd seen those eyes, he'd never been able to forget them.

How long had it been? She'd been sixteen, a senior at Fortune High, when he'd gone off to the University of Texas at El Paso, and while he'd come back that first summer, he'd been too busy helping Dad around the store to do much more than nod and say hello once in a while. He hadn't grown into his body yet, and while the acne had improved, he'd still been too shy to ask any girl out. He'd fantasized doing so, and in his dreams she'd always said yes, but the reality was, he might as well have had elective mutism when it came to talking to her.

Those afternoons when he worked in the back unpacking boxes of reproductions and other souvenirs, he hid behind the bookshelves, closed his eyes, let her voice wrap around him, and listened to her sharing her dreams.

Casey, the shorter name suited her, exuded confidence and poise, and wasn't afraid to take risks, as her motorcycle proved. It took a lot of self-assurance to stand in a courtroom and question witnesses let alone address the jury. Looking at her now, he tried to picture her in a staid business suit and failed. No, this new Casey would wear "look at me clothes" and do it with pizazz. She wouldn't hide from the world ever again.

Despite his best effort, he was having a hard time controlling his body's response to her, something that rarely happened to him. Taking a deep breath, he tore his eyes away from her leather-clad bottom, and returned to sorting the new shipment of books, trying to immerse himself in the jacket blurbs, but failing. He jumped when he heard her shout.

"Holy shit!"

Dropping the book he was holding, he pushed his way through the boxes of candles, books, and other items crowding the aisle to see what had upset her.

"What's wrong?" He hurried to her side, worried that she'd somehow hurt herself. While it was true, the worse injury you could get from a book was a papercut, this close to the desert, unwanted insects and reptiles sometimes managed to sneak in. Last week, he'd returned a tarantula to the great outdoors. The big, hairy spiders might be harmless, but they scared the daylights out of the tourists.

"Nothing's wrong, but you have all of CJ Coleson's books shoved back here where no one can see them. They should be out front."

The look of disgust on her face made him laugh.

"I take it you're a fan."

"Well, duh! Of course I'm a fan, isn't everyone? He's a great author even though he's the Howard Hughes of writers—a total recluse. How come you have his latest book? It isn't due out in paperback for another two weeks."

Cole ran his fingers through his hair, a nervous gesture he made when he was caught off guard. "I know the author." The white lie slid off his tongue before he could stop it.

"Get out of here! You know CJ Coleson?" she asked, excitement lighting up her face. "How?"

"We went to school together." Another half-truth.

"In Texas?"

He nodded, hoping she would change the topic soon.

"Well, he's Arizona born and bred, I'm sure of it. He's either from around here, or he's spent time here. Reading those books is like coming home—better even. Is that his real name?"

Turning away from her, he tried to think of an answer that would help him out of the quicksand in which he'd inadvertently stepped. The truth always came out, and usually at the worst possible moment. Sharing his secret with a virtual stranger wasn't an option, but he was pretty sure she wasn't going to let it go.

"He's from Arizona and has spent considerable time in the area, but he uses a pen name. CJ and I are very close. I get advance copies of his books when his publisher releases them. Technically I'm not supposed to display them yet, so don't go broadcasting it," he answered, more sharply than he'd intended, hoping that would end her snooping.

"Who would I tell?" The look on her face told him she thought he was being ridiculous.

"I don't know. Maybe some of your friends in New Mexico." He'd put a little more heat into his voice than he'd needed, but he was dying here, sinking deeper and deeper by the minute.

She rolled her eyes and snorted. "Let me get right on that. I'll tell them to drop everything, and drive almost seven hours to Fortune, Arizona, to buy a book they'll be able to pick up at home in a matter of days."

Sarcasm dripped from her voice again. He would hate to be on the stand if she was questioning him. She would rip a liar to shreds in seconds.

"I get it. My comment was a little over the top, but if you're a fan, you know he doesn't like the spotlight. I'm a little protective of our friendship."

"A little protective? There are she-bears who could take lessons from you," she scolded. "I know how close some of you frat buddies can be. Knowing you know my favorite author, and won't tell me who he is, will probably drive me crazy, but I'll let you off the hook—this time."

He exhaled and relaxed, grateful for the temporary reprieve, knowing damn well she wouldn't let the matter drop and would try to ferret out the secret sooner rather than later. His gaze still fixed on her, he watched as she picked up two books, including the CJ Coleson one not yet released.

Grinning at him, she walked back to the cash register. "Getting to read *Black Widow* early will do for now, but I'll be back. When I am, I'll get you to tell me all about the talented man behind Sheriff Tate Silvers."

Knowing he would see her again, even if it were only to pry information out of him, pleased him more than he expected it to.

"Maybe I can convince you to get a book autographed for me." She smiled sweetly. "After all, you and I are old friends, too ... sort of." She batted her eyelids rapidly.

Chuckling, he stepped behind the counter to conceal the evidence of his lust.

"I'll see what I can do." He hoped he'd managed to hide the way she'd affected him. "Are you ready to check out?"

Instead of answering, she stared at him as if she could somehow see into his soul. He could see how that might intimidate a reluctant witness. At last, she handed him the books and her credit card.

Within minutes, he'd scanned them, totaled the sale, placed her purchases in a reusable bag and handed her the slip to sign.

"Compliments of Walker's," he said as he handed the bag to her.

"Thanks. Maybe I'll see you around town while I'm home."

As she took the sack from him, their fingers touched and desire barreled through him as it never had.

"Maybe. Come back anytime," he said, surprised by how much he meant the words.

Standing at the store window, he watched her cross the street to her bike. Once there, she secured the package in the motorcycle's tank bag, donned her helmet, and threw her leg over the seat. The bike started smoothly. She glanced back toward the store as if she knew he was watching her, waved, and then eased the bike into traffic.

Sighing, he turned back to his sorting, but the image of the woman in black leather wouldn't go away.

CHAPTER TWO

Twenty minutes later, Casey pulled into the driveway of her childhood home, turned off the engine, and engaged the kickstand. Mom had mentioned the town had grown, but she hadn't expected what she'd seen. Hotels and motels, many of them with "No Vacancy" signs lit, shared the land with low-rise condos, houses, mini malls, and fast food restaurants.

Fifteen years ago, the large adobe and stone, two-story house, its veranda on stilts providing a storage area beneath it and ready access to the storm and storage cellar, had been isolated, surrounded by acres of land kept reasonably green by irrigation, land that had been in her family for more than one hundred and fifty years. Today, the laneway to her home had become a road, and while there was still grassland to the south and west of the house, a large condo development stood no more than two hundred yards east of it with a few houses built across the street where cattle had once roamed.

Unlike in days past, there were no horses or cattle dotting the landscape, no chickens scrambling in the yard. Most of the outbuildings, including the bunk house where the hired hands had slept, were gone. The stable, where she'd spent the few happy hours she hadn't spent at Walker's, was now a garage, and the corral had been replaced by a fenced, in-ground pool, desert willows at one end of the compound providing much needed shade. Gazing to her left, she realized she'd missed her home, but she still doubted the wisdom of coming here for a two-week stay. Dismounting, she removed her helmet, took her suitcase and backpack out of her saddlebags, and added the books from Walker's to her backpack. Braced for the inevitable, she walked toward the veranda.

"Cassandra Maureen Stevens! You lied to me." Her mother's righteous anger was palpable, the screen door slamming hard behind her. She unlatched the child security gate and stormed down the stairs. "You said you were driving home. You didn't say you were riding that death machine here."

Casey took a calming breath. Arguing wouldn't help—it never had. While she loved her mother dearly, they were like oil and water—great together, but they just didn't mix.

"Hi, Mom. I've missed you, too," she answered, approaching the veranda steps. "I knew you would worry if I'd told you I'd decided to take the bike instead of the car. In my defense, when I made these plans, I didn't know it would be ready in time, so I didn't lie. I just withheld information."

"Lawyers. You say one thing and mean another, but I'm glad you're here." Her mother shook her head. "Lying by omission is still lying, Casey, and you know it, but you did the right thing. Had I realized you were coming home on that thing, I wouldn't have slept a wink."

Her mother, dressed in denim crop pants and a blue and gold print top, stood with her hands on her hips, staring menacingly at the motorcycle, obviously fighting the urge to walk over and kick it.

Helmet and suitcase in one hand, backpack slung over her shoulder, Casey moved to the bottom of the steps, and pulled her mother to her with her free arm. "Mom, like it or not, it isn't only my hair that makes me a throwback to Great-Grandma Stevens. When I'm riding, it's like I'm on Ginger again, and we're tearing into the wind. I wish I could make you understand that."

"You always did have a way with words." Her mother

stepped back, a worried smile on her face, her eyes filled with concern. "I love you, sweetheart. I don't want to get a call one night from the police telling me they had to scrape you off the pavement somewhere."

"You won't. I'm careful, really I am, and Harley's are the best bikes out there."

"That may be, but it isn't *your* driving that worries me."

Subject closed.

"I know you told me things had changed, but … I didn't expect all this." Casey indicated the nearby condos.

"Despite what you've always believed, time moves on, even in Fortune," her mother said tucking her arm in hers and walking up the stairs. "We may not have intended to do it, but once your father sold some of the land and gave up ranching, we were both happier. Working full time at the university was your dad's dream come true. He didn't mind the commute, and I could spend more time sewing and indulging my passion. Today, we might miss the peace and quiet we had, but that's a small price to pay for helping you and Randy realize your dreams."

Not wanting to dwell on the past, Casey nodded.

"I see toys." She pointed to a miniature riding tractor, large orange construction vehicles, and other tiny cars. "Where's my nephew?" Although Mom and Dad had met her in Phoenix in April, she hadn't seen Randy or Jaxon since Christmas, eight months ago. Photographs helped, but they weren't as good as the real thing.

"Jaxon's gotten so big," her mother answered, as though the fact the child was growing amazed her. "I swear I put him to bed in pajamas that fit, and he outgrows them overnight." She chuckled. "Dad took him fishing on Canyon Lake this morning. They caught a few bass and some trout which I'll cook for supper tonight. Jaxon's excited about eating his own fish. He made me promise not to mix it up with the others. Randy came home early today. She's upstairs getting him cleaned up for supper now."

"After raising two daughters, I'll bet Dad loves having a boy around."

Her mother chuckled. "He says it's his duty to do guy things with him," she answered a note of sadness in her voice, "but believe me, he adores every minute of it."

Casey didn't comment. With the child's father dead, the Stevens family was the only family Jaxon had. She followed her mother into the house as anxious to see her nephew again as her mother was to show him off.

"Randy, Austin, Casey's here," her mother called loudly.

Her sister's delighted scream echoed from upstairs. "We'll be down in a minute."

Heavy, hurried footsteps announced her father's arrival, a huge welcoming smile on his face. He was thinner than she remembered, but when he opened his arms, she pulled her backpack from her shoulders, dropped it next to her suitcase and helmet, and ran into them.

"Hi, Daddy," she said softly, wrapped tightly in a warm, familiar hug. "I've missed you."

"We've all missed you. Welcome home, baby."

The scent of his aftershave as well as the familiar pet name brought back memories of her youth and his unwavering love.

"Let me look at you." Holding her at arms' length, his eyebrows lifted quizzically as he took in the suit she was wearing, and he whistled. "Nice outfit. It's too bad they didn't have one small enough for you."

"Very funny," she said, scrunching up her face at him. "It's for protection. It has to fit snugly."

"Sure it does," he replied with a wink. "I just hope you can breathe in it. Let me guess … those heeled boots help your feet stay in place, too."

"Nah, I wear them because they make me look taller." She giggled. "You've lost some weight. I guess chasing after a four-year-old is good for you."

"What on earth have you got in here, girl?" her mother complained, hefting the heavy backpack off the floor.

"Leave it, Mom. It's got my laptop, toiletries, and a couple of new books in it. I'll carry it up in a minute."

"Don't tell me you took the time to stop at Walker's on the way home?" The disapproving tone of her voice promised a reprimand.

"Well, I did drive right by. I wanted to say hello to Mr. Walker, but he wasn't there. I did speak to Cole Junior though. I guess he runs the place now."

Mom nodded her head. "Senior semi-retired about five years ago, but still helps out now and then, since young Cole is a police officer and one of our volunteer firefighters."

That explained the muscles. The sound of footsteps hurrying down the stairs filled the room, yanking her away from thoughts of the new store manager. Miranda, who, like herself, had shortened her name, looked happier and more alive than she had in ages. No doubt the miniature Spiderman at her side had a lot to do with that. Losing David in Afghanistan had almost destroyed her, but discovering she carried his child had pulled her back from the brink.

Randy, fifteen months younger than Casey, favored their mother, her Mexican roots clearly evident. Her sister had brown hair, so dark it was almost black, her mother's olive complexion, and their father's deep blue eyes. Her tall, lean body belied the fact she'd had a child. As a teenager, she'd been outgoing and popular, everything Casey had wished to be. Smiling, her sister disengaged the little, tow-headed boy hiding behind her leg and squatted down beside him.

"What's with you, Spiderman? You remember Aunt Casey, don't you?"

Her biological clock, which had been ticking annoyingly loud lately, sent a pang of regret through her. "That can't be Jaxon," she said, smiling at her nephew. "You've gotten so big."

Jaxon laughed and jumped at her, almost knocking her down.

"You look like Batgirl without a mask," he stated, as if that settled everything.

Casey smiled. "Thanks, I think." She struggled to speak because of the unexpected lump in her throat.

"Be prepared for him to talk your ear off if you let him," Randy said with a grin. "Especially if you know anything about superheroes."

"Aunt Casey, do you want to see my *Lego* collection? I made most of them all by myself," Jaxon stated proudly.

Her mother shook her head. "That little guy is into those blocks the way you were into books at that age."

"I'm learning to read all by myself, too," he boasted.

"Let me get these off, and I'll come and see what you have," Casey answered, melting in the leathers she still wore.

Quickly removing her protective garments, she hung them in the hall closet, and returned to the living room, eager to spend time with the newest member of her family.

Jaxon waited on the steps for her.

"I've got another loose tooth," he said, grinning broadly to show her the space where he'd already lost one of his lower incisors. "The tooth fairy gave me five dollars for it. I'm saving for another *Lego* set."

"Wow. I think I had to lose five teeth to get that big a pay day." She chuckled.

"It's called infation. Money isn't worth as much now as it was in the olden days," he parroted. "That's why Grandpa and I had to bring home supper tonight."

Casey burst out laughing at the way the words rolled smoothly off his tongue. His facial expression and voice intonation mimicked her father perfectly, even if there was a missing letter in his special word.

"And I thank you for that. Fresh fish is one of my favorite meals." She reached over and hugged her sister. "He's great, sis. You've done a wonderful job of raising him. I'm really proud of you."

"He is pretty wonderful, isn't he?"

"Yes, and he looks just like David. I wonder when his hair will darken, if it ever does."

A momentary look of sadness crossed Randy's face. It was gone almost as quickly as it had appeared.

"We'll see. David's never did. If it's okay with you, I'm going to grab a quick shower while you're entertaining him."

"Take all the time you need," Casey answered. "Shall we?"

Following her nephew into what used to be Mom's craft room, now clearly a boy's play area, she admired the various red, blue, yellow, and white *Lego* sets displayed proudly on the shelf, next to some of the gray ones she knew were for older kids.

"And you put these all together by yourself?" she asked.

"Grandpa helped with the harder ones," he admitted. "I've got a new one started. Want to see?"

It had been ages since she'd played with plastic building blocks. "Sure do."

She grinned. Ryan was right. Coming home had been the right thing to do.

* * * *

The bell above the door tinkled, indicating a customer. Glancing at his watch, Cole frowned. It was almost six. He sighed, stepped away from the boxes he still had to unpack, and walked through the archway to the front of the store.

"Afternoon, Hal," he said smiling.

Despite the twenty-five-year age difference, Hal Rankin, chief of the small but highly effective Fortune Police Department, was not only his employer but also one of his closest friends. Normally, such a small town wouldn't have its own police force, but while the population was just over twenty-five thousand, the large number of tourists constantly moving through the area made local policing necessary. Knowing the emporium wouldn't be enough to support him when he'd returned to Fortune, Cole had applied to the Police Department, grateful for the part-time position he'd gotten. Of course, that had been before CJ Coleson hit it big. Lately balancing his writing career with the demands of his job on the force, his volunteer firefighting responsibilities, and the emporium was getting to be too much.

"I was just about to close for the day. What can I do for you?"

"I won't keep you long. Nice to see you aren't any worse for the wear. I heard you and Drew Macintosh had a few last night."

Cole chuckled. "You could say that."

He remembered Casey's comment about the gossip mill. Knowing he was the topic of conversation for the day didn't bother him, but it would've annoyed her.

"The morning was rough, but by noon, I'd more or less gotten over the aftereffects of self-induced alcohol poisoning."

Hal laughed. "That's one way to put it. I'm glad Drew made it back in one piece. Wish to hell David had, too. Is he home to stay?"

"Not sure yet," he answered, shrugging his shoulders. "He's stationed at Camp Waterdog, but he's finished next month. I know his mother would like him to stick around now that his dad's gone, take over the helicopter sightseeing business, but from what he told me, he hasn't made a decision. Apparently someone else is involved, and as drunk as he was, he wouldn't say more."

"Well, you tell him that if he decides to stay, I've got an opening for a full-time officer. Cletus is retiring at the end of September, and I could sure use another man who knows how to handle himself in a fight and use a gun. The fact that he can fly doesn't hurt one damn bit. Search and Rescue want to park a bird here, and if we had a pilot available, we'd get up in the air that much faster. Might've saved those hikers a few years ago. You're sure I can't talk you into coming on the force full-time? I heard you've got your pilot's license, even though you don't like people to know about it."

"That has to be Mom bragging again," he said displeased. One of these days, his mother would let a little too much slip.

SUSANNE MATTHEWS

"Sorry, Hal. I pilot planes, not choppers. Considering the hours you've been working me lately," Cole answered shaking his head, "I *am* full-time, but I'll pass along your message."

Hal nodded. "Before I forget, Melba wants me to get a couple of books for Corrina. She's staying at the house until the baby comes."

"I've got a few medical thrillers she might like, and the new CJ Coleson book Melba wants is in. You might as well pick that up, too. Follow me."

"Melba's not the only one who reads those," Hal said. "I'm partial to the adventures of Tate Silvers myself. He's quite the lady's man." He winked. "If I spent as much time in the saddle as he does, I'd be too bushed to do much else. That man has stamina."

Feeling the heat rise in his face, Cole led Hal over to the section of books he knew Corrina enjoyed, eager to avoid a discussion about CJ Coleson for the second time today. Why had he presumed Melba was the only one reading those books? He had hundreds of male fans ... He just hadn't expected Hal to be one of them.

"Was there anything else you wanted?" he asked, pulling a couple of books off the shelf and handing them to Hal, before moving farther along to get a copy of *Black Widow*. "I expect you've got next month's shift schedule ready."

"I do, but that's not the reason I'm here. I finally got the results about those bones we found back in May. The forensic anthropologist consulting with the Arizona Department of Public Safety in Phoenix had a surprise for me. She identified the remains based on dental records."

"Dental records?" Cole asked confused. "The bones we recovered were from the lower body."

"Those were, but a bunch of forensic tech students from the university combed the area two months ago and found a lower mandible with the teeth intact. They eventually matched it to dental records. DNA testing proved all of the bones belong to the same person."

24

"If he had dental records, then the body couldn't be as old as we thought. I figured he was some ancient prospector who'd disappeared on the mountain decades ago."

"So did I, but the man's name was Leon Turner, age seventy ... used to live in Fortune, but moved to Apache Junction when he retired about ten years ago—retired, nice way to say the man lost his job when the bulk of the remaining mines closed. He worked security for Skansen Mining. My guess is knowing the lay of the land like he did, the old fool decided to increase his pension by doing a little prospecting. He could've been looking for the Lost Dutchman Mine for all I know, but my guess is he was snooping around Skansen's deserted mineshafts, must've gone out on a ledge and slipped off. Doesn't take much for a man to lose his footing, and the guy was past his prime. Since *Lucky Seven* is still viable, rumor has it there's gold in the other pits too, and while the company doesn't deny it, they claim modernizing the equipment to get it out would be too expensive for the return they'd get."

Cole carried the copy of *Black Widow* back to the cash and set it down next to the other two.

"It's amazing we don't find more damn fools out there with broken necks. Superstition Mountain and the wilderness are dangerous at the best of times, but around those old mines, the ground's unstable. Some of those pits were holes in the ground they've just backfilled." He shook his head. "Ever since those guys dry-panned a small fortune in gold nuggets last summer after the quake, we've had more and more prospectors coming through town, desperate to hit it rich. The campground's still overflowing, just as it's been despite the hot summer we've had. I guess there's still no cure for gold fever."

"Unfortunately, no, nor for stupidity, and I think it takes more than a little of both to go off into the mountains when the temperature's well above one hundred and ten degrees in the shade, if you can find any. The quake really shook things up, and then those two days of rain ... Those nuggets could've come from anywhere, including the Skansen mines. It's a real shame, but it all comes down to greed no matter how you sugarcoat it. I've had Eddy Ramos in complaining at least a dozen times in the last two months. Sometimes he doesn't seem to be firing on all cylinders, but he's incensed about this. It seems people are trespassing all over the place, and he wants me to make an example of them."

"Of course he does. Just because he's the company's CEO doesn't mean he actually has to do anything, like posting signs or hiring more security."

"Security costs money, and if he can get us to do it for free..." He shook his head. "No matter how many no trespassing signs Skansen Mining posts, if someone wants to get into the mine, they will." Hal frowned and huffed out a frustrated breath. "I talked to Ms. Minerva a couple of months ago when he came to me the first time and asked her to consider cementing the entrances to those old shafts, but she refused. She's got this thing about the historical significance of the area and her legacy. Eddy's on my side, claims keeping the shafts the way they do costs them a fortune in liability insurance. He's looking into solar-powered security cameras, but so far that hasn't happened. He mentioned selling off some of the excess land and a few of the unpatented mining claims from the early strikes."

"Eddy can say that all he wants, but we both know he can't do it. He may have the title of CEO, but when it comes right down to it, Ms. Minerva runs that company, and everyone knows it. She won't part with as much as a grain of sand. I don't understand why she hasn't cut him off. When she dies, he'll blow through that money like a hot knife through butter."

"I agree." Hal tipped back his Stetson and leaned against the counter. "He's got two ex-wives to support, only because he was smart enough not to marry the others. He's moved in with Minerva, claims it's his responsibility to watch out for her, but my guess is his latest skirt gave him the heave-ho and kicked him out of that fancy condominium, and his aunt is too damn nice to do the same."

Cole chuckled and rubbed his chin. "That man just doesn't learn." He frowned. "When does the anthropologist think Leon died?"

"Twelve to fifteen months ago, probably closer to twelve. That's about the time of the quake, so it's possible the mountain shook him off, just like it did those nuggets. The animals had lots of time to scatter his remains, but the jeans kept most of his lower half intact."

Cole shook his head. "Got to hand it to denim for durability. I figured, given the shape of the bones, they'd been out there for years. Didn't anyone report him missing?"

"Apparently not. Since we have no proof Leon's death was anything but an unfortunate accident, Apache Junction PD have taken over the case, but they've run into a little problem."

"What's the issue?"

"According to government records, Leon's living in Apache Junction and still collecting his pension and social security. His bank account's been active—rent paid, regular withdrawals made—but that's damn hard to do when you're scattered all over hell's half acre."

"Are we looking at identity theft?" he frowned.

"Maybe, but he'd have to be one brave son of a bitch to move into the guy's apartment. No. They've found family—a nephew you might know—Trent Gibbs."

"That's a name I haven't heard in a while. He was never one of my favorite people. Obviously he and his uncle weren't close if he didn't even know the man was missing." The idea the poor old guy might've lain there alive but injured, before eventually succumbing to the heat and lack of water, twisted his gut.

"Can't be sure of that. Gibbs works for Skansen Mining, and they want me to have a talk with him—see what I think of the guy. The police have called the bank and have put a hold on the account. Apparently there's a safety deposit box, too. AJPD will get a warrant for it and follow up with the landlady, see when she saw him last or at least describe the person who's been using the apartment. Trent works for Skansen Mining, so I'll go over there and talk to him tomorrow."

"From what I remember of him, Trent wasn't exactly Mr. Reliability." Cole scratched his head. "I can't see him going out of his way to help anyone. He looks after Number One, and that's it. Mom told me his wife finally got fed up with his antics, took the kids, and went back to her family somewhere in the Midwest, I think. What does he do at Skansen's?"

"He's their head accountant."

Cole burst out laughing. "Seriously?"

Hal nodded.

"As I recall, he and Eddy were thick as thieves in school, which is probably how he got the job, but he's the last man I'd put in charge of my books. Hell, if I shook hands with him, I would count my fingers afterwards and check for my watch. He almost got kicked out of school for taking bets on the high school football team." Using the electronic scanner, he totaled the sale. "I realize this was labelled an accident, but it's possible whoever's using that money knows what really happened. Maybe they had something to do with his fall."

"True enough, but unless someone confesses to the crime, we'd never be able to make a murder charge stick. Not enough evidence."

Cole shook his head. "And they say there's no such thing as the perfect crime."

"Well, whoever's using that bank account may get away with murder, but they'll face fraud charges for sure. Which brings me to the main reason I'm here. I want to take a run out to the abandoned Skansen mines on Sunday to make sure everything is properly sealed and posted with no trespassing signs. I know you aren't supposed to be working that day, but can you come with me? I'll bring some lumber to reinforce the barriers sealing off the entrances. The last thing I need is for someone else to end up dead out there. Those damn fools looking for the Lost Dutchman figure they can dig anywhere, and we always get more people snooping around Superstition

Mountain on Gold Rush Weekend."

"Sure. Mom and Dad are away until Tuesday, the store's closed, and I've got nothing planned. By the way, did the forensic anthropologist come up with cause of death?"

"Pretty much what we figured, although with bits and pieces of him missing, including most of the skull, the theory is that he was climbing, slipped, and fell. With the fluidic timeline, he could easily have been a casualty of the quake. Pete Putnam fell off his ladder and broke his leg that day, remember?" He picked up a copy of the *Fortune Examiner*, the town's weekly newspaper, and added it to his purchases. "What do I owe you for the books?"

"Eighteen-fifty," Cole said, ringing up the sale. "Melba paid for hers ahead of time. I'll see you Sunday morning. What time?"

"Around nine. I'll pick you up. Remind me to check the Morris place when we drive by. Chester's been seen hanging out there again. He claims he's seen aliens in the mountains."

Cole chuckled. "Aliens? Why not? He and those kids spend enough time combing those mountains for gold and artifacts, it's amazing he doesn't see ghosts, especially the ones he finds in that damn mescal he drinks. My guess is that he's got one hell of a still operation out there. That poison could make the poor bastard see just about anything, including UFOs and the Lost Dutchman. I'll see you Sunday."

Hal left and Cole locked the door behind him, going back to unpacking boxes and thinking about a certain redhead he'd met earlier today. He hoped she would stop by again while she was in town, because that was one high school friendship he would gladly renew ... Trent Gibbs? Not so much.

CHAPTER THREE

Casey sat on the porch swing, pleasantly full after an excellent chicken dinner. Since she'd been home, all the meals had been leaner and healthier than those Mom had served years ago—as delicious as ever, but less fatty. The lighter meals suited her palate, since not a day went by that the image of her portly self didn't manifest itself in her mind.

Sipping the coffee she'd brought out with her, savoring its richness before placing the cup on the side table, she reached for the *Fortune Examiner*.

When was the last time she'd been able to sit down after a meal and relax? In Santa Fe, she usually ate in front of the television, catching up on the evening news before going into her home office to work on briefs. Occasionally, she'd meet a client or another attorney for a business dinner. The only leisure activity she indulged in, other than the half hour each day on her exercise machine, was her weekly motorcycle rides with Ryan and Sally. There was no room in her life for personal relationships, and while she wasn't lonely, she did miss friendly companionship once in a while, which was no doubt why Cole was still hovering on the edge of her mind.

Spending the last two days with family had been easier than she'd expected. Arizona was the sunniest state, and thanks to the gorgeous weather, Saturday had been spent out by the pool, her coated in sunblock, playing with Jaxon. This morning, they'd all gone to church just as they'd done all those Sundays ago. In the afternoon, per Jaxon's suggestion, they'd taken the ATV and had explored the southwest section of the ranch, land her dad hadn't sold, searching for fossils, arrowheads, and dinosaur bones. While it was a crime to disturb any artifacts on public land, as long as they were on their own property, anything unearthed out there was theirs for the taking.

Casey had been surprised to see several sections of the far pastures sporting solar panels, but given the need to find alternative energy sources, it made sense. Combing the rocky slope at the edge of the property, she and Jaxon had found a few interesting rocks, including a small clump of desert rose quartz and pyrite Jaxon believed contained gold, as well as a teardrop shaped-stone with veins of malachite running through it that she'd brought back with her. Wrapped in silver wire, it would make a gorgeous natural pendant, something to remind her of home when she left again—not that she needed anything concrete to recall the tears she'd shed here.

The screen door opened, and her father stepped outside. He pulled the glider rocker over near the swing, and turned on the porch lamp hanging from the ceiling.

"Sorry, but I can't read without it," he said, opening his worn Bible.

"What happened to the table lamp Mom had out here? That thing was older than I was."

"It fell off the table and broke during the quake last summer. We've lost a few doodads over the years, but I loved that lamp. This one isn't bad, but it does attract the moths."

She nodded. "When did you start reading that again?" She indicated the book that had once belonged to her grandfather.

"I never stopped ... You stopped noticing. Sometimes, a body needs a little advice from the Good Book."

He handed her a brass key. "I meant to give this to you on Friday. With the activities later in the week, you might want to go out on your own—maybe meet up with old friends."

31

If I had any, I might.

"I don't know if you still have your old key, but I had all the locks changed last spring. The code for the alarm system is the same as the one on the gate for the pool. Your mother didn't want to have too many numbers to remember."

"Locking the gate to keep Jaxon safe is a great idea, but since when do you lock the doors? I don't think I ever used the key I had."

He shook his head, his face tense. "Probably not, but things have changed. While we've got a good number of people from the Northern States and Canada wintering in Fortune, since they found those Columbian Mastodon fossils south of here, the paleontologists have started to outnumber the anthropologists looking for Indian artifacts and petroglyphs."

"Surely they aren't the people you're worried about?"

"The reputable ones? No, but Eddy Ramos has complained about people stealing things up around the old mines—bits and pieces of machinery—some even going through the refuse piles. I don't always trust the man given his history, but he could be right. Given the current economic climate, we've got a lot of transients coming through town, too. A couple of prospectors claim to have dry panned a thousand dollars' worth of gold in a wash only fifteen miles from here a few months ago, just before they found part of a skeleton up near one of the deserted Skansen mines. I doubt the two are related—at least there wasn't any mention of foul play in the paper—but..." He shrugged. "The idea of finding the Lost Dutchman or striking it rich somehow never seems to pale. I can't imagine what it must've been like for your great-great-granddad having to deal with all of those men struck by gold fever back then. Hell, they're a pain in the ass now."

She chuckled. "Come on, Dad. You know he came out here looking for gold just like everyone else."

"True, but eventually, he realized the wealth was in the land, not just its minerals, and he had the good sense to give up and settle here. Too many of them didn't and died a lonely, miserable death at the hands of Mother Nature or some claim jumping miner."

"And don't forget the curse. Those mountains are sacred Apache land."

"Now, Cassandra, don't tell me you believe in that curse."

"Hey, *you* named me after a Trojan muse. There are too many unexplained things that have happened in those hills not to be wary. When I used to skirt the mountain on Ginger, I always felt I was being watched."

He laughed. "That might've been me and my binoculars. I never liked you riding out there alone, even on our land. But I need you to be extra careful, baby. I've found a few of those die-hard prospectors camping at the far end of the west pasture, called Hal to move them out of there since you can't be too careful these days, and had to post no trespassing signs."

"You can't be serious. They were looking for gold here? On the ranch? Don't you own those mineral rights?"

"I do. In fact, I still own those rights on the land I sold, but if you think private property will stop them, you've got another think coming. If they dry pan, there's no way to prove where the gold came from. The last thing I need is one of those idiots damaging the solar panels or getting electrocuted." He shook his head. "Things have been unsettled around here lately. We've had a few unexplained fires, probably set by squatters bedding down in some of the abandoned houses along the mining road. With Randy and Jaxon in the house, it seemed foolish to take chances." He put on his reading glasses and flipped his book open, ending the discussion.

Reaching for the town paper, she perused its pages. Judging by the amount of advertising, Louis Lamont, the publisher, must finally be turning a profit.

She sighed. "I don't remember crime being much of an issue when I was growing up, but I see the police have their own column."

He put down the Bible. "That's because you had your nose buried in a book all the time—not that it was a bad thing—and you certainly didn't run with the wild crowd. Fortune had its problems just like every other town. For the most part, life was good, but it wasn't perfect. We had brawls on Saturday nights, domestic disputes, petty thefts and break-ins, horse and cattle rustling, and of course drinking and driving. Every now and then, some kid would decide they'd had enough of the rules at home and would run away—just like you did. Most found their way back; some never did."

"Dad, be fair. I didn't run away. I went away to school, and you knew where I was."

"True, but you were gone a month before you called. It was all I could do to keep your mother from filing a missing persons' report, but you're right. You didn't run away, but you haven't come back either."

"According to the *Police Blotter*, you've got a crime spree— break and enter, trespassing, shoplifting, arson—why there's even someone in here who's been charged with possession with the intent to sell," she said, not wanting to discuss why she would never come back to stay.

Her father pursed his lips, chewing on the stem of his pipe, one she hadn't seen lit since she'd come home. Dad had quit smoking years ago, but the pipe went with him everywhere.

"Hal Rankin and his officers do the best they can, but it's an uphill battle. Some of the men named in there work the mines, others are drifters. They'll be even more trouble come the weekend. Last year, we had a crew of pickpockets who made off with a tidy sum. Never caught them either. We'll have some ADPS officers helping out this weekend for the festival, but the more people think they can get rich by finding gold or copper, the higher the crime rate. The price of progress can be steep."

"It certainly can. Looking at this, I'd say Matt Gunderson, your prosecutor, has his hands full with misdemeanor criminal cases."

"The big cases go to Phoenix, you know that, but he handles most of the petty stuff including traffic violations, and city code and by-law offenses. The one who's snowed under is poor old Horace Stone. His partner retired three years ago, and he's on his own now. He's also the public defender, so he handles most of what you see there. That man's older than I am. If you ever wanted to come back here—and I know you could since you've passed the Arizona bar—I'm sure you could open your own office and be busier than you are now in Santa Fe in no time."

"Dad," she set down the cup she'd just picked up, the coffee in it untasted. "You do know that's never going to happen, right? Sometimes, my firm sends staff out of state to assist on specific cases. That's the only reason I was in Phoenix at Easter."

He reached out to take her hand and smiled sadly. "I know that in my head, Casey. You've got your reasons for not wanting to come back, and I accept that, even if I don't like it, but my heart still wishes it could be different. I miss having my oldest girl around."

Casey looked down at her hands, blinking to keep the tears away, and then glanced up. Her dad was staring out into the night. Scrutinizing him for the first time, she noted that not only had he lost weight, he looked tired and worried. It was true Jaxon expended a lot of energy, but...

"Dad, is everything okay? I mean, now that you've sold off most of the ranch and quit teaching, do you and Mom have enough money?"

He chuckled. "We're fine, honey, financially fit, and doing well. That's why I was able to take early retirement. The energy collected by those solar panels will keep us nice and comfortable for some time to come. Until the Good Lord calls us home, between the rents I get on the land I lease, my stocks, and my pension, we'll stay out of the poor house. Don't you worry about us."

"But you look worried."

Knowing her parents were set financially did ease her guilt somewhat, but her gut said something was going on.

"Maybe I do, but it isn't about anything to do with money. I worry about Randy, your mother, and you, girl. It's an ugly world out there. If it's this bad here, how much worse is it where you are?"

The door opened, and Randy came out. "Well, he's finally settled. I had to leave the light on in his room again. I hope he outgrows whatever this stage is soon. Dad, Mom needs you for something—not sure what—but she says it's important."

He shrugged. "There's probably a spider in the laundry room." He chuckled. "Still scared to death of the damn things. I'll see you both later."

Casey leaned back on the swing, propelling herself back and forth with her toes, musing on what her father had said.

"What are you thinking about?" Randy asked, dropping down beside her, throwing off its smooth rhythm. "You look so serious. Not a case I hope. You're supposed to be on vacation."

"Not a case, no. I was reading the paper, and Dad was explaining about the changes around here. He mentioned the trespassers and overeager prospectors."

Randy nodded. "Yeah, I had to have that talk with Jaxon about not speaking to strangers. You can't seem to escape the increased crime rate, but so far it's not as bad as it was in Phoenix. That city has one of the highest violent crime rates in the country. When David was around, I didn't even think of it. We lived in a safe neighborhood, not too far from the restaurant but after … That's why I came back when I was expecting Jaxon. Now, while it isn't the way it used to be, I'm glad I did."

"How often do you see Cole Walker?" she asked, deciding Randy might know something about Cole and his friend CJ. As much as she'd tried to put the enigmatic store proprietor out of her mind, she couldn't quite do it. Those golden brown eyes of his kept coming back to her, and he'd had a starring role in her dreams the last two nights, much the way he had in her girlish fantasies fifteen years ago. Part of it had to be being around Jaxon and her biological clock, but she needed to turn that damn thing off before it got her into hot water.

"Every day when he and Noella are in town. They come in for coffee each morning."

"Not Cole Senior, Cole Junior," Casey said, a touch too sharply.

Randy frowned. "Cole Junior? I didn't realize you two were friends."

"We aren't … exactly, but I was talking to him on Friday when I stopped by the emporium to see his father. I picked up the new CJ Coleson book, and he told me he knows him. Apparently they went to school together."

"I don't pay attention to gossip, but I haven't heard that before. Cole really keeps to himself, so I don't think he'd want that little tidbit getting around."

Casey chuckled. "If he's half as reclusive as CJ is, I can imagine letting me know that was a mistake. He also fessed up to the fact that CJ's visited here once or twice. I wondered if you'd ever seen him hanging around with a stranger."

"It sounds like you two had quite the *tête à tête*. As I said, Cole keeps to himself, so if he's had company, I wouldn't know about it. He came back a couple of years before I did. If he's got any kind of social life, it's a mystery to all of us. There hasn't been anyone visiting him in the last year, not since *Cookies and Cream* opened its doors. I think he bought a cabin on Apache Lake, but I'm not sure. That could've been his father."

Casey nodded, disappointed that her quest to know more about her mysterious author had hit another dead end, and annoyed with herself for hanging on every word Randy had uttered about Cole.

"He travels—goes back to El Paso or Dallas, where he worked before joining the Fortune Police Department—but that's all I know," Randy continued. "He doesn't date, and believe me, it's not because no one's interested. A lawman and fireman combined in one? That's yummy in any woman's book. He's been hit on more times than a punching bag. There are all kinds of theories about his celibacy, too—everything from an

SUSANNE MATTHEWS

ex-wife who broke his heart to a dead lover he can't forget. I heard his mother complaining to Mom that she doubts he'll ever settle down."

"Well, marriage isn't for everyone, I guess," she answered. Cole's mother wasn't the only one bemoaning the fact that her child hadn't tied the knot. It had been one of the questions Mom had asked at supper last night, right before the "please pass the potatoes."

"Not for me, either," Randy agreed sadly, "I did it once, but … What do you plan to do with yourself Tuesday?"

"I don't have any plans, why?"

"Selma Gomez, my employee, has a dentist appointment in Phoenix. Her daughter needs orthodontic work that can't be done locally. I was wondering if you wouldn't mind pitching in for the day. It's okay if you can't, but it would save my neck. There's really too much work for one person."

"Sure, but if you're that busy, you should consider getting more staff—maybe a part-timer."

Casey smiled to mask the terror filling her. Working in the coffee shop would expose her to any of Fortune's denizens who deemed to drop in—possibly some, if not all—of the ones she hoped to avoid.

"I've got a teenager starting next week. She'll work after school and Saturdays. I appreciate you helping me out. Coming in? That new Sandra Bullock movie is on."

"In a minute. I want to check out the stars. I don't see them often in Santa Fe."

"Okay. I'll make the popcorn. It'll be like old times."

Casey smiled, the pleasant childhood memory easing her worries. "And we can eat it lying on blankets on the floor."

"You've got it. By the way, Cole usually drops in for coffee and a muffin around one." She winked and entered the house.

Great, now she thinks I'm interested in Cole.

But her sister couldn't be more wrong. Cole was a means to an end, and that end was CJ Coleson.

* * * *

Cole recognized the sound of Casey's bike coming along Main Street. He hadn't been able to get her off his mind, and he's spent most of Saturday night and the better part of Sunday working on a new Tate Silvers novel, one inspired by her. Crimson Manners, a reformed outlaw, as colorful as Belle Starr, would be the main character in *Firebrand*, and she would give Tate a run for his money.

Until Sunday, he hadn't had a chance to take a good look at the place where Leon's remains had been found, but once he did, the acid in his stomach had gone into overdrive. At the beginning of his second book, *Rattlesnake*, Cole had killed off a nosy prospector in that same area. The weirdest thing was that he'd modeled the gambler in his story after Trent Gibbs, and here it was his uncle who was dead. It had to be coincidental, but that nagging feeling just wouldn't go away.

Basing the imaginary town of Prospect on Fortune during the gold rush and his characters on the people he saw each day, gave his books the authenticity he wanted. As Casey had put it, reading a CJ Coleson novel was like coming home. He wanted that realism in his stories, but he needed to be careful that, should his secret ever get out, the people of Fortune would be flattered, instead of voting to tar and feather him before they rode him out of town.

The trek out to the mines yesterday with Hal had been productive, even if it hadn't yielded any new information concerning Leon's death. Each summer, determined tourists trespassed onto the mining sites—some just to look, others to try and find that elusive gold dust, but sadly many went out there to get some bit of machinery as a souvenir. While Skansen land wasn't public land where removing any kind of artifact was illegal, it was private property and an integral part of the area's history. Theft was theft, even if the stuff was just left lying around to rust.

The company had donated many old pieces of mining

equipment to area museums, but drew the line at people helping themselves and selling their wares on *EBay*. It wasn't the first time it had happened, and no matter what he and Hal did, it wouldn't be the last. The other danger involved miners bent on claim jumping who just might go down into the old shafts, regardless of the dangers, and try to find the gold rumor claimed was still down there.

It had been almost eighty years since the company had closed some of the oldest shafts, and nature had taken back most of those areas, but until Skansen gave back those patents, that land was theirs. Since Leon had been found near the first Skansen mine, they'd started there. They were no more than a thousand feet up from the desert floor, but the area was rugged, filled with basalt outcroppings, clefts in the rocks, and sheer rock faces that would be a challenge to climbing enthusiasts. There was an old dirt road part of the way, but rock slides and new growth cacti made it hard to take a regular vehicle all the way in. Even the four by four they were using was having a tough time of it.

In addition to climbers and prospectors, this section of the mountain was popular with naturalists in the spring, fall, and winter when it wasn't as hot. A small herd of Nelson's desert big horn sheep made its home in the region. Looking up, Cole had seen a ram, alone on a crag, staring down at them. He'd taken a picture of the majestic beast. If he made prints, he could have them framed and sell them in the store. There was a rough trail heading farther up the mountain, one that while steep might be navigable by a sturdy ATV. He'd pointed it out to Hal, but since it technically wasn't on Skansen land, there wasn't anything they could do. In the end, while they couldn't post a "No Trespassing" sign on it, they had put up a "Danger Unstable Ground" sign there.

When they arrived at the second wave of shafts, those closed between ten and thirty years ago, the ones people believed still had gold in them, they'd reinforced the barriers on the mine entrances, using newer, stronger boards, but a determined person with a crowbar could get in easily enough. Someone had busted the chain locking the gate on the roadway leading into the mining area, and Hal was supposed to speak to Eddy Ramos, the company's CEO, about it today. Without a locked gate, it was just too damn easy for anyone to wander too close to the pits. Even with the no trespassing signs, if someone got hurt, they could be sued, and if the judge found the mining company negligent, they could be out thousands of dollars.

Finally, they'd driven up to *Lucky Seven*, the Skansen mine still producing substantial amounts of high quality ore. Mining operations continued as usual. In fact, both he and Hal had been surprised by the number of men working on a Sunday. Hal had spoken to a couple of the security men on duty, but they hadn't seen anything or anyone in the area. The sound of the machinery would be enough to keep any prospector a safe distance away, and since the area was occupied twenty-four hours a day, no one could get near the place even at night.

On their way back to Fortune, he and Hal had stopped by the Morris place. This house was the one closest to town along the old mining road, and the only one still standing after the recent unexplained fires. The shed, a structure so dilapidated it was amazing it still stood, boasted a new combination lock. The main house appeared deserted and more run down than ever. It was always possible that Chester was using the shed as a base of operation for his daily trip up the mountain, but without a reason to look inside, Hal had left the place alone.

Shaking off his unease, Cole stepped over to the window to get another look at last night's inspiration. When she got off the motorcycle and removed her helmet, his body stirred, much as it had the first time he'd seen her. As she bent and shook out her long red hair, he swallowed a flash of desire so great it pained him. Raising her face to the sun, she stretched. He wanted her more than he'd ever wanted a woman.

After edging her way through the cars lining the street, Cole burst out laughing when she stuck her tongue out childishly at the driver who honked at her for crossing in the middle of the road. What would happen if he went out there and kissed her the way he wanted to? She would probably bust his balls, and the tattlers would have a field day.

As Hal had proven yesterday, gossip traveled as quickly in Fortune as wildfire. It was another reason he kept his writing career a secret. He might never have a minute to himself, and writing was a solitary occupation, one he intended to pursue as long as he could.

CHAPTER FOUR

Cole was still chuckling when he held the door open for Casey.

She nodded her thanks.

"I saw that," he said, using his head to indicate the street. "Classy."

Stepping inside, she shrugged. "What is it about coming home that brings back all your bad habits? I thought I'd outgrown childish gestures. Mom will get a call any minute complaining about my outrageous behavior."

"Maybe not. I'm not sure you've been recognized yet. You have to admit, you've changed," he said, looking her up and down and smiling.

"I guess, but at times, I still feel like I did fifteen years ago. Things haven't changed much in here. How's the book business treating you?" She walked over to the checkout counter and leaned against it.

For a moment, he thought she'd somehow discovered the truth, but when she spread her arms to encompass the emporium and the shelves of books nearby, he realized what she meant.

"It's a part-time gig, but I like it, and business is steady. I'm open four days a week."

He forced himself to concentrate on the store and not on

the way her T-shirt clung to her breasts as she removed her leather jacket and laid it on the counter.

"When the mall opened, Dad wanted to close the store so he and Mom could travel. I hated that idea, and moved back five years ago to give him a hand and keep the emporium up and running. We still carry pretty much the same things we always have, but I've expanded into educational toys and locally produced decorative items."

"You don't mind being back in Fortune after Dallas?"

"How did you know I'd lived in Dallas?" He watched her cheeks pink. Blushing women, especially when they were as outgoing and confident as she appeared to be, were a novelty. He wondered how far down her body the flush went, and fought to get the image out of his mind.

"Randy told me the other night," she admitted. "I'd mentioned seeing you."

"You talked to your sister about me? Should I be flattered?"

"Maybe a little. I asked her if she'd ever seen you with a stranger. I mean if she had, she might've been able to describe CJ Coleson."

Ego deflated, hoping the disappointment didn't show on his face, he nodded. "It's all about CJ for you. I'm hurt." He placed his hand over his heart.

Casey giggled.

The sound made his heart beat double time. It was as crisp and pure as a crystal bell, and he wanted to hear it again.

"Please," she said, rolling her eyes. "I'm a seasoned attorney, remember? I know a load of bull when I hear it."

Swallowing his desire, he focused on the woman in front of him. She could make the Pope break his vows of celibacy.

"So what did she say?" he asked, hoping to keep her here a while longer. He had things to do, but nothing that couldn't wait.

"Not much. The gist of it is you were a lawman in Dallas, and came back here to work the shop and keep the peace. I can almost understand that. I've had a few cases in Texas. They do everything big there, including crime. She did mention you were a bit of a recluse, something you and the elusive CJ have in common, which probably explains why you're such good friends. It seems you're still the strong, silent type." She shook her head. "Frankly, I was surprised to discover you weren't married." She bit her lip as if by doing so she could take back the words. "I'm sorry. That's really none of my business. Like I said earlier, since I've come home, it seems I've picked up a few bad habits. My common sense must be on vacation, too."

"Don't worry about it. I should be grateful the gossips haven't fabricated a story to explain it." He chuckled. "I like girls, if that's what you're wondering," he continued, watching her turn an even deeper shade of red. "I just haven't met the right one."

Dating the women from Fortune wasn't an option, and while it might seem odd, it was simply a case of self-preservation. During his years away, he'd filled out and matured, but he hadn't expected the homecoming he received. Many of the girls who wouldn't have given him the time of day in high school had flocked to him, even some of the married ones.

While he enjoyed female company as much as the next guy, he didn't jump another man's claim. He limited his dating to the women he saw when he visited his publisher or dropped in unexpectedly on old friends. There was always a wife or a sister ready to hook him up with someone single on short notice. Was he lonely? At times, sure, but he could always lose himself in a book.

He drank in the sight of her in skinny jeans and a tight, blue, T-shirt. It might be courting disaster, but damn, he wanted her. When she smiled at him and tilted her head questioningly, he suspected he'd been staring at her, probably with that starving puppy look on his face, the one he'd seen on other guys' faces over the years. It was a bad idea to even consider hooking up with her, despite the fact she was going back to Santa Fe in a week or so, but he couldn't stop thinking of what it would be like.

Reining in his desire, he smiled. "Did you come in for more books?" he asked, as she fidgeted uncomfortably in front of him, chewing her lower lip, making him want to do it himself.

She blinked twice as if coming out of a trance. "Not books, no. Actually, Jaxon's birthday is Wednesday, and while I bought him some clothing, I wanted to get him some *Lego*, too. Mom said you were the one to see about that."

He smiled. "I am. Jaxon is one of my best customers. I have a list of all the sets he has, so if you want something in particular that I don't have in stock, I can order it for you." He hoped that would be the case. It would give her another reason to come into the store. "Follow me."

He led her through the doorway leading to the addition he'd put on the store last year.

"Wow! This is like walking into Santa's workshop at the North Pole."

"That's the response I was hoping for. Come Christmas, I hire a few people to dress up, and of course, I bring in the jolly old elf himself. Your mother made his costume for me. She's a hell of a good seamstress. I even have a mailbox for letters to Santa. Mom and a few other women from town answer them for me. Not only do I have fun, but it raises my sales for the quarter, and the kids love it. I've had people come in from Phoenix just to see the place."

"I'll bet." There was no mistaking the admiration in her voice. "Fortune can always use another tourist attraction, especially if it doesn't have anything to do with gold."

"You say that as if prospecting is a bad thing." He stepped over to the counter and pulled out an old-fashioned ledger.

"What? No computerized list?" she asked.

"Sorry. Around here, Santa still does things the old-fashioned way. Here we are." He opened the book wider for her to see. The name Jaxon Stevens was printed at the top of the page. "I keep a list of everything your parents and Randy buy for him—*Lego*, books, cars, you name it." He looked down the list. "He's really very good at putting together those sets. I think

I have a couple in stock he might like ... he's still into superheroes, right?"

"He certainly is. I learned more about that subject last weekend than I ever expected to. Apparently, in my leathers, I resemble Batgirl."

Chuckling, he reached up and pulled down two sets. "That's quite the compliment. Either of these would do."

Cole watched her eyes light up as she examined the boxes he'd set on the counter. She'd wondered about him being single, but what about her? Was there a man in Santa Fe waiting, counting the minutes until she returned? If there was, he was a fool for not staking his claim. There was no gold band or diamond ring on her finger, although she should have something special—nothing as common as diamonds. Emeralds, maybe, or sapphires.

"I'll take this one, thanks."

"Okay," he answered a second too slowly.

She tilted her head at him, a questioning frown on her face.

"Sorry. Wool gathering. Let's go and ring it up out front."

She handed him the bag from yesterday. "Here. Might as well reuse it, right?"

"That's what it's for. So what have you got against prospecting? This town exists because of it." He wanted to keep her here talking as long as he could.

"I know, and for the most part it still does, but Dad mentioned the number of transients around, and I noticed the crime rate seems to be increasing as well."

"If you're thinking of coming back home and starting a practice, I can guarantee you would be busy enough. I'm sure Horace Stone wouldn't mind the competition."

"As attractive as that proposition might be, you can be damned sure it's never going to happen." There was no denying the conviction in her voice, and that disappointed him.

"Never say never. Despite what you see as our escalating crime rate, Fortune's a good place to settle down and raise a family." He wasn't as comfortable with the topic as he'd been a few minutes earlier.

"Is that why you came back? Pretty hard to do if you don't date." She reddened once more.

"Touché."

"None of my business," she said and licked her lips. "Dad mentioned you'd found a body on the mountain a few months back."

"Not a body, more like parts of one. Some hikers found it and called it in. I figured we would never know who the bones belonged to, but the forensic anthropologist in Phoenix managed to identify him." He relaxed, glad she'd changed the topic, even if it wasn't the usual chit-chat he was used to. "The man lived in Fortune years ago. Leon Turner. You would know his nephew, Trent Gibbs. I think he graduated the same year you did."

"I knew him, but we weren't friends by any means. You might remember I wasn't too popular back then."

"I never understood why. You were smart and—"

"Outweighed the competition by fifty pounds," she interrupted bitterly. "Sorry, most of my memories of high school aren't pleasant ones. So good old Trent still lives around here, does he?"

"That's not what I remember about you, but yeah. He works for Skansen Mining."

"That's not surprising. He and Crazy Eddy were close, although I never could understand why. Eddy was different, you know?"

He moved to the cash register, ran up her purchase, and put the money she handed him in the till. After closing the cash drawer, he tore off the sale's receipt, stepped back out from the counter and handed her the bag. "He was and still is. One day he's like the *Energizer Bunny* and you can hardly keep up with him, and the next, he's a victim of the *Zombie Apocalypse*. If you want, I can lay aside that other set for Christmas."

"I'd like that. When I see him so rarely, it's hard to get the perfect gift. I'll pick it up before I leave next week."

"I don't mind keeping it for you until the holidays. You can pick it up when you come back."

"I won't be back," she answered with conviction.

"That's a shame. I would've liked you to see this place at Christmas."

She gnawed her lower lip as if she were struggling with some tough decision. "I'm sure it's lovely. Listen. I know you don't go out much, but would you like to have coffee with me later? This is the most interesting conversation I've had in a while. We could talk about crime or books ... I don't have any friends here, and Randy's busy with the shop and Jaxon. I feel like Mom's been cross-examining me for more than seventy-two hours. It wouldn't be a date or anything." The flush in her cheeks returned.

At the hint of self-consciousness in her voice, all of his good intentions vanished.

"I would like that."

"Great." Her relief was palpable, almost as if she'd expected him to decline.

"What time do you close?"

"Six. We could meet around seven-thirty—make it dinner if you like," he offered, ignoring his conscience.

"I wish I could. I'm sure the conversation would be more pleasant, but if I skip out on a meal, Mom won't be happy. Since it's my first time back in a while ... you know." She pushed her hair behind her right ear. "How about I give you a call when I know when supper will be over?"

"That sounds good," he agreed.

Leaning in, he trapped her body between his and the hard surface of the wooden counter, and reached across for a notepad and pen. Standing flat against her like this, he could feel her heart quicken. Reluctantly, he stepped back, and handed her the slip of paper.

After tucking away another wayward strand, she glanced at the number and smiled. "See you tonight," she said huskily, her voice betraying the fact their body contact had affected her, too.

"I'm looking forward to it."

She turned and walked out of the store, helmet and bag hanging at her side.

Cole stared at her sassy wiggle as she walked away, but this time she didn't look back. He was probably going to regret this, but tonight couldn't come soon enough. She might not think this was a date, but before the night was out, he would make sure it was one she would never forget. Whistling, he went out to the store room to unpack the last of the boxes he hadn't unpacked on Saturday.

* * * *

Once she left the downtown core, Casey pulled her bike over to the side of the road in front of some of the newer stucco bungalows, part of a retirement community according to the sign she'd passed, noting the electronic gate across the driveway. Palm trees had been planted, a strange site in the area that had once been desert scrub. No doubt underground irrigation pipes were responsible for the green grass. In the distance, Superstition Mountain rose up toward the sun.

"Cassandra Maureen Stevens, are you insane?" she mumbled aloud, removing her helmet.

Her latest encounter with Cole had left the acidic butterflies in her stomach fluttering madly. With her mind still at the bookstore and not on her driving, she needed to calm down and look at things in perspective. What the hell had she just done?

Engaging the kickstand, she got off the Harley and walked up and down the sidewalk, trying to make sense of things. Pacing helped her think clearly—she'd worn a path in the rug in her office to prove it.

Over the years she'd become confident and wasn't afraid to go after what she wanted, but she'd never been this bold in her entire life. At thirty-three, she'd just asked a man out for the first time—oh, she'd made appointments with other lawyers and clients, but this was different. It wasn't a date, but it was the closest thing to it. Where the hell had she gotten the nerve to do that?

Here she was, back in Fortune of all places, arranging to spend time with a man who attracted her, probably the last man on earth she should even consider seeing. While she might tell herself it was the fact he knew CJ Coleson, the truth was something about Cole drew her like a moth to a flame.

"I've got to be out of my mind," she mumbled, shaking her head, hoping none of the security conscious people living in these new homes were looking out the window.

What was it about this guy? Sure she'd had a crush on him, painful since she'd been sure he hadn't even known she was alive, but that had been years ago. She couldn't think straight when he was around, and that scared the daylights out of her.

Escaping another round of questions from her mother by going to get Jaxon a gift had seemed like a good idea at the time. Ever since she'd asked Randy about Cole, his name kept coming up in the conversation. Her mother couldn't say enough about what a wonderful asset he was to the community and she swore, if her dad could adopt the man, he would.

For a while yesterday, she'd wondered if CJ had used the name Coleson because it was a variation of Cole's name, a way of honoring and old friend. If that were the case and the two were that close, it would be hard to get him to give up any information about her literary hero.

She'd become addicted to the western crime novels when she'd picked up a copy of *Fool's Gold* at the airport in Santa Fe on her way to Denver where she'd sat second chair at a murder trial. Prospect, the town Sheriff Tate Silvers called home, could've been any of the towns in Arizona in the mid-nineteenth century, but it reminded her of Fortune, not the way it had been in her teens, but the way her grandfather had described it when she was young. In CJ Coleson's prose, she could let the beauty and mystery of the Superstition Mountains, Apache legends, and the ghost towns carry her away.

His second book, *Rattlesnake*, the one with the sleazy

gambler who reminded her of Trent Gibbs, one of the boys a year ahead of her, had cemented what she hoped would be a life-long relationship between herself and her new favorite author. In his third book, *Fistful of Silver*, her distaste for the killer had been so strong, she had trouble reading the sections he was in, but she was positive Goldfield, now a ghost town, was the setting. She'd worked there as a tour guide the summer before her final year of high school.

Over the course of the past four years, she'd morphed into a groupie, haunting his website, signing up for his newsletter, participating in every contest and giveaway he hosted. She had a CJ Coleson bookmark and magnet, and a neat little fake gold nugget paperweight on her desk. Knowing she had *Black Widow* even if she hadn't been able to start it yet, was almost the best part about coming home. The other part had been meeting Cole, but only because he was CJ's friend. She shook her head. It was probably just as well he wouldn't tell her who CJ really was. If she met him in person, with the way her libido and biological clock were behaving at the moment, she would probably do something really stupid—like offer to have his baby.

At least she was safe from that mortifying notion, but damn it, the minute she'd stepped into the store, any thoughts about CJ Coleson had taken a back seat to the reality of the man in front of her. She might admire CJ, but he wasn't real—not real like Cole. He'd looked even sexier and more appealing than he had on Friday and in her dreams, and she'd come unglued. Instead of digging for information as she'd intended, she'd flirted with the guy. Sure, she'd managed to remember to get Jaxon's gift but…

It was easy to understand why Randy had come back, but Cole? Why give up the glamor and excitement of Dallas to work as a small-town cop and run a store? Even if crime in Dallas had disillusioned him he was still at it here, probably because the profits from the emporium couldn't support him. Maybe she should call and rescind her invitation. After all, she was home to spend time with her family, not a stranger, but something about that idea bothered her. She wasn't a quitter anymore. Rationalizing, she decided keeping the date would be the only polite thing to do. Besides, if she didn't, how else would she learn more about her favorite author? She ran her hands through her hair. Thoughts of CJ would probably go right out the window the moment she laid eyes on Cole.

"Whatever!" she said aloud, annoyed when the little voice inside her head laughed at her.

Without another moment's hesitation, she jumped back on her bike and headed home, putting as much distance as possible between herself and the man who had her acting in the weirdest way.

Ten minutes later, Casey opened the door and stepped back in time into a dressmaker's studio. Her mother, the town's go-to person for custom clothing, had been busy putting the final touches on Gold Rush Days' costumes. Several, on wire hangers and encased in plastic garment bags, hung from a metal bar, no doubt waiting to be collected by their new owners. Casey skirted what had to be Dad's miner's outfit next to a miniature version that had to have been made with Jaxon in mind. The green gingham dress and bonnet, her mother's favorite, were freshly washed and starched. Next to them stood a similar dress and bonnet in navy cotton trimmed with white lace. The last gown, a pale green Swiss dot, more formal in styling with puffed sleeves and a low cut bodice, had a straw hat trimmed with matching fabric. It reminded her of something Scarlett O'Hara might've worn in *Gone with the Wind*.

She'd been so busy working and trying to find an excuse not to come to Fortune that she'd forgotten how important this celebration was to her mother. As a descendant of one of the founding families, Mom believed it was her duty to participate to the fullest. Maybe she could slip into Phoenix and see if the costume shops had anything remotely suitable left. She would probably end up with the standard saloon girl outfit, but whose fault would that be? It was too late to ask Mom to make her something now.

Glancing at the anniversary clock on the mantel, she frowned. It was way off. Sniffing the air, Casey could smell fresh bread and pies. Her mother's love of cooking was what had prompted Randy's own interest in the subject, whereas she was addicted to salad and frozen meals. She could cook—not as well as her mother and sister—but cooking for one held no appeal. Besides, after working late five nights a week, and sometimes on the weekends as well, who had time to cook?

Following the aroma of hot bread, Casey found her mother chopping vegetables for a salad. Next to her, two large round pizza pans waited to go into the oven once the fresh ingredients were added to the dough. Her stomach grumbled. "Pizza for supper. What kind?"

There'd been tension between them since her arrival home, and while she'd tried to minimize it, she was convince Mom had something on her mind. Since it might be another lecture, Casey opted not to ask.

"One garlic, chicken, and mushroom with three cheeses and a pesto sauce. The other one mushroom, pepperoni, bacon, and green pepper on a standard red sauce with mozzarella. Glad you're home in one piece. Did you get what you wanted?"

Her mother's quip made her smile.

Casey walked over and kissed her cheek. "I did."

And then some.

"What was that for? Not that I'm complaining."

"Just because. I told you the bike is as safe as Ginger was. You weren't afraid of the horse … You'll get used to it. Maybe I should take you out for a spin one of these days and prove it." The look of absolute terror on her mother's face made her laugh. "It smells fantastic in here. By the way, the clock on the mantel's way off. If you've got batteries, I can change it. Where is everyone?"

"The clock can't be fixed. It fell during the quake last summer. Since it was a gift for our twenty-fifth anniversary, we've kept it for sentimental reasons, but one of these days, I'll declutter, and it'll be the first thing to go. We joke that the damn thing isn't completely useless since it is right twice a day—noon and midnight." She chuckled. "Your father's in his study, and Jaxon's taking a nap. Randy won't be home for another couple of hours. I've baked my pies for the contest and more bread for sandwiches and toast."

Casey's mouth watered. Mom had never used store-bought bread, and there was nothing like the taste of the real thing fresh from the oven. "I'm going to gain ten pounds while I'm here. The costumes look fabulous by the way. I can't wait to see Jaxon in the mini miner's outfit."

"Bread's not as fattening as people think," Mom said with conviction. "I made your father a new shirt this year. I was going to alter the other, but it was worn and, since I was making a whole outfit for Jaxon, I thought he might as well have a matching shirt. What do you think of the navy dress I made for Randy? I wanted a younger, brighter color, but you know how fussy she can be."

"Be grateful it isn't black or gray. The dress is beautiful, and that lace cap will look great given the color of her hair, but you outdid yourself on that pale green one. It's the loveliest dress I've seen yet. Who's it for?"

Her mother licked her lips. "I know you said you didn't want to dress up, but I thought—"

Casey squealed. "You made that for me?"

"I did. I know you think dressing up is childish, but maybe just this once?"

Casey's heart filled with regret, and she hugged her mother once more. "Mom, I'm sorry for being such a bitch all these years. The dress is beautiful, and I'll be very proud to wear it."

Her mother smiled. "I know wearing homemade clothes wasn't something you liked doing as a teenager."

"It was never the clothing, Mom, it was the body. I was always proud of the clothes you made me. I've kept most of the skirts—I had them tailored of course after I lost the weight. The dressmaker in Santa Fe said they were better made than

55

anything she'd ever seen. That red shirtdress you made me is still my go-to outfit for closings. I add a jacket and a scarf ... A couple of the other attorneys at H. L. and D. claim that when my opposing council see the 'lady in red' enter the courtroom, they know it's over. Maybe I should get you to make me a couple more in different colors and confuse them."

Her mother beamed, and Casey felt like an ungrateful brat for never having mentioned it before.

"Can I help with anything?" she asked, knowing the answer would probably be no, but she wanted to hold onto this relaxed feeling between them.

"Not really, I'm almost done anyway. Why don't you go up and wake Jaxon. If he sleeps too long, he's hard as the dickens to put down again at night. Lately, he's had this fear of what he calls the 'big dark' and claims there are monsters in the mountains with fiery eyes." She shook her head. "Such an imagination. Maybe he would like to play in the pool before supper."

"You've got it."

She left the kitchen and headed up the stairs. So far, coming home hadn't been as bad as she'd expected. The image of Cole came to mind, and as much as she tried to ignore it, she had to admit the emporium's new owner might well be part of the reason.

CHAPTER FIVE

Slowing her steps when she reached the second floor, Casey glanced at her watch. Before waking Jaxon, she needed to call her secretary and see how Ken was managing. If those papers hadn't been filed by ten this morning, she would be ruined. No jury of her peers would convict her for murdering the incompetent fool.

Closing the door to her bedroom, she bathed in its familiar comfort, once more astounded at the way her mother had preserved it as if it were some kind of shrine. Nothing had changed in the fifteen years since she'd walked away. The handmade white and green quilt and matching shams covered her pine double bed, the coordinating drapes hung from the window, and the green braided rug warmed the floor. The pine dressers, waxed to a mirror shine, held the pictures and other souvenirs of her life here, the things she'd abandoned when she'd escaped. The books she'd cherished, including more than a few by Louis L'Amour and Zane Grey, explaining why she loved CJ Coleson's work, filled the bookcase. While the walls had been repainted, they were still the same shade of sage green she'd chosen when she'd turned sixteen. On her bed, the pink teddy bear holding a book of fairy tales, her most prized possession fifteen years ago, sat in his position of honor, but like her family, she'd left him behind, too.

Pulling her smartphone out of her pocket, she dropped into the rocker by the window. At this time of day, Wanda would still be at the office. She pressed the speed dial number and heard the phone ring.

"Hi, Casey," her cheerful secretary, Wanda Wilson, dubbed Wonder Woman by Ryan, answered on the third ring. "How's home?"

"Better than I thought it would be. I didn't realize how much I missed the place. How's the case going?"

"We filed all the affidavits on time this morning, including the one Ryan brought in Friday afternoon. The judge said he would have a ruling by September seventh, so relax. We've got this. You did a great job putting this case together. When the judge rules in our favor, that junior partnership is yours."

The news should please her, since she'd been angling for that partnership for the last two years, but lately, she'd felt discontented. She hadn't had an interesting case in months, and while corporate law was a big part of her firm's cases, she missed the excitement of criminal law. Getting stuck with Ken had intensified that dissatisfaction, and then she had the whole "I'm not getting any younger" thing going on.

"You know me. Worry is my middle name. How's Ken doing?"

"Baby Boss, as you call him, is doing fine," she answered warmly. "He just needs a chance to prove himself. Don't worry. I'll keep a close eye on him."

"Please do. Well, I guess if everything is good, I'll let you go. Call if something comes up. Give my best to Ken."

"Will do, and for Pete's sake, do something exciting and daring. I know Fortune isn't your favorite place, but give it a chance. Time changes everything. Meet new people or renew old friendships. You're on vacation. Forget about this place. Enjoy yourself. You're too young not to have fun with a capital F."

Casey chuckled softly as memories of Cole filled her mind. "I'll try. While Fortune may have changed and grown since I left, it hasn't necessarily been for the better, although some things are looking up."

"Hey, aren't you the one who always told me not to judge a book by its cover?"

"Right." If Cole were a book, she would read him cover to cover, over and over again. She shook her head. "I'll check in later in the week. Have a good night."

Ending the call, she changed into her one piece maillot, grabbed her cover-up and sunblock, and left the room.

By the time supper rolled around, Casey was a nervous wreck. She'd thoroughly enjoyed her time in the pool with Jaxon, even though she'd been terrified when the tremor had struck. Playing in the water, Jaxon hadn't even noticed it, but all the crooked pictures on the walls inside attested to the fact she hadn't imagined it.

Throughout the meal, she tried to follow the friendly conversation, much of it devoted to last year's earthquake, but kept drifting off, pondering the wisdom of meeting Cole for coffee. She did her best to do justice to the delicious pizza, but the fluttering in her stomach wouldn't abate, and she was glad no one commented when she only had two pieces.

This wasn't a date—they both agreed on that—Cole didn't date and neither did she. This was simply a chance to discuss books with him the way she had with his father and collect vital information about her favorite author ... knowledge he was withholding from her.

Think of it as a pre-trial interview with a reluctant witness.

But the butterflies in her stomach didn't believe it any more than her common sense did.

Once the meal was over, in an effort to escape anyone's notice, Casey offered to supervise Jaxon's bath while Randy helped Mom clean-up, a task the two of them had down to a fine art.

After stripping off sand-caked socks and shorts, wondering if she should vacuum the floor instead of sweeping it, Casey filled the tub to the six-inch mark and helped Jaxon dump in all the toys in the mesh bag hanging from the bar in the corner.

"Do you really need all these toys?" she asked, tossing the tenth rubber fish into the tub and checking the water's temperature.

"Yup. I'm a whale," he giggled, splashing about like a fish on land, sending water out of the tub, showering the room.

"Whoa, Moby Dick. Try to keep some of it in there with you."

Twenty minutes later, despite the fact the bathroom was probably wetter than it normally was, Casey wrapped Jaxon in his fluffy Superman towel, and carried him into his bedroom. Once he was dressed in another superhero-themed pair of pajamas, she settled down beside him to read the two books he'd chosen.

"Here's Mommy," she said, closing the second book. "Goodnight, sweetie." She bent and kissed the child.

"G'night, Aunt Casey. Love you." Jaxon yawned, tucking what was surely the largest blankie any child had ever had under his chin.

That ache that had been festering inside her, the desire for a child of her own, flared up again, but she forced it away.

"Love you, too," she answered, her voice clogged by a lump of regret.

Casey walked back to the bathroom, repaired as much of their damage as possible, and returned to her room. Earlier, between dessert and bath time, she'd called Cole to see if their rendezvous was still a go. His suggestion to hook up in front of the store had suited her fine, but she'd moved the time to eight, grateful that she had since it was after seven now. The last thing she wanted was for him to pick her up at the house. The less her parents knew, the better. They'd already spent an unhealthy amount of time praising Cole, so if they knew she was meeting him for coffee, they would probably make a big deal out of it. It wasn't a date, but her parents and sister would read more into it than there was.

Three outfits later, she heard her door open, and Randy

walked in uninvited.

"Don't you knock?"

Randy made a face. "Why should I? Wow! You look nice. That's a gorgeous sweater. Is it cashmere? Where are you going?"

"It is. I thought I'd go for a ride—maybe grab some fresh coffee," she said casually.

"Dressed like that?" The way Randy cocked her eyebrow showed she didn't believe her.

"Yup," she lied, avoiding her sister's curious eyes. "I'm used to dressing up. Besides, I often do this in Santa Fe."

"Bull! I can't see you trolling for men anywhere, and in that outfit, that's what you're doing. As far as fresh coffee goes, there's some in the kitchen, and you know it."

Randy could tell when she was lying or hiding something. She'd been able to fool her once, but that time, the stakes had been too high to lose. Casey had hoped she'd gotten better at it over the years, but she doubted it. The one thing she'd never acquired had been a poker face, which was ironic considering her occupation. Somehow, she managed to pull it off in court, at depositions, or settlement meetings, but anyone who knew her well could read her like a book. Ryan claimed her basic honesty was one of her more endearing qualities. "Naïve as a rube fresh off the turnip truck" was the way he'd phrased it. She didn't consider it a compliment.

Randy stood there watching her as she put in a fresh pair of contact lenses and added the finishing touches to her makeup. Casey risked a glance and knew, from the skeptical look on her sister's face, she wasn't going to get anything past her. Randy wasn't going to let her go until she fessed up to the truth. Time was running out, and unless she hurried, she would be late.

Damn.

Staring at her, Randy crossed her arms, looking more like their mother than ever. She even had the jutting chin to match.

Casey burst out laughing.

"Man, Jaxon won't stand a chance. You've got Mom's glare

down pat."

"What do you mean by that? I may look like Mom, but I'm nothing like her."

"Said the pot to the kettle!" Casey mimicked the pose her sister was holding.

"Whatever." Randy dropped the pose and replaced it with a pout. "Are you going to tell me where you're really going or not?"

Casey felt guilty for teasing her. There seemed to be more to Randy's curiosity than she was letting on, but she didn't have time to explore it. Other than Sunday night's conversation— most of it about Cole—she hadn't spent much time with her sister. She would make up for it by helping out at the shop tomorrow.

"I'm going to meet Cole Walker for coffee, okay?"

"What?" Her sister actually squealed and bounced up and down. "You're going on a date with Cole Walker Junior?" Randy reverted to the seventeen-year-old she'd been when Casey had left home.

"That's what I said, but it's just coffee. We were discussing the recent increase in crime and the body they'd found and decided to continue the conversation. You said yourself, he doesn't date." Even to her, the statement sounded false.

"Oh, it's a date, even if it is based on something as gory as an old dead guy," Randy insisted. "No wonder you're all gussied up. How did you manage that? Believe me many women around here have tried to get his attention, and none of them has succeeded."

"I didn't do anything special. We were talking, I asked, and he said yes." She stepped around her sister who was blocking the bedroom door. "I have to go or else I'll be late."

"You actually asked him out?" Randy's eyes were the size of silver dollars.

"What? It's the twenty-first century. It's not like I've never asked a man to meet me for a drink or coffee before. Lots of women ask men out, but this isn't a date. It's just two old friends meeting for coffee."

"Sure it is, but I want details when you get home." The shrewd look on her face promised a grilling the likes of which Casey hadn't had since she'd graduated law school.

"Fine, but it's not a date."

"What's that line from Shakespeare Dad used to quote? You know, the one about protesting too much?" Randy chuckled.

Casey shook her head and stepped around her. As she headed down the stairs, her sister called out. "Have fun!"

Great. By the time I get home, Mom and Dad will probably be sitting in on the inquisition, too.

* * * *

Tucking his shirt into his jeans, Cole hoped he'd made the right decision. While Casey had suggested meeting for coffee, unless they drove into one of the shops in Apache Junction, the chances were they would be seen together. While the thought of giving the ladies' sewing circle something knew to jaw on didn't bother him, he was certain Casey wasn't ready to add another tidbit to this week's rumor mill.

From what he'd seen the last couple of times they'd spoken, a ride out into the wilderness was more her style. It was a beautiful night, and she would be surprised to discover he rode a Harley, too. That gave them something else in common. Table Rock was the place to go, and while he hadn't been there at night in months, he knew the place would be the ideal setting for them. She might not consider this a date, but he did, and he intended to make it a memorable one, one where they would be alone without anyone watching them and gossiping about it later.

Satisfied with his decision, he grabbed his wallet, keys, and cellphone and was just leaving his bedroom when his phone rang again. For a brief moment, he considered letting it ring in case it was Casey calling to cancel. If he didn't answer, he didn't think she would stand him up.

Force of habit had him glancing at the call display. This wasn't a call he could ignore. To do so could bring on the wrath of the gods.

"Hi, Mom. Is everything okay?" he asked, not hiding the concern in his voice.

"Yes, everything's fine. Fallon, Tom, and the boys send their love. What have you been up to while we were gone?"

"Nothing much. Business at the emporium's been steady. Lots of tourists in town for Gold Rush Days. You can tell Dad those bags of 'gold' dust are selling really well. The kids love them although that candy powder is way too sour for me. The gold nugget bubble gum flew off the shelves. I had a couple of extra shifts with Hal, and there was another fire last month. No serious damage, but one more of those shacks east of town is in cinders. Drew Macintosh is back from Afghanistan. We met for beers the other night. Oh, and they identified that body found out near the mine. You might know the guy—Leon Turner— Hal figures he was out prospecting, more than likely at the old abandoned mines, where he had no business, and slipped. Could've been during the earthquake last summer. That would fit with the time range the medical examiner gave us."

"I remember Leon," she said, her voice filled with sorrow. "That poor man. His life ground to a halt when they closed that mine ten years ago and let him go with nothing but a handshake. He'd spent his entire life working for Skansen Mining and then … Hard to believe he could slip and fall like that. The man was as agile as a mountain goat, but the quake was a strong one, and as we get older, our balance isn't as good as it was."

"Not you, Mom. You're as spry and nimble now as you were when I was a kid."

She chuckled. "Liar. I have to say all of these fires bother me. How many is that now? At least four in the last six months. I hope Hal can find whoever's setting them soon before they decide to move on to bigger and better things."

"So do I. So far, no one's been hurt, but it's just a matter of time."

"How is Drew? I'm sure his mother is relieved to have him back on US soil."

"Drew's fine. He's leaving the air force, but isn't sure what he'll do."

"It was hard on him losing David like that. Those two were thicker than thieves. So what are you doing tonight?" she asked, always interested in what he did since she complained he didn't socialize enough.

"I'm taking a night off and going out on the Harley. I started a new book over the weekend. Maybe I'll get inspired."

"Already? You usually wait longer between books. I know the more you publish the better it is, but I worry about you. You spend too much time alone. You really need to get out and mingle more."

"Well, I plan on mingling tonight," he answered, although he hoped he might find fodder for a scene or two. "I'm going riding with Cassandra Stevens."

"Really?" Her voice went up at least two octaves. He could hear the wheels turning in her head and sensed her excitement.

"Don't read anything in to it, Mom. It's just a motorcycle ride," he cautioned. "Casey's home for Gold Rush Days and has her own Harley." Knowing that fact probably wouldn't stop her from thinking and planning.

"Fine. Have it your way, but you're not getting any younger. It's time you settled down. Any woman would be lucky to have you."

"Yeah, that may be, but I haven't found one I want to spend my life with. Casey's home for two weeks, and since we reconnected only Friday, I think a marriage proposal tonight would be a little premature," he joked.

"Ha, ha. Very funny," she said, and he knew his sarcasm hadn't pleased her, but he doubted she would let go of her matchmaking ideas. After visiting Fallon, her desire for more grandchildren always increased.

"I have to go, Mom. I'm running late."

"Wait. Are you still picking us up at the airport tomorrow afternoon?"

"Yes, I'll be there. Four o'clock, right? Don't worry." It wasn't a problem since the emporium was usually closed on Tuesdays and Thursdays, and since he'd put in extra hours on Sunday, Hal had given him the day off.

"In a minute. You're always in such a rush. Did you speak with Mrs. Harper?"

"I did," he said, resigned to the fact she wouldn't let him go until she was good and ready. "I assured her the volunteer firefighters would be there first thing Saturday morning to help set up the stage."

"Thank you, darling. I knew we could count on your help."

Cole enjoyed living in Fortune and being part of the close-knit community. He'd spent five years in El Paso and another seven in Dallas working as a police officer, reaching the rank of sergeant before he'd resigned. Despite seeing the dark side of humanity, for a while he'd been happy in the city, but eventually, loneliness and homesickness had crept up on him. Instead of reaching out and becoming more social, he'd retreated into himself as he'd done during his teenage years. As an avid reader, he'd known the market was ripe for western adventure stories, and so, he'd filled his lonely nights with writing, but something had been missing.

When he'd returned to Fortune, the town and its people had inspired him. He'd revised one of the manuscripts he'd worked on in Dallas and submitted it. The last thing he'd expected was for his Tate Silvers' novels to become an overnight sensation. Four books and two movie deals later, a third one pending, he was still awed by his success. Sure he wrote westerns, but he was no Zane Grey or A. B. Guthrie. The money was an unexpected bonus, and although he could choose to go anywhere he wanted to, no place drew him like Fortune. This was where he'd created Tate, and this was where he would stay. There was enough inspiration around here for a hundred novels.

Realizing his mother was going on about something and having no idea what it was, he glanced at the clock. It was almost seven-forty.

"Mom, you can tell me all about it when I see you tomorrow. I have to go now."

"Okay. Be careful tonight. Love you," she said, smacking a kiss into the phone.

"Love you, too." He ended the call and hurried downstairs.

The last thing he wanted to do was have Casey wait for him, worrying he might not show up.

Twenty-five minutes later, Cole paced nervously up and down the sidewalk in front of the store. Where was she? Checking his watch for the second time in as many minutes, he wondered if he were being stood up. Wouldn't that make an interesting scene? Tate left high and dry watching the sultry redhead ride away from him, dressed in a velvet riding outfit, her breasts spilling from her white linen blouse, nipples hard—

"Cole, you're working late."

The familiar voice startled him out of the daydream. Pete Putnam stood just behind him with Bullet, his Jack Russell Terrier, straining on his leash to get moving again. How a man his size, with a limp left over from his fall last year, could move so quietly never ceased to amaze Cole. The burley, white-haired man had delivered the mail for more than forty years before retiring, but that hadn't changed him. He still knew everything happening in Fortune. He was the inspiration behind Len, the bartender at Prospect's *Lucky Slipper Saloon*. So far Len ran the saloon on his own, but maybe he would add a dog to the next book, one determined to protect his owner at all costs. Bullet might not be big, but he would be tenacious.

"Hi, Pete. Not working late, just had to pick up a couple of things I needed. How's your wife?"

"Maize's fit as a fiddle. That new hip works just fine. She would've joined us on our walk tonight, but that dancing program was on television, and she never misses an episode."

Society's obsession with so you think you can—fill in the blank—programs and reality shows stymied him. He glanced down the street and then turned back to the elderly man. "That recipe book she ordered came in today. Is Trevor coming home for the weekend?"

"Yup. Should be here next day or so—bringing the new baby, too. They'll probably need to rent a truck to take back all the stuff Maize's bought." He laughed. "It's amazing how much stuff a three-month-old needs nowadays. Years ago, when we traveled, we put Trevor in a drawer on the floor. Well, I'd better get going. There's going to be a meteor shower early tonight. Normally I miss them since they happen after midnight, but I'm looking forward to seeing this one. Nice clear night for it. The local channel made a mistake and announced it for tomorrow night. I'll get a great view from the balcony off the spare bedroom. I'll tell Maize about the book. See you later."

Cole nodded and watched the large man shuffle down the sidewalk as silently as he'd approached and stared into the twilight, second-guessing himself once more.

What if this was all a mistake? So what if it was the first date he'd had since high school with someone from Fortune? It wasn't as if he'd lived the life of a monk or anything. He just didn't like messing around in his own sandbox.

Tonight was all about spending a few hours together getting to know one another. Besides, they had a lot in common, including CJ Coleson and being involved with the law. Lots of women enjoyed being passengers on his motorcycle, but Casey was the first girl he'd met who rode her own—and not just any motorcycle. That bike was one of Harley Davidson's latest models.

Another glimpse at his watch showed she was almost ten minutes late. Pulling out his phone, he looked to see if he'd missed a call, but there were no messages. Unlatching his saddle bag, he checked its contents for the third time. Everything he needed for his surprise was there, except his date. He gave a sigh of relief when he heard the sound of her bike approaching.

Hunched over, she made it seem as if she and the machine were one, and a jolt of desire ran through him. Taking Casey out into the desert in the moonlight might not be the wisest thing to do, but it was definitely what he wanted to do.

The motorcycle eased to a stop beside his, and she lifted the visor on her helmet. Her beautiful, large, hazel eyes twinkled with excitement and curiosity.

"Sorry, I'm late. It took me longer to get out of the house than I'd expected. Have you been waiting long?"

"Nope, just got here a few minutes ago." Thirty was a few.

"Nice ride. Is it yours?" she asked admiring his Harley.

Cole closed the flap on his saddle bag and walked over to where she sat astride. The warm sensation he'd felt watching her approach pooled in his gut, and he envied the bike.

"Yes, it's mine. I thought we would go for a ride. You've been gone a while, but you must remember what an awesome place the wilderness can be at night. I want to show you one of my favorite spots. It's about half an hour from here."

"I don't know," she said, a frown marring her face. "My last experience in the desert at night wasn't a good one. Besides, I was really looking forward to a cup of coffee."

"No worries. I filled a thermos with my favorite blend, and promise this desert experience will be great. Trust me?"

She laughed softly, the insecurity she'd shown earlier evident.

"Well, if you think so ... since you've got everything under control, which way do we ride?"

"West, along the Apache Trail, and then we'll turn into the Last Dutchman Campground and ride south to the Superstition Mountain Wilderness trails. How's your gas?"

"Filled up this afternoon. Let's go." Flipping down her visor, she started the engine and rode off down the street.

Cole shook his head ruefully, jumped on his Harley, and took off after her. Keeping up with Casey wasn't going to be easy, and not just because of the bike. He had a feeling any time he spent with her would be one hell of a ride.

CHAPTER SIX

Cole enjoyed himself as they sped along the road. The setting sun turned the blacktop into a golden ribbon stretching endlessly ahead of them. Depending on how things went tonight, he just might use what he'd always considered his private place as one of the settings in *Firebrand*. He could picture Tate and Crimson, alone in the desert, just as he and Casey would be tonight.

Pulling ahead, he turned onto the road leading into the campground, and then onto a trail anyone would miss in the twilight unless they knew it was there. He slowed his bike to make sure Casey was behind him, and to accommodate the change in road conditions. Like many of the paths leading into the wilderness, the hard-packed dirt road was better suited to ATVs and other off-road vehicles. Maybe this wasn't such a good idea after all. This kind of terrain probably wasn't what she was accustomed to. If anything happened to her, her father would have his neck, and a few other choice parts of his anatomy.

When they reached the end of the trail, they shut down their bikes and made sure they were secure on the uneven ground. Cole took the backpack full of supplies out of his saddlebag and, like Casey was doing, fastened his helmet and riding gloves to the bike. He loved it here, and he hoped she would, too. The desert wasn't for everyone, but in his case, it was in his blood.

The waxing gibbous moon bathed the landscape in an eerie silver wash. Flipping the switch on the LED flashlight he carried, he held out his hand to Casey. Her hand was small in his, and since he stood almost a foot taller than her, he felt like Jaws in *Moonraker*. He hadn't realized how petite she was.

"How far do we have to walk?" she asked, breaking into his thoughts.

"Not far." Shouldering the backpack, he made a point of tamping down the excessive excitement running through him. "Maybe two hundred yards. Most of the ground is even enough between here and there. Just hang on to me, and you won't have a problem."

"Okay. I just don't want to step in a trapdoor spider hole or something equally disgusting."

He chuckled. "Don't worry. I'll stay well away from those."

As they walked farther away from the bikes, Cole pointed out the buckhorn cholla, hedgehog, prickly pear, brittle bush, and barrel cacti. The plants, so familiar to him, were alien shapes rising out of the desert floor—beauty and danger combined.

"Watch out for the teddy bear cholla. They stick to you before you even know they're there."

"Yeah. We have some of those growing on the ranch. My favorite is still the Saguaro. I have a much smaller version potted in my condo in Santa Fe," Casey said, pointing to the tall cactus plant in front of them. She chuckled softly, the slight sound loud in the stillness around them. "At first, I got a tiny bit homesick, but having the plant around helped."

Cole gently squeezed her fingers in understanding. "You can take a person out of the desert, but you can't take the love of the desert out of a person. I learned that in Dallas. I might've had a cactus or two in my apartment and in my office."

Something flew above them, low enough that he felt the need to duck.

71

She clutched his arm and looked up. "Tell me those aren't what I think they are."

Cole laughed. "Spotted and pallid bats. They're harmless."

"Says you," she said, holding his arm more tightly. "I'm not a fan."

The hoot of an owl broke the ensuing silence. She clung to him, avoiding the obstacles in their path, and checking the sky every now and then. Maybe for their next date, he'd invite her over to watch scary movies. That would keep her tucked into him nicely.

"How was the rest of your day?" he asked.

"Okay, although I did just about lose it when we had that quake this afternoon. Jaxon was in the water and didn't even notice, but I was like, whoa!"

He chuckled once more. "Big city girl afraid of having the earth move under her feet?"

"Hey, if I wanted to live in an earthquake zone, I would've chosen to practice law in California. Dad said the quake was a small one—3.9 on the Richter scale. I'd hate to be in a big one."

"It shook things around at the store, but I had no casualties. As far as a sizeable quake goes, we should be safe. The last big one around here was in 1887."

"So we aren't due yet. What are you? A trivia expert? That's something I would expect CJ to know. Let me guess. He gets you to help with his research."

Cole nodded. "Something like that. Research takes a lot of time away from writing, but a good author knows he or she has to do both. You must have to do some for your cases, right?"

"Yeah, while we have paralegals on staff, I usually look for precedent myself."

Luckily, they'd arrived at their destination, a large, flat rock rising some two feet above the desert floor, and the conversation ended. Cole let go of her hand, stepped onto the flat surface, and then turned to help her up.

"It's incredible," she said, the awe in her voice matching the way he felt every time he came out here, no matter what time of day.

Table Rock, as he'd christened the place, was about ten feet in diameter and stood on a rise, overlooking the wilderness. On its right side, the stone was barely two feet above the desert floor, but on the left, the land dipped and their stone island stood a good six feet above the ghostly landscape. Below them was a forest of buckhorn cholla, their long spikes reaching up like fingers toward the sky.

Superstition Mountain, the tall volcanic hill that gave this particular chain of mountains their name, was no more than a mile or so east of them. In the moonlight, the rough remnant of an ancient volcano looked dark and mysterious.

"I can see why you like it here." Her voice was barely above a whisper. "It has an unearthly, haunting beauty that calls to the soul. Was that body on this side of the mountain?"

"Yeah, but farther south than where we are." Cole flashed the LED across the surface of the rock. "Just want to make sure there aren't any bark scorpions around before I put down the blanket. They don't like the light, so if there are any up here, they'll disappear quickly."

Casey wrapped her arms around herself. "I'm not fond of creepy crawlies, even if they are only two inches long. Mom's terrified of spiders."

"I had a tarantula in the store last week, and before that a yearling rattler sunning himself on a rock out back." He chuckled at the look of horror on her face. "You can relax. Nothing will bother us up here tonight, I promise."

"I can see this is a great spot for a date that's not a date," she commented, her face betraying her concern, "but if you keep telling me about bugs and bats, not to mention reptiles, I'll change my mind."

Cole moved closer to her once more, stopped in front of her, and placed his hand on her cheek. Her skin was warm beneath his palm.

"This is a date, one I hope you'll remember long after you've gone back to Santa Fe."

She smiled uncertainly and nodded. "You're pretty confident," she said softly. "I've had dates before."

"But never like this one."

"You're probably right. It's definitely the first time I've been wooed with talk of bats, tarantulas, and scorpions."

Cole laughed, shook his head, and pulled a couple of blankets out of his backpack, wishing the two of them had come together like this years ago.

"I could regale you with the gory details about the body and its missing parts if you prefer."

"No, thanks. You can keep the Halloween conversation for broad daylight."

He chuckled and spread one of the heavy wool coverlets on the rock. As soon as he finished, he removed his leather jacket, unzipped the sides of his leather pants, and folded them together to make a pillow. The long sleeved, crew neck, cotton shirt he wore with his jeans would be plenty warm enough for a while. If he got lucky, they would be cuddling later, sharing body heat, and watching that meteor shower Pete had mentioned.

"Usually, even though it's the end of August, the desert cools down at night," he said, smiling at Casey, wishing she would relax. "Tonight's not too bad. It was one of the reasons I thought we could make this work."

"I'm surprised it's so warm. What have you got in there?" she asked, as one by one, he pulled the rest of the things he'd brought with him out of the backpack.

"Just a few things I figured we would need." Standing so that she couldn't see everything before he was ready to share it with her, he pulled out a battery powered LED lantern and turned it on, allowing the light to create an island of radiance amid the darkness. "This will definitely keep the scorpions and bats away."

"You smooth talker," she said, chuckling softly. "That's the most romantic thing you've said yet."

He turned off the flashlight and looked up at her. "I aim to please. Why don't you get comfortable while I finish unpacking?"

"Are you planning to be here all night? You certainly seem to have a lot in that bag. While I'm at home, Mom expects me to honor my high school curfew." She shrugged her shoulders. "I may be on the wrong side of thirty, but if I'm out past midnight, she'll turn me into a pumpkin."

"Don't worry, Cinderella. I'll get you back before curfew. It's just after nine. We've got lots of time. Now, settle back and relax. You don't want to ruin the surprise, do you? We can stay out here for a while yet. I brought an extra blanket in case it gets colder."

"It looks like you've thought of everything. For a man who doesn't usually date, you've certainly come prepared."

"What can I say? It's my boy scout training."

While he continued to rummage in his bag, he heard her unzip her leather pants and jacket. He pulled the thermos out of the bag, along with a small container of cream, and several packets of sugar.

"How'd you take your coffee?" he asked, turning to face her. The deep azure blue sweater brought out the blue in her hazel eyes, the neckline low enough that he could see the swell of her breasts. The skinny black jeans and knee-high leather boots made it seem as if her legs went on forever. "You're so beautiful." The words spilled out of him before he could stop them.

For a moment she looked too surprised to speak. Had no one ever told her she'd grown into a gorgeous woman?—not that she hadn't been attractive back then.

She looked away, breaking eye contact, as if being complimented made her uncomfortable.

"Cream and sugar, please."

The huskiness in her voice told him more than she probably wanted him to hear.

"You take my breath away," he whispered.

"You don't have to keep saying things like that, you know.

This is a great place. I'm glad you brought me here, even if it does have some peculiar and scary residents."

Cole turned away, not only to prepare the coffee but to cool his ardor. The last thing he wanted to do was scare her with the strength of his desire—hell, it scared him. Never had he wanted a woman the way he wanted this one. He handed her a mug and sat down beside her closer to his pile of leathers than she was.

"From reading his books, I would say CJ knows almost as much about this area as you do." She sipped the brew he'd given her. "This is really good. Has he ever seen this place? He's described parts of the Superstitions I recognize but...?"

Cole choked on his coffee. Damn, the woman had a one track mind. The problem was with each question she asked, he was digging himself a deeper hole.

"It's one of his favorite places," he admitted. What would she do if he blurted out the truth?

Expecting her to ask another question, he was surprised when she didn't. Sipping coffee, they sat there deep in their own thoughts, comfortable with one another, looking up at the moon and the stars, and listening to the desert's night sounds. Few people understood that sitting quietly, side by side, didn't mean something was wrong.

"Do you come to this place often?" she asked as she finished the last of the coffee in her mug.

"Yeah, but sadly, it's been a while." He leaned against his makeshift pillow, feeling more content than he had in ages. "I come out here whenever I need to clear my head. You know—get away from it all. While it's part of the Superstition Mountain Wilderness, for some reason, most of the hikers tend to drive in closer to the mountain over toward the petroglyphs, and leave this section alone. It can get hotter than hell here in the summer, but ... When I'm here, I can think straight. Things fall into place. I've never been one for crowds, and I feel as if I belong when I'm out here. When I lived in Dallas, I'd go up onto the roof of my apartment building, hoping to find this sense of peacefulness, but I never did. Riding was the only way I found the harmony I needed to counteract the ugliness of my job. But you ride, so you have to understand that. Is that your first Harley?"

"No, but it's the first new one. When I moved away to school, I missed riding. Horses are a little hard to look after in the city, even in Texas. A friend got me hooked on Harleys, and I've never looked back. Mom hates it. Calls it a death machine, but I've promised not to let someone scrape me off the pavement, so we're good."

"My mom was like that when I got my first Harley. It seems they lost a good friend in a motorcycle-car accident. At first, everyone thought it had to be the biker's fault, but the truth came out. The car driver, some rich kid from Phoenix, was drunk and lost control. The guy's family tried to get him charged, but he walked on a technicality."

"They often do. The law isn't perfect, but now that I know what's bothering her, I'll try to be more understanding. People die that same way in cars, too," she said, her brow creased in thought. "Drinking and driving … too many people drink and act like idiots without considering the consequences of their actions. They don't care who gets hurt, who dies."

"Yeah, but things are slowly improving."

"Once the damage is done, it can't be undone."

He had the feeling she wasn't talking about her mother's dead friend any longer.

"For what it's worth, I don't think I've pulled a drunk driver over in months."

"That's a step in the right direction." She looked up at him. "How many other women have you brought out here for coffee?"

"Actually, you're the first," he admitted, glad she'd changed the topic.

"You're kidding. With that moon and all these stars, this is probably one of the most romantic places I've ever seen. What makes me so special?"

"I've never met anyone I wanted to share this place with before," he confessed. "I thought you'd appreciate it—kindred spirits, I guess."

Suddenly, the sky was ablaze with streaks of white light as several meteoroids tore across it in the natural fireworks display Pete had mentioned.

"Did you know that was going to happen?" she asked.

The sense of awe in her voice pleased him.

"I'm impressed. Moonlight and fireworks—what a way to set the mood. And you've never shared this with another girl?"

"Nope. Did I know there'd be a meteoroid shower tonight? Not when I decided to bring you here, but Pete Putnam mentioned it when I was waiting for you."

Putting down his empty mug, he stretched his body along the blanket, lifting his arms, and lacing his fingers behind his head. He watched the joy blossom on her face as she observed the heavenly shower.

"Well, it's incredible. I can't imagine any girl not being impressed in such a setting."

Reaching up, he pulled her down so that she rested against him. He breathed in the floral scent of her shampoo.

"Good thing I'd finished my coffee," she scolded, her voice catching as she spoke, but she didn't pull away.

He nestled her head more deeply into his chest.

"How come we weren't friends when I lived here?" she asked a few minutes later.

"I didn't have the nerve to talk to girls back then. I was rather shy. Can you imagine what cradle-robbing would have done to what little reputation I had?"

"Seriously. I don't think anyone would've accused you of cradle-robbing. Two years isn't that big a gap."

He twirled a strand of her silky hair around his finger. "We did talk once." He closed his eyes, savoring the memory. "It was during my senior year. There was a carnival in town, and I'd watched you for over an hour trying to win a pink teddy bear. You came close, but then I heard you tell your friend that you'd run out of money. When you walked away, I decided I was going to win that bear for you."

"I still have it. It's on my bed at home," she admitted shyly.

He chuckled. "A man likes to know his gifts are appreciated. Once I'd won it, I looked everywhere for you afraid you'd left. When I finally found you I said, very macho-man-like, 'Here you go,' and tossed it at you. You looked stunned. I walked away before you could say anything."

"That was one of the happiest moments of my life. Thank you, Cole," she whispered.

The soft brush of her lips surprised him, but like food offered to a starving man, he wasn't going to refuse it. He groaned deep in his throat, entwined his fingers in her silky hair, and dragged her closer, pulling her body into his.

When she didn't pull away, he deepened the kiss, giving free rein to the urgency within him. She moaned into his mouth fueling the fire burning through him. He shut his eyes blocking out everything but the sensation of her lips on his.

Casey was intoxicating and definitely the most wonderful thing he'd ever savored. He feasted on the flavor of his favorite coffee mixed with the tang that was hers alone, supped from the sweetness of her mouth, absorbing her very essence, and knew no other kiss had ever matched this one, and none ever would.

Her mouth was made for kissing—lush and full, pulsing and throbbing with life beneath his—lips he suckled and sipped, leaving them swollen and trembling, something he'd dreamed of doing from the second she'd sauntered into his store. He ran the tip of his tongue along them, and when she opened to him, he slipped into her mouth, intensifying the kiss, moving the encounter up a level and feeding from her nectar.

Swallowing her moans, he took them deeply into himself and wrapped his arms tightly around her. When she positioned herself to fit him, he hardened to the point of discomfort, but he wasn't going to do anything to end this until he had to. His hands began to explore the softness of her body, moving up under the smooth fabric of her top to skim the silkiness of her skin, the edge of her breasts.

Being here with her like this had him on sensory overload. They continued to explore one another's mouths, Casey suddenly taking and giving with an energy that matched his. His libido screamed for more, but his common sense warned him that if he didn't stop now there would be no turning back. This wasn't what he'd been expecting, and he wasn't prepared for it. He wasn't a randy teenager intent on getting laid on the first date. She deserved more than a quickie on a rock in the desert.

Gently, he untangled his hands from her hair and pulled his lips away from hers.

"I'm going to regret this, and it may very well kill me to do so, but we need to stop." Contrary to what his words said, he continued to feather her face with gentle kisses.

Casey giggled against his lips, and the vibration ran through his torso.

"If you want me to try and control myself, you'll have to stop kissing me like this," she murmured, running her fingers lightly through his hair, exciting him further, and sending a surge of desire through his body.

"Believe me, I *am* trying, but you taste so good. I just can't seem to get enough of you. You're addictive. From now on, you're my drug of choice."

Giving him a quick kiss, she pushed herself up and straddled him. He suppressed a groan as he felt her heat against his hardness, sending wave after wave of need crashing through him. A man could die this way. She wasn't making this easy, and he couldn't stop a moan from escaping his mouth.

"Drugs can be dangerous," she said, a mischievous grin on her face.

Her body squirmed atop his, enticing another growl from him.

"Casey…" Unable to utter another word, he concentrated on keeping it together. He had a feeling she was enjoying herself at his expense.

She leaned down, pressing her chest to his, bringing her

delicate hands up slowly to caress his face. Her warm breath tickled his lips as she ran her fingers through his hair again. He ached for her.

She whispered his name against his lips, and his control broke. He captured her mouth in a ruthless, hungry, demanding kiss. Fisting her hair in his hands, he savaged her mouth, dragging all he could from her as payment for the way she'd tortured him.

With what little willpower he had left, he lifted her from him, cradling her so he wouldn't hurt her, and gently flipped her onto her back, straddling her so that she bore none of his body weight, but pinning her to the rock beneath them. His eyes met hers, surprised by the level of heat and desire he saw there.

"Seducing you tonight wasn't what I'd planned. When I make love to you, it'll be in a soft bed on silk sheets, not on a rock in the desert."

"Promises, promises."

He kissed her quickly. "It's a promise you can take to the bank. Now, are you going to behave?"

Her swollen mouth turned into a pout. "If you insist."

He kissed her one last time—a long, drugging kiss that promised more because he knew he would never get enough of her.

Slowly lifting himself off her, he reached for the backpack and removed the book he'd brought. He turned back toward her and stopped, awed by what he saw.

She hadn't moved and lay where he'd left her, her tangled hair spread across the blanket, her lips, ruby red, swollen from his kisses, her eyes sparkling dark blue and amber gems in the light of the lantern. Without a doubt, she was the most alluring woman in the world, and at the moment, she was all his.

Piling her discarded leathers on top of his, he leaned against them and pulled her into and slightly onto him, so she could rest her head against his shoulder. They belonged together—even if it was only for a little while. Her breathing was still ragged, and he knew it wouldn't take much to send them both tumbling into oblivion again. He wasn't sure he would be able to stop the next time.

"We could talk shop if you insist, but I brought a book, and I thought I would read to you," he said huskily, trying to ignore the softness of her body molded to his—the peak of her breasts hard nubs against his chest.

"You're going to read to me?" Her voice was shaky and surprised.

"Yeah, I thought you might like that. Was I wrong?"

She shook her head. "No. What did you bring?" she asked snuggling into him. Her body trembled slightly, and he pulled the blanket over her.

"One of the short stories CJ published and distributed only to family and friends. He wrote a few of them loosely based on Apache legends before he created Tate Silvers."

"You've definitely made this the most romantic date I've ever had. Since I've been home, I haven't had time to read anything but Dr. Seuss," she said. "He's Jaxon's favorite author."

Cole laughed. "Hey, there's nothing wrong with that. He used to be mine, too. I still read him now and then, but don't tell anyone." He winked.

"Your secret's safe with me." The rock beneath them shook slightly. "What was that?" she asked, her eyes large with fright.

"Probably just an aftershock because of the quake we had earlier. I could say you felt the earth move because of me, but I'm too modest for that."

She giggled. "Modest? I don't think so."

Stroking her hair, twisting the silken strands around his fingers, he smiled.

"How about unassuming? I often wondered what your hair would feel like. It looks like lava, and yet, it's so soft and silky."

She chuckled softly. "That's only because you've never tried to comb it first thing in the morning. Sometimes, I think barbed wire would be easier to work with."

"Anytime you need it brushed, just ask." The image of her

naked in front of a mirror, with him brushing her hair, the flame-colored locks spilling down her white back had him uncomfortably aware of her once more. That scene would definitely go into the book. He cleared his throat and started to read.

"Liluye sat in front of her tepee watching the moon rise. In the distance, she heard the hungry howls of the coyotes and shivered. Her own belly was so empty, she was ready to eat anything she could find..." Before he'd finished chapter one, he heard her soft snores.

So much for his engrossing prose. Closing the book softly, he stretched his arm behind his head making himself comfortable, listening to Casey's soft breathing, and, leaned back to watch another round of meteorites fill the sky. Letting his fingers run through Casey's silky-smooth curls, he sighed and closed his eyes ... If this wasn't one of life's perfect moments, it was damn close.

A rumbling, similar to rolling thunder, resonated in the distance, reminding him of the Apache legend that the thunder gods resided in these mountains. The sound grew louder, rousing him from his reverie. While it could be slight activity echoing off canyon walls, it sounded more like the engine on an ATV. Clicking off the lantern, he looked toward Superstition Mountain, amazed to see lights in the distance, appearing and disappearing on the mountain almost like a boat on a heavy sea.

The old abandoned Skansen mines he and Hal had visited yesterday were out that way, as was the area where Leon Turner had died. That section of the mountain hadn't been worked in years, so what the hell was going on?

While there was always the chance it was teenagers, risking life and limb in some foolish game, there was a possibility someone was claim jumping, going into those old Skansen pits, and using small gasoline-powered diggers to extract ore, hoping to find gold. It had been more than eighty years since anyone had looked for it down there, and with modern equipment ... What if the Skansen Mining Board of Directors were wrong?

Maybe Leon Turner hadn't been the only one prospecting out that way, and if that was the case, the old man's death might not have been an accident, nor might it have anything to do with his social security payments.

Red lights moved away from the mountain and dipped down, hovering no more than fifty feet off the desert floor, well below radar range, slowly creeping toward them, growing larger by the second, a whoop-whoop sound coming to him on the breeze. Cole prayed no one over there had noticed their light. Heart pounding at the sight of what had to be a helicopter, its lights, both red and white, giving the illusion of a monstrous creature moving in the night sky, he held his breath. Cold sweat slithered down his back. If Chester had seen lights like those, accompanied by the sound of the rotor blades, he could easily have believed he'd seen aliens landing or taking off in the desert.

If whoever was in that chopper was coming to investigate, they were defenseless. Tucking Casey closer to him, he covered her with his jacket and the dark blanket hoping to hide them, but at the last minute the bird veered south, away from them. He let out the breath he'd been holding, grateful Casey was a sound sleeper.

The loud cry of a big cat somewhere nearby sent goosebumps crawling along his flesh, reminding him that men weren't the only predators out tonight. Turning on the flashlight keeping the light pointed at the surface of the rock, he reluctantly roused Casey. While he would willingly lie with her in his arms like this for hours, tonight wasn't the night to do it. The desert could be hazardous at any time, but right now those dangers were multiplied.

CHAPTER SEVEN

Cole shook Casey gently, hoping he could mask his concern. "Wake up, Sleeping Beauty. If I let you rest any longer, you'll miss curfew."

She opened her eyes, blinked sleepily and then sat up quickly, her teeth gripping her lower lip in horror, her eyes wide open.

"I'm so sorry. I can't believe I did that," she stammered, her cheeks red in the LED light spilling from the flashlight. "Please don't say anything to CJ. It wasn't the story. I haven't been getting much sleep lately. I had to burn the midnight oil at work to get this time off, and I guess I was just so relaxed and…"

"Hey, don't sweat it. I was dozing, too. Besides, if you were comfortable enough to nod off in my presence here, knowing how you feel about the area's residents, then that's a compliment. Let's get this picked up and head back into town."

The loud, unexpected crack of a rifle made them both jump, reminding Cole of their immediate danger.

"What the hell was that?" she asked, her voice filled with fear.

"Probably a poacher out after deer," he lied, hoping to reassure her and knowing they needed to get the hell out of here a.s.a.p. That shot most likely came from a rancher or a Bureau

85

of Land Management ranger hunting for the mountain lion he'd heard. Having the big cats this close to civilization didn't happen often, but when it did, it wasn't usually a good thing. Last spring, a rabid cougar had wandered into the campground and attacked a camper. The rangers had caught the animal and destroyed it, but the man had lost his leg. The other possibility, the one where that shot had come from whoever was responsible for the lights he'd seen earlier, wasn't one he wanted to think about.

"Is he near us?" the nervous tremor in her voice convinced him she didn't need the truth.

"No, that shot was miles away. Sound really carries at night."

"Well, it sounded really close. It's getting cold." She shivered and reached for her leathers.

"Let's pack it up. As much as I would love to spend more time with you, I don't want you to catch your death out here."

As soon as the words left his mouth, he regretted them, but Casey laughed.

"You don't have to worry about that. I rarely get sick. Mom claims I have the constitution of an ox."

He chuckled, some of his disquiet vanquished by her innocuous comment. "I guess that animal can be considered red, but it's the last one I'd have compared you to. I'd envision a fox, a red panda, or some exotic red-haired rabbit—small, and adorable.

She laughed. "You are so full of it. No wonder your eyes are brown."

Stopping what he was doing, he reached for her.

"You're without a doubt the most beautiful, puzzling woman I have ever met. One of these days, I'll convince you of that, and believe me, I have outstanding powers of persuasion, but it's getting late. I don't want to ruin my chances at a second date."

Shaking her head, she smiled sheepishly. "You're good, but you might need to have your eyes checked."

She stood on tiptoes and kissed him quickly, a mere brush of her lips on his, and while he might want to take it deeper, the faint sounds of those engines floated over to them.

"I didn't realize we were so close to the highway," she said as they moved apart.

Shrugging, he picked up the backpack, and lied again. "Maybe we aren't, and it's the Apache Thunder Gods moving around." He wiggled his eyebrows.

She giggled.

Cole jumped down from the rock and held out his hand to her. "Come on, Cinderella. We've got to get back before the witching hour."

"Very well, my prince. I found you quite charming tonight." She held out her hand.

Reaching for it, he brought it to his lips and kissed it before helping her down from the rock.

"I try. I'm looking forward to my next chance to show you how appealing I can be," he whispered, wanting to keep their voices down just in case. "Maybe someplace with candles and silk sheets. I know one only thirty minutes away. I've got more coffee, too."

"Coffee's good," she answered, biting her lip once more.

Cole took her hand in his and, using the flashlight to illuminate the ground before them, led her back through the cacti to the trail. As soon as they reached their Harleys, he did his best to hurry her without making her notice the furtiveness of his actions. The sooner they were back in town, the better he would like it. He worried the entire ten minutes it took to follow the path, get to the campground road, and then back onto Highway 88. Watching for signs they were being followed, he saw no one, but he was glad they'd agreed earlier to go to his place. The problem would come later when he would try to convince her to let him escort her home without revealing the possible danger.

It was shortly after eleven when they pulled into his driveway and got off the bikes. Casey removed her helmet and stepped into his open arms.

"You bought your parents' home. That's great. I always loved this place," she said, putting her arms around his waist and resting her head on his chest.

He blinked. "What? No. They still live here, but they aren't around much, so it doesn't make sense for me to have a place of my own when this one's empty most of the time."

She released her arms from around his waist, and moved away.

"I guess. I'd better get going. Thanks for a wonderful evening," she said, but the words sounded off somehow. "I enjoyed every minute. It's definitely been a night I won't forget, and the most romantic date I've ever had—tarantulas and bats notwithstanding."

He chuckled, trying to figure out what had her shying away. "I thought you were coming in for coffee," he said, unable to mask his confusion.

"Not tonight. I need to get home."

"You don't have to go. My parents aren't here right now, if that's what's bothering you."

He pulled her tightly against him, but something had changed between them. She was stiff in his arms, and damned if he understood why.

"Nothing's bothering me," she answered, a touch too quickly. "It's getting late. You made me forget about all the things I have to do tomorrow. Randy's waitress is off, and I promised to help out at the shop. I haven't worked as a waitress since I got my degree. I'm sure I'll be dead on my feet by noon. As you saw earlier, I really need to get some rest, and the last thing I want to do is let her down."

But she could crush his hopes. He released her. She gave him a quick kiss, and mounted her bike.

"Are you sure you don't want me to come with you?" he asked, worried she might be followed. Just because he hadn't noticed a tail didn't mean they didn't have one.

"Absolutely. What could possibly happen to me in Fortune?

Besides, two motorcycles pulling into the driveway might wake Jaxon, and he's really hard to get back to sleep if he wakes up during the night. He's going through that monster phase."

Since he didn't know enough about the sleeping habits of four year olds, and vaguely remembered Fallon's fear of the dark when she was a child, it was hard to disagree.

"I'll call you. You were right. It was a date that I'll never forget." Donning her helmet, she dropped the visor in place, and started the bike. Within seconds, all he could see were her taillights.

Despite his desire to follow her, Cole moved his bike to the garage and locked it up, reminded once more that Fortune wasn't the town it had been when he'd grown up here. Climbing the steps, he unlocked the door and punched in the alarm code. Too wound up to sleep, he poured himself a drink and turned on the television to catch the late night news, hoping to hear that Skansen Mining had reopened those old mines, but the redhead who'd kept him enthralled ever since her arrival wouldn't release her grip.

* * * *

Casey pulled away from the curb without looking back, intent on getting home as quickly as she could. Tonight had been one of the most wonderful nights of her life ... until he'd invited her into his parents' house. Seriously? What the hell was he doing living with Mommy and Daddy?

Cole was an adult. He should want to have his own place, be independent, cut the apron strings, but he hadn't. The fact he'd given up what must've been a lucrative job in Dallas to come back to Fortune spoke volumes, yet it made no sense. The last thing she'd have taken him for was a momma's boy. After dating a couple of trust fund sons in Santa Fe, she'd learned to avoid the type. The last thing she wanted was to get involved with another one of those—spoiled brats with a sense of entitlement, men still living at home, unwilling to step too far away from the family purse strings, and who wouldn't know honesty and trust if it bit them on the ass. The last thing she'd expected was to find another one here.

While she could understand his reasoning about them traveling so much, the whole thing just didn't sit right with her. He hadn't mentioned a separate apartment in the house, which might make it less weird, but still, a man of thirty-five should have a place entirely his own.

Just the thought of living with Mom and Dad made her shudder. She wanted her own space, with her own things around her, and the ability to come and go as she pleased. What about laundry? Imagining the look on her mother's face if she saw some of her racier undergarments made her laugh out loud. She might not live on the edge, but she had a penchant for sexy bras and panties—all of which she'd left tucked in her Santa Fe drawers, safe from prying eyes.

Randy lived at home, but that was different. As a single mother with a four-year-old to look after and her own business to manage, she needed help.

Pulling into the driveway, she parked the bike under the veranda on the west side of the house, chaining it to the metal bar there the way Dad had told her to, and ignored the voice in her head telling her she was overreacting. On tiptoes, she climbed the stairs, preventing the heels of her boot from making a staccato sound against the wooden steps and veranda. She unlocked the door, eased it open, and punched in the alarm code, grateful when bells and whistles didn't sound announcing her arrival. No one sat in the living room waiting to play twenty questions as to where she'd been and why she was so late. Relief washed over her when she reached her room undetected.

Opening the bedroom door quickly and confident she would soon be in bed, she smothered a scream when she saw someone or something sitting in the old rocker, bathed in the silvered moonlight coming in through the window.

"Holy crap, Randy! I thought you were a frigging ghost. You scared the bejesus out of me. What are you doing here? It's almost midnight."

"Shush! You don't want to wake Mom or Jaxon," her sister whispered. "I told you I wanted details, so give."

"I don't believe this. Miranda Maria Stevens, are you telling me you camped out in my room, sitting in the dark like some insane psycho waiting for me to come home, just so that you could grill me on my evening?" Her voice rose on the last word. She shook her head. "You need a life, girl."

"I did, and for the record, I have a life," she answered quietly. "It may not be the one I wanted, but…"

Guilt flooded Casey. Of course Randy had a life. It was all wrapped up in her gorgeous son and her new business. Neither of those commitments would give her much time to date—if she even wanted to. She'd taken David's death hard, and was still in mourning.

Casey plopped down on her bed. While Randy might want details about the most romantic evening she'd ever had, all she wanted to do was sleep and forget the man who'd made her feel like no one else ever had—the one who still lived with his mom.

"You know someone who doesn't know you as well as I do might think you're certifiable."

"Not crazy, Casey, just lonely. I still miss him."

The sadness in Randy's voice had her opening her eyes and looking at her sister. The longing on her face broke Casey's heart.

"Humor me, please," Randy begged.

Casey motioned to the bed beside her. The irony of the situation didn't escape her. In years past, it had been Casey who'd sat anxiously waiting to hear all about Randy's dates. While David had been born and raised in Fortune, he and Randy had met in Phoenix where Randy had worked as a pastry-chef. Casey hadn't been privy to the details of the whirlwind courtship that had led to a hasty wedding before David had gone overseas, and she realized she'd missed these tête à têtes more than she'd suspected.

Her face awash with excitement, Randy scrambled to get

comfortable, grabbed an extra pillow to place on Casey's chest, and rested her head on it.

"Tell me everything, don't leave out a single detail," she commanded as Casey unconsciously began to twill a strand of her sister's hair around her finger the way Cole had done with hers tonight. Before she could say anything, her cellphone vibrated in her pocket, making Randy giggle.

"Who calls you so late at night?" she asked, her eyes twinkling.

Casey pulled out the phone, saw it was Cole's number, and smiled not because she was pleased but because of the way Randy was staring at her. There were some things she wasn't ready to share, not that they were special in any way, but they confused her, and if there was anything she despised, it was feeling off-balance the way she did now.

"He seemed concerned about me getting home safely, as if anything bad could happen to me here." She rolled her eyes and pressed the call answer button. "Hi, Cole."

"How was the ride home?" he asked, his voice warming her, despite the fact she didn't want it to.

"Uneventful, just like I expected it to be."

"That's good. What are the chances we can repeat the adventure tomorrow? I still owe you a cup of coffee." The seductive way he spoke brought the image of silk sheets and candles to mind, but she forced them away.

"Look, I'm getting ready for bed. I'll talk to you tomorrow. Goodnight." She ended the call, not answering his question nor letting him say anything else.

Randy frowned. "That was kind of rude."

"Not really," she lied. "Besides he was interrupting sister talk, now where to begin. It was most definitely a date, but we didn't exactly go for coffee," she began.

Randy sat up so quickly Casey cried out in surprise. "Watch it! You almost hit me. The last thing I need right now is a bloody nose."

"Sorry." Her sister shrugged and sat cross-legged on the

bed facing her. "I want to see your face while you talk. Go on."

"Did you know Cole had a motorcycle?" Casey asked.

"Yes, I've seen him on it more than once. A few of my friends would give their eye teeth to go for a ride with him, but he doesn't offer. As I mentioned Sunday night, he's considered quite the man of mystery around here. The fact he doesn't date—make that didn't date—still hits the rumor mill now and then, especially when he comes back from one of his trips. I swear the man can be more closed-mouthed about his comings and goings than Father Bob about sins heard in the confessional, but it adds to his appeal." She chuckled. "Drives some of them crazy, but still … You do realize that if anyone finds out about tonight, you'll be the talk of the town."

Casey cringed. That was the last thing she wanted. While she wasn't sure exactly how she felt about Cole, the first man to ever make her lose control the way she had tonight, she did know she didn't like the idea of him with another woman, even her own sister.

"Are you attracted to him?"

Randy laughed and shook her head. "I wish."

Her sorrowful response piqued Casey's interest. "What do you mean?"

"Nothing. Cole's one of the best. Have you seen his version of Toyland?"

Casey nodded. "I was impressed. He seems right into the whole Santa and Christmas thing."

Randy nodded. "He is. The man would make a great father, and Jaxon adores him."

"And you?" she asked, her breath catching on the words.

Randy sighed. "There's no chemistry between us, not like there was with David. I like him well enough, but to me, he's just a customer and fellow business owner. I'm not even sure that qualifies as friendship. So if you didn't go for coffee, where did Cole take you?"

"Don't tell Mom and Dad because they'll have a hissy-fit, but we went for a ride out into the Superstition Mountain

Wilderness. We left the bikes at the end of the trail and walked to this incredibly romantic spot. He brought a thermos of coffee, and we chatted and watched the meteor shower."

Shyly, Casey described her unbelievable, ultra-romantic date with Cole, omitting only the gunshot since she didn't want to worry Randy or her parents, and instead dwelling on the earth-shattering kisses they'd shared. "I can't explain it, Randy, but when he kissed me, it was like I was a different person, alive for the first time. It was the most fantastic evening. Can you believe it? He purposely won this bear for *me*." She reached for her teddy. "I always thought he'd won it and simply didn't want it—not exactly a masculine toy."

"Why wouldn't he have done it for you? You've always been way too hard on yourself. So what happened when you got back to town?" Randy asked, excitement evident in her words.

"Nothing. I left him at his place and came home."

"That's it?" A puzzled frown marred her brow. "Seriously? All that heat and poof! Goodbye?"

"Well, he did invite me in for coffee," she admitted, "but I said no."

"You said no?" Randy's stunned words, louder than any she'd spoken so far, echoed in the room.

"Shh!" Casey said quickly. "You'll wake Mom, and I'm not ready for the Spanish inquisition."

"Sorry." Randy lowered her voice once more. "Why on earth did you do that? What you've described sounds like the most romantic night I can imagine. You've just said you could barely control yourself when he was kissing you. I know you don't date a lot, but don't expect me to believe you're a virgin. Heating up the sheets with that hottie sounds to me like the perfect way to end the night."

"I don't know—maybe it would have been too much, too soon—besides, what's the point of starting a relationship that'll go nowhere?" she asked, using the excuse as a way to avoid the real reason she'd fled, one she herself didn't really understand. "I'm only here for two weeks, then it's back to Santa Fe. I'm bushed, Randy. I need sleep."

"Bullshit."

"Go to bed, Randy."

"Casey? There's more to it. Give."

"Fine," she huffed out the word. "I'm not a player. Don't get me wrong, but I don't do one-night-stands. While it might've been a night to remember, I've got my principles," and that included avoiding spoiled men who lived at home. "Maybe if I see him again … That's it, I swear. I have to get some sleep. You've got to be up early, too. Goodnight."

Randy nodded. Without another word, she let herself out of the room and closed the door behind her.

Casey undressed and climbed into bed, but sleep eluded her. She punched her pillow repeatedly, tossed and turned trying to get comfortable, wanting to forget the way her body had reacted to Cole's touch. Gently stroking her lips, still sensitive and swollen from his kisses, she realized the truth.

As she'd told Randy, she wasn't into slam, bam, thank you ma'am sex. No, she wanted it all—love, marriage, kids, a dog, the damn white picket fence—but not until she made partner. Cole lived at home for Christ's sake. He wasn't ready to move on, and there was no way in hell she would come back to Fortune. A relationship between them would leave her craving more, and it just wasn't in the cards. She would eventually find someone to love in Santa Fe; if she didn't, she would never find her happily ever after, and that was too sad to contemplate. For the first time in ten years, she had to admit that a fulfilling career just might not be enough, but loving and losing the way Randy had would destroy her.

The sound of her phone vibrating against the surface of the bedside table attracted her attention, and she glanced at the clock. It was well after one. Who could be calling at this hour?

Not even Ken. Baby Boss would have the decency to wait until morning. Checking the call display, she recognized the local number—Cole.

She stared at the phone. He probably wanted to know why

she'd brushed him off, and she wasn't ready to discuss it. Damn, she didn't even understand why she'd done it, but she had a feeling it was another case of cold feet. Her heart told her he wasn't really a mama's boy, but there had to be a reason beyond convenience for him to live with his parents.

This wasn't the first time she'd pulled back, afraid to commit emotionally or physically, but the last thing she wanted Randy to know was the truth. There had only been one man in her life, the one she'd given her virginity to, and they'd both agreed, their friendship was more important than their sex life. How pathetic was that?

The phone vibrated again. Should she answer it or just let it go? Rolling over, she pulled the pillow over her head, and prayed she'd made the right choice. As long as Cole was rooted in Fortune, they had no future. Since they didn't have much of a past, it was probably better not to have a present, too.

When the alarm on her phone sounded six hours later, Casey opened bleary eyes, as tired if not more so than she'd been last night. She blinked twice. Focused on Cole and their impossible future, she'd pushed her promise to help Randy at *Cookies and Cream* to the back of her mind, but now it was front and center. How the hell was she going to get through the day in one piece? She would rather battle in court with Santa Fe's misogynistic district attorney than face the residents of this town even for five minutes.

While it was true she'd never met more than half of them, there was a small number of those who'd grown up here she'd hoped never to see again. There was a slim chance the less than stellar individuals in her class no longer called Fortune home, since she hadn't been the only one who'd gone away to school. Surely others, like her nemesis who'd wanted to be a star, had stayed away, too—although, unless she'd made it big in pornos, that dream had never been realized.

Sighing, she threw back the covers. It was a work day. Maybe most of those she knew wouldn't have time to drop into the bakery. With any luck, the worst of her tormentors was far,

far away from here. She would probably have to face some of the town's older residents, but if there was a God, they wouldn't recognize her; after all, Cole hadn't.

Getting up, she made her bed and headed into her en suite bathroom. Dad had added the toilet, sink, and shower stall to her room and to Randy's as a Christmas present the year she'd started high school. It must've been expensive at the time, but by doing so, since he commuted into Phoenix to teach a couple of English courses each semester at the university campus there, he'd guaranteed himself the bathroom time he'd needed.

Showering quickly, she dressed in a pair of jeans and the white blouse Randy had left for her with the bakery's name stitched in navy blue on the pocket. Pulling her wet hair into a tight chignon, she applied her makeup and then went downstairs to get coffee and a bite to eat. No doubt her mother had questions about last night.

"Once more into the breach..." she mumbled. The words from Henry V, another of Shakespeare's plays her dad often quoted, seemed appropriate right now. If there was ever a time she needed to prepare for war and facing the enemy, it was today.

CHAPTER EIGHT

Tired after a restless night, Cole stepped into the sheriff's office before going to the emporium for the morning to catch up on paperwork. It had been after eleven when he'd called Casey to ensure she'd actually made it home safely. She'd answered and brushed him off so quickly, had he been in a car, he would've had whiplash. He called a little while later, too upset by her behavior to let it go, but she hadn't answered. He reasoned she was either asleep or had turned off her phone for the night—which made sense in a house with a four-year-old. The way she'd up and left so quickly bothered him, since he could've sworn she was as aroused as he'd been. She would be working at *Cookies and Cream* today. Maybe he would drop by for muffins and coffee before leaving for the airport.

The other thing that had kept him awake was the memory of what he'd seen and heard while Casey slept. Cougars this close to town could be dangerous, but whatever was happening on the mountain was something Hal needed to know about. He might have the exact location wrong, but that helicopter had been in the vicinity of the abandoned mines. And then there'd been that gunshot.

"Morning, Cole," Rita Hynes, the dispatcher and receptionist, said, smiling at him, pulling him out of his head.

She'd been in his class in high school and had married

Jason, the captain of the basketball team. Three kids and twenty pounds heavier, she still resembled the cheerleader she'd been. Like Casey, and quite a few others in town, she was a big CJ Coleson fan.

"Morning. Is he in?"

She chuckled. "Yeah, and he's had two cups of coffee, so you're good to go."

"Thanks." Hal wasn't a morning person by any means, and his grouchy bear persona was one of the town jokes. Having gone on a few fishing trips with him, Cole could testify that it really wasn't as bad as gossip implied, but the man was definitely more pleasant after a jolt of caffeine. "I've got a copy of *Black Widow*, the new Tate Silvers novel, set aside for you at the store."

She beamed. "That's great. That last one, *Fistful of Silver*, kept me up all night reading. The next day, I dragged Jason and the kids over to Goldfield and pointed out all the stuff I recalled from the novel—we even found a burned out shack up there. I could just imagine poor Justice ... Lordy, the man who writes those books has a way with words that can make an ice queen spike a temperature." She giggled. "But you know that. Can I pick it up at lunchtime?"

He nodded, a touch uncomfortable with her conjecture, but reasoned she'd probably assumed he read the books instead of writing them.

"I'm closed today, but I've got paperwork to do before I go to the airport to pick up my folks. Just knock."

"Thanks. I'm planning a barbecue in a couple of weeks. Jason and I would love you to come. His sister will be in town."

"I'm not sure I'll be here then. With Mom and Dad back, I was planning to visit friends in Dallas—if the boss can spare me."

Or maybe Santa Fe since Casey would be back at work by then. Grinning, he shrugged. He'd used Rita's blatant matchmaking efforts to create Sarah, Tate's sister and housekeeper, who was always looking for a way to get her wayward brother to settle down. One of these days, she'd succeed, but her efforts brought a touch of levity to the books, something he didn't want to lose just yet.

"Well, if you're around, you would be more than welcome. You can go right in."

Cole nodded and rapped his knuckles on the oak door. Like many of the buildings on the town's main strip, the outside face of the sheriff's office was more or less as it had been a hundred and fifty years ago, but the inside had been modernized, with a sizeable addition built onto the back of the structure.

"Come in," Hal called out loudly.

Cole opened the door and entered.

Hal sat behind his desk checking information on his computer. He didn't look happy, but when he looked up, he smiled.

"Morning, Cole. Didn't expect to see you in today. I just got some information from AJPD. They spoke with Leon's landlady. It seems Trent Gibbs is the one who's been using his uncle's apartment. He told her Leon had gone east to visit an old friend, which we both know is a load of bull. Another man's been staying there with him. She described him as tall, brown-haired, and shifty-looking."

"Now, that's a hell of a description," Cole said, shaking his head in frustration. "She would make a lousy eyewitness. Did she happen to mention skin color? A limp? Piercings, a tattoo? Anything that would distinguish him from a significant portion of this country's population?"

"According to my contact, no, but they're going to hook her up with a sketch artist. Given the right questions, she may be able to come up with a composite," Hal said, "but the woman's in her seventies. What she was sure of was that Gibbs and his friend left the apartment a week ago Monday and haven't been back. That matches what I was told when I called Skansen Mining. Gibbs is on vacation and not due back until after Labor Day. The receptionist didn't know any more than that."

Dropping into the chair in front of the desk, Cole smiled. "So you think he's been misusing the old man's money?"

"It certainly looks that way. The withdrawals were all local, and we both know Leon isn't back east."

"I'm not making excuses for Trent, but what if Leon himself fed him that lie? Gibbs could have a perfectly legitimate reason for doing what he's done—paying the old man's rent and his bills."

"It's possible. The police are opening the safety deposit box this afternoon. Maybe that'll shed more light. But you aren't here to talk about Leon. What's up?"

"Maybe nothing. Did you hear anything about Skansen reopening any of their older mines?"

"No, why?"

Cole explained what he'd seen last night, omitting the fact he hadn't been alone.

"Damnation! You're sure it was a helicopter?"

"Yeah. It flew south, maybe toward Tucson, but I could be wrong about the exact location on the mountain. It's hard to pinpoint something like that in the dark. It's possible they were on public land. Has anyone filed a claim in that area?"

"A new one? I don't think so. Chester has a stake out that way, not too far from Skansen land. He's been bragging about it for years—claims he'll find the gold vein they lost. Over the years, he's found a little gold, but nothing substantial. If he had, his home wouldn't have been repossessed by the town for back taxes. By the way, he claims aliens landed in the area last night. Came in to see me not half an hour ago." He chuckled humorlessly. "If he saw a helicopter, in his usual drunken state, he could've mistaken it for a spaceship. At least we know he hasn't lost his marbles. I can go out and have a look out that way this afternoon if you like. Do you want to come with me?"

"I can't. Mom and Dad are arriving in Phoenix at four, and I promised to pick them up. You know what she'll be like if I have a car service waiting for them."

Hal rolled his eyes. "Yeah. She tore a strip off me the last time for working you too hard. If I did it again, neither one of us would get any peace. Today's Ramon's day off, but with the new baby on its way, he can use the overtime. We'll go out and see what we can find. I'll give Eddy a call, too. Make sure he doesn't know about it, and I'll call the base. You could've stumbled onto air force maneuvers. Chester may be out there with his sidekicks looking for proof E.T. dropped in, but I don't see the Harvey boy doing anything but sketching or painting. If he comes back with a drawing of a flying saucer, I'll eat my hat."

Cole laughed. "I definitely want to see that. There's a couple of Kyle's watercolors at the store. The kid's talented and will probably get rich off his art long before Chester does on gold." He sobered. "You know Hal, if something illegal is going on up there, Chester and those boys could be heading for trouble. Hell, it's possible Leon stumbled onto something last year that got him killed. There's no proof what I saw hasn't happened before."

"Don't even think that way," Hal answered grimly. "That would turn an accidental fall into a murder investigation, and land the case right back into my lap. It's the last thing I need before Gold Rush Days. You're working Thursday, right?"

Cole nodded.

"Okay. I'll look into this and get back to you then."

"I hope there's a logical explanation for what I saw," he said, standing and reaching out to shake Hal's hand. "I'll let you know if I see or hear anything else."

Cole left the office hoping there was nothing covert about what he'd seen. More than one man had died when another prospector had jumped his claim. He shivered. *Rattlesnake* had been based on that. If Leon had been pushed ... He was all for fiction imitating real life, but it wasn't supposed to work the other way.

* * * *

Casey swiped at the sweat beading on her forehead, hoped

her hair wasn't the frizzy mess she feared it was, and sighed. She loved her sister and was incredibly proud of her success, but she sincerely regretted agreeing to help her out today. While so far, she'd only seen a couple of people she knew, the day was young, and she was already exhausted.

How her sister managed to do this, day after day, was one of life's unsolved mysteries. Randy came in before six each morning to mix the dough for the sweet breads and make up the batter for all the cookies, muffins, and rolls she sold each day. She also took care of the specialty cakes people ordered, always having one or two extra creations on hand for walk-in sales. Those that didn't sell by the end of the day either made it to the seniors' home in town or the dessert menu at home. Saturday night's carrot cake had been the best Casey had ever tasted. Hidden in the refrigerator in the kitchen was a superhero cake that was going to thrill a certain five-year-old tomorrow.

A steady stream of people had stopped by to sample some of Randy's treats or pick up bread and rolls for dinner. Her butter tarts, with or without pecans, were a big seller, and after sampling one earlier, Casey could understand why. The delicate pastry melted in your mouth. If Randy wanted to leave Fortune, she could make a real fortune in Phoenix or even Santa Fe. She chuckled at the pun.

There were two skills Casey hadn't inherited from her mother—baking and sewing. Instead, she'd acquired her father's love of reading and her Grandma Maureen's passion for riding, something she now indulged on her bike rather than on a warm animal beneath her. The death of her beloved Ginger had been the straw that had broken the camel's back as they said. Without that animal, once she'd graduated from Skansen High, there'd been nothing to keep her in Fortune ... well other than family, and forced to choose, she'd left them behind.

"Well, well, well."

A voice, reminiscent of fingernails drawn across a chalkboard, a voice Casey had hoped never to hear again, replaced the buzz of conversation in the bakery.

"Look what the cat dragged in. Cassandra Stevens. All that plastic surgery and liposuction must've cost you a fortune. Nice of you to deign to visit us small-town folk."

And just like that Casey was eighteen again, an insecure teenager, wanting to hide. Kristal Jameson had been head cheerleader and the girl who'd made her life a living hell.

When Casey refused to help her cheat on an English test their freshman year, Kristal had sworn vengeance, and the torture had started. Name calling and fat jokes were just the tip of the iceberg. Things were written on her locker, people in the hallway jostled her books out of her hands, and vicious rumors caused whispers and laughter, which followed her throughout every single day of high school, all the way to the moment that had all but destroyed her. Today, that level of bullying wouldn't be acceptable, but back then, even if the adults in her life had been aware of it—and she was sure some of them knew—nothing would've been done about what was considered character building. From the sound of the venom in the woman's voice, she hadn't changed from the bullying bitch she'd been.

But I've changed. Sticks and stones…

"Hello, Kristal. How nice to see you again. How have you been?" Casey smiled sweetly, calling on every ounce of courtroom poise she possessed. There was no way she was going to allow the woman to ruin her day.

Kristal frowned, obviously surprised by her reaction. The woman wore way too much make up, and with her dark-red artificial nails, looked like a female vampire out for blood. She was thin, too skinny by far, and her face was gaunt making her look far older than her thirty-four years. While she'd falsely accused Casey of having work done, there was no doubt Kristal had had more than one procedure. Those had to be double Ds. It was amazing she could actually walk upright.

Maybe she did make it as a porn queen.

Casey smothered a giggle by clearing her throat.

"I've been great," Kristal answered too enthusiastically and more than a little off-balance.

Casey recognized the lie. At the moment, she didn't care if Kristal's life was the stuff horror movies were made of. Grateful she didn't have time to talk to her since the place was a zoo, she nodded and picked up the cups on the table in front of her archenemy, setting them on the nearby tray which Ruis, Randy's helper, would carry into the kitchen as soon as it was full.

"That's good," she said to be polite and moved away from her teen years' nemesis, but the woman, her designer handbag dangling from her wrist, grabbed her arm, her claws sinking into the flesh.

Casey glared at her, and Kristal released her, mumbling an "I'm sorry" she probably didn't mean.

"I married Rick Harvey. He owns his father's car dealership now," she gloated, but while the words might be true, something in the tone belied them.

Icky Ricky, as Casey had come to think of him over the years, had almost ruined her life. It was his fault Ginger had stumbled in that hole and broken her leg. If ever there was a match made in hell, this was it. They deserved one another. Maybe God had cared after all.

"Congratulations," Casey said in her best courtroom false-friendly voice, praying she could get away before she got sick. It wasn't the mention of Rick the Dick that had caused her stomach to churn. It was simply that her feet were killing her, and the last thing she wanted to do was make nice-nice with Kristal.

She glanced over her shoulder, grateful to note the crowd had gone back to minding its own business, and hoped Randy could come to her rescue, but her sister seemed to be having an argument of her own with a man in a black t-shirt. The guy looked familiar, but Casey couldn't place him. Suddenly, Randy turned away and hurried into the kitchen. The man got up and left, but judging by the determined look on his face, he would be back.

What the hell was that all about?

Casey had all but forgotten Kristal when she spoke again.

"Things not going as well as your mom's been saying in Santa Fe? Too bad, but at least your little sister can give you a job. There must be mountains of dishes to do."

Swallowing the words she would like to say, Casey grinned as if having this conversation was an everyday, friendly occurrence. "Things in Santa Fe are great, Kristal. Thanks for asking. I'm just helping Randy out until Selma's back tomorrow—great workout by the way, you should try it. It amazes me she can do all this and look after Jaxon."

"Well, she does have help, doesn't she? Get me a coffee. Black."

Casey fisted her hands at her side to stop from clawing the woman's eyes out. She wasn't the little mouse Kristal had shit on. While she'd taken a lot of crap, Randy shouldn't have to.

What a bitch! Someone needs to put her in her place, but it won't be me—at least not here and now.

"I'm sorry, but you have to place your order at the counter like everyone else," she answered, her voice saccharine sweet. "You should consider adding a tart."

You could use a little sweetening.

"I hear you're still single," Kristal said, ignoring Casey's comment, but seemingly unwilling to end their conversation. "You look a bit better than you used to, but I wouldn't be too picky if I were you. You're not getting any younger, you know."

"Thanks for your concern," she answered, on the verge of losing her hard-earned composure. "Getting married *is* on the bucket list, but I've got a few other things ahead of it."

"Well, if you don't have looks, I guess you have no choice but to lie to yourself and work your ass off," Kristal said sweetly.

Witch!

Hanging on to her self-control by a thread, Casey heard a familiar voice, one that made her cringe and wish she'd stayed in Santa Fe. How much worse could today get?

"Hello, Cassandra," her old English teacher said. She was

certain that man had been put on the earth for the sole purpose of torturing her. No matter how hard she'd tried, he'd always expected more.

"Hi, Mr. Lowell," she forced out, turning away from the woman she hated more than anything, smiling, and hoping she sounded friendly.

He nodded. "I almost didn't recognize you. You've grown into a beautiful woman, and your hair—Titian fire." He turned to the other woman. "Kristal, I didn't see your broom parked outside."

Casey choked back the guffaw that threatened to spill out. Had Mr. Lowell really just called Kristal a witch?

The color drained from Kristal's face, and she actually snarled at the older man, before getting up and walking straight out the front door, bumping into a woman on her way in.

"Wow. What was that all about?"

Mr. Lowell shook his head. "That girl hasn't changed a bit. In fact, she's worse than she ever was. Once a bully, always a bully, acting as if she's better than everyone else, when the truth is she's as fake as those boobs she's lugging around."

Casey burst out laughing, unable to contain her mirth.

He chuckled and reddened. "One could almost feel sorry for her. Being a bossy know-it-all might've kept her on top in high school, but it doesn't work now. That husband of hers is no prize, and everyone in town knows it. Some people just don't know enough to grow up. Unlike you, Miss Stevens," he said smiling at her. "You're as diplomatic and well-mannered as ever. You were always one of my favorites. According to your parents you're doing very well in Santa Fe. Congratulations."

Casey stared at the man, not trusting herself to speak without her voice cracking. His favorite? How was that possible?

"Thank you, sir," she croaked out, her calm having deserted her.

"You're welcome." He bobbed his head. "I suspected the girl was making your life miserable back then, but you rose above it. Maybe I should've said something," he acknowledged, "but those were different times. Come home more often. We all miss you."

"I will," she said and actually meant it.

The next hour was a blur. Feeling run off her feet, she was glad to see Randy come back into the café area. Casey made a mental note to ask her later about the man in the black T-shirt. Something about him had upset her sister, and she wanted to know exactly what that was.

She'd just grabbed a cup of coffee and sat down for a much needed break when someone tapped her on the shoulder.

"Casey, welcome home. Do you remember me? Carmella Rankin? Like you, I've shortened my name. I go by Ella now. Can I join you?"

Casey nodded. "Of course." The bakery was still crowded, and it would be churlish to refuse anyone a chair, especially someone who'd been nice to her back then. "Ella suits you."

"Thanks. You look fantastic—better than a few people I could name—but you were always kind of cute—painfully shy—but sweet. I'll bet Randy's thrilled to have the extra help today. Crazy Kristal almost knocked my mother down in her haste to leave earlier. Mom's still miffed about it." She shook her head, short chocolate curls bouncing around her face. "I don't think there's a single person in town she doesn't rub the wrong way."

Ella had been her lab partner in senior year. They'd worked well together, and while neither she nor her twin Corrina had ever openly teased her, Casey had considered the sisters to be on the fringes of Kristal's cadre.

"You should drop over and see my sister. Rina's staying with our folks until the baby arrives. I insisted on it, and for once she's listening to me. I may be a nurse, but she's a doctor, even if most of her patients have four legs instead of two, and she's the world's worst patient right now. Her husband, Blake, is in Afghanistan."

"That's tough. I hope he gets home safely."

She nodded. "He's flying Evac helicopters. It was hard on everyone when David was killed. Do you remember Drew Macintosh?"

Casey frowned. The name was vaguely familiar, but she couldn't put a face to it.

"I don't think so," she admitted.

"That's not too surprising, I guess. He was a couple of grades ahead of us. He was in here a little while ago. Mom mentioned seeing him on her way in, looking madder than a horse with a burr under his saddle. He just got back and visits Rina almost every day, trying to cheer her up. Did you know he was David's best friend?"

"No, I didn't." Casey stored that tidbit of information away for later consideration.

Carmella pinked slightly. "You know, you were my hero that last year of high school."

"Seriously?" Casey couldn't imagine why.

"Yup. You were so driven, focused on your studies. Nothing bothered you. Do you remember when someone blew up the chem lab? We had to listen to a week of lectures from the principal on lab safety. I'll never forget the way you used that science book cover to hide your novel. While the rest of us sat there, bored to tears, way too afraid of incurring Mrs. Drumheller's wrath to try anything, you calmly read your book and finished that English assignment."

Casey laughed a little uncomfortable to realize her actions had been misinterpreted that way, and even more so to be seen as some kind of maverick.

"I didn't realize anyone knew what I was doing."

"Rina knew and so did a few others, and we admired your act of rebellion, more so because you were the one doing it. But then, you were the only one with a backbone, the only one who didn't let Kristal and Heidi control your life."

"I'm not sure I remember it quite that way. I'll try to drop over to see Rina," she continued, using the short form of the other twin's name. "I'm only here for the two weeks, but I'll do my best."

"I really hope you can. She'll get such a kick out of seeing you. She's the class historian, you know, and has followed your career in Santa Fe. As much as I would love to stay longer, I have to get to work. Maybe we can meet for a drink during Gold Rush Days."

"Sure, I would like that," she answered, too surprised to refuse.

"Great. I'll call you."

Ella hurried out the door, leaving a stunned and bemused Casey staring after her.

CHAPTER NINE

Still reeling from her encounter with Ella, Casey went back to work. It was funny how her memory differed from her classmate's. The last thing she'd ever expected anyone to believe was that she was gutsy. According to her recollections, she'd avoided Kristal and the others to save herself from embarrassment. Never had she considered people might think she had done so because she simply hadn't cared to be part of her group.

She was cleaning off one of the tables when she noticed Ms. Minerva Skansen, Fortune's oldest and probably its wealthiest citizen, waving at her from one of the tables, her order number sitting in the small holder in front of her. The only time Old Maid Skansen, as some of the boys had referred to her, had ever made a comment to Casey, it had been to tell her to get her nose out of her books and watch where she was walking. That statement had been followed by a disapproving tsk-tsk, and laugher from Kristal and Heidi walking by.

"Cassandra, you've grown into a beautiful young woman, just as I knew you would," Ms. Skansen said when Casey placed the cup of tea and scones she'd ordered in front of her.

"I *was* a bit of an ugly duckling," she agreed, shrugging. "I'm surprised you recognized me."

"What nonsense!" the elderly woman exclaimed, brushing

the words away with her hand, displaying a gorgeous silver and turquoise ring that had to be a family heirloom. "You certainly weren't an ugly duckling, although one could argue you've become a graceful swan. You're a mite thin for my taste now, better though than some I could name, but you've always had those golden green and blue eyes that bespoke intelligence and that lovely, curly, copper hair. I'm so glad you didn't cut it short as so many professional women do."

Casey felt a familiar sense of self-reproach. She'd been planning to do exactly that when she got her promotion. It could shave as much as fifteen minutes off her morning prep time.

"I've followed your career with interest, young lady. You've done very well for yourself, as I knew you would. I mentioned you to Horace Stone just last week. Can you sit a minute?"

"Unfortunately, I can't. We're swamped right now. Can I get you anything else?" she asked, noting the disappointment on the elderly woman's face.

"No, I'm good, thank you. You always were conscientious to a fault, worth so much more than a few I can think of. I'm so glad you've come home, even if it is just to visit for now. Drop by the house before you go back to Santa Fe. My nephew, Edward, is staying with me," she said, the disdain on her face matching the tone of her voice as she said his name, "but we can still have a nice, long visit."

"Will do." Casey moved away, hoping that if she did decide to drop by, Eddy Ramos would be far, far away. A year older than Cole, he hadn't been the sharpest pencil in the box, having failed a few too many courses. She remembered him as one of the Three Stooges. Instead of Moe, Larry and Curly, she had Eddy, Ricky, and Trent. At least the first three had been funny. While Rick and Trent were mean and vindictive, there was something about Eddy that had always scared her. Somehow, she had managed to stay off his radar. He had shark's eyes, vacant and deadly. While he hadn't been a fixture in Fortune as a child, he did occasionally visit and she'd made a point of staying on the ranch when he was in town. He'd moved in with Ms. Minerva the year she'd started high school and had turned the Disgusting Duo into the Three Stooges. He called the shots because he had money, something the other two worshiped.

Hurrying to clear tables and deliver orders, she couldn't imagine how Randy and Selma did it. Casey had waitressed in university, unwilling to let her mom and dad pay the entire cost of her schooling and living expenses in Austin, but that had been more than ten years ago, and her feet, back, and legs loudly protested the torture she'd inflicted on them today.

As business slowed to a more a manageable level, Casey's mind returned to Cole. Randy had mentioned he usually came by for muffins and coffee-to-go around one. Would he show up today? He knew she was working ... She'd told him so.

That hasty parting in his parents' driveway was all mixed up in her mind along with the reasons she'd fled Fortune in the first place. She wasn't sure about her feelings right now—she was no longer sure of anything—but the thought of never feeling his arms around her again dismayed her. If he asked her out again, her common sense said she should refuse, but her heart and her hormones begged her to reconsider. At the very least, she owed him an apology for her behavior when he'd called.

She tried to convince herself that she didn't need a man like him in her life. A man who made her feel alive and more aware of herself as a woman than anyone ever had. A man who'd gotten under her skin as no other had ever done. A man who wouldn't be easy to leave behind when she returned to Santa Fe, and that was the crux of the problem. Wanting Cole was a good thing, but she didn't want Fortune—even if today had shown her that life hadn't been as bad as she remembered it—but she had a feeling the two were inseparable. So, for the next hour, each time the bell sounded, she practically got whiplash looking to see if the newcomer was him, and was deeply disappointed when it wasn't.

It was well after four before business slowed enough for

Randy and Casey to sit down and relax. She savored every bite of her lemon blueberry muffin and sipped the rich dark coffee similar in flavor to what Cole had produced last night.

"We did well today," Randy said, her voice filled with pride. "It's probably the busiest weekday I've had since Christmas, and I think the fact that you were here brought in a few customers I haven't seen before. I hope they'll come back now that they've sampled my wares." She chuckled. "Maybe I should consider having a celebrity work here once a month."

Casey laughed. "What celebrity? Me? No way. If you want a celebrity, try getting Cole to invite CJ Coleson for an autograph session. You'd have to stockpile goods for a month to handle that."

Randy chuckled. "Probably. Let me know if he reveals the author's identity, and I'll take you up on the challenge."

"You don't need any gimmicks to be a success," Casey assured her sister. "If this muffin and the tart I ate earlier today are any indication, your goodies are what brought them here. By the way, this coffee is delicious, better than anything I can get in any coffee shop in Santa Fe. What's your secret?"

Randy laughed. "I've always had a knack for baking, but before I added the coffee shop, I made the world's worse cup of coffee. David compared it to army mess dishwater. I've learned to use top quality, freshly ground coffee beans. The secret is in making small pots that don't last long. I've even learned to make tea. Ms. Skansen says mine's as good as any she's ever had."

Casey yawned, last night's lack of sleep catching up with her. "I don't know how you do this. I'm beat. Speaking of Ms. Skansen, she wants me to drop over for a chat before I leave town." She chuckled. "I can't imagine what we would discuss."

"Maybe she wants to hook you up with Eddy the creep, or perhaps get free legal advice on how to get rid of him," Randy suggested.

"Short of murder? I take it he hasn't changed? He's always been a little off."

"Off? That's like saying food filled with botulism isn't going to kill you. The man scares me. Every time he comes into *Cookies and Cream*, I do my best to avoid him, and I'm not the only one. Kristal gives him a wide berth even though Eddy and Rick spend more time in Vegas or at the Apache casino than Rick does at home. I really feel sorry for their son—he's a shy, quiet boy. I don't think either one of his parents give him much of their time. Rick's a jerk and Kristal's too full of herself to even notice the poor kid." She shook her head. "Please be nice to Ms. Minerva, even if it means be civil to Eddy. She's one of my best customers and the one who approved the renovation money I got to get the upstairs refinished so Jaxon and I can have a place of our own."

Casey sat up straighter. "You could've asked me for money. Do Mom and Dad know what you're planning?"

"I didn't ask you because you've already done so much for me. Giving me that new van for my birthday … This is free money. I only have to repay it if I sell within five years of fixing up the place. Believe me, *Cookies and Cream* is here to stay. And, yes, Mom and Dad know and understand. Jaxon starts kindergarten in two weeks. It'll be easier in town. We both hated that school bus ride, and you know it. I've lined up a teenager to watch him after school. Not having to drive to work and back will give me an hour more time each day. Besides, if he gets hungry, think how easy it'll be for him to rob the cookie jar."

Casey enjoyed the animation on her sister's face. Randy loved the shop notwithstanding the long hours that went with it, but she loved her son more. If this made it easier for her, Casey was all in favor of the move.

"Let me know when it's ready, and I'll help out with the cost of furnishing and decorating the place." She sipped her coffee. "They'll miss him, you know."

"I know," Randy said, "But they'll still see lots of him, and Dad needs to slow down."

Before Casey could ask what she meant, the front door

opened. Randy hopped off the chair as if it was burning her, and flashed her million-dollar smile.

"Hi, Mr. Stone." Her voice was full of enthusiasm as if seeing this particular customer was the high point of her day. "Busy day in court?"

"Too busy. How was yours?"

"It was great. Casey was here helping. You remember my sister?"

"I certainly do. Nice to see you, Casey. Welcome back. Randy, can I have a coffee and a couple of your chocolate chunk cookies?"

"You certainly can." Randy turned to fill his order.

"I'll go over and sit with your sister."

His words surprised Casey, but she sat up straighter and smiled as he walked toward her. She'd always admired Horace Stone. He'd come to the school in her junior year to talk to her citizenship class. It had been that class that had led her to pursue a career in law. He'd spoken of the need for equality and justice for all, regardless of race, religion, or economic status. The law wasn't only for the rich. She'd gone in with the idea of defending the underdog. Sadly, things didn't always work out that way.

"I was going to call the house to talk to you, young lady. May I?" he asked, indicating the seat Randy had vacated.

Casey nodded, more than a little curious. "Of course. It's nice to see you again. Ms. Minerva was in here earlier and mentioned you wanted to talk to me."

Randy brought over his coffee and cookies and began washing tables, but Casey knew her sister was eavesdropping.

"Since we're both professionals, I won't beat about the bush. I have a proposition for you," he said, using what she was sure was his best courtroom voice. "One I hope will please you as much as it pleases me. When your mother mentioned you were coming home for Gold Rush Days, I realize what a fortuitous coincidence it was. Ms. Skansen is my most important client, and she's very much in favor of this. In fact, the initial idea was hers. 'Give a local girl a chance,' was the way she put it."

Casey frowned in confusion. A local girl? Maybe once, but not now.

"I don't understand. A chance at what?"

"An equal partnership in my firm," he said and beamed as if he'd offered her exactly what he knew she wanted.

"But—"

"Hear me out, please. Three years ago, when Stuart Holmes retired, I was able to handle the work by myself, but things have changed. There's simply too much work now for one man. I want to bring in a partner—equal in every way. This town is growing, and it needs new blood, but there's no one to say that blood can't be part and parcel of its heritage. I plan to retire in five years, at which point the firm would be all yours."

Randy brought over the coffee pot and refilled both cups. The happy glow on her face was almost blinding.

Mr. Stone continued. "I'm sure we can work out suitable terms for your buy-in. I wouldn't expect you to pay it all up front."

Before she could fully grasp what he'd said, Randy squealed.

"Oh my God, Casey! That would be wonderful. You could come home to stay, and we could be a family again."

Damn!

This wasn't going to end well. Why hadn't Mr. Stone waited to have this discussion in private? A full and equal partnership. It was an incredible offer, the kind she wouldn't get in Santa Fe for years to come, but it meant returning to Fortune, something she just couldn't do. Smiling to take the sting out of her words, she spoke softly.

"Mr. Stone, thank you for considering me for what I know is truly a great honor, but at the moment, I have to decline. I love my job in Santa Fe. It's everything I've worked for. I don't see myself coming back to Fortune to practice law. I hope you find the right person, but it won't be me." There. She'd said it.

Let the cards fall where they may.

Casey avoided looking at Randy, knowing she would see pain and accusation on her sister's face.

"Now, let's not be hasty," Mr. Stone said, obviously surprised by her quick decision. "You may think Santa Fe is more exciting, but you would be amazed at how well you can do here in Fortune. I know I've sprung this on you rather suddenly. Think it over. Have a look at my books. It isn't all real estate law, filing land claims, and wills. We could work well together, and I know my clients would be comfortable with you handling their affairs. Skansen Mining pays me a hefty retainer each year. Minerva wants to talk to you as well. She wants to discuss her legacy, and she's making some changes ... I also have clients in Apache Junction and Phoenix. There's something for everyone: criminal cases, divorces, trusts, and law suits." He chuckled. "I like to think I'm well-rounded."

Casey wanted to tell him not to waste his time, but she couldn't. She'd be lying to herself if she didn't admit the proposition was fascinating, and not more than a little tempting, but it was in Fortune, which was the kiss of death for it. There was no way she was going to move back here to stay—ever— but arguing with Randy in front of Mr. Stone wouldn't be the smartest thing to do.

"All right, I'll think about it and see you before I leave town," she lied. Casey hated prevarication, though it was often a lawyer's bread and butter, but at the moment, she saw no alternative. She'd given him her answer, and he'd refused to accept it. Her decision was made, and it wasn't going to change.

Mr. Stone smiled broadly. "Wonderful. I'll let Sylvia, my office administrator, know. She can answer all of your questions. Once you think about it, you'll see the benefit of owning your own firm. Now, I have to get going. Clara is waiting for me. It's our forty-fifth anniversary. I'm taking her to a resort for few days. We'll be back by Sunday." He stood. "Before I go, Randy, do you have any of that twelve grain bread left?"

"Of course." Randy winked. "I always set aside a loaf for you."

Casey could see her sister was forcing herself to be pleasant. Randy was angry and disappointed, but that was too bad.

Once Mr. Stone left, Randy came over to her and stood beside her, arms folded across her chest. Casey had hoped to avoid this conversation until later—maybe even avoid it altogether—but the shop was empty, and there was nowhere to run.

"Are you going to consider his offer?" Randy asked point blank.

"No, I'm not. I gave him my answer. He might not like it or want to accept it, but it isn't going to change." Her words inflicted pain, but they were the truth. "I have no intention of ever returning to live in Fortune."

"Why not? Fortune's home. It's been our family's home for five generations. That should mean something to you. This would be a great opportunity. The business is established, and you wouldn't have to work such long hours. You would be a full partner, not a junior one the big boys can load down with even more work. We could be a real family again." Randy pleaded.

"You're not being fair, Randy, and you're missing the point. I like the life I've made for myself in Santa Fe. I'm proud of what I've accomplished, and while it won't happen tomorrow, I will make partner one day. This shop is your dream, a partnership in Santa Fe is mine. I don't want to give it up."

"Aren't you lonely? Don't you miss us?" Randy's eyes filled with tears.

"Of course, I miss you guys. Don't be ridiculous."

Tears rolled slowly down her sister's cheeks, and she stood there, as still as a statue.

"I've worked really hard to get where I am, just as you have," Casey implored, begging Randy to understand. "If I quit now, it'll all have been for nothing."

"Don't say that." Randy's anger was palpable. "It would be

for us, for our family. When you passed the Arizona bar, I thought you would come home again, but you didn't. Your hours at work seemed longer than your classes at law school had been. If you said yes to Mr. Stone, you would be part owner of the firm, your own boss, and in five years, it would be all yours. Plus, we would be here for you, just as you would be here for us."

Sorrow filled her. "I wish I could, you know that, right? I just can't."

"I don't believe that. You could if you wanted to—you just don't want to. If Dad—"

The door opened cutting Randy off mid-sentence.

"How are my girls?" Her father entered the shop and stopped cold when he looked at them.

"Fine," they answered in unison, one defiant, the other emotional.

He looked from one to the other, a scowl replacing the smile he'd worn on his way in the door.

"What are you arguing about now? You know I don't like it when you fight." He stepped farther into the store letting the door shut behind him.

"Blame Casey," Randy said self-righteously. "Mr. Stone offered to make her his partner, and she declined without even giving it any thought. She doesn't care about any of us."

"Randy, this is Casey's decision," he said surprising her.

"It shouldn't be. It affects all of us. She's so selfish. The only thing that matters to her is her career." She turned back to Casey, her face an angry mask. "Go, leave us the way you always have. We've never mattered to you, so why did I think it would be any different now? We've managed without you before, and we'll do it again."

"I don't need this," Casey said, pushing past her dad. Tears brimmed in her eyes. She stepped out of the coffee shop into the bright Arizona sunlight, but Randy's last words followed her outside, chasing her away just as surely as Ginger's death had done fifteen years ago.

"Honey, wait," her dad called after her. But she'd reached her bike, blinded by the tears she couldn't hold back any longer. Grabbing her helmet and gloves, not even bothering to take the leathers out of her saddle bag, she started the bike and drove off.

* * * *

Cole focused on the highway and not on the two people inside the car conspiring to drive him insane. He'd hoped to drop by *Cookies and Cream* before heading to Phoenix, wanting to clear the air with Casey, but it hadn't worked out. Now, he was hungry and tired, and Mom wasn't making things any better.

"Dad, can't you turn her off?" he pleaded, hoping he sounded amused and not irate. What he wouldn't give for a pair of earplugs right now. From the second he'd picked them up at the airport, his mother hadn't stopped grilling him about his date with Casey.

"Not me," his dad answered and chuckled. "When your mother gets going on an idea, she's like a dog with a bone. Besides, I happen to agree with her. You and Casey *would* make a nice couple. I can see those curly redheaded, hazel-eyed grandchildren of mine right now. It's time you settled down, and since she's an avid reader, she would appreciate your second career."

Cole glared at his father and saw the twinkle in his eye. He shook his head. While last night had been earth-shattering for him, he'd decided based on the fact she hadn't called that it had meant nothing to her. It had been a date, one with a couple of fantastic kisses, and a dismal, disappointing ending, but the way his mom was going on, she would soon be planning the wedding.

"Mom, cut it out, please. We had one date. I'm not sure there'll even be another. Don't go spreading rumors. Casey's home for Gold Rush Days—that's it," he said, resigned to the

121

fact and regretting it.

A motorcycle, weaving in and out of traffic, came toward them. Cole frowned when he recognized the girl on the Harley tearing passed them way too fast for road conditions, and definitely not dressed for riding.

He rubbed his forehead. Where the hell was she going?

"Headache?" his dad asked.

"Yeah," Cole jumped at the excuse and pulled over. "Why don't you drive the rest of the way? My eyes are going wonky. I missed lunch..." The headache was a mild one, probably brought on by lack of sleep more than anything, and it was catching up with him.

"Sure thing," his dad answered, concern evident in his voice. "You work too hard. The emporium, your job with the police, and then there's the volunteer fire department ... Your mother told me you've started a new book. Staring at a computer screen hour after hour can't be good for you, either." His father opened the passenger door and stepped out of the car.

Cole did the same and met him in front of the vehicle.

"The new computer glasses help with that aspect of things. It's not that bad, but I might as well nip it in the bud if I can." He smiled at his father and continued around to the passenger door. "Mom, why don't you move up here? You'll be more comfortable, and I want to get out of the sun. It's not as bright back there."

"Are you okay, honey? It's my prying. I didn't mean to upset you," his mother apologized softly, concern etched on her face.

"I'm fine, Mom," he answered sheepishly, feeling remorse for worrying her. "You were just kidding around. I haven't been sleeping too well lately, and I forgot my sunglasses. I guess the glare off the tarmac finally got to me."

Once she climbed out of the back seat, his mother reached up and stroked his face.

"Are you sure you're okay? How come you didn't eat?"

"Rita came in to pick up a book, and we got talking about Leon and everything. Since I was late leaving to pick you up, I figured I'd get something at the airport, but I just wasn't interested in fast food. I'm fine. It's not as bad now that I'm not driving."

After pecking her on the cheek, he crawled into the back seat, and focused on the real reason he couldn't drive. Something was wrong. Casey was too smart a rider to go off halfcocked. As soon as the car was on the road again, he pulled out his phone and dialed Casey's number, knowing her helmet was equipped with Bluetooth. No answer. Redialing, he frowned when the call went straight to voice mail. The headache nagged at his temples, threatening to intensify at any minute.

The reckless speed at which Casey had been traveling had him on edge. Visions of her wrapped around a telephone pole or worse played through his mind. Most likely she was fine and simply didn't want to talk to him, and while that hurt, he would just have to learn to live with it. It wasn't the first disappointment in his life, and probably wouldn't be the last.

As soon as his dad pulled into the driveway, Cole unloaded the car and ushered his parents into the house, but he couldn't get Casey out of his mind. He called her cellphone a half a dozen times before phoning her home, but her mother said she wasn't there yet. He tried *Cookies and Cream*, but there was no answer. Something had happened—something that had sent Casey out on the road, hell-bent for leather, and he needed to find her and figure out what that was.

CHAPTER TEN

Casey wove in and out of traffic, her vision blurred with tears, knowing she was moving well above the speed limit. Her Bluetooth buzzed repeatedly, but she ignored it. The last thing she wanted to do was talk to anyone right now. Like any injured animal, she needed to lick her wounds before stepping back into the arena. Her gashes might be invisible to others, but the pain they inflicted was immeasurable. Even boxers got to go to their corners between bouts.

She'd had to get away and ride, but the Harley wasn't calming her the way it usually did. The entrance to the Lost Dutchman Campground came into view, and on impulse, she turned onto the road. As much as she wanted to head back to the safety and security of her Santa Fe apartment, that kind of flight wasn't an option this time.

She let out a long, shaky breath and loosened the death grip she had on her bike's handlebars. If she didn't calm down, she could very well end up road pizza, and that wouldn't help one damn bit.

The bitter exchange with Randy after her sister had blurted out Mr. Stone's offer to her father had wounded her, but it had been her sister's final words that all but crippled her emotionally.

"Just because you don't want to be here with us doesn't

mean I'm going to make it easy for you to leave us this time. You broke our hearts once. I won't let you do it again. We matter, Casey. We matter as much as you do. We always have."

Of course they mattered, how could Randy think they didn't?

Fifteen years ago, she'd been too humiliated, too embarrassed, too hurt to realize the pain she'd caused her sister. She'd known Mom and Dad had been upset, but as she'd told Cole, staying in Fortune would've killed her. Knowing her rash behavior had cost her the life of her horse had broken her spirit, but the thought her shame might become public knowledge, something that would devastate her mother and father, had torn her apart. The only solution had been escape. Away from her tormentors, the horrid mistake she'd made might not feed the rumor mill, but if she were around, too many people would relish her humiliation. It had taken years for her to realize she hadn't done anything wrong, but understanding it, accepting it, and admitting it were all very different beasts. It looked like she'd chosen flight over fight once more, but her reprieve would be temporary at best this time. She would have to face her family and try to explain without letting them know the truth.

Seeing the sign for the Superstition Mountain Wilderness, she turned in, following the path she had with Cole last night. He went to Table Rock to think, to clear his mind. That's what she needed to do. She looked up, noted the clouds rolling in from the east, but above her, the sky was blue. It was only five. She had plenty of time to get there, ponder the situation, and come up with a viable plan. Once Randy understood how much she cared for them all, she'd accept that Casey had to leave. She would promise to come back at Thanksgiving, maybe even Christmas, but she couldn't live here.

Spying the Harley tire prints in the soft sand, she turned onto the rough track. The clouds were massing on top of the mountain. She chuckled bitterly. Maybe the spirits were as upset as she was.

Stopping her bike at the end of the trail where they'd parked last night, she secured her helmet, grabbed the water bottle from her tank bag, realizing she hadn't refilled it the way she'd meant to.

It was hot out here, but thanks to the clouds, a haze was filling the sky above her, and since she'd be back home in a couple of hours, there wasn't really anything to worry about. Even the clouds could be ignored. It rained so rarely around here. She drained what little was left in the bottle, and replaced it in her bag.

Turning in the direction they had last night, she spied the path they'd used and headed into the desert, mindful of spider holes and hot rocks that might harbor predators. Ten minutes later, she stopped next to an unfamiliar rock below a stand of Saguaro. She looked around. The path that had been so clear when she'd started in wasn't quite so easy to see now. The desert floor was rocky, dotted with a variety of cacti, but try as she might, she couldn't see the footprints she'd noticed earlier. The gentle breeze had intensified, whipping up miniature dust devils now and then. What was if Grandpa had always said about east winds?

Stopping and leaning against the rock, she swallowed awkwardly. She didn't have a hat or sunscreen. The skin on her arms was already pink, and she could feel her nose burning. Would she never learn to stop and think before doing something stupid?

Gazing into the distance, she could see the waves of heat dancing above the desert floor. Squinting, she saw Table Rock in the distance and pushed off the rock, but just when she thought she was close, the rock seemed to change shape. Leaning against another boulder, trying to relax, she realized she'd gone and done something far worse than she had that fateful night.

Staring ahead, the desert vanished, replaced by the images from fifteen years ago.

"Cassandra," Rick Harvey calls her name as she closes her locker

door. *"Wait a minute."*

She turns and smiles quizzically, watching the captain of the football team and the most sought after guy in school, jog toward her. He hasn't always been nice to her, but he looks friendly enough.

"Everyone's meeting out near the old Skansen farmhouse south of town for the bonfire tonight. Are you going with anyone?" he asks, putting his arm up to lean against the locker, trapping her between his hard, T-shirt-covered chest, and it. He inhales deeply. "You always smell so fresh and clean."

For someone like her, this is a dream come true, but one for which she's ill-prepared. No boy has ever been this close to her. Trying to act blasé when her heart is beating a mile a minute, she shrugs. "I wasn't going at all. I rarely get invited to any of the crowd's activities. As you know, Kristal and I aren't exactly friends."

"Stuff that bitch." He chuckles, his breath warm against her face. "I know you don't date, but just this once, make an exception. Say you'll come with me." He nuzzles her neck, and whispers softly in her ear. "It'll be a blast. I've wanted to do this for a long time, little muse."

The nickname, one that started earlier in the year, isn't one she likes, but coming from him, it's almost an endearment.

"You want to take me to the bonfire?" she asks, unable to believe this isn't a cruel jest. It's not that she doesn't date ... no one's ever asked her out before. She looks around to see who's watching, but the hallway is deserted. "Me?"

"Yes, I want to take you to the bonfire. I wanted to ask you out before, but things were ... complicated. Say yes, sweet Cassandra. We'll have a great time."

Joy wells up in her soul. Her first real date. "I ... I would like that. When will you pick me up?"

"Here's the thing. Since I live east of town and in the opposite direction from where we're going, it would be hard for me to pick you up so that we could be on time. My dad makes me slave away washing cars at the dealership until six. Why don't we meet at the old Morris place around eight? I'll be on horseback as will some of the others, but it's no big deal if you aren't. Some kids are going in the back of Eddy Skansen's new pick-up. He's bringing the wood for the fire. They could pick you up if I asked."

"*No, that's okay,*" she says, grateful not to have to make that choice, even though she should refuse the suggestion. Dad has a rule that all of Miranda's dates have to pick her up at the house. That rule no doubt applies to her, too, even if she's never had occasion to test it. "*I've got Ginger. I'll see you there.*"

"*It's a date.*"

He drops a quick kiss on her hair before he pulls away, and hurries down the hall.

Kristal and her witches come around the corner looking smug, but she doesn't care. Let them do their worse. She has a date. A real date.

Giddy, she hurries out to the school bus stop.

Mom will have a fit if she know she's going riding on the mining road at night, so this will have to be her special secret for now. If Miranda were here, she would tell her, but she's in Phoenix completing some pre-admission test for the culinary school she plans to attend next year.

Casey smiles dreamily as she boards the bus and settles in her customary seat near the back.

"*I have a date!*" She wants to shout out loud, but doesn't, preferring to savor the wonder in silence, the way she always does.

The scene shifts to one of her and Rick sitting around the largest bonfire she's ever seen. She hasn't missed the way he's been glaring at Kristal and the guy she's with—some other football player whose name she can't recall. Like many of the others, Rick's been drinking, and while she's had a couple of bottles of beer, she doesn't care for the taste of it or the way it makes her woozy.

"*Have a shot of this, babe,*" he says, passing her the bottle that's been making the rounds. She pretends to take a mouthful, but just the smell of the tequila nauseates her.

"*What is this stuff?*"

"*Some home-made mescal. One of the guys got it from Chester. Come on. Let's take a walk,*" he whispers, nuzzling her neck, then standing. He sways, and she stands to steady him, letting him drape his arm around her possessively. Part of her is uncomfortable with the situation, but just for tonight, she wants to believe she's like everyone else.

Darkness replaces the fire and a suffocating weight presses her into the sand. Rick's on top of her, groping her, getting rougher and rougher.

"Stop, please stop," she begs, trying to avoid his invasive kisses, the taste of the alcohol so vile she would vomit if she wasn't so scared. This isn't what she'd expected. Her dream date has become a nightmare. Her heart pounds.

"Relax," he slurs the words. "It'll be fun, you'll see."

"Get off me." He frightens her. She pushes him away, but he's more forceful now, angry.

"Damn it, Cassandra. You can't tease a guy and then call it quits." He grabs her breast painfully, the delicate fabric of her blouse tearing under his assault.

She's terrified. She hears laughter nearby—maybe she can call for help, but as she looks over, a lighter momentarily illuminates the scene, and the truth dawns on her. A couple of boys stand just a few feet away. That hooked nose is one she can't mistake. They're watching them. Was this all planned? Furious at what she believes is meant to be a public display of her rape for their entertainment, she fights harder.

"Come on, Cassandra, don't be like this," Rick says angrily, as he tries to force her legs apart.

Her terror explodes exponentially. "No, stop, get off me." Tears run down her cheeks.

Are they taking pictures? She hasn't seen flashes, but ... Desperate, she manages to pull one leg close to the other, raises her knee, and hits him hard in the groin. Groaning, he rolls off her, doubling in two, giving her a chance to scramble away.

Laughter erupts from her left. Humiliated, she gets to her feet and runs toward the place where she left her horse.

"What the hell did you do that for, you frigid bitch?" Rick yells, his voice almost drowned out by the sound of the music playing near the fire where some of the kids are still sitting. "I only wanted to have a little fun. Go ahead, run home to Mommy and Daddy, but if you say anything, no one will believe you. You've been asking for it. Kristal was right. I don't know why I bothered."

Panicking, she runs toward the tree where she tied her horse. Rick calls her name, begging her to come back, saying he's sorry, but the sound of his voice betrays the fact he's getting closer and closer ... Fear pushes her, and as soon as she reaches her horse, she mounts it. Tears of pain and humiliation flow down her face. Her shirt is ruined. She doesn't know how she'll explain it, but Rick doesn't have to worry about her telling on him. To do so would mean admitting how stupid and gullible she's been. Right now, all she can do is pray there's no evidence of her shame.

Riding away into the darkness, she searches for the trail they followed to get here. In the background she can hear the music and the laughter, the glow of the flames of Eddy's enormous fire sends shadows dancing around her, camouflaging the path. No one cares about her. Rick doesn't like her; he never did. He only said that to get into her pants. It was all one big joke—another way to degrade her. She's riding fast, too fast, but blinded by her tears, she doesn't care. She needs to escape—get away from here—get away from Fortune itself, and never look back.

Suddenly, Ginger stumbles and falls. She screams as she goes flying over her horse's head. The impact with the ground knocks the wind out of her. Pain fills her. She hears people running, their excited voices looking for the cause of the screams. Forcing her eyes open, the aching in her head unlike anything she's ever felt, she sees someone kneeling beside Ginger.

"Call 9 1 1." A voice she vaguely recognizes says, coming from the shadow kneeling beside her. "Cassandra, speak to me." But instead of answering, she slowly descends into oblivion.

The roll of thunder pulled Casey back. The clouds had darkened, filling the sky. The wind whipped the sand around. Fear filled her. It might not rain often in this area, but when it did …

Among the lessons on desert safety instilled into her all those years ago was the danger of flash flooding. Severe thunderstorms in the mountains often caused serious runoff from the heavy rains moving down the slopes. While she'd never witnessed one, she'd heard of water walls, sometimes more than twenty feet high, barreling through canyons, ripping up mud, rocks, trees, and cacti along their way. More than once, the Apache Trail had flooded, stranding motorists along its length. Even if it didn't rain here, a storm in the Superstition Mountains could be deadly.

She stepped away from the rock, intent on retracing her steps, but in the gloom, she couldn't see a path to follow, nor could she see her footprints. The trail was north of where she was, but which way was north?

Swallowing her terror, she pulled the cellphone out of her pocket, dismayed to discover her power level was below half. Looking through her contacts, she found the local number and dialed, noting he'd called a dozen times. She prayed he would answer this time.

"Hello?" Cole's anxious voice echoed loudly in her ear, and she leaned back on the rock.

"Cole, it's me." Her throat was dry, making her voice huskier than usual.

"Casey? My God, where are you? I've been calling and calling."

"I know. I'm sorry…"

"Damn it. I was worried," he said angrily. "Why didn't you answer your phone?"

"Look. I said I was sorry. I didn't feel much like talking," she admitted, knowing that an apology wouldn't be enough, but she needed his help. If he hung up … It was still light out, but she would never find her way back on her own.

"You scared the daylights out of me," he continued, more calmly. "I was on my way back from Phoenix when you flew by me, moving like a bat out of hell on a mission."

"I had to ride. You know how it is," she said, praying he would know the feeling and forgive her.

"Are you feeling better now?"

"No, not by a long shot. In fact, I've probably made things worse."

"Do you want to talk about it?"

"No. I want to forget about it all, but I sincerely doubt that'll happen."

"Maybe I can help. I've been there once or twice."

She giggled nervously, fighting to tamp down her fear. "Actually, you're probably the only one who *can* help me."

"Tell me what's wrong."

"I'm lost," she whispered, her voice clogging with tears she couldn't hold back.

"Casey, I know how hard it can be to come home, wondering if you still fit in—not knowing whether you should stay or go. Why don't you tell me what happened to make you feel so lost?"

"What kind of psycho-babble are you selling, Cole?" she asked, frustration giving her voice an angry bite. "I'm lost, as in I don't know where the hell I am, you numbskull."

"Lost? Where?" he asked, the sound of his Harley engine coming over the line.

"If I knew where I was, genius, I wouldn't be lost, would I?" she challenged. Were all men this dense? "Randy and I argued, and I had to get away, so I decided to go to our place and clear my head. You said you went there when you needed to think. After I parked the bike, I headed toward the rock, following our footprints and the path, but I got turned around somehow. I thought I saw the rock in the distance and headed for it, but it must've been a mirage I tried to go back the way I'd come, but now that the sky's overcast, I can't figure out which way is north. I'm lost in the frigging desert, it's windy, there's thunder and, and it looks like rain." She ended on a mournful note.

"Casey, wherever you are, stop walking, and stay put. Do you have a flashlight?"

"Just the one on my phone, but the power's down to half."

"Okay. Turn off as many apps as you can, and when you think it's too dark, turn on the light, and flash it around you, but whatever you do, don't move. Can you tell me what the terrain looks like around you?"

"What do you think it looks like? It's the frigging desert, for God's sake. There are a lot of big rocks here—I don't remember seeing any of those last night. There's Saguaro, and those buckthorn things you pointed out. I passed prickly pear and teddy bear cholla on the way here—wherever here is."

The line went dead.

"Cole? Cole?" she screamed into the phone, before

common sense told her to end the connection and try again. Hopefully, he'd done the same thing, but before she could redial, her phone rang.

"Cole?"

"Yeah. Listen. If you look at the mountain, what can you see?"

"The main mountain and the tip of Weaver's Needle. I don't think we could see that Monday night, or maybe it was just too dark."

"I know where you are. I'm on my way."

"Okay, but please hurry. It's getting dark fast, and I don't think my flashlight will last long. I'm not wearing my leathers, and it's getting cold. You told me sound carries in the desert, but I swear I just heard some growls and snarls that sounded awfully close. There's more thunder and I'm sure I saw some lightening. I can't believe how stupid I am."

Panic edged her voice, but she couldn't suppress it.

"You're not stupid. You needed time to think. I'll be there as soon as I can. I'm—"

The line went dead once more.

"Damn! What the hell am I supposed to do now?"

She huffed out a breath. Cole knew where she was. He was on his way. She had to stay still and relax. That wouldn't be too hard. Thunder rumbled again, and the tears she tried to hold in slipped down her cheeks.

"Please God," she said aloud, her voice a mere whisper. "If there's even the tiniest bit of compassion in you for me, please let him find me before it gets dark."

* * * *

Driving as fast as he could toward the campground road, Cole prayed the dropped call was because of the erratic cell service caused by the incoming storm. If he didn't get to her before the flashlight went out, he knew all too well what could. Mountain lions weren't the only predators out there. His mind filled with images of the dangers Casey faced at night in the Superstition Mountain Wilderness, and he had to keep reminding himself to slow down. Crashing his bike and getting killed wouldn't help her. When the turnoff for the campground road finally came into sight, it didn't lessen his fears.

Cole couldn't stop the horrible scenarios from taking shape in his fertile imagination. At times like these, his creative writer's mind was a curse, not a blessing. He slammed his palm against his handlebar. This was all his fault. If he hadn't taken her into the desert last night, she wouldn't be in this mess. If she'd needed to ride, she would've stayed on the highway, ending up in civilization, not at the mercy of Mother Nature or shady human beings.

As much as he loved the area, this land was harsh and unforgiving. The Apache had known it. Legends and sacred beliefs gave them a reverent respect for the mountain, but settlers, miners, and prospectors paid little attention to and had even less admiration for the land's original inhabitants and their ways. Few of the prospectors who'd died searching for gold had done so from natural causes.

There were several dirt tracks leading off the campground road. Even if she thought she'd found the right place, she could easily have been mistaken. As soon as the trail he needed came into sight, Cole turned onto it. If anything happened to her, he would never be able to live with himself. When he reached the end of the trail and saw her Harley, he parked his ride next to hers, and relaxed slightly.

Casey had been away a long time, and she'd only been to Table Rock once, in the twilight, with a flashlight illuminating only the section of the land they'd needed to cross. In the daytime, everything would've been different. To the uninitiated, desert rocks and cacti looked alike, and more than one person had died of exposure or dehydration after going around in circles, thinking they were moving in the right direction. He'd marked his path to the rock, not that he'd explained that to her last night. If he had, she might've found it easily enough. Now, she was out there, somewhere, and darkness was moving in far more quickly than he'd like.

After dismounting, he looked around, but he couldn't see light anywhere. The land between here and the mountain face might look flat, but it wasn't. If she were in a depression, he wouldn't see her, but her enemies didn't hunt by sight, they hunted by smell. His heart constricted. If she'd fallen into a ravine, rolled down an embankment, twisted an ankle in the entrance to some creature's underground lair, or been bitten by one of the desert's venomous snakes, she could be hurt and that would bring the predators even more quickly to her side.

Cole made call after call, but her phone kept going to voicemail. Maybe it was just the storm messing with the signal, but the possibility she was injured and unable to answer continued to eat at him. Carrying his LED flashlight and her leather jacket, he headed into the wilderness toward Table Rock. She wouldn't be there, but he had to start searching somewhere. Thunder reverberated in the mountains and lightening lit the distant sky.

Moving deeper into the desert, he continued to try the phone. If he didn't find her within the next half-hour, he would have to contact Hal and have him bring out the volunteer fire department's search and rescue team. If the weather held off, Drew could use one of his family's sightseeing helicopters with a searchlight. If it didn't, they had a hell of a long, wet night ahead of them, but he wasn't leaving until he found her.

As expected, there was no sign of her when he reached Table Rock. He scanned the area, checking to ensure she hadn't gone down below the outcropping. Standing on the stone, he used the camera function on it like a pair of binoculars, searching for an area that might have more boulders than they had around here. Noting a place that seemed promising, and convinced she would be able to see part of the needle from there, he started walking south, yelling her name as loudly as he could. He would have to walk at least fifteen minutes before Weaver's Needle would be visible from this vantage point, but knowing she could see it spurred him on.

If there were predators in the area—human or animal—it might scare them off. Listening carefully, he heard the sounds of the desert resume, but no human voice, and moved deeper into the wasteland, closer to the mountain itself. Overhead, bats swooped, feeding in the early dark, and remembering her aversion to them, he hoped they weren't anywhere near her.

When Rita had collected her novel, she'd mentioned fielding call after call from people in town, including Pete, who'd been adamant they'd seen lights on the mountain last night. While Chester Morris insisted it had been aliens, most didn't believe in extraterrestrials. Some had blamed ghosts or illegal immigrants looking for someplace to stay on their journey north, but others were convinced it was the air force conducting maneuvers. Hal had verified that hadn't been the case. Hopefully, all the talk would convince whoever was involved to lay low for a few days, and if that didn't work, the bad weather tonight might.

Hal had called just after Cole had returned from Phoenix. He and Ramon had taken a ride out to the abandoned mines, but they hadn't seen anything there. While he couldn't be positive, it appeared as if something large had gone farther along the narrow trail away from Skansen land. There were tire tracks from at least one ATV. It could simply be someone from the campground trespassing on Skansen land to get where they wanted to go, or one of the prospectors looking to stake a claim out that way. But that didn't explain the helicopter.

Forcing himself to focus on the matter at hand and not all the mysteries facing them at the moment, Cole walked deeper into the desert, using the powerful flashlight to search the unfamiliar ground ahead of him. The last thing he needed was to step in a stand of teddy bear cactus or injure himself. Calling her name repeatedly, he figured he was attracting attention to himself since the animals could sense fear, but he didn't care. This was an area he rarely traveled, but the ground was firm and the cacti few and far between. It was rocky, with large outcrops, which provided excellent hiding places for hungry animals. Swallowing his anxiety, he trudged on.

Considering the heavy cloud cover, darkness fell far sooner than he would've liked. Cole continued calling her name, stopping each time he did, listening for her answer. Hearing her faint reply, his heart, which had been pounding its way out of his chest, slowed, and he veered in that direction, walking as quickly as he could.

"I'm here, Casey. I'm coming to you. Just hand on a little longer."

CHAPTER ELEVEN

"Casey, sweetheart, where are you?" Cole yelled. Hearing nothing, he took a calming breath, and called out to her again. This time there was a faint sound in response.

"Honey, I'm here, but I can't pinpoint your light. Can you flash it around so I know where you are?"

Forcing himself to stay calm, he turned full circle trying to catch a glimpse of light, but saw nothing. She had to be around here. If he could hear her, why couldn't he see her?

"Can you see my light? Do you know where I am? Please, Cole, for the love of God, see me." He heard the panic in her voice. "My phone's almost dead."

"I can't see you yet, but I can hear you clearly, so that's a good sign. Don't worry. I may be in a depression or you could be behind a rock. Keep moving your light around and take small steps in front of you. Something may be blocking the light."

"Okay."

Hoping his hunch was correct, Cole walked forward. Every few steps, he would call out to her. He had to keep her talking.

"What did you do today before riding?"

"I helped out at Randy's shop," she answered, her voice louder than before.

"See anyone you knew?"

"Lots of people, including Kristal Jameson Harvey."

Cole whistled. "The Wicked Witch of the West? That

couldn't have been fun. I'll bet she didn't have anything good to say." The widow in his novel had taken more than one of her character traits from the town's queen bitch, but knowing what she had to put up with, Cole had given her a number of redeeming qualities as well. "So, who else did you see?"

She rattled off the names of people they'd known in school, and after what seemed like hours, but was no more than a few minutes, Cole spotted her weak light.

"That was quite the trip down memory lane, but I can see you," he said, trying for a relaxed friendly tone. "Stop moving now. I'm almost there."

Sprinting toward the faint light, he thanked whoever was listening for letting him find her.

Only a few feet away from scooping her up into his arms, swearing he would never let her go, his breath stalled as the shadow behind her moved and his worst nightmare came into view.

No other predator evoked mixed feelings in Cole the way the puma did. Although the big cat was at home in this part of the desert, it tended to stay at higher elevations where the deer, sheep, goats, and wild horses were plentiful. What had dragged this fellow out of his usual habitat? Knowing the animal was still lying in wait, after all the noise they'd been making, scared him. This had to be one very hungry cat or one who'd found an easy way to feed in the campground garbage dump. If it was the one who'd torn Leon's corpse apart, it would have to be destroyed. If it hurt Casey, Cole would hunt it down and kill it himself.

Unlike other big cats, puma were lazy hunters, preferring to lie in ambush, until their prey moved close enough for them to leap on. This animal was biding its time, waiting patiently for Casey to step within range. Cole swore he could see the old feline lick its chops. If he were any closer to it, he could probably hear the big cat purr.

Cole stifled his fear and moved toward Casey, eyes glued on the shining orbs in the distance behind her. This cat was old and quite large, and he didn't look underfed.

"Casey, stay exactly where you are. Whatever you do, don't move." If she started to run, the cat would be on her in seconds. Puma could sprint as fast as fifty miles an hour when they needed to. The fact she stood still probably had the animal confused.

"What? Why?" Ignoring his words, she moved forward. The animal stood and matched her steps, slowly decreasing the distance between it and its dinner.

"Cassandra Stevens, stop this minute! For God's sake, don't move another foot," he called loudly, unable to keep the terror out of his voice, knowing he'd frightened her, but she complied.

Slowly, never taking his eyes off the creature, he bent and picked up a loose rock about the size of a baseball. Back in high school, he'd had a good pitching arm. With any luck, he hadn't lost his touch. A rock wasn't much of a weapon against a one hundred and eighty pound killer, but it was all he had. He'd never been this scared in his life, and he knew by now the animal had scented his fear, too.

The thought of that monster jumping on Casey, sinking its razor sharp teeth and claws into her neck almost had his knees buckling under him. Show no fear! He wouldn't let her get hurt even if he had to wrestle that damn cat himself.

"Casey, I'm coming," he yelled loudly, flashing the full force of the LED into the animal's face causing its eyes to shine an eerie yellow in the bright light.

The cat stood its ground and bared its teeth, emitting a low growl that made the hair on the back of Cole's neck stand on end. Stopping suddenly, he dropped the flashlight at his feet and fired the rock at the animal, landing the stone with a heavy thump right beside the beast's feet and sending sand up into the animal's face. With an angry snarl, furious about losing what he'd seen as an easy meal, the puma turned into the desert and disappeared into the night.

Would he be back? It was hard to say. It would depend on how hungry he was. Satisfied they were safe for the moment, Cole picked up the light and focused it on Casey noting the terror in her eyes, but she'd done as he'd asked. Moving the last few feet to her side, he gathered her trembling body in his arms, grateful to feel her there.

"It's okay." He pressed a kiss into her hair. "You're safe now."

The floodgates opened, and she cried, no longer able to control the emotions pulling at her.

If he could, he would be crying too, but one of them had to stay strong and get them the hell out of here. Holding her tightly, he murmured words of comfort. When his breathing returned to normal, and her crying jag subsided, he eased her away from him.

"You're safe now. Feeling better?" he asked, not releasing her completely, but holding her, knowing how close he'd come to losing her.

"Why do people assume a person feels better after they've cried?" she answered. "I don't feel better, Cole. I'm terrified. What the hell was behind me? A bobcat? I heard that growl. It was so close..."

"A puma." He couldn't mask the fear in his voice.

"Oh my God," she whispered. Her knees buckled, and if he hadn't been holding her, she would've crumpled to the ground.

Cole held her tightly, giving her a minute to settle her nerves. She had to be able to move under her own steam for them to get out of here safely. Given the terrain, as much as he might like to, he couldn't carry her out. And there was always a chance that cat wasn't the only predator in the area tonight. Taking out his compass, he watched until the needle settled and then turned to retrace his steps toward Table Rock. They couldn't linger here. While the wind had eased slightly, thunder continued to rumble.

He kissed her face and hair. Her breathing wasn't as ragged now, and she seemed to have put some starch in her backbone. She had every right to her fear, and he didn't blame her one bit. He was just glad he'd gotten to her in time.

Casey pushed him away and reached for the jacket he'd

brought with him.

"I'm really sorry you had to come out here and rescue me," she said, putting on her coat. "I'm not usually the damsel in distress type. It was silly of me to come out here alone." She was trembling still, reaction not having loosened its grip on her.

Her choice of words was like a red cloth to a bull. Fury filled him. Silly? Had she just said silly?

"It was more than that, Casey, it was extremely stupid and irresponsible, and I'm not going to sugar coat it. The desert is dangerously deceptive at any time of day, but especially at night, and coming out here by yourself when you don't know the area was reckless." As he spoke, he grew angrier, his voice filled with rage, the images of what might've happened fueling his ire.

"I said I was sorry." Indignation screamed from every pore of her body. "Don't worry. If I'm ever in trouble again, I'll be sure not to bother you."

She turned away and started walking. He grabbed her arms to stop her and spun her around to face him, angrier than he'd ever been in his entire life.

"What the hell's wrong with you? Haven't you learned anything tonight? You're going the wrong way," he yelled at her when she tried to pull out of his grip. He tightened his hold, aware of the fact he was scaring her, but she had to understand how dangerous this had been. "Listen to me." His voice rose, filled not only with his fury but with fear.

"When I think of how close you came to being seriously injured or killed—that puma wasn't looking for a tummy rub. He was looking for supper, and you were on the menu. Do you understand? Another few minutes, and I would've been too late. You could have died!"

"Damn it, Cole. I'm not an idiot, I know that," she cried, tears coursing down her cheeks. "I wanted to get away. I didn't think I would get lost, and I'm sorry. Now forget it."

Cole stared at her, and unable to stop himself, pulled her into his arms and kissed her roughly. She stood woodenly in his arms, forcing him back from the edge of his terror.

He released her, stunned by the depth of his rage. What the hell was he doing?

* * * *

The depth of Cole's fury, obvious in the punishing kiss he'd given her, scared Casey as much if not more than the puma had. His fingers dug painfully into her upper arms, and for a moment, she thought he would shake the life out of her—not that she didn't deserve a dressing down after getting herself into this mess. The panic she'd felt earlier filled her, threatening what little composure she'd found.

Instead of acting on his rage, Cole let out an unsteady breath and relaxed his grip, but he didn't let go of her. His voice softened, his underlying terror still there.

"I'm sorry if I hurt you. This is my fault as much, if not more, than yours, since I should never have taken you here in the first place. My ego outweighed my common sense. I knew the dangers, and I ignored them." He hung his head. "People have died out here, and some have disappeared without a trace. Last year, I helped carry out four hikers in body bags. They got lost and the heat got them, but it could've been anything. We're over two hundred miles from the border, but they've arrested illegals over near Apache Junction and Mesa. I told you about Leon Turner. That puma might've been one of the predators that feasted on him. We still haven't found all of him."

Dread filled her, and her stomach roiled at the thought.

"I don't know what I'd have done if I'd been too late." Cole's voice hitched as he pulled her back into his arms, but this time, there was no anger, just self-recrimination and guilt.

She didn't resist. Appreciating the way he blamed himself, she understood his need to hold her as badly as she needed to be held, and realized she'd run away from her problems just as she had fifteen years ago, once more endangering not only herself but someone she cared about—and she did care for Cole. If that puma had chosen to attack, they would both be dead now. Instead of talking, she stood in his arms, bathed in the light of the flashlight Cole had dropped at their feet.

She gazed up into his eyes and placed her quivering hand along the side of his face.

"I'm so very, very sorry. Don't blame yourself. I needed to be alone, and God knows where I might've ended up. At least you knew where to look for me, and I had someone to call to help me out." She lowered her hand. "You're right. What I did was so far beyond stupid, it doesn't even have a name."

She sighed. As memory had reminded her, the last time she'd ridden off the way she had today, her horse, and eventually her family, had paid the price.

"I've always known the desert was hazardous, filled with hidden pitfalls. Everyone growing up in this area is grilled on those dangers. Hell, I didn't even have a hat or a bottle of water with me, and until the clouds rolled in, my skin was burning quite nicely. By tomorrow, my nose will look like Rudolph's and come Sunday, I'll be peeling." She swallowed and licked her lips. "Coming home to Fortune was a mistake. I don't belong here. The woman I become isn't someone I want to be ever again. Thank you for saving me," she whispered before leaning forward, placing a soft kiss on his mouth, and pulling back.

"I happen to think there's nothing wrong with the woman you are right now, and as far as I'm concerned, you definitely belong here, in my arms. I want to be the person you call when you need help, Casey. I want to be the one you turn to always," he said, his face serious, his eyes shining with moisture from unshed tears that matched hers. "I know it seems too early to even be thinking this way, but you matter to me. You always have."

Casey smiled unsteadily at him, unfamiliar emotions filling her, making her heart ache, longing for something she'd never experienced.

Cole bent his head and captured her mouth once more, but unlike his last kiss, this one was tender. After running his tongue across her parched lips, he plunged into her mouth, and she rejoiced in the taste and texture of him—something she'd considered throwing away earlier today, but realized she needed more than ever now.

Eagerly, needing to feel alive after her near-death experience, she returned his kiss with a passion she hadn't known she possessed. All the need, loneliness, and fear she'd felt over the past fifteen years poured out of her and into him. Their tongues dueled, and heat pooled in her lower abdomen. She wanted him as she'd never wanted a man before, and had they been anywhere else, she would've torn his clothes off and hers, and made love to him right this second, an Amazon claiming her mate. But this was not the time, and definitely not the place.

Releasing her lips slowly, he smiled at her. "I don't know about you, lady, but I'm ready to blow this Popsicle stand. Let's get the hell out of here."

"Good idea, and as soon as we get back to town, I'm going to need more than coffee to settle my frazzled nerves. Think you might be able to find something stronger?" The idea of joining him on those silk sheets like he'd suggested last night held enough appeal that she would overlook whose house it was. After all, he'd said they were away.

"I've got a well-stocked liquor cabinet, or we could go to the *Golden Nugget* for a while."

Moving out of his arms, she picked up the flashlight, handed it to him, and wrapped her fingers tightly around his, the heat comforting her.

"We'll try your place first."

"Yes, ma'am." He kissed her softly and turned, following the compass, retracing his steps to Table Rock.

Lightening flashed over the mountains, and thunder rumbled, shaking the earth, making her cringe.

As they passed Table Rock, she shivered. What had been a supremely romantic place had lost its magic, and that was her fault. Maybe they could come back one day and try to recapture it, but not any time soon. Holding Cole's hand tightly, she moved beside him, her feet following the circle of light shed by the flashlight in his hand, her head turning left and then right, searching for eyes in the desert. There was always a possibility that puma was watching them, waiting for his chance to pounce.

Casey was still shaky when they arrived at the motorcycles.

"Can you ride?" he asked as she untied her helmet from the saddle where she'd secured it.

"I think so, but I'm looking forward to that shot."

And maybe finishing what they'd started in the desert last night. She needed the validation that she was alive, but more importantly, she needed him. It was a simple and as complicated as that. Desperate to get away from here, she opened her saddled bag and took out her leather pants, putting them on quickly.

"I wish I'd left my extra boots in there," she pointed to the other saddle bag, "but they're in Randy's office."

"Runners aren't the best for riding, but we'll take it easy. We can leave the Harleys in my garage. Whether we have drinks at the house or go on to the *Golden Nugget* doesn't really matter, but I don't drink and ride."

"Neither do I," she answered, once more ashamed of her reckless behavior.

"Do you want to talk about why you came out here in the first place?" he asked, his brow furrowed as if he thought she might do it again.

"No, I don't. But I promise not to repeat the incident. Let's go get that drink."

"You're sure you're okay to drive now?"

"Yes, I'll be fine."

Watching Cole settle on his bike, she did the same, but for the second time today, riding gave her no pleasure. Coming out here had been a foolish, reckless thing to do, and when she got home, she would have to face the consequences. Since Cole insisted she go first, she started her Harley and headed up the trail, nervously watching the shadows beside her. As soon as they hit the tarmac, the skies opened. Riding in the rain was no

146

fun, but it beat the hell out of filling some cat's belly.

Casey let out a long, shaky breath. Cole was right behind her, and while that should make her feel safe, she was terrified. She'd almost been eaten by a freaking puma tonight. Kitty chow, and for what? Because she was a coward unwilling to face her sister and the pain she'd seen on her face, pain echoed in her own heart. Randy's words had ripped her heart apart as easily as a bullet would. Facing her family would be far more difficult than facing the fact that she'd almost gotten herself killed again. Who said people learned from their mistakes?

* * * *

Cole stayed beside Casey as they drove along the highway, unwilling to let her out of his sight even for a second. Rain pelted them, but so far, the thunder and lightning seemed to be staying in the mountains. Thanks to the heavy rain, the only light they had to guide them were the lights on their Harleys, and they hadn't seen another vehicle since they'd passed the BLM ranger car entering the campground. They'd both be soaked by the time they reached his home, but it couldn't be helped.

Even though Casey maintained she was fine, he doubted her words. Hell, he was shakier than a newborn colt, and he hadn't been the one who'd practically been dinner. He'd nearly died when he'd seen those glassy eyes. If he'd taken the time to grab his service weapon—something he knew damn well he should've done—he could've chased that cat away quickly and easily. What kind of fool faced down a puma with nothing but a rock? He couldn't believe it had worked. While the whole scenario had a David and Goliath feel to it and would make a great scene for his new book, he doubted he would be able to write it any time soon.

He glanced at Casey, noted the death grip she had on her handle bars, and sighed.

Yup, she's just as unsettled as I am.

Maintaining a steady speed below the limit in concession to the road and weather conditions, it took them well over half an hour to reach the house. Knowing how she'd reacted last night when he'd asked her in, he was fairly certain she would refuse again, once she discovered his parents had returned, but he wanted her to come inside. He needed time alone with her, even if it wouldn't be the intimacy he craved.

Pulling ahead of her, he motioned she should follow him and pressed the garage door opener, the door creeping up in front of them, revealing a brightly lit space next to the SUV. He turned off his engine and steadied his bike. She did the same. He pulled off his helmet, secured it to the bike, and removed his leathers, hanging them on the coat hooks he'd installed for that purpose.

"You can leave your gear here," he said as she removed her helmet and shook out her hair, reminding him of flames in a campfire. "It's locked, and there's an alarm. Everything will be secure for the night."

"Thanks." She removed her wet leather pants. "My phone's dead. As soon as we get inside, I have to call home. They'll be worried sick. I've definitely earned whatever tongue-lashing I'm going to get this time."

"Of course, but they know I was looking for you," he admitted. "I phoned when I couldn't reach you."

She nodded, but before she could answer him, his mother opened the kitchen door.

"Cole? Where have you been? You left in such a hurry. I've been worried sick."

He glanced over his shoulder at the stunned look on Casey's face, telling him clearly that had she known his parents were home, she would've refused to come here.

"Sorry about that," he said, suddenly wishing he did have a place of his own. Mom meant well, but she did tend to be overprotective. "Casey called. She got herself lost in the desert and needed help."

"Oh my God," his mother exclaimed, forgetting about him and hurrying over to Casey. "Well, for heaven's sake, Cole, get her into the house. You're getting wet—we all are. Come on.

You poor thing. I'll get you something to warm you up." She took Casey's arm and led her toward the steps.

"That's okay, I'm fine, really," Casey protested. "I don't want to be any trouble."

"After Casey uses the phone, we're going over to the *Nugget*," he added coming to her rescue.

"Nonsense. You can stay for a while. The *Nugget* isn't going anywhere," his mother answered, her 'don't argue with me' tone evident. "Cole Senior will be happy to see you."

Casey turned to him for support. Knowing there was no easy way out of this, he shrugged and winked.

"We won't stay long," he whispered, although he would gladly keep her by his side all through the night.

"I suppose we could go in for a bit," Casey said, the look she gave him promising retribution. "I do need to call my mother."

Mrs. Walker beamed at her and led her toward the house. "Of course you do. Have you eaten?"

"I'm not really very hungry, thanks."

Cole stood a few feet away, waiting as Casey made the call, ready to jump to her defense if she needed him.

Dialing the number, he noted the surprised look on her face when no one answered right away.

"Hey, Mom, it's me. Sorry I didn't call sooner. I met up with Cole," she said.

Her phrasing startled him. He watched her expressive face as she listened, obviously surprised by whatever her mother was saying.

"Yeah. I'm at his place now. Sorry about missing dinner. We were talking, and I lost track of time."

She glanced at him, her eyes pleading for his understanding.

He reached for her hand and squeezed it. Maybe they didn't need to know what had really happened to her tonight.

"His parents are here. I'll be home in a couple of hours," she continued, obviously confused by her mother's response. "I will." Casey hung up and stared at the phone.

"That was weird. Where are my real parents, and who answered that call?" She laughed, but it seemed strained.

Cole chuckled. "Maybe she's just glad you're okay."

"Maybe, but more than likely she's saving up to give me both barrels when she sees me in person."

Cole pulled her to him. "Stay with me, and you can avoid it." But he knew she would say no.

CHAPTER TWELVE

Casey held Cole's hand as he led her into the living room where his father sat watching television. She wished there were some way she could avoid this visit. What she really wanted was to stay with him as he'd suggested, feel his arms around her, his lips on hers, and make love with him, but considering his parents were here now, that definitely wasn't going to happen tonight.

Like so many of the other long-time residents of Fortune she'd seen today, Mr. Walker's face lit up the moment he saw her.

"Well, look at you," he said, turning off the television with the remote, standing, and pulling her into a bear hug. He released her and stepped away. "It's a good thing your mother has pictures all over the house or I wouldn't have recognized you … although you are much prettier in person. Welcome back, Casey."

"Thanks, Mr. Warner. It's good to be back," she said, wishing Cole still held her hand.

"Now, now, no more Mr. Warner. Call me Senior. Everyone else does."

Nodding, she took a good look at the man who'd been such a powerful presence during her teen years. He was a bit more wrinkled than she remembered, no doubt from the hours spent fishing on Canyon or Apache Lake. His hair had turned white, making his olive skin seem darker, and he'd gained a few pounds, but he looked fit and healthy. Seeing the two men side by side, the resemblance between father and son might be a slight one, but it was there.

"Noella said you got lost out in the desert," Senior said. "I'm surprised Austin didn't warn you to stay away from there. Too many people coming through town these days, and with the fair later in the week, they won't all be here to help us celebrate. Now tell me exactly how you managed to get yourself lost.

"Dad did warn me not to go into the wilderness at night, but it wasn't dark when I decided to do that," she lied, amazed at how easy it was to do. It seemed the more you skirted the truth, the easier it became. "I rode west to a place I remembered, but I guess my recall wasn't as good as I thought it was."

She described her ordeal, omitting what had sent her there in the first place, and focused on Cole's valiant rescue.

"Now that I think about it, it would make a great scene in a CJ Coleson book." She giggled nervously at the surprised look on Senior's face. "You should've seen him. Scared the living daylights out of me—not that I wasn't already terrified. He started to yell, ran toward me, and tossed that rock…"

"You faced down a puma with nothing but a stone?" his mother said, her eyes mere slits in her angry face, as she entered the room carrying a large tray with a bowl of fresh salsa, a larger bowl of tortilla chips, an ice bucket, four glasses, and a bottle of whiskey. She set the serving platter down on the table and put her hands on her hips, her face a mask of shock and disapproval. "Who the hell did you think you were? Tarzan?"

After pouring a generous amount of the amber liquid into the glass, she added a few ice cubes, and gave it to Casey. "I have lemonade and tea, but I think after your nightmare out there, you'll appreciate this more. And you," she used the glass to point at Cole before handing it to him. "Don't ever do anything that stupid again."

He chuckled. "Not by choice," he agreed. "But if Casey's in danger, I'll do whatever I have to."

Choosing not to comment, Casey took a sip and rested against the couch, letting the soothing whiskey burn away the residue of her shock.

"So you know about Cole and CJ Coleson," Senior said, smiling his approval.

"That they're friends and went to school together? Yes, Cole told me when I saw Coleson's new book on the shelf at the emporium."

"I see," he said, glaring disapprovingly at Cole. "He doesn't usually share that."

"Don't worry," Casey answered, "I won't tell anyone. I did mention it to Randy when I got home, but she can keep a secret, too." She turned to Cole, whose face seemed redder than it had. "Maybe, once this isn't as scary as it is tonight, you can describe the rescue to him, and he can write the scene into his next book. But if he does, I'll expect an autographed copy for being his inspiration."

"I'll definitely see that you get one," Cole said quietly.

"You'll have to tell Hal Rankin about that puma," Senior said pointedly, his eyes fixed on Cole. "He'll need to organize a hunting party. They may be able to tranquilize the cat and move it, but—"

"I know," Cole answered, before his father could finish, and Casey got the impression there was more being said than the words implied. She vaguely remembered the last time one of the desert cats had come too close to town. They'd managed to relocate it, but sometimes the animals returned to their old hunting grounds. With the increased popularity of the Lost Dutchman Campground, a large puma could easily walk off with someone's pet or worse. She thought of Jaxon playing alone in the yard and felt her stomach roil. A six-foot fence wouldn't keep one of those killers away if it was hungry enough. They'd been known to jump more than fifteen feet high. She shuddered.

The emotional highs and lows of the day, coupled with the previous night's lack of sleep, had taken their toll on her, and suddenly, she was bone-tired. Cole leaned back, put his arm around her shoulders, and pulled her into his side. His mom raised her eyebrows in approval and smiled at the gesture. If Casey weren't so tired, she would probably let it bother her, knowing the fact that the two of them were dating would be all over town in no time, but she didn't care. Being close to Cole like this was comforting, and she would hang onto the feeling—and the man—as long as she could.

"It's getting late," she said, a couple of hours later, reluctant to leave Cole's side, but well aware of the fact she had to. "This has been great, but I've got to get home." She sobered. "Mom will have a fit when she hears about this. I don't suppose we could keep it our little secret?" The pleading in her voice was loud, but she was fairly sure it was a useless request. This was Fortune after all where everyone's business was someone else's.

"Of course we can," Noella said and smiled. "You're fine, and there's no point getting Maria all worked up about it. I'm sure she has enough to worry about as it is, and she's none too fond of motorcycles. None of us are."

"That's putting it mildly," Casey said, remembering what Cole had told her.

After saying goodbye, she followed Cole outside to wait for her cab. The rain had ended and the moon smiled down on them. Wrapping his arms around her waist, he pulled her close, kissing her gently. "The offer to stay the night still stands."

"I know, but it's not possible. My mother would have a fit if I didn't come home, and knowing your parents were in the next room, I wouldn't be able to sleep a wink."

"I wasn't planning on getting any sleep," Cole said with a chuckle.

"I definitely wouldn't be able to do *that* with your parents in the house. It would just be too weird," she answered, her earlier concerns about his living arrangements coming back.

"That's why you took off last night, isn't it? I don't understand why my living here is a problem. They're away a lot. It's just practical."

"That may be true, but right now they're home, and I just can't … you know … I can see how it all makes sense to you, but to me, it's just odd. I need my space and my privacy, neither of which you seem to have here, at least not tonight. I could never picture myself living with my parents again under any circumstances. Don't get me wrong, I love them. I just don't want to live with them."

"Living with my parents, or rather having them live with me, has never been an issue before."

"Are you telling me that having your parents in the next room has never bothered your girlfriends?" she asked, unable to grasp the idea that a woman could make love to him with his parents two doors away.

"Since I've never brought another woman here before, it hasn't been an issue."

Casey was speechless. How was she supposed to respond to that? Cole didn't date—at least he hadn't dated until yesterday. First, he'd taken her to his special spot in the desert. Now, he'd brought her home.

"From the way you kiss me, I know you're not inexperienced," she said, trying to make sense of what he'd revealed.

He gave her a sexy smirk that made her melt. "Oh believe me baby, I've had plenty of experience. The things I could do to you…" He winked. "I've dated, just not in Fortune. I've never met anyone until now that I cared enough about to bring home. I think we've got something special going on here, something worth pursuing. I hope you do, too. Some people can make long distance relationships work. I'd like to give it a try."

Struggling not to show him how giddy she felt inside, she stood on tiptoe and gave him a quick kiss as the cab pulled up to the curb.

"So do I. It won't be easy once I return to Santa Fe, but …

155

I'll get someone to bring me over to collect my bike in the morning. Will you still be here?"

"It depends on the time. I usually open the store at nine."

"Okay, I'll try to get here before then. Goodnight."

"Goodnight, sweetheart. I'll see you tomorrow."

He bent his head and kissed her, but unlike the other kisses they'd shared, this one was full of hope and promise. He pulled away, and Casey got into the cab. Cole couldn't see the huge smile on her face as the taxi pulled away. Coming home to Fortune had definitely been the right thing to do. Now, all she had to do was convince Randy that she wouldn't be deserting the family when she returned to Santa Fe.

* * * *

Cole watched the lights of Casey's cab vanish around the curb much the same way he'd observed her bike do last night, but tonight, the feelings were different. How could he have become so emotionally involved with the woman after spending so little time with her? Love at first sight was for fairytales and star-struck teenagers, but whatever was going on here was stronger and a hell of a lot scarier than anything he'd ever felt for a woman before.

Turning toward the house, he walked up the stairs to the porch and settled onto the swing where he often sat when a trek out into the desert wasn't possible. He liked Casey, admired her, and enjoyed her company, but there was more to it than that. Lust was definitely a factor and had been from the moment he'd set eyes on her, but there was something deeper, something that had sent him into the desert terrified he would lose her. Whatever this fascination was, he needed to explore it, but he was working within a limited time frame. He had ten days left to convince her they belonged together, at least in the short term.

The slow swaying of the swing was relaxing, but his conscience nagged at him. Sooner or later, he would have to tell her the truth about his alter ego, and the longer he waited the more difficult it would be. Glancing at his watch, he reasoned she'd be home by now. He entered the house, locked up, and unable to squelch the need to hear her voice, he went up to his room and reached for his cellphone.

Unlike last night, she picked up on the first ring.

"Hello?" The sound of her hushed voice warmed him. He had to find a way to make this work.

"Hey, did I wake you?" He pictured her lying in bed in some diaphanous nightgown, and his body reacted.

"No. I was just about ready to turn in," she whispered.

"Sorry. I forgot how late it was." He glanced at the clock. Almost one—the same as last night. He should've considered that before calling, but given when she would be leaving Fortune, he didn't have a second to waste.

"Don't worry about it. What's up?"

Cole lay back against the pillows of his bed wanting to get more comfortable.

"Nothing really. I just wanted to hear your voice and make sure you got home in one piece."

"That's so thoughtful of you, but like last night, my ride home was uneventful. Unlike the cab rides I take in Santa Fe, there wasn't any traffic to contend with. The cab driver was a sweet, old man who stayed well within the speed limit, and charged me less than half of what I would've paid in the city."

He chuckled. "You've got to watch those charming, quiet ones. I know … I'm one of them. Did the family give you a hard time when you got home?"

"No, thank God. I was sure Mom would be pacing the carpet, but everyone was asleep, so I came straight upstairs. It'll probably come up in the morning, but I just don't want to fight about it anymore. I want them to accept and understand that I'll never move back to Fortune. I'll definitely visit more often, but I can't come back here permanently. This small town would eventually destroy me. Their badgering me about it won't change that."

Disappointment filled him, cooling the ardor he'd felt, and

erasing the delectable image from his mind. So much for his dream of a future together here. On the heels of that thought came another.

"Are you telling me that's why you went off like that, why you could've been killed tonight?"

As the seconds ticked past, he wondered if she was going to answer him. The dead air between them weighed heavily on his heart.

"I suppose, since you rescued me, you do have a right to know, but I'm not a very open person, Cole. I usually keep my life and my feelings to myself." She chuckled. "I guess your friend CJ and I have that in common. You don't tend to get hurt that way."

Guilt nagged at him. He knew that only too well, but sometimes protecting yourself came at a heavy cost as she'd almost learned tonight. The silence was profound. Had she ended the call?

"Casey?"

"Sorry. Things went well at the bakery until Mr. Stone came in, and then Randy and I argued and—"

"What does Horace Stone have to do with this?" he interrupted. The town's lawyer was a stand-up guy, one of the four people who knew the truth about CJ Coleson.

"Mr. Stone told me he's looking for a partner and offered me the job—equal partner, sole proprietor in five years when he retires."

"That's a hell of an offer," he said, stunned by how much he would like her to accept it, realizing she probably hadn't.

"It is, but I said thanks, but no thanks. He refused to accept my answer and made me promise to think about it. I said I would, but I have no intention of doing so. Randy was upset about that, and we argued."

He listened as she related her side of the confrontation that followed. When she'd finished, he spoke quietly. "Casey, you can't blame Randy for feeling the way she does. You two were as close as the Rankin twins at one time. When Dad told me you'd gone to school in Austin, I'd expected her to follow. It shocked the hell out of me when she didn't. It shouldn't come as a surprise that she would want you to take the offer and come home."

"Thanks for the support, Cole. I have to go now." The anger and hurt in her voice took him aback.

"Hold on, Casey. You're misunderstanding me."

"What did I miss? Did you want to add that I'm a heartless, selfish bitch for wanting a life of my own? I've already figured that one out, thanks."

"You should know me better than that," he answered quietly, hurt that she would even suggest such a thing. Casey might've put her career ahead of her family for a while, but he was convinced there was something else at the root of her refusal to come back to Fortune. People didn't avoid towns; they avoided people.

"You're as prickly as barrel cactus, so instead of going off halfcocked again, be quiet for a minute and give me a chance to explain myself."

Expecting her to hang up, he was surprised when he didn't hear the dial tone. Weighing his words carefully, he tried to plead not only Randy's case, but his.

"I can understand where Randy's coming from. Hell, I can't deny I would be thrilled if you decided to take the offer. Family's important, and when its members are spread far and wide, it's easy to feel disconnected. If my sister Fallon could come back, she would."

"I'm not your sister, Cole. At the moment, I don't have a burning need or any desire to be in Fortune."

"Ouch. That's putting me in my place, and I probably deserve it. No, you're not my sister. Otherwise, those kisses yesterday and earlier tonight would be highly inappropriate. I'd love to prove it too you in a room with candlelight, a bottle of fine wine, and a large bed covered in silk sheets."

When he heard her low giggle, he let out a sigh of relief.

"That doesn't sound so bad," she said, the edge to her

voice gone. "Maybe I'll dream of that instead of hungry cats."

"I'd like to make that dream a reality. You're entitled to whatever you want out of life, but try to put yourself in Randy's shoes. I can't imagine what her life is like. I may not have dated here, but I do have a social life. I hang out with the guys, play pool, have beer, and go fishing. I have lots of friends, not only here in Fortune, but in El Paso and Dallas. From what I understand, Randy hasn't had a date since David died. Her life consists of that bakery and her son. She doesn't spend time with her old friends, even though she could if she wanted to. I'm sure your parents would watch Jaxon. I can't imagine how lonely she must be. Right now, she's hurt and angry because to her there's no difference between a partnership in Santa Fe and one here. That's all she sees. Can you understand that?"

"I'm glad I'll never have to face you in court," she said. "You would make a hell of a lawyer. I understand what you're saying, but ... For me, Fortune holds few happy memories of my childhood and teen years. School was its own kind of hell. I've learned today that I was a much better actress than I thought I was, or else people just didn't want to admit or accept what was happening. It doesn't matter now. The only time I felt alive was in the store talking to your dad, or riding Ginger, and when they put her down, there was nothing left here for me."

She stopped talking, but he had a feeling there was more to come.

"I can't go back to living that way again. Can't you understand that?" Her voice pleaded with him.

"I don't think you're giving yourself enough credit. You have to realize that you're not that shy teenager anymore. You're a strong, self-reliant, and competent woman. You would excel anywhere you wanted to, including Fortune."

"Thanks for the vote of confidence," she said and laughed, but it wasn't the joyful laughter he loved. "As much as spending time with you is a definite plus, I'm not ready to face the Ricks and Kristals of this town. I've got to go. I'm tired, and it's been a long day. Don't forget, I'm not used to being the blue-plate special."

"I wouldn't mind having you for dessert."

Although he joked about it, the vestiges of his earlier fear twisted his gut. "Before you hang up, I wanted to ask you something."

"Sure. Go ahead. My savior should be entitled to ask a question."

"Will you have dinner with me tomorrow night? We can ride into Apache Junction if you want to avoid the gossip, but as far as I'm concerned, I don't have a problem with people knowing we're a couple."

"I'd like to, but I can't. I have a date tomorrow."

He felt as if she'd sucker punched him.

"I promised Mom I'd help out with Jaxon's birthday party," she continued. "Six exuberant five-year-old boys in the pool is too much work for her alone, and they'll be here a good two hours before Randy can get away from the bakery. Since I'm a strong swimmer, she's put me on lifeguard duty."

Able to breathe again, he chuckled in relief, his earlier vision morphing into one of her in a string bikini.

"Lucky boys. Any objection to my dropping by after supper to bring him a gift? Maybe by then you can sneak off, and we can spend some time alone."

"I'd like that, as long as it isn't in the desert. I've had my fill of it for a while."

"Believe it or not, so have I," he answered, his earlier fears returning.

"Then, it's a date. Goodnight, Cole."

"Dream of me."

She giggled. "I'll try."

The line went dead.

Cole set his phone on the side table, got undressed, and climbed into bed, his mind going over what Casey had said. Kristal and Rick. What the hell had those two done to make her so determined never to come back here? They'd been bullies back in school and that hadn't changed, but he'd managed to ignore the queen bitch and her consort. And Ginger? Dad had mentioned they'd had to put her horse down when it had broken its leg. Casey had sustained cracked ribs, a broken wrist and a concussion at the time. As soon as she was on her feet, she'd left Fortune and hadn't returned until now. What the hell had happened that night? With the image of Casey's smile in his head, he closed his eyes.

After what felt like mere seconds, Cole's volunteer firefighter beeper sounded. Wide awake, he sat up and reached for the device, checking the display for the message. Nothing chased sleep away faster than knowing something in his town was burning. Too much of it was still old wood.

Getting up, he went into the bathroom, splashed cold water on his face and then got dressed. Stepping out into the hall, he met his father.

"I heard the beeper. Where is it?"

"The old Morris place."

His father frowned. "Must be those damn vagrants."

"Dad, there was lightning earlier tonight. This could be just an unfortunate accident. We don't know who set the other fires, and as unlikely as it seems, we don't even have proof they were all set by the same person. It could be prospectors looking for a place to sleep out of the rain, or vagrants going across the country looking for work. Although it's far from the border, it could even be Mexicans on their way north. Just because we found gasoline doesn't mean they weren't using it to start a fire that got out of hand." Not that he believed that—once maybe, but four times? "My biggest concern right now is that Chester was seen out there. In spite of everything, he still considers it his home."

His father pursed his lips and nodded. "I hope he wasn't. Despite what people think of him, Chester's a damn fine man when he's sober. As I told Casey earlier, things are too unsettled around here these days—these unexplained fires, Leon falling like that and lying out there God knows how long before he died, and now Pete and a few others swear they've seen mysterious lights out in the desert. You were out that way riding with Casey on Monday—did either of you see anything?"

"I saw lights just before I headed home and mentioned them to Hal this morning. Go back to bed, Dad. Hopefully we'll have this out within the hour."

"Be careful," his father said.

"Always."

Cole let himself out of the house and into the garage, taking the SUV instead of his bike. It looked as if Casey was right about one thing. If his dad had heard the beeper through the walls, he would've heard something else. It was definitely time for a home of his own.

CHAPTER THIRTEEN

As tired as she'd been when she'd lain down, Casey couldn't sleep. The conversation she'd had with Cole kept replaying itself in her head. It was better than nightmares of being eaten by a giant puma, or reliving that horrible memory of Rick, but not by much.

Cole had laid out the pros and cons of Randy's dismay clearly, something that, in her emotionally-charged state, she'd been unable to do. What had really hit home had been his question concerning how her family would've reacted if he hadn't found her. That realization had scared her even more than the puma had. The laws of physics didn't change for her. For every action there was an equal and opposite reaction, and sometimes the consequences of that reaction were daunting.

Why was it she could stare down a boardroom full of lawyers intent on protecting their clients and succeed in winning her arguments, and not be able to plead her case to her family? Had nothing changed in fifteen years? Today's quarrel had been like stepping back in time, only back then, she'd argued with her mother, not her sister.

Despite the painful words they'd hurled at one another that August, Casey had packed her bags and left Fortune, with only the contents of her meagre bank account and an acceptance letter to the University of Texas, vowing never to return.

Determined not to look back, she'd gotten a part-time job working in a Mom and Pop restaurant in Austin, had found a small apartment to rent, and had applied for a student loan.

After a month or so, homesickness and guilt had driven her to call her parents, but after that one tearful conversation, Mom, Dad, or Randy had called regularly. Dad deposited money in her account to help her with her education, and the family had come to her in Austin or Santa Fe or they'd met elsewhere for holidays and extended visits. This was the first time Mom had insisted she come home, and she'd almost refused.

She sighed. Why couldn't life be black and white like the law? In a courtroom, she knew exactly where she stood. Here in Fortune, everything was colored some variation of gray. Earlier today, when Mr. Stone had made his offer, the answer had been clear, but now, after listening to Cole, she wasn't so sure. In the past, she'd buried her head in the sand, worrying only about herself and her needs. Randy was right. She'd been incredibly selfish and insensitive, pretending to herself that her family accepted her choice of lifestyle, but deep down, she knew they missed her and didn't understand why she despised Fortune. Fifteen years ago, putting herself first had been necessary for her survival and peace of mind. Now?

Would returning really be so terrible? It was true the people who'd made her life hell were still here, but as she'd learned today, she was stronger than she'd been, and she wasn't alone. There were people like Ella, Rina, and Mr. Lowell that she'd misjudged. And of course there was Cole. Tossing and turning, she searched for answers, wanting a sign that would tell her exactly what to do.

As she'd told Randy, she'd spent the last ten years working incredibly hard to get where she was. Was she willing to give up a potential junior partnership in Santa Fe and the prestige that went with working for such a large, well-respected, national firm? Too much blood, sweat, and tears had gone into her current job for her to dismiss it just like that, even if she found it less satisfying lately than it had been. The end game had always been to have a husband and children and make it to the Bench someday. Would that happen if she buried herself here in Fortune? Sure, the town was growing and the money would be more than adequate, but would that be enough for her?

Being with Cole was an added bonus she hadn't considered this afternoon, but who knew where that relationship could go? She'd fantasized a 'happily ever after' with him before, and it hadn't worked out. And she still had at least one dragon to slay, the memories of which were clearer in her mind today than they'd been in a long time. It had been a sexual assault, something swept under the rug back then, but more and more, such crimes were being investigated and tried. She'd assisted on an attempted rape case only last year. Strangely, she hadn't equated Rick's assault and what the frat boy had done to her client, but the similarities were overwhelming. Settling on her side, punching her pillow, wishing it was Rick's face, she closed her eyes once more, trying to relax and stop overthinking things. She'd made the only decision she could. Now, like everyone else, she would have to learn to live with it.

Casey awoke to the sound of someone tapping on her door, but unwilling to argue again, especially after the difficult day and night she'd had, she feigned sleep. When the door didn't open, she let out the breath she'd been holding and nestled under the covers, hoping to grab a few more zees. The second time she woke, sunlight streamed in through the window. A quick glance at the alarm clock told her it was barely after seven.

Getting up, she showered and dressed. Randy would've left long ago, but the other two members of the inquisition would be waiting for answers. Not only would she be on the hot seat over her decision to reject Mr. Stone's offer, there was her little vanishing act afterwards and her relationship with Cole. At least she could keep her desert misadventure to herself.

Braced for the worst, she stepped into the kitchen. Dad and Jaxon sat at the table finishing their cereal, and Mom was at the sink washing dishes.

"Morning, dear," her mother said, turning around when she

entered the room, a huge smile on her face. "How was your evening?"

"It was fine," Casey answered, waiting for the other shoe to drop. "We sat around, talked about the places they'd visited in their travels, and then watched a movie. Noella and Senior said to say hello."

"They love traveling. Did they have a good visit with Fallon? It's hard having a child so far away from home."

"Yeah. The weather was cool and rainy, but they managed to take the boys to a couple of theme parks. Noella is pretty excited since it looks like Fallon and her family will be home for Thanksgiving."

Here it comes.

"That's wonderful. Breakfast is toast and cereal or muffins this morning. I've got tons to do before..." she nodded her head in Jaxon's direction.

"A muffin and coffee will do nicely, thanks," Casey answered, reaching for a banana, more confused than ever. What was going on here? No questions, no third degree? She dropped a kiss on Jaxon's blond hair before sitting across from him. "Happy birthday, kiddo. Do you feel older?"

"I think so. When Mommy woke me up, she said I looked older. That's good, isn't it?"

"It is," she said, her face fixed in mock severity. "I think you're taller, too." She turned to her father. "Dad, can you drive me over to the Walker house? I left the Harley there last night. I can call a cab if it's not convenient."

"It's fine. I need to go into town to pick up a few things for your mother." He winked. "Eat, and we'll go when you're finished."

Her mother set a cup of coffee and a warm bran muffin on the table in front of her. "There's butter and jam right there ... I must say, I'm really happy to see you and Cole have become friends. I often wondered why you hadn't years ago. Mrs. Bloomsbury told Noella all about that teddy bear you have in your room. Her son was there that night trying to win one for his sister. It was such a sweet thing for Cole to do, but then he left for school, and then you left Fortune … Randy said you saw a lot of people at the shop yesterday, including that nasty Kristal Harvey."

"Yeah, she didn't exactly make my day, but she didn't spoil it either," she answered, refusing to comment on the bear. The fact he'd purposely won it for her was still too precious to share. "Mr. Lowell really put her in her place." It was too bad no one had done it seventeen years ago, when the bullying had been at its worst.

"Well, as much as I've always disliked that girl, and the ten pound chip on her shoulder, I feel sorry for her. She lost her parents in a car accident just before her son was born, and that husband of hers is no prize. She's so busy putting on airs and treating everyone like dirt, she doesn't realize she's driving away the very people she needs the most. That son of hers is a sweet, sensitive boy."

Casey took a mouthful of coffee. Not wanting to talk about Rick and Kristal or their son. "Most of the people I spoke to were glad to see me. I was a little surprised they knew so much about my life in Santa Fe."

Her mother blushed. "I'm sorry about that, but your father and I are so proud of you, you can't blame us for wanting people to know."

"It's okay, I'm not upset with you. It made some things easier. I suppose Randy told you about our argument." Waiting for them to bring it up was killing her.

"Your dad did, and we spoke to her last night. What she said was uncalled for," her mother admitted, shocking her. "We might like you to consider Mr. Stone's offer, but it's your life. You've done a fine job of it so far. We would just like to be a bigger part of it. We aren't getting any younger."

Casey thought her mother was going to add something, but she turned back to the sink.

"Cole made me look at things a little differently, and while I'm not ready to change my answer, I'll try to be more considerate and come home to visit more often. I've been selfish, and I realize that now. I love you all, but some things about this town will never change."

She shoved the last bit of muffin in her mouth, chewed, and swallowed. After draining her coffee mug, she stood.

"Let me get my extra boots, Dad, and we can go. I want to come back and help Mom get ready for later. Cole said he might stop by after supper if that's okay."

She chewed her lower lip nervously. A long-term relationship with Cole would be difficult, but she liked him—maybe a little too much, considering they'd only been together twice. If he thought they could make a go of it, then he deserved a chance to try. In the end though, geography mattered, and Santa Fe was seven hours away.

"This is your home, Casey. Your friends have always been welcome." Her mother dried a cup and put it back into the cupboard. "By the way, if Cole decides not to come by, don't read anything negative into it. There was another fire last night out at the old Morris place. Cole and the volunteer firefighters were there several hours. I understand someone was staying in the house."

Casey glanced up, and from the look on her mother's face, she realized there'd been a fatality.

"Bad news travels fast. Anyone I know?"

"I don't think so. Chester Morris," she answered. "Take your time, but when you get back I'll look forward to your help. Austin, can you take Jaxon with you? It'll give me a little bit of quiet time before the festivities start."

"Festivities mean a party," Jaxon said, shoving the last spoonful of cereal into his mouth. "I'm having a birthday party."

"Yes, you are," Casey agreed. "So, do you want to come for a car ride?"

"Can we stop and see Mommy? She gives me cookies."

Her father smiled. "I don't see why not. She wants to see Aunt Casey, so we can do that before going to get the motorcycle."

Casey smiled and held out her hand to her nephew, praying seeing Randy wouldn't end up in another argument.

"Sounds like a plan. Maybe you can talk her into giving you one of those butter tarts."

Jaxon shook his head. You can have the tart. I want chocolate chip cookies."

She smiled. "Maybe I'll try one of those, too." Then, she would drop in on Cole. If he'd been out all night, he might still be home and seeing him would be a great way to start the day.

* * * *

The alarm woke Cole. Glancing at the clock, he noted it was just after eight. When was the last time he'd gotten a decent night's sleep?

Stepping into the shower, he hoped the hot water would wash away his tiredness, knowing it probably wouldn't, but it was the only option he had this morning. In the last few months, Fortune's volunteer firefighters had battled four blazes, fires some people considered a public service. All of the buildings had been dilapidated eyesores, ready to be demolished, including the original Skansen homestead. Over the years, various extended members of the family had lived there until the mid-nineteen seventies. Once abandoned, the house had become a gathering place for Fortune's teenagers, and when it had burned down, Cole had assumed it had simply been an accident, like the one a year earlier where campers had failed to properly extinguish their campfire.

Someone had died in last night's inferno and that changed everything. The arson investigator would arrive later today, but there was no doubt in Cole's mind that this fire, like the others, had been deliberate.

They'd found traces of gasoline at previous arson sites, but hadn't found anything to connect anyone to the torchings. This time they'd located prospecting equipment along with art supplies, a container of anti-freeze, an empty jerry can of gasoline, and a couple of green bottles of homemade mescal locked in the old dilapidated shed near the house, the door secured by a combination lock, similar to the ones the high school sold each fall.

Three years ago, after the authorities had cut off the power to the Morris house for non-payment, the local building inspector had condemned the structure, and forced Chester to move out. As far as Cole knew, he'd been living at the Golden Goose Motel, one of the cheaper places east of town. Why had he gone back to the house last night?

Two years ago, after a minor stroke that had left him with a weak left side and a limp, Chester had befriended three young boys. Most likely, the art materials belonged to Kyle. During the summer months, probably the worse time of the year for it, the four of them would go off into the hills for a week at a time. It was a damn shame no one paid attention to those kids, but from what he'd seen, those boys doted on the old man as much as he did on them. He was the grandfather they'd never had.

Despite the hot water, Cole shivered. Chester was a gentle soul, an old bachelor, who'd spent his entire life combing Superstition Mountain searching for the seven golden cities of *Cibola,* Peralta's mine, or the Lost Dutchman mine, but like so many others, he'd failed. Coronado himself had named the mountain, *Monte Superstition,* back in 1540 when he'd given up hope of ever finding any gold there. Over the years, many men had searched for that elusive rock. Some had been lucky for a while, but eventually, it seemed everyone who struck it rich there, didn't live to enjoy the spoils of their labor.

In his younger days, between minor finds of gold, turquoise, or some other marketable mineral—never in quantities large enough to make him rich, Chester had supplemented his income guiding archeologists onto the mountain to search for artifacts or study the petroglyphs. Occasionally, he did heavy work for some of Fortune's older residents, but as he'd aged, it had been more difficult to do any kind of physical labor. In time, during the day he'd satisfied himself pretending to be an archeologist à la Indiana Jones, complete with the battered fedora, and spent his lonely nights at the bottom of a bottle of the mescal he brewed at a secret still. He was a harmless old man, the butt end of more than one joke, but no one deserved to die that way.

Once the fire was under control, Cole and one of the other firefighters had gone in and had found Chester, face down, on the bed upstairs. It would take a medical examiner to give the exact cause of death, but the odds were it would be smoke inhalation.

Maybe some vagrant had decided to camp out inside for the night and accidentally set the fire, escaping before he himself got burned, not knowing old Chester was snoring away upstairs. It didn't make sense for those kids to do it, but Hal would have to question them. They'd obviously been using that shed, and then there was the empty jerry can. He'd researched pyromania for one of his novels and knew the disease often affected disenchanted teenagers. While he wouldn't have pegged one of those kids for that, people hid their pain and secrets deep inside. He was the perfect example of that.

Cole turned off the shower and dried off. He would like to stay home long enough to see Casey this morning, but time was a luxury he didn't have.

Dressing in his sand-colored police uniform, he went downstairs to get what he hoped would be strong, black coffee and something to eat. When he moved out, he would miss Mom's cooking, but he wanted Casey in his bed, and if that was the price, so be it.

Twenty minutes later, he got out of the SUV.

"Thanks for pitching in today, Dad," he said. "I'm not sure how long Hal will need me, but I have to meet with the arson investigator. I'll call when I have some kind of timeline."

"Don't worry about the store. If he doesn't need you all day, go home, and get some sleep. Any idea what caused this one?"

"Nothing conclusive. We hope to know more after the inspector checks it out. I'll see you later. I have to stop by the store to pick up something for Jaxon. I'm heading over to Casey's after supper, and it's the little guy's birthday."

His dad nodded. "See you later."

Cole watched his father drive off and then climbed the steps two at a time. Opening the door, he smiled at Rita, who hung up the phone, the look on her face similar to what he'd expect to see if he caught her with her hand in the cookie jar.

"You must be absolutely exhausted," she said, speaking quickly. "Jason crashed as soon as he came into the house. I got to thinking this morning that last night's fire was a scene taken straight out of *Fistful of Silver*, when Justice ends up in that old mining shack, threatens to expose Wilkes as a cheat, and the man kills him and sets fire to the place. It was so similar, I got goosebumps, but I can't imagine Chester blackmailing anyone. No one would believe anything he had to say."

Cole nodded, the acid in his stomach churning just as it had when he'd found the body last night. If Rita saw the similarities then he couldn't be imagining them. He swallowed his anxiety and smiled at her.

"Has he had his coffee?" He indicated the closed door to Hal's office.

"He has, but it didn't make much difference. He got a call from AJPD. Some hikers called in a body last night over by Weaver's Needle."

Cole frowned. It had been years since anyone had died on the mountain and now two bodies had been discovered within months.

"Maybe the tremors we had on Monday shook something loose and whatever it was came down the mountain in last night's rain. The rangers often find bones and other stuff after a bad storm."

"True, but these weren't just bones. Apparently they've had to sedate the woman." Rita leaned in to whisper conspiratorially. "The body had no head." She shuddered.

Cole burst out laughing. "Good one, Rita, You had me going until you brought up the curse."

Rita frowned. "Fine. Don't believe me. You'll see, but isn't it a strange coincidence? I mean, first Leon, then Chester, and now a body by Weaver's Needle. It's as if CJ's books are coming to life."

"You've got a good memory for detail," Cole said, the acid in his stomach bubbling up again. "Although I didn't think the place was called that."

"Of course it wasn't. He changes all the names to protect our privacy and his, and believe me, we're grateful he does. This place would be a zoo if we had his fans lining up for autographs on top of all the other tourists here. God, we would never get a moment's peace. I'd like to know what he thinks of all these coincidences. I mean if we could interview him—on the phone or on the Internet. Maybe we could charge admission to the broadcast and raise money for new football uniforms for the school." She smiled conspiratorially, as if they shared a secret.

"I'd better get in there," he said, wishing he could go back home and sleep this nightmare away. Rita couldn't possibly know the truth, could she? He'd have Horace make a donation to the school in CJ's name. If the boys needed new football jerseys, he didn't mind paying for them, but an interview where someone might recognize his voice? No way.

Knocking on the door, he waited for Hal's answer before entering.

"You don't look bad for a man who's only gotten three hours' sleep," Hal said, reaching for the large coffee mug on his desk and indicating the pot on the small table in the corner. "It's strong and less than an hour old."

Cole helped himself to coffee. "No worse than you." He noted the man's haggard face. "Hell of a night, wasn't it?"

"That's putting it mildly. And so far my morning hasn't been any better. Gold Rush Days start tomorrow, and it seems someone's hell bent on reenacting the worst aspects of them. I'm going to need everybody on the clock, including you."

"I can work days tomorrow, but I'm hoping to have a date tomorrow night, and I can't work on Sunday."

"Get out of here. You're going on a date? With a woman?"

The stunned look on Hal's face made him laugh, something he needed right now.

"I haven't asked her yet, but I certainly hope she'll agree." He chuckled. "Don't look so surprised. I'm hoping to take Casey Stevens to the opening ceremonies for Gold Rush Days tomorrow night, and my folks expect me to be part of the Sunday celebration."

"There are going to be scores of disappointed women in this town, but good for you. As far as Sunday goes, I'll make you a deal. I've got a gun belt, a Colt single action pistol, a white Stetson, and a tin star for you to wear. You can be Tate Silvers. He's as big a part of this town's history as its past. I sure as hell could use his help right now, but I won't call on you unless all hell breaks loose. Fair enough?"

Cole choked on his coffee. "I suppose I could manage that," he answered when he could speak again, "but you should be Silvers. After all, he's a sheriff, and I'm just a lowly officer of the law."

Hal laughed, as if what he'd said was the punchline to a joke. "Sure you are."

Cole swallowed. It was the second time this morning that he got the impression someone was onto his deception—first from Rita and now Hal. Was he dreaming it? Sure he was tired, but … It almost made him want to come out and ask them if they'd figured it out, but if he was imagining it all, he might be giving himself away.

"Knowing how much you enjoy solving mysteries, this one should be right up your alley."

"You mean the body those hikers found?" Cole asked. "Rita mentioned it when I arrived. Claims the body was decapitated. It's a little early for Halloween pranks."

"Damn that woman. She's getting to be as big a gossip as Heidi."

Cole sobered. "Let me get this straight. She wasn't kidding around? The rangers have verified a headless body at the base of Weaver's Needle?'

Hal nodded. "Not quite at the base, but close enough. It'll probably be all over town by noon."

Cole coughed, trying not to laugh at the look on Hal's face. What had Casey said about gossip?

"The BLM rangers called a few minutes ago. The man was shot in the back, and yes, his head was missing. The rangers found it a good thirty feet away. The poor woman who found him probably won't sleep for weeks."

"The Apache ghosts strike again?"

"I doubt it. The last I heard, gods and spirits, even disgruntled ones, don't carry guns. Whoever's behind whatever the hell's going on here is messing with us to confound things. But it gets better. The man's wallet was in his pocket. It looks like our John Doe is none other than Trent Gibbs, Leon's nephew, which makes me think Leon's fall might not have been an accident after all. What if those two knew what was going on out on the mountain? Just because I haven't been able to find any trace of that helicopter doesn't mean it doesn't exist. Too many people saw those damn lights for it to be your imagination, as creative as it is."

Cole frowned. That was an odd comment for Hal to make, another one that hinted at the fact he might know the truth.

"You think Leon saw something he shouldn't have and was murdered?"

"It's possible."

"How would Trent fit in?"

"That's what I don't know. Maybe he was looking for his uncle and stumbled across whatever the old man had found. Why else would he be in the mountains? The man was an accountant for Skansen's. If he thought something was going on out there … Leon worked for Skansen Mining too, remember?"

Cole nodded. "Maybe it's a Skansen employee helping

himself to the leftovers? Wouldn't be hard to borrow some machinery from *Lucky Seven* and bring it back if you were someone no one would suspect. But that doesn't explain the helicopter. I'm assuming you checked with Macintosh Tours?"

"I did. All their birds were accounted for Monday night. So here's what I've been asking myself. Was that chopper doing a pick-up or a delivery?"

His thoughts jumbled and confused by this new possibility, Cole paced. "If it was a pick-up, who and why?"

"Not sure. If someone were pilfering gold out of the abandoned pits or robbing someone else's claim, it would be an easy way to move nuggets, but I'm inclined to think it was more likely a drop off. Think about it. Phoenix and Apache Junction have had an increase in the amount of drugs hitting the streets. I busted a kid for possession with intent to sell only a couple of weeks ago. He wasn't local either. What if the cartel brings in its product here, drops it on the mountain, and someone masquerading as a miner or hiker carries it back to the city?"

"That's a hell of a theory, but you don't have proof and whoever was involved would need local talent to help. As far as I know, there isn't anyone around here or in Apache Junction who's in bed with the cartel." Cole chuckled. "Besides, Weaver's Needle is a good ten miles from where I saw that chopper."

Hal huffed out a frustrated breath. "I know it doesn't make a damn but of sense, but my gut says everything is related. When I called Skansen Mining this morning to talk to Eddy, I was told he wouldn't be available until Monday—she wouldn't tell me where he was, either. I asked again about Gibbs, but got the same song and dance."

"Any guess at how long Trent had been out there?" Cole asked.

"At least a week. They're going to do their bug thing to be sure. Coyotes got to him, so he isn't a pretty sight. Probably just as well the woman didn't see the head."

"Maybe not just coyotes," Cole said and described Casey's encounter with the puma, omitting the reason she'd fled into the wilderness in the first place.

"Damn stupid of her to wander into the desert like that. I hope you told her so." Hal ran his hand through his hair, messing it up, and then took a mouthful of coffee. "This is more bad news I didn't need this morning. Most cats prefer fresh meat, but an old, hungry puma won't be fussy. The forensic examiner in Phoenix mentioned something had been gnawing on Leon's bones. I just assumed it had been coyotes or wild dogs. I'll get the rangers to go after that puma. We don't have the manpower, especially not now. They'll probably need you to show them where you saw the cat, but after that, once they find scat, they'll take care of him." He added more sugar to his coffee. "In the meantime, the arson investigator will meet you at the Morris house at ten."

"Okay. I'm on my way. I'll call in when I know something."

"In the meantime, I'll notify Chester's band of merry men."

Cole nodded and left the office. For their sakes, he hoped those boys weren't involved with that fire. Even if it had been an accident, something like this would haunt them for the rest of their lives.

CHAPTER FOURTEEN

After settling Jaxon into his car seat, Casey sat up front next to her father. He started the SUV and pulled into traffic.

"I noticed you still have that old blue sedan you bought me," she said.

"Yes. Randy used it right up until you bought her the van. It's in great shape, and I didn't have the heart to part with it. It would be like losing another part of you."

Casey looked away. All of the maudlin opinions her parents had voiced this week had to have been festering in their hearts for a while.

"Mom seemed upset about the fire," she said, not wanting to pursue the current train of thought. Jaxon's attention was focused on the DVD playing in the backseat, and with his headphones on, he wouldn't be privy to their conversation.

"That's because it's the fifth one we've had this year, and like a lot of folks around her, she liked Chester. I saw him as a tragic hero. He spent his entire life trying to win the heart of the woman he loved."

"I thought he was the town drunk," she said, trying to put a face to the name.

"That, too. He wouldn't be the first man to try to mend a broken heart that way, but I think your mother's concern is because the Morris place was the one nearest to us. Whoever's been setting those fires is getting too close for comfort."

"Could they be insurance fires?" she asked.

"Not likely. The first house belonged to Minerva Skansen—the old homestead where you had your accident—and was probably insured, but the others were old abandoned places, most of them taken back by the town because of back taxes, including the Morris place, and all of them southwest of the city."

"Come to think of it, I noticed a few when I was out on my bike." She chose not to comment on her accident, having firmly locked that night out of her mind once more.

"The town council votes next week on demolishing what's left of those buildings and trying to sell the land."

"Is that land particularly valuable? I mean could a developer have paid someone to torch those places, looking to cash in on the building boom?"

"I doubt it. In case you didn't notice, Fortune is expanding north toward the lakes. There hasn't been much development in the south. Other than a few standard housing lots out that way, most of the land belongs to Skansen Mining, and I can't see Ms. Minerva selling any of it, not even the ranch. If someone did manage to get her to let it go, they would have to deal with the forest service, since all the land in this area is technically part of the Tonto National Forest. They've got serious restrictions on the number of animals allowed to graze. Hell, they've even been rounding up the wild horses when they can catch them. The place would be ideal for a solar farm though—faces southwest. As far as the Morris place goes, the town condemned the house years ago."

She shuddered. "Then why was he there?"

"Don't ask me. Maybe he just wanted to go home. Cole may have more answers for you tonight."

She'd been out at the Morris house on the night that had ruined her life, and the place had been falling apart back then. Yesterday, she'd barely noticed it as she'd driven past it on her way to and from the wilderness. It had been raining hard the second time. Wood, even old dry lumber didn't spontaneously catch fire when it was wet, and the lightning had stayed in the mountains.

"So what are we looking at arson? Pyromania?"

"I don't know," he said, "but now that someone's dead, Hal will have to look into it more thoroughly. It might have something to do with the lights people saw out on the mountain Monday night, but who knows?"

Casey frowned. Lights on the mountain? She hadn't seen any lights. Maybe whoever had seen them had been up much later than she'd been. Dismissing that thought, she focused on a far more troubling one. If the town did have a firebug, sooner or later, someone else would die.

Fifteen minutes later, Casey followed her father and nephew into *Cookies and Cream*, stepping aside to let a man walk out, the same man Randy had argued with on Tuesday. He nodded at them, looking as if he'd just lost his best friend.

"Who was that?" she asked her dad, watching the man walk away, noting the dejected slump to his shoulders and his clenched fists.

"Who was who?" her father answered.

"The man you just said hello to," she said, trying to curb her frustration. Why did people answer a question with a question?

"Oh, that was Drew Macintosh. His family owns the sightseeing helicopter business over near Tortilla Flats. He and David were in the same unit. He was his wingman. In fact, Drew introduced David to Randy. She'd been dating him at the time. Your mother and I thought he was the one, but then she and David eloped. Those two boys were closer than brothers. Losing David was as hard on him as it was on your sister. He keeps asking her out, but it looks like she turned him down again."

"Mommy," yelled Jaxon.

Randy turned around, eyes filled with unshed tears, swallowed whatever had upset her, and smiled at her son. "Hey you," she said, opening her arms to her son and hugging him fiercely. "You're just what I need right now."

"Too tight," Jaxon said, struggling to get away. "I'm bigger now, remember?"

Randy laughed. "Of course you are and as handsome as your daddy was. You're not too big for a chocolate chip cookie, are you?"

He giggled. "I'll never be too big for cookies and chocolate milk," he added.

"Coming right up, sweetie. Coffee for you, Dad? Casey?"

"Coffee's great," she answered, hoping her sister's dismay wasn't because of her. "And maybe one of those butter tarts?"

"Coffee and a cookie are fine by me," her father said, his slight frown and the tone of his voice indicating his concern.

"Let me get Selma, and I'll sit with you for a few minutes. She's going to close for me tonight, so I'll be home around four. That should help."

Within a few minutes, Randy returned with three cups of coffee, a glass of chocolate milk, and a plateful of cookies and a tart.

She handed out the drinks, but didn't sit down, and stood next to her. "I won't apologize for everything I said yesterday, Casey, but I'm sorry I hurt you and sent you running off like that. I don't understand why you feel you can't stay here. I didn't see why you had to leave after the accident either. But, as Mom and Dad have explained, whether I like it or not, I have to live my life and you have to live yours. Drew just reminded me that despite everything, I'm still alive and need to move on. I'm not sure I can, but maybe you have the same problem. Being stuck in the past isn't good for either of us." She took a deep breath. "Can we forget yesterday happened, well, at least that part of it, because the time before that was great."

"It wasn't all your fault, Randy," Casey said standing once more. "Cole helped me realize that, and I'm sorry. You were right. I've been selfish, not for the reasons you believe, but I'll try to do better. It's all I can offer right now."

She hugged her sister, blinking away tears, more emotional than she'd been in a long time.

"I guess that ride Monday night wasn't a complete bust," Randy said, changing the topic.

"No, it wasn't. Cole will be dropping over later tonight after supper," she said shyly. "I'm going to ask him to take me to the opening ceremonies tomorrow night and then maybe we can stay for the midway. I haven't been to a fair in years. You should come with us. I'm sure Cole wouldn't mind."

"Two's company, three's a crowd, but thanks for asking. I've just turned down Drew's offer to go with him, and I doubt it'll be the last time he asks. He seems to think Jaxon and I are his responsibility—some promise he made to David—but that's my problem, not yours." She shook her head, unable to hide her sorrow. "I'll get my fill of the fair when I take Jaxon on Saturday. It'll be Bracelet Day—ride as much as you want for twenty dollars."

Casey stored away the comment about Drew and David, and shrugged. "In that case, if tomorrow night doesn't pan out, I might just come, too."

Randy smiled. "I'm sure tomorrow will be fine, but if you want another midway fix, we would like that."

"We'll see. So far my social calendar has lots of room on it."

They both sat and Casey leaned back, watching mother and son. While Randy might not understand why she had to leave Fortune, at least she'd accepted it. It was the first step. The next one would be up to her. If she and Cole were to make this work, she had to be willing to come home more often.

Once she'd finished her coffee and tart, Casey stood.

"Dad, I know you've got a gazillion errands to run for Mom, so I'll leave you two now," she said indicating Jaxon, "and walk over to the Walker house. It's just a couple of blocks from here, and considering the way I've been eating since I got home, I can use the exercise."

Her father chuckled. "If that's what you want, go ahead.

I'm not sure Jaxon's ready to leave yet." He indicated the cookie on the plate. "After we finish here, we have to head to the mall. We'll see you at home."

Casey hugged them all, bought a bag of assorted cookies to take to Noella, and left the shop. It was another warm, dry, sunny, Arizona day, perfect weather for a pool party, and she looked forward to an afternoon playing lifeguard, even if it meant coating her nose and shoulders in zinc oxide based sunscreen. The aloe vera she'd slathered on her face and arms last night had helped, but more sun today wouldn't.

Walking at a steady pace, her leather jacket hooked over her left shoulder, the bag of cookies in her right hand, she was half a block from the Warner house when a black convertible sports' car—something James Bond might drive—pulled up to the curb in front of what she realized was the Skansen house. Seated behind the steering wheel—right handed drive—was none other than Edward, Eddy, Ramos, heir apparent to the Skansen mining empire, one of the people she'd desperately hoped to avoid. Swallowing her disquiet, she smiled and nodded.

"Hello, gorgeous. Mm, mm, mm." He smacked his lips in appreciation and grinned. "Cassandra Stevens. If Aunt Minerva hadn't shown me your picture, the one she cut out of the paper a few years ago, I wouldn't have recognized you," Eddy said, stepping out of the car beside her, and pulling her into a bear hug as if they were old friends.

The combined stench of alcohol, cologne, tobacco and marijuana nauseated her. She pushed him away.

"Hello, Eddy. It's been a while." And she'd hoped it would be even longer.

"I heard you were home," he said, raking her with what she'd always considered dead eyes.

When Eddy looked at you, you were never sure what he was thinking, what he was feeling; you just knew you needed to get away. Being his object of interest for the moment made her skin crawl.

"You're looking damn fine, girl. Life in the big city must agree with you. I'll bet Rick wouldn't mind getting to know you again." He was twitchy and sniffled as if he had a bad cold. More than likely he'd graduated from marijuana to some cocaine-laced designer drug.

Casey swallowed the bile rising in her throat.

I will not let him upset me. I'm better than this, stronger than this. He doesn't scare me now.

She silently repeated the litany that had been part of the first few days after she'd fled Fortune.

"So how long are you here for?"

"I return to Santa Fe after Labor Day. I spoke with your aunt yesterday. She mentioned you were staying with her."

He pulled a pack of cigarettes out of his jacket pocket, slipped one between his lips, and patted himself down, looking for a lighter. Not finding one, he reached into the car and pulled out a book of matches. His hands trembled as he lit the cigarette, no doubt from the overuse of alcohol or the need for another fix.

"You haven't changed much," she lied, pasting a plastic smile on her face.

Whereas she'd lost almost fifty pounds, Eddy had gained at least that many. His dark curly hair was now heavily sprinkled with gray, and his once golden complexion was pasty from too many hours spent indoors. The hooked nose that had always reminded her of an eagle's beak stood out prominently on his face, his cheeks and skin covered in black stubble. The heavy, dark circles under his eyes spoke of too little sleep, too much alcohol, and too much of whatever he was on. His clothes were wrinkled as if he'd slept in them, the belt on his pants doing double duty as it held up a pot belly bigger than the baby bump on a woman carrying triplets. He flashed a yellow smile at her, and held up a hand with too many rings on it to be anything but his way of bragging and showing off, and glanced at the Rolex on his wrist.

"Listen, I'd love to get together and talk about the good old days, but right now, I've got to go. Aunt Minerva is waiting for me." He sighed as if he were suffering. "I moved in with her a few weeks ago." He made a circle at his left temple with his index finger. "The old girl's losing it, if you know what I mean, and someone has to watch out for her. She leaves things on the stove unattended, and the place is an absolute mess inside. I've seen neater hoarders. Being forced to live here cramps my style, but she is my only living relative." He shrugged. "The things we do for family. She goes on and on about that cockamamie idea she's come up with concerning what she considers the Skansen Legacy. I'll humor her, but when it comes right down to it, those decisions are mine now, not hers. The Board hasn't come right out and told her, but … Listen, why don't I give you a call, and we can get together before you leave?"

Casey fisted the hand holding her jacket and fought to retain her self-control. There was no way Minerva Skansen was losing it. If anyone had delusions, it was Eddy, and the two of them going out for drinks? That was definitely a psychotic fantasy. As far as the rest of what he said, if there was a slob in that house, it was him.

"Why not?" she lied, her heart pounding, unwilling to annoy him, knowing agreeing with him would send him on his way faster. It always had. If he did call, she would find some excuse to put him off, something easier to do on the phone than in person. The last thing she wanted was discuss the "good old days" with him. There hadn't been a damn "good" thing about them.

"It'll have to be next week since Rick, Trent, and I have business in Vegas this weekend. I hate leaving Aunt Minerva alone, especially with all the extra people in town, but a man's got to do what a man's got to do. I'm always on her case to lock the doors, but you know how stubborn old people can be. Damn shame to miss the Gold Rush Day Celebrations, but what can I do? Business comes first."

She didn't give a rat's ass about what he and Rick did, but she would continue to be as civil as she could. Knowing the

Three Stooges would all miss the celebration lifted her mood considerably.

"That's too bad," she said. "We could've joined Ella Rankin at the saloon. I'm pretty tied up while I'm here, but we'll see."

"I wouldn't mind tying you up," he said and winked.

The very notion of some kind of bondage fantasy with him brought back the nausea and fear she was trying to suppress. He looked like a man who enjoyed inflicting pain—he always had. Memories of the way he'd butchered that frog in science class came back to her. While the rest of them had used specimens preserved in formaldehyde, Eddy had brought in a live one and dissected it alive. When the science teacher had realized what he was doing, the tortured reptile was dead and Eddy faced a two-day suspension. She swallowed, trying to think of something to say.

"Listen, why don't we make it an impromptu high school reunion? I'll give Kristal a call and see what she thinks. If that won't work, maybe the four of us can have dinner?"

Throat suddenly dry, Casey scrambled for something to say. Dinner with Rick, Kristal, and Eddy?

Over my dead body!

"I may not be able to get away for a meal. I'm visiting the family after all, and as you said, the things you do for family, but we'll see."

Eddy didn't seem to notice anything unusual in what she'd said, and shook his head in agreement.

"I know. By the way, what are you doing in this neck of the woods? As I recall, you live west of town."

She noted the intensity in his cold eyes, and his voice no longer held the friendly familiarity it had.

"Did you come by to see my aunt?"

She wasn't imagining the suspicion in his voice, and it puzzled her. What business was it of his if she were?

"No. She did ask me to drop over, but I visited the Warners last night and left my Harley there."

"You ride a Harley?" He seemed to relax slightly. "You've

turned into a wild woman. I wouldn't mind getting a ride," he said and leered at her, suggesting the Harley wasn't part of his desire.

She wanted to vomit all over him, but swallowed the bitter taste in her mouth.

"Maybe another time. I didn't bring a spare helmet with me."

He burst out laughing. "And you wouldn't want to do anything illegal, but honey, you don't need a helmet for what I have in mind. The things I would do to you ... I've got to go. I'll call you. I have to keep the old bitch happy a bit longer. See you."

For a man his size, Eddy moved swiftly along the front walkway, climbed the stairs, and disappeared into the beautiful old brick and clapboard house.

Casey unfisted her hand, noted the deep crescents in her palm put there by her nails, and took a deep breath. Poor Minerva. She wouldn't wish Eddy on her worst enemy. If anything was going to make Minerva's health take a turn for the worse, it would be putting up with that man.

Seeing Eddy, imagining him touching her, served to remind Casey why coming back to Fortune would never work. Feeling depressed once more, she continued to the Warner house.

* * * *

"Cole, unless you've got something else, I'm going to rule this an accidental fire," Clay Winston said, stepping off what was left of the back porch of the house and crossing to the SUV.

Cole closed the passenger door. This wasn't what he'd expected.

Clay was the best fire investigator in the area, and the one who'd examined the last four blazes. While he'd inspected the ruins of the house, Cole had searched the shed again, looking for anything they might've missed last night. The place was ready to fall down on itself—an accident waiting to happen—and as unlikely a storage spot for what they'd found in there as he could imagine, but what he'd discovered in a small leather pouch tucked inside an old rusty toolbox astonished him. Not wanting to share this until he spoke to Hal, he put the pouch in the SUV's glove compartment, and locked it.

"You're sure? What about the traces of gasoline on the back porch?" he asked, since the portable hydrocarbon sniffer had detected the accelerant.

"Coincidental, and not the point of origin. I'd say someone spilled the stuff refueling a generator or some other gas powered piece of equipment. The gasoline could've been embedded in those old, dry boards years ago. There isn't any trace of it inside the house, and we both know that whoever started your other fires spread the stuff around. This was just a case of carelessness. The fire started downstairs. Here, let me show you."

Cole followed Clay as he retraced his steps into the house, avoiding the blackened beams and puddles of water on what was left of the main level of the dwelling. Here and there, the fire had burned through the wooden planks, but this house, like so many others had been built without a basement, so the biggest danger was falling six inches through the rotten, burned boards to the muddy earth beneath. Bits and pieces of old furniture, mostly metal springs and bits of charred wood, rose monster-like out of the floor. Clay stopped beside what must've been a recliner. He pointed to the floor.

Cole glanced at the blackened object lying on its side next to the chair. "A liquor bottle?"

"Might be wine, but I'd guess liquor of some sort. There's no label on it. There are several bottles like that throughout the house. I haven't found any screw tops, so whatever it is, was probably homemade, and the bottles corked. This guy had one hell of a drinking problem," Clay said, shaking his head. "This is where the fire started. That window was open, and considering the wind we had last night, it fanned the flames. Odds are, your dead man was smoking and left the cigarette burning on that ashtray, which had to be on the arm of the chair. Damn stupid place to put it, but I've seen this before. Drunk, he put the cigarette down without extinguishing it and went to bed. The damn thing rolled out of the ashtray and down onto the seat of the chair. The stuff in here looks like it was manufactured long before the rules for fire retardant fabrics came into play."

Cole nodded, unsettled by Clay's explanation. "We figured Chester has a still somewhere and made his own stuff. Lord knows the man couldn't afford to buy tequila, not the way he drank it." But if there was more of what he'd found in that toolbox, the man could've bought himself a whole distillery. "Thanks, Clay. How about we stop at *Cookies and Cream* for coffee before you head back?"

"Sounds good. My wife asked me to pick up some cinnamon buns," he said, stepping out onto the porch. "This place needs to come down sooner rather than later."

They had just reached the SUV when Cole's cellphone rang. Pulling the Smartphone out of his pocket, he glanced at the display, momentarily disappointed it wasn't Casey, and answered.

"Yeah, Hal, what's up?"

"Are you still out at the Morris place?"

"We are. Clay just finished. You can relax. This one was accidental, but what's left of the building is unstable."

"He might want to rethink his decision," Hal said, the anger barely suppressed in his voice. "I just got the coroner's report. Doc Creighton says there was no smoke in Chester's lungs."

"How is that possible? Clay claims the fire started in the living room, and we found Chester in his bed upstairs."

"Doesn't matter where the damn thing started now. It had to have been set to cover this up. The doc assures me Chester was poisoned. He found large amounts of ethylene glycol in the man's system. Looks like someone added it to his mescal."

"Anti-freeze?" Cole asked, stunned.

"Yes, and that container in the shed is likely the source of it. That damn stuff is the number one substance used in homicidal poisonings. The man was murdered, and because he was, there's no way that fire was an accident."

"Damn," Coles gut twisted.

"I need you to bring back any empty liquor bottles in the house. We'll have the full ones we took out of the shed tested along with the anti-freeze. Right now, it looks like I've got three suspects and believe me, I want to be wrong. Why on earth would those boys want to kill Chester?"

"I may have an idea, but I need to test it. I'll check the place again with Clay and then get back to the station. If I'm right, I may have found the reason for a lot of what's been going on."

Ending the call, Cole turned to Clay. "We have to take another look at all of this. It seems our victim was dead before the fire started."

"That changes things," Clay said, tearing up the document he'd just completed. "The chief is certain?"

Cole nodded.

"Then I'd better fill this out again. The fire started just as I said, but now it's arson by persons unknown. Not sure that helps you. I can't say whoever set this one set the other four, too. I'm sorry. Let me have another look around."

Upset to realize that Chester's death mirrored Justice's in his book even more than he thought it had, Cole stepped back over to the investigator's truck and reached for the ladder. If someone was somehow trying to recreate the crimes in his books, more people would die before this was over.

"We'll need this again, too. I've got to go upstairs and collect any liquor bottles up there. Chester was poisoned."

Clay pursed his lips and nodded.

Heavy-hearted, Cole moved back into the house. What the hell was happening to his town?

CHAPTER FIFTEEN

It was almost eleven when Casey let herself into the house, surprised to see Dad and Jaxon weren't back yet. She'd passed on a second cup of coffee with Noella, but now knew that Cole, despite the fact that he'd had barely three hours' sleep, would be working with the sheriff all day, wrapping up last night's loose ends.

"Mom, I'm back, sorry I'm late," she called, stepping into the kitchen.

"Did you see Randy?" her mother asked, coming in from the pantry.

"I did, and we're good. Where are Dad and Jackson?"

Her mother smiled, but Casey read the worry etched into her face.

"He took him to the mall to visit the pet store and buy him a goldfish." She shook her head. "Apparently, if he can take care of the fish, Randy will consider getting him a puppy for Christmas. Sit. There's still some coffee or there's lemonade in the fridge. We need to talk."

That phrase never boded well. Here was the lecture she'd expected earlier.

"I'm glad you and Randy made peace. I know the idea of coming back to Fortune is a touchy subject for both of you. I hate to see your father upset, especially now…"

"Why do I get the feeling there's more going on than I've been told?" Casey asked, realizing that whatever her mother was going to say had nothing to do with yesterday's adventures.

Her mother hung her head. "Austin wanted to wait until later next week, but I'm afraid you'll cut your visit short once Gold Rush Days are over, and I can't have that."

Casey's stomach roiled. At one time she'd considered leaving on Monday, but that had been before Cole. Moving back was out of the question, but for now, she would stay as long as she could.

"Are you sick, Mom?" she asked, anxiety filling her.

"Me?" Her mother shook her head. "No, of course not. I'm as healthy as a horse. I'm afraid it's your father."

Casey gasped. "What's wrong with him?"

Her mother's face filled with so much sorrow and worry that Casey began to tremble.

"Your father had a weak spell back in April, just after we got back from visiting you in Phoenix, another in late May, and then a syncope six weeks ago. Randy found out because she was with him when it happened. Fool man didn't mention the first two episodes to us. Scared us all half to death."

Casey felt as if the bottom had dropped out of her world. Her heart beat so fast it hurt.

"What's a syncope?" She wrapped her arms around her middle as if she could somehow protect herself from what she was certain would be bad news.

"It's a fainting spell caused by a sudden drop in blood pressure. The brain doesn't get the oxygen it needs, and the patient loses consciousness."

"Isn't that the same as a stroke?" Her mouth was so dry, she couldn't swallow. Not her dad. He couldn't be sick. It was true he'd lost a little weight, but he was strong and alert.

"Not a stroke, Casey, but he's had a couple of minor heart attacks. The cardiologist in Phoenix found a couple of blocked arteries in his heart. He's taking the right medication and will have two stents inserted to clear the blockages next Friday.

That's why I wanted you home for two weeks. I would've asked for three, but I couldn't push my luck. We were going to tell you about it at dinner last night, but then Horace made his offer and Randy overreacted to your refusal to consider it. The surgeon says there's no danger, but I wanted my girls here for me—for him. Your father insists he'll be fine, that this is a routine procedure in this day of high cholesterol and blood pressure readings, but it's a wakeup call for all of us, especially for Randy. She's lost so much ... I'm sorry she took her fear out on you."

Casey let the tears slip down her cheeks. Knowing this, Randy's accusations made more sense, but realizing her family didn't want to bother her about anything, including her father's illness, filled her with pain, guilt, and sadness. Did they really believe she was that selfish, that heartless? All the little things she'd noticed but dismissed since coming home fell into place.

"That's why you changed the menu to provide leaner, healthier meals. It explains Dad's morning swims and those walks he takes after supper, even why he's started reading his Bible each night. I guess it's why you wanted us all to go to church on Sunday. None of it is for Jaxon—it's for him."

"When you're feeling your mortality, you turn to God, but Jaxon will benefit from this, too."

"That's why Randy's moving out, isn't it?" The final piece of the puzzle fell into place.

Her mother nodded. "We told her she didn't have to, but she feels that as Jaxon gets older, it'll be harder on Dad to keep up with him. He's not supposed to lift anything over ten pounds as it is, but try to explain that to a forty-pound child. And, you know how stubborn your father can be. Being in town will be easier for her, and of course we're just a phone call away. We'll be helping her as much as possible, and I'll miss having that little angel underfoot, but your father and I want to travel while we can. In February, assuming your father gets a clean bill of health from his doctor, we're going to Hawaii with Noella and Senior."

The door opened, and Jaxon raced into the kitchen. "Look at what Grandpa bought me."

He held up a clear, plastic, water-filled cup in which swam the most gorgeous blue betta Casey had ever seen. The fish's body glimmered like multi-hued sequins.

"Wow, he's really pretty," she said.

"He's a fighting fish," he told her proudly. "Like a ninja." He made several attempts at karate moves, making the appropriate grunts as well.

Casey bit her lip to keep from laughing.

"He needs to live in a bigger bowl with a plant," Jaxon continued, expounding on what he'd been told by the person who'd sold him the fish. "But he's got to stay by himself. He's a lone wolf. I've named him Blue Lantern. Is it time for my party yet?"

Her mother suppressed a laugh. "No, sweetheart, not yet, but I like the name, and since he needs to be alone, it's a good thing he'll have you for a friend. I assume Grandpa has the rest of his paraphernalia?"

He nodded. "And I won't feed him too much like the boy in my book did."

"That's good. I thought you were getting a goldfish?"

"I was, but they were kind of puny. This one was way cooler."

"I see. Why don't you go and watch television? As soon as we get Blue Lantern settled, I'll come find you and we can decide where to put him and his new home."

"You can call him Blue, for short. Can I watch my Batman cartoons?"

"Yes, you may, now scoot."

The door opened once more, and her father came in carrying three bags of groceries in one hand and a large, clear vase holding a lily planted inside a smaller vase fitted into its neck.

"Austin, for heaven's sake. You shouldn't be carrying all that."

195

"I'm fine, Maria, relax. There isn't anything heavy in them. Here, take this." He handed her the plant.

Casey jumped up, swiped at her tear-stained cheeks, and reached for the bags. She deposited them on the table and put her arms around her father, holding onto him, realizing that she would lose him one day.

But not today.

"You should've said something," she scolded. "I would've come home."

He returned her hug. "That's exactly why I didn't. There are enough females monitoring my every move as it is. Your mother is worrying herself sick for no reason, and your sister … well, you know how emotional Randy can be. There's nothing you could've done. Doc Creighton fixed me up with a top-notch cardiologist at the hospital in Phoenix, and the man's had excellent results. I'm glad we didn't tell you before Horace Stone made his offer. If you'd known, you might've made a choice based on all the wrong reasons. I want you to live your life following your heart, not mine."

"I love you, Dad," Casey said, hugging her father, bitterly regretting the circumstances that had stolen the last fifteen years from them. What if she'd been brave enough to accuse Rick? She swallowed her tears. "Being with you, with my family when they need me, *is* following my heart."

He squeezed her tightly and then released her, "I know you believe that, baby, but you have to do what makes you happy, too, and I don't think that's coming back to Fortune, not that I'm not mighty glad you came home for this. Now, someone's having a birthday party today. No more doom and gloom. You two have work to do. I'll just get the newest member of the family settled in his bowl, and then I'll do my best to keep Jaxon occupied and out of your hair until lunch."

Casey watched her father pick up the fish and the plant before leaving the room. Her heart was heavy, and she was more confused than she'd been earlier. Would knowing about his health have affected her decision to reject Mr. Stone's offer?

Of course it would have. The sacrifices her parents had made for her over the years were humbling. Even when they wanted her around, they'd put her needs above theirs. Almost choking on a fresh round of tears, she turned to her mother.

"What would you like me to do?"

"How are you at blowing up balloons?"

Casey laughed, tears still slipping down her cheeks. "Mom, everyone knows that to be a lawyer, you have to be full of hot air, and as you know, I'm a hell of a lawyer."

* * * *

It was almost three when Cole returned to the station, after making one extra stop. Just about every inch of his body ached, his gritty eyes burned, and his muscles screamed their fatigue. He hadn't slept well Monday night, and with no more than three hours last night, he was exhausted. The only thing that kept him going was the thought of seeing Casey later.

Whoever had started this fire had hoped to obliterate all evidence of the crime, but they didn't know enough about fire to do it right. While the average house burned at approximately eleven hundred degrees Fahrenheit, you had to raise that another five hundred degrees to cremate a body. Neither gasoline nor alcohol would do it—they would destroy the flesh, but the bones would stay, as would the evidence of the crime.

"Hi, Rita," he said, closing the door behind him. "Have you got any more mysteries for me?"

"Not really. What have you got there?" She indicated the bag he carried. "Judging by the bulge at the bottom, it looks heavy."

"Just evidence collected at the Morris place." She would find out what it was soon enough, but right now, he hoped Hal would agree to keep this a secret—at least until they figured out exactly what was at stake.

"I hear he was poisoned." She shook her head. "Why would anyone want to kill that sweet old man? The chief said to tell you to go right in. There's an officer in there from AJPD."

Cole nodded, knocked on Hal's door, and opened it.

"Cole, there you are," he said. "Did you get everything we needed from the crime scene?"

"Yeah, Clay and I collected half a dozen empty liquor bottles. I dropped them off at the crime lab before coming in here."

Hal turned to the man beside him. "Jones, this is Cole Warner."

Cole shook the man's hand.

"We had another fire last night," Hal explained. "One with a fatality. Our crime lab moved over to a new facility on Buckhorn three months ago. The coroner convinced the town he needed more space, and since surprisingly enough Minerva Skansen funded half of it, he got what he wanted. I can't imagine her nephew was too happy about that donation, but she still holds the purse strings. They put her name on the building again. Quite the legacy that family has left this town. Doc Creighton is thrilled with his state of the art facility, but I doubt he was expecting the influx of bodies he's got."

"I doubt anyone was. My captain said to offer whatever help you might need on this one. There'll be six men here tomorrow morning to help out for the weekend, and another six later in the day for shift change. Call if you need anything else."

"Thanks for bringing this in, although I wish you hadn't," Hal said and chuckled bitterly. "This was one gift I would gladly have done without."

Jones shrugged and left the office.

"What did he bring you?" Cole asked, wondering about the way Hal had spoken.

"Everything they collected on Leon Turner. It looks like we have three murders to solve."

"So, he didn't fall? Did they find something else?" Maybe the rest of the bones had turned up.

"You could say that. Here's the content of the man's safety

deposit box." He emptied the manila envelope onto his desk. A bunch of black and white printed photographs sat on the table next to a bulging white envelope.

Cole reached for the envelope and opened it, almost dropping it in his surprise.

"Holy shit. How much money is there?"

"Close to fifty thousand, and you can rest assured it wasn't reported to the IRS."

"Where does it come from?"

"My guess? Blackmail. Have a look at the prints."

Cole put down the envelope and picked up the sheets of paper. The images were poor, but it was easy enough to identify the helicopter although its call letters weren't visible. Three men were unloading duffle bags from it, but not one snapshot showed their faces clearly. The grainy photographs, taken at night with a cellphone without the flash, captured some of the scenery around the chopper and the men. He tried to place the exact location from what little of the scenery he could make out. It looked like a plateau on Superstition Mountain, but it that's where it was, it wasn't a place he'd visited.

"This isn't near the mines or where we found Leon's body."

"Agreed, but it does prove your helicopter exists, not that I ever doubted you."

"Did they dust this for prints?" He held up the envelope.

"They did, but matching them will be a real problem. That money's changed hands way too many times. The only prints on the envelope were Leon's." Hal reached for the ever-present coffee mug on his desk, drained it, and made a face. "I hate cold coffee."

Cole shrugged. "You drink way too much of it anyway. Well, this does verify your theory that the helo was making a drop off. Those could easily be drugs they're unloading. You know, if Trent knew about this, it would be a hell of a motive for murder."

"Maybe, but I doubt he was aware of it. There's no way he would've passed up those fifty gs. The bank records indicate it's been thirteen months since the box was opened."

Cole frowned. "You know, Chester spent a lot of time on that mountain. He claimed he'd seen aliens on Monday night. What if whoever's involved in this decided he might draw the wrong kind of attention to their business? It would give them a reason to shut him up."

"I agree. At least we have a lead. We just need to figure out where the hell this place is. I'm going to bring in Chester's boys and show them the pictures. They've been all over that damn mountain. They might recognize it. I thought it might be out near Weaver's Needle since they found Trent there, but there's no mesa out that way that would be large enough to land a chopper. What have you got there?" Hal asked, noticing the bag in his hand.

"What I thought might be the motive, but now it's just going to confuse things more." He pulled the two old leather pouches out of the bag he carried and dumped the one he'd found in the toolbox in the shed on Hal's desk.

"Holy shit," Hal exclaimed. "Where the hell does this come from?"

"A toolbox in Leon's shed. This, Clay and I found hidden in his mattress." He dropped the second bag unopened next to the pile.

Hal stared at the items, his mouth opening and closing like a fish blowing bubbles in his bowl. He reached for a gold coin.

"Is this real?" His voice was barely a whisper.

"I don't know about that stuff, but I would say it is. The gold nuggets are. I took this one up to the assayer's office near the mine. He says it's the real deal, and richer in quality than what they pull out of *Lucky Seven*. He wanted to know where it came from. I told him I'd found it in some belongings left behind by a transient." The nugget, just a bit bigger than a child's fingernail, lay on his palm. "He says it's worth about five hundred bucks."

"For that?" Hal picked up the bag and dumped it next to the other loot. "Then there has to be a small fortune here."

"Exactly, and whoever killed Chester couldn't have known about it. If they'd had even an inkling this existed, there's no way they would've left it behind."

"That's for sure, so the motive wasn't theft, not that I would've expected Chester had anything to steal. So where did he get this stuff? Some of those coins are more than two hundred years old. This one's dated 1809."

"My best guess? Chester found Peralta's mine," Cole said, "and if he did, once this gets out, all hell's going to break loose around here."

Hal ran his hand through his hair, the color leeching from his face. "Son of a bitch. I need a drink." He opened his bottom drawer and pulled out a bottle of whiskey and two glasses. After splashing a half-inch into the bottom of each glass, he offered one to Cole and downed the other before refilling it.

"If you're right, how do we find it with Chester dead?"

"We don't, but I'll bet those boys know where it is."

Hal downed the second mouthful of liquor. "Damn. Does that make them suspects or potential victims?"

Cole shook his head. "I don't know, but once this gets out, someone will need to watch their backs."

"Then we'd better make damn sure it doesn't."

It was after five when Cole entered the house, feeling like something the cat dragged in.

"You need to go to bed," his mother scolded as he entered the kitchen, annoying him in a way she never had before. Was it because he was beat, or had Casey's comments about lack of privacy and independence finally sunk in?

"No, I just need something to eat, a cup of coffee, and a shower. I've got a gift for Jaxon, and I'm going over to see Casey tonight."

He'd called her earlier in the day, and while she'd begged him not to bother and get some sleep, he needed to see her, to hold her in his arms, and feel her lips on his.

As well, he wanted her help and her legal expertise. With her quick mind, and without having to divulge the truth at the

201

moment, she might be able to tell him whether or not Rita's idea that the deaths and his CJ Coleson novels were connected made any sense.

Then there was Chester's death and what he'd found at the Morris place. Clay had been sworn to secrecy until he and Hal could figure out what the hell was going on. Horace Stone might have some answers, since apparently he'd been Chester's lawyer, but those kids knew something, too. For now, he would be keeping Leon and Trent Gibbs out of it.

His mother smiled. "I really like her, Cole. I always did, and she's become such a beautiful, self-assured, young woman. I'm glad you two have finally gotten together, but you really need to tell her the truth about CJ Coleson, and you should do it soon. She's not going to be happy with you when she finds out, what woman would be? We don't like being lied to."

"I didn't lie, Mom," he answered defensively, unable to keep his exasperation out of his voice. "I may have misled her, but to my credit, when I told her that story, it was the first time I'd seen her in seventeen years. How was I supposed to know she would come to mean something to me? I've worked hard to keep my secret, and I'm not about to give it up just like that. You know better than anyone exactly what's involved."

His mother harrumphed. "Casey hardly seems like the kind to gossip and go around broadcasting your secret. She likes her privacy, and I'm sure she would respect yours, but as far as your secret goes, I still think you're making a mistake. The people of this town, especially those you model your characters around, have a right to know you're the one writing those books. I know you think some of them will be upset, but they might surprise you. I've heard nothing but good things about CJ Coleson."

"Maybe you're right," he admitted, "but I never expected *Fool's Gold* to become a best seller and once it did, I couldn't go back. ... What's for supper? I'm starving." His mother meant well but sometimes she needed to give him a little more credit.

"Meatloaf, mashed potatoes, and peas," she answered, her lips compressed. "Call your father to the table. He's been waiting to find out what you've learned about the fire."

Cole filled in his parents on what he could, keeping the gold, Trent's identity, as well as Chester's cause of death confidential the way Hal had insisted. He'd talk to Casey as he'd reluctantly promised, but until they interviewed the boys and the results came back on the items in the shed, it was all conjecture. He'd been with Hal when he'd gone to see each boy in turn to tell them about Chester. They were crushed, leaving no doubt in his mind that they'd loved the old man.

"I stopped by Apache Trail Realty before meeting Clay," he said, knowing his parents needed to know he was planning to move.

"Whatever for?" his mother asked, taking away his empty plate and placing a piece of pecan pie in front of him. "Aren't you happy with the cabin?"

"The cabin's fine, Mom."

"Noella, don't be naïve," his father said and chuckled. "I think he's looking for something in town. Cole's an adult. He needs his own place, and now that he's seeing Casey..."

"Oh ... oh," his mother said, her eyes growing wide. "I see. But you can always bring her here—"

His father burst out laughing. "Sweetheart, you aren't that old. Sometimes a couple needs privacy. We may be gone a lot, but right now, we're here."

She reddened. "I've gotten a little dense, haven't I? Did you find anything?"

"Maybe. There's a four-bedroom, Spanish-styled house west of town, just before you get to the Canyon Lake Road. It's on the south side and belongs to the guy who built the retirement village over there. He and his wife split up last year, and he wants to sell it. The price is well below market and within my range, and it's partially furnished. It's bigger than I need, but the three-acre property is fully fenced, and from the pictures, it has a lanai, deck, and in-ground pool, with a spectacular view of the desert and Superstition Mountain." The view wasn't unlike the one he had at Table Rock. Now that he'd decided he wanted his own place, he wanted to move sooner rather than later.

"That sounds perfect for you," she said. "I know how much you love being close to the desert, and yet you would still be nearby."

"I've arranged to see it on Friday afternoon, so if it works out, you two will be honeymooners in no time."

The twinkle in his dad's eye made him realize that he might've been cramping their style, too.

Twenty minutes later, Cole stripped, stepped into the shower, and allowed the water to ease the tiredness from his muscles. The only thing keeping him from collapsing exhausted on the bed afterwards was the thought of seeing Casey and feeling his arms around her, his lips on hers again. How he would love to have her here in the shower with him. In his writer's imagination he pictured the scene.

The water flowed down her lithe body, leaving glistening beads on her skin. Taking the soap in hand, he rubbed it into a lather and using both of his hands, soaped her back, moving his sudsy hands down her spine to cup her delicious derrière. Leaning into her, he smacked his forehead on the shower wall.

Damn!

He rubbed his brow. Considering the way she felt about having his folks around, that scenario wasn't going to happen any time soon. Turning the water from hot to cold, he hoped to douse his ardor and get rid of the rock-hard erection he sported.

His body almost back to normal, he dressed quickly and grabbed the gift he'd picked up on his way home eager to see the woman who monopolized his thoughts. Chuckling, he realized this was his second date with someone from Fortune—third, if he counted his chivalrous rescue in the wilderness. It was funny how things changed. Here he'd vowed never to date a woman from town, and he was on the verge of turning his life upside down for one.

The only downside to his upcoming date was the promise he'd made to Hal. He knew some people abhorred shop-talk. It didn't bother him, but his brother-in-law was an accountant, and he constantly complained about so-called friends milking him for free advice on their taxes. If Casey felt that way, this case might well cost him more than he wanted to pay.

Going into the kitchen, he opened the freezer and grabbed two ice packs, and then took the six-pack of beer he'd picked up on his way home out of the fridge.

"I won't be late," he said to his parents as he grabbed his jacket and headed out the door.

CHAPTER SIXTEEN

Casey stretched her back, leaned against the counter, and watched Jaxon playing in the tub. She'd had no idea how exhausting four hours spent entertaining six five-year-olds could be. From the moment the little tykes had arrived, it had been go, go, go. They'd spent enough time in the pool to have withered hands and feet. Games, especially the water balloon war, had been loud and boisterous, and while Casey was tired, the look of joy on Jaxon's face made it all worthwhile.

The tiny figurines from the superhero-themed cake now shared the bathwater with their owner along with the inevitable rubber fish, and a box of soap crayons Jaxon was using with enthusiasm as he drew pictures not only on himself but the porcelain tub. He didn't look ready to come out any time soon.

The afternoon's activities had kept her from dwelling on her disquieting encounter with Eddy and her mother's equally frightening revelation. Before the boys had arrived, she'd looked up syncopes and stents on the Internet, and while she was still worried about her father, she understood he was getting the care he needed. As much as he claimed it was no big deal, she contemplated extending her vacation for another week or two. The only case she had was the one Ryan had guaranteed would be a slam dunk, and Ken, with Wonder Woman's help, could probably manage that. If she were lucky, Baby Boss might even be someone else's problem when she got back. Not only would she feel better watching her dad recover, it would give her more time to figure out how she felt about Cole.

The other troubling bit of news involved rumors that a body had been found out near Weaver's Needle, and apparently the man had been shot. Of course, that could be an embellishment supplied by the gossipers, but she'd heard that gunshot the other night, and while she hadn't seen any lights, it was possible someone had gone back to look at their dirty work. Despite what Cole had said, she couldn't help wondering if they'd actually heard a man being murdered. While this might've been an accident with two men hunting the puma who'd almost made a meal of her, it could easily be a case of greed and claim jumping, like in CJ Coleson's books.

Many men had died on Superstition Mountain, some by gunshot, others by strange and inexplicable ways, and of course some had simply vanished. She'd always believed the stories of severed heads and mutilations Grandpa had dredged up each Halloween had been just that. It was several years later before she realized they'd all been true. One way or the other, Cole and the police chief would get to the bottom of it. She couldn't help wondering what CJ would make of recent events. As Grandpa used to say, there were more stories on Superstition Mountain then men could tell.

But while she could ease her worries about her father, the way she felt about Cole continued to puzzle her. Although he might live at home—and that was still a sore point—he wasn't like the pampered, trust fund men she'd dated in Santa Fe. He'd been honest and upfront with her right from the beginning. Plus, he was a volunteer firefighter, a part-time police officer, and a store owner who loved the magic of Christmas. On top of that, he was a loyal friend as his protection of CJ Coleson's identity showed. Like Ryan, the only man other than her father that she'd ever trusted, Cole had integrity. If she were looking for a baby daddy, he was it.

She sighed. No one knew what the future held, but maybe,

as her father had said, she should give her head a break and follow her heart. When she'd arrived in Fortune, all she'd thought of was leaving again as fast as she could and never looking back. Now, there was her father's health, Randy's loneliness, Jaxon's exuberance, and the way she responded to Cole in the mix. Maybe part of that was the biological clock, but at the moment, while her body definitely wanted Cole, she didn't know what her heart wanted, and that was the problem. How the hell could she follow it if it didn't know where to go?

"Casey," her mom called, snapping her out of her reverie. "Cole's here."

Damn!

He was early. After being up most of the night and then working all day, he had to be exhausted, but he'd said he would come, and Cole was a man of his word. She smiled, warmth spreading through her. If she was going to trust someone with her heart and her happiness, then he was the one she would choose.

"Jaxon's still in the tub," she answered, vain enough to be horrified at the prospect that Cole was about to see her in the most unflattering clothes she owned. While the baggy shirt and track pants were comfortable and perfect for supervising Jaxon in the bath, they were a far cry from anything sexy or stylish. She'd expected to have time to clean herself up and change before his arrival, but the party had gone overtime, and now Picasso was taking longer than he usually did.

"I'm here," Randy said, coming to her rescue. "If I were you, I'd make him wait and change into something else." She chuckled. "Wet, baggy, and wrinkled isn't a good look for you."

Casey made a face. "You're mean—accurate, but mean." She turned to Jaxon. "See you later, kiddo."

Hurrying to her room, Casey rummaged through the clothes she'd brought with her, wishing she'd added something sexy instead of just practical, opting to wear the blue sweater again, but this time with a pair of denim crop pants and matching flats. She fluffed her damp hair, knowing that if she tried to brush it, it would become an unholy mess, and fixed her makeup. Adding a pair of gold hoops, she used tortoiseshell combs to pull her hair behind her ears.

Taking a deep breath, using all of the self-control she possessed, she walked calmly down the stairs, wanting to run into his arms, but forcing herself not to.

"Hi," she said, annoyed by the breathless sound of her voice.

He'd showered and shaved, and while there were shadows under his eyes, he looked good enough to eat—man candy at its best, and while she knew candy wasn't good for her, Cole was.

"Hi, yourself." The heat in his gaze told her he wanted to kiss her as much as she wanted him to, but he wouldn't act on the impulse in front of her parents.

"Jaxon's still in the tub painting himself. Why don't we go and sit on the porch?"

Casey stepped around her mother and led Cole onto the veranda. They'd barely made it away from the windows when he dropped the package onto the table next to the swing and pulled her into his arms.

"I missed you," he said. "I've waited all day to do this."

His lips met hers in a soul-melting kiss that chased away whatever doubts she had about the rightness of this relationship. His tongue licked her lips, and she opened to him, savoring his taste. The long, lingering kiss was one of promise, but when he pulled away, his eyes were filled with worry rather than passion.

"How did your day go?" she asked, trying to understand the contrary emotion. Perhaps he was just tired, concerned about this latest crime.

"Not good. I'm sure you heard about last night's fire."

"And the body discovered in the mountains. That's all anyone's talking about. Even the return of the prodigal daughter has taken a back seat to it."

"Yeah, well, what can I say?" He chuckled. "Fortune's like Hollywood. You get your five minutes of fame, and then, the limelight moves on." He sobered. "The fire was a bad one, Casey."

"I know. Was it an accident?"

"No. It was deliberate." His brow was furrowed, his lips pursed.

"Like the others?" she asked, concern eating at her.

Before he could answer, the screen door opened, and they came apart quickly as her mother stepped onto the porch with a jug of ice-cold lemonade and two pieces of birthday cake.

"Thanks, Mom," Casey said, watching the care vanish from his face as Cole's eyes lit up at the sight of the chocolate treat. Did every man have a sweet tooth?

"It looks delicious, Mrs. Stevens. Did you make this, or is it one of Randy's?"

Her mother chuckled. "I may still bake bread and make pies, but Randy has the cake concession in this family. Even if she didn't, she would insist on making her son's birthday cake. Eat. Jaxon will be down shortly. He's pretty much tuckered out, but Casey said you had something for him, and despite all the gifts he's had today, he's definitely eager for one more." She turned and went back inside.

"It's delicious," Cole said, finishing the cake at lightning speed and smiling when Casey handed him the rest of her piece. "What can I say? I love chocolate cake."

Had he even chewed before swallowing? The boys had wolfed it down much the same way.

Before Casey could comment, Jaxon burst through the open screen door, wearing his new Batman pajamas, obviously having gotten his second wind. He looked nervously out at the darkness, but stood his ground.

"Hi, Mr. Cole. Mom says you brought me a present, and I'm supposed to say thank you."

Standing behind him, Randy rolled her eyes. "I try."

"As a matter of fact, I did," Cole said. "Happy birthday, Jaxon, and you're most welcome." He handed her nephew the small package.

With all the enthusiasm of a five-year-old, Jaxon ripped off the paper. "Look, Mom. It's the new Lego movie. Can I watch it now, please?" he begged, his eyes imploring her to say yes.

"For fifteen minutes only, young man. It's been a long day, and you have to get into that school routine we talked about."

"Yay!" He turned to Cole. "I'm going to kindergarten in two weeks."

"Already?" Cole asked, sounding impressed, and the child preened.

"Yup. I'm bigger now." He edged toward the door, looking out nervously into the darkness, betraying the fear he felt, and reached for his mother's hand. "Let's go inside; it's too dark."

"I hope you like the movie."

Jaxon nodded and pulled Randy inside. As soon as the two were gone, Casey turned to Cole, expecting him to take her into his arms again now that they were alone, but he didn't.

Instead, he stood there, staring down at the veranda floor, and ran his hand through his hair in his signature nervous gesture.

"What's wrong?" she asked, knowing instinctively that there was more than tiredness at play here. "Don't tell me you're afraid of the dark, too." She hoped the jibe would lighten his mood.

"We need to talk," he said, the tone in his voice ominous.

There was that phrase again. Twice in one day, and the last time she'd heard it, the bottom had all but fallen out of her world. She'd seen men sentenced to life in prison who looked less grim than he did at the moment. Sitting on the swing, she took a deep breath, worry making her heart beat faster.

"Did something else happen? Something the grape vine hasn't latched onto yet?"

He nodded, his tired face etched with anxiety. "Yes, but it isn't really something else … it's probably the reason for a hell of a lot of what's been happening, but I can't put it together in any way that makes sense. I need your advice."

"You've got it, but I don't know much about fire and

arson."

"It's more than that, but that's definitely involved. I brought the SUV instead of the bike, so we could have some privacy." He held out his hand to her. "Want to go for a ride?"

"Sure, as long as it's not into the desert," she said and chuckled. "I've had my fill of dirt and cacti for a while."

"Duly noted, but I was thinking of driving to Canyon Lake. It's only twenty minutes from here. I know a spot where we can park the car overlooking the water, and no one will disturb us. I brought some cold beer—not a lot—I thought we could have a can or two while we talk."

"Sounds like a plan." She forced the memory of the last time she'd had beer in the moonlight to the back of her mind. That had been a lifetime ago, and despite the fact seeing Eddy and listening to his lewd suggestions had brought back that night, this was Cole, not Rick. He wouldn't lie to her, take advantage of her. "And after the hijinks and noise of six five-year-olds, a quite spot overlooking the lake sounds heavenly. What do you want to talk about?"

"I know how lawyers hate being pumped for information, but this is important, Casey, otherwise I would never presume on our relationship to do this. I need legal advice."

Casey frowned. This wasn't what she'd expected, and it sort of explained his discomfort. Another woman might feel slighted, but her career had always come first. "For you?"

He shook his head. "No, for Hal and the three boys under sixteen he may have to arrest tomorrow."

She gasped, her ability to speak stolen by his unexpected words.

"I need to tell you what I know and then, I need you to tell me what I'm up against, and what I can do about it." He smiled humorlessly. "This is unofficial, you understand, and no one can know anything—not until we figure out what the hell's going on. Believe me, something's happening here, and I haven't the slightest idea what it is and who's in charge, but it could be very bad, not only for three young boys, but for all of Fortune."

Cole ran his hand through his hair again, and Casey's fingers itched to straighten the curls in disarray.

"If this is a police matter, Cole, should you be discussing it with an outsider?"

"This was Hal's suggestion. He agreed we needed to talk about this right now, and since Horace Stone is out of town, you're the only lawyer around. The way I see it, that's probably the best thing that can happen to those kids."

Furrowing her brow, she nodded. "I'll say one thing for you. You have a way with words."

He held out his hand once more, pulling her to her feet. Bending his head, he kissed her softly. "I'm sorry about this, believe me, I had very different plans when I hung up the phone last night."

"I'll bet you did," she said, chuckling. "Maybe after we play Q and A, we can get to them."

She was enthralled by what he'd said. Saving innocent people was the reason she'd chosen to become a lawyer. "Let me tell Mom we're leaving and then, I'm all yours."

Casey hurried into the house. After informing her mother that she was going with Cole and telling her not to wait up, she went up to her room, used the bathroom, and then hurried back out to the veranda. This certainly sounded like the kind of case she'd missed working. Maybe, if she did stay for a few extra weeks, she could sign on with the police department as a special consultant. She would love to sink her teeth into something as captivating as this. While she didn't know exactly what 'this' was, the fact that Cole was so worked up about it meant it had to be serious, and if she were going to stick around until her dad was on his feet again, having something interesting and productive to do would help pass the time.

* * * *

Once Casey was settled in the SUV, Cole started the engine and drove back to the Apache Trail. He needed to make her understand what was involved here, not only for the boys but for Fortune. Once this news got out, things would never be the same again—that was if this was the real deal—and as hard as that was to believe, Chester had definitely found something. He turned north onto Canyon Lake Road. The sky was clear and the moon, now full, rose slowly in the east.

"So, now that you've got me here, talk," Casey said. "You've got me on pins and needles waiting to hear more."

"Patience. This is important, and I want to make sure you understand everything that's at stake. You've got a quick mind, and what I need is someone who can think outside the box and yet stay within the intent, if not the rule, of the law." He reached for her hand and squeezed it.

"There you go saying those sweet things again." She chuckled, but left her hand in his. "I have to admit, my dates with you have been anything but ordinary. I don't think I ever truly appreciated how gorgeous the moon is out here," she said, "and while I'm sure the scenery will be spectacular, I'm dying to find out what this is all about."

"Okay," he said, knowing how single-minded she could be, but he would do this his way. "You win. Before I share my information, why don't you tell me what you know about the local legends?"

"Legends? As in Hezekiah Skansen or your friend, CJ Coleson?" she asked, her brow furrowed, her nose scrunched up.

She looked so cute and yet sexy, he'd like nothing better than to stop the vehicle and kiss her senseless, but this matter was too important. He shook his head.

"No, legends as in Peralta's mine."

"Peralta's mine? Are you serious?" Her voice rose so high, the word ended on a squeak. "You want to test my knowledge of Arizona myths and legends now?"

If the situation hadn't been so critical, he'd have laughed at the stunned look on her face.

"I wish it was just that. Indulge me. I really need to know

everything you know about the Superstition Mountains."

Casey shrugged, angled her body toward him, and let go of his hand, since holding it now was awkward.

He missed the contact with her, as slight as it had been.

"Let me see." She pursed her lips and cocked one eyebrow. "Do you want me to start with *Cibola*?"

He nodded. "Why not? It all began there, right?"

"You're going to regret this," she said and giggled softly. "Giving a lawyer the floor is always dangerous, but for something like this? My best friend calls me a fountain of useless information."

"The right knowledge is never a waste," he answered, trying not to sound preachy, but from her raised eyebrow, he'd failed.

"Okay," she said, stretching out the word. "I've always been a history buff. My grandpa used to tell me stories about the *conquistadors* and their never-ending quest for gold when I was younger, and of course Mr. Lowell did that unit on myths and legends in twelfth grade. From what I remember, the original myth dates back to the sixteenth century. The Spaniards living in Cuba decided to try and colonize Florida and the Gulf Coast of what's now the United States. Not realizing how unfriendly the natives and the animals could be, six hundred men left their ships to explore the land. Long story short, they ran out of supplies, were hounded by the local tribes, not to mention some pretty hungry crocodiles in southern Florida and then alligators in the rest of the state and southern Louisiana. Eight years later, after what must've been hell, Vaca, the expedition's treasurer and three other men made it back to Mexico. They had some gold with them, but what really caused a stir was a baby rattle made of copper."

He nodded. "Yeah, the copper had been smelted and worked. At the time, copper like that was even more valuable than gold." He smiled. "If you remember that, then you know the story didn't end there. After Vaca returned to Spain, he wrote about his adventures, no doubt embellishing them, and eventually the tales caught the attention of the Viceroy."

She nodded, and smiled, obviously pleased with herself. "The Spanish Viceroy, always interested in expanding Spain's influence and filling its coffers, heard about Vaca's ill-fated expedition. He found Estevan, a slave who'd made it to Mexico with Vaca, and sent him to guide a Franciscan monk back to the area to investigate Vaca's story."

"Yeah, the monk's name was Friar di Niza."

"I'm impressed. So if you know the story, why the quiz?"

He chuckled. "I looked it up. I need to know what you know."

Shrugging, she leaned back. "Fine. Believe it or not, I enjoyed learning about all this stuff and remember most of it. Since Estevan, di Niza's guide, knew the lay of the land and could communicate with some of the natives, he was readily accepted by them—apparently he was some kind of healer. Di Niza was jealous of the way the natives treated the guide, and that caused issues between Estevan and the rest of the party. He started moving farther and farther ahead of the group, communicating with them through messages attached to crosses. In one message, he claimed he'd heard of seven great cities north of where they were. The people there were rich and lived in multilevel buildings, and wore clothes made from cotton. He named the cities *Cibola*. According to the legend, that was his last message. He was supposedly killed by the Zuni, but that's open to interpretation. My grandpa believed the Zuni, who respected the slave, hid him among them, and he lived out his life there."

"Yeah, it doesn't make sense for the Zuni to kill off a gifted healer and translator. The tribes often fought among themselves and having someone who could mediate would be a valuable asset. To continue the story, without a guide di Niza had the choice of going on or returning to Spain, back the way he'd come. So, with nothing but his faith to guide him, he traveled through hostile territory, and claimed to have found this *Cibola*, with its walls shining in the sun. When he returned to Spain with a little gold, he described this incredible city so well, that everyone really believed he'd found it. More than likely, he was lying through his teeth. The monk, not renowned for his courage, probably turned tail and ran back to Spain as fast as he could once Estevan disappeared. And, not wanting to upset his benefactor, made up this wild story. But the damage was done, and people believed those cities existed."

Casey nodded. "Grandpa felt the same way. The Church was a powerful influence back then. If a man of God claimed he'd found these cities of gold, no one was going to call him out on it." She chuckled. "Man, he must've been thrilled to discover he was to be the guide for the next expedition." She cocked her head to the left. "You're good at telling stories—not as good as CJ Coleson, of course—but we can't all be writers."

Cole swallowed a laugh at the backward compliment. He should probably tell her the truth, but to do so now might complicate things. He had to think of the boys. Casey would understand when he could reveal himself.

"I'll bet he could really do something with this legend," she continued. "You should suggest it to him. Maybe Esteban fell in love with a Zuni princess, or lived out his days in *Cibola*."

"I'll do that," he answered. "Let's get back to the story, shall we? Your turn."

She shrugged. "The Viceroy wanted someone to get that gold, so he put Coronado in charge of the expedition with di Niza acting as guide. Coronado had a couple of hundred men with him and some natives, and he set out to find *Cibola*. He attacked a Zuni village expecting to find gold, but all he found were people living in adobe houses, some of them multi-storied, and while they had a little gold, silver, and turquoise, it wasn't what he'd expected. Furious, convinced the Zuni were lying to him, hiding their wealth, he tortured them. Eventually realizing there was no fortune in gold to be had there, he continued his explorations, reaching not only as far north as the Grand Canyon, but maybe into the Midwest as far as Kansas. I think his men were the first Europeans to ever see a buffalo. Eventually, he ended up in this region. The Apache told him that the mountain held great stores of gold, but that the land belonged to the Thunder Gods, and was sacred. Not ready to give up, Coronado and his men explored the mountain on their own. Soon, his men started vanishing, and predisposed by the Apache to believe spirits inhabited the hills, the men were afraid, especially when they started to find their missing compatriots' bodies mutilated—you know, the missing heads, or heads far from the rest of the body. Coronado named the mountains, leaving the area with very little to show for his troubles. Over the years, the legend of *Cibola* has persisted, but no one's ever found the seven golden cities."

"Excellent," he said, impressed with her knowledge. "You get an A plus for that. Experts think di Niza may have seen the Zuni pueblo cities gleaming in the sunlight, and embroidered his tales on that. From a distance, the baked adobe could look like gold."

"True, but that doesn't explain where Vaca's fancy copper rattle came from. The natives were incapable of producing copper like that at the time. What does all this have to do with anything? Don't tell me the body found at Weaver's Needle was looking for Coronado's golden cities."

"Maybe, maybe not. What else do you know about the Spaniards and their quest for gold?"

She made a low growling noise in her throat. "You're driving me crazy. Fine! Nothing happened for three hundred years and then a Mexican, Don Peralta, somehow got hold of one of Coronado's maps, and went looking for gold on Superstition Mountain. He struck it rich, and named the place Sombrero Mine, because the area around it resembled the broad-brimmed hats. He pulled lots of gold out of his mine, sending it back by wagon-load to Mexico. When the Apache realized the extent to which he was stealing from them, desecrating their sacred land, they got mad. Peralta packed up as much gold as he could and got ready to leave the mine until tempers cooled, but it was too late." She went on to describe the subsequent massacre at the hands of the angry tribe.

Cole pulled the car to a stop, parking it so that they looked out over the silvered lake.

"The Apache didn't take the gold since it belonged to their gods. They left it and the animals there. Burdened as they were, the mules and donkeys roamed the mountains until they all died. Years later, prospectors searching for gold came across the animal skeletons, the mined gold still in bags and baskets on their backs, but no one's found the Sombrero mine itself. Some people think the Skansen mines might be the tail end of the vein Peralta found, but apparently the gold they mine isn't the same quality as the samples people recovered from the remains of donkeys—although it's been almost a hundred years since anyone has found one of those. Satisfied?"

"Yes. Want to get out and sit on the grass? I've got a blanket in back."

"Sure, but you still haven't told me what this is about."

He opened the car door. "That's because we haven't finished the history lesson."

Casey got out of the SUV and followed him to a spot a few feet away, closer to the water, and waited for him to spread the blanket. He went back to the vehicle, and returned with a small cooler. Opening it, he handed her a beer.

She reached for it. "Thanks. I must say you've picked the perfect place for ghost stories, but what does any of this have to do with the boys you mentioned?"

"Humor me just a little longer. Despite or maybe because of Hezekiah Skansen's strike, many prospectors have searched for Peralta's mine, using a variety of maps. Some people thought his sombrero looked more like a finger pointing to the sky and renamed it the Finger of God. After Paul Weaver carved his name in it, it became known as Weaver's Needle."

"So you think the man found there was looking for Peralta's mine?" she asked, her face contorted in confusion. "No one's found that one either. And before you ask, there's the Lost Dutchman Mine that may or may not have been Peralta's mine, but it's vanished, too. People have been searching and dying, trying to find those damn mines for over a hundred years." Her tone implied she'd reached the end of her patience. "Now, what the hell has all this to do with sixteen-year-old kids?"

"I'm not sure, but the physical evidence says they may have killed Chester."

CHAPTER SEVENTEEN

"Get out of here!"

Casey stared at Cole and snapped her jaw shut. Of all the things he could've said, that was the last thing she would've expected. He looked serious, but...

"Let me get this straight." She took a mouthful of beer. Over the years, thanks to Ryan, she'd learned to enjoy the brew without associating it with that night. "You think three teenagers set fire to Chester's house and killed him in the process? Why? What's the motive? What kind of physical evidence have you got to support that? And why the trip down memory lane?"

"Before I answer any of your questions, I want you to look at this." He handed her a small leather pouch. "The contents aren't all there, since it's evidence in a murder case, but I convinced Hal you wouldn't believe me without seeing some of it. I know lawyers need proof. You tend to be like Doubting Thomas in the Bible," he chuckled softly.

"Maybe a little," she admitted reluctantly and shrugged. She did belong to the 'seeing is believing' cadre. "But, to win a case, you need tangible corroboration. You can't rely on supposition and hearsay. I'm not one for playing games, but you obviously enjoy them and you do seem to like keeping secrets. Cole Warner, Man of Mystery." She hefted the bag. "Where did you get this?"

"I found it hidden in a toolbox inside a locked shed next to Chester's house."

"Odd place for three kids to hide stuff."

"I didn't say it was theirs."

Casey scowled, opened the bag, turned it upside down, and gasped. Four items dropped onto her lap: a set of rosary beads made of turquoise and silver, the cross, a turquoise stone at its center, partially cleaned to remove the years of tarnish, a gold nugget roughly as big as a baby's fingernail, and two coins, one of them a dollar-sized-silver coin, the other an eight centavos gold one. She picked up the silver coin first, examined it, and then reached for the gold one.

"It's hard to believe Chester had something this valuable hidden in an old shed. I've got a friend in Santa Fe who collects coins. Considering the condition of this thing, he could've gotten at least fifty dollars for the silver one, but the gold one has to be worth a couple of grand."

"There were fifty-three coins in the bag, some gold, others silver—different sizes and denominations—all this age or older. They've been cleaned and don't appear to have been in circulation long. The engraving is still crisp and clear. We haven't had an expert look at them yet, but they look like the real deal to me."

Casey nodded. Not that she was any kind of adept, but Ryan had taught her a little about numismatics. Those coins would be worth a hell of a lot of money to a man supporting himself with his social security. She put down the coins and reached for the rosary, noting the fine craftsmanship of the cross, especially the Spanish detailing.

"Do you think this is from the same era? If it is, it's probably worth a few hundred dollars, too."

"We do. I've never seen anything like it. It doesn't seem like something a soldier would use, but maybe it was meant as a gift for a wife or sister. The bag contained other pieces of turquoise jewelry, several silver rings, a couple of copper bracelets, and a man's gold ring with a bloodstone in it, as well as forty arrowheads. Hal will have someone take all the items into the university in Phoenix along with the coins for authentication."

"Good." She frowned, examining the detailing on the cross once more. "I've seen something like this recently." She shook her head. It must've been in Santa Fe. "If you think these things are your motive, then knowing the value will be important when it comes to laying charges, but usually a thief takes the booty with him. That gold nugget is a good size, too. It must be worth a couple of hundred dollars." She stopped speaking and turned to him, as the truth dawned on her. "Is this real?" She indicated everything in her lap. "This stuff is all mid-nineteenth century. Are you suggesting Chester found Peralta's mine? Do you know what the historical significance of that would be? Not to mention the financial repercussions."

"I know; believe me I know, and so does Hal. According to the assayer over at Skansen Mining, the nugget has a higher quality of gold than anything they get out of *Lucky Seven* and is worth five hundred dollars." He stuck out his tongue and licked his lips. "There was a second bag full of nuggets stuffed in Chester's mattress. Altogether, we found more than five pounds of gold."

"My God! That's more than one hundred thousand dollars' worth at today's prices. Nobody leaves that kind of money behind." She held up the chunk of gold. "I assume you dusted this for fingerprints before you had me touch it?"

"We did. The surfaces were too rough to yield any viable prints." He ran his hand through his hair before taking a swig of his beer. "It's more complicated than you think. Chester didn't die in the fire. He was poisoned first, and the building was torched to cover it up."

"Damn! Then you're talking premeditated murder," she said, her stomach plummeting at the implications. "You do realize a sixteen-year-old can be tried as an adult, don't you?"

"I know," he said sadly, "and Arizona still has the death penalty."

"Pretend I know nothing and lay out your case for me. Why do you suspect the boys are behind this?"

She listened intently as Cole relayed the information he'd learned from the arson expert, listed the evidence they'd found not only in the shed but in Chester's bed, and then explained the relationship the boys had with Chester.

"Chester bought every single book I had or could get about *Cibola*, Coronado, Peralta, and the Lost Dutchman. He was obsessed with finding that gold. It's funny I never realized how much money that amounted to, and never questioned where he'd gotten it. Like everyone else in town, I assumed the guy never had a buck in his pocket he didn't spend on booze. I just don't get it."

"Maybe he was a miser or a hoarder. He had a drinking problem." She shrugged, wishing she could think of something else to help him figure this out. "Sometimes an alcoholic's brain doesn't function normally, but I agree. Having all this wealth at his fingertips and living hand to mouth like that makes no sense."

"If you think that's confusing, try adding this to the mix. According to Melba, Hal's wife, Chester went to see Minerva Skansen about six months ago. Apparently, they were engaged to be married when they were young, but her father squelched it. Some say that's when Chester caught gold fever, started drinking, and disappeared for weeks on end on the mountain."

"And Minerva never married. If that's true, it's just so sad," she said, reminded that she could easily end up a lonely, old, spinster herself. "Maybe he went to see if she could help him sell his gold. Dad mentioned Chester might've turned to drink to ease a broken heart. How does Melba know about the visit?"

"She was there the day he went to see her. Minerva seemed excited to see him and asked her to leave, so she doesn't know what they discussed. Melba was working with some of the local women organizing the stuff in Minerva's attic. She's turning a bunch of items over to the town on Sunday. I don't know much more, and since Mom's been away, she isn't involved."

"I can ask my mother. If it's something to do with Fortune's history, she'll be in it up to the eyeballs. Poor Minerva. If she still has feelings for Chester, this will be incredibly hard on her." Casey sighed. "I'll make sure to go and see her before I leave."

"Here's the other thing that makes very little sense. Hal got a call in the early afternoon from Horace Stone's secretary, which is why we knew he was out of town. She'd heard that Chester had died in the fire and wanted to verify the information for Mr. Stone. It seems Chester was a valued client. By valued, I assume that means he paid his bills on time."

"It could mean that," she said and chuckled, "or Chester could be an old acquaintance. He wasn't that much older than Mr. Stone. Most lawyers do some work pro bono for friends and family."

"Either way, Sylvia verified that Chester had filed several claims for mineral rights over the years, some dating back to the 1970s. According to Sylvia, in the last six months Chester visited the office three times. The first time, the boys went with him. The other times, he was on his own. She didn't know why. There are a few matters Mr. Stone handles personally, not even sharing them with her."

"That's strange. I understood the man was swamped. That was why he wanted me to consider a partnership with him. I don't do any of my own paperwork—paralegals handle most of that—and believe it or not, there's a lot of paperwork involved in filing mineral claims. That might be why he went to see Minerva—to find out how the process works. The gold would have to be assayed, and he would need a buyer. Horace could've been acting as his agent in the matter." She stopped and chewed her lower lip. "If he had the knowhow, Chester could've refined some of the nuggets himself and had Horace sell them for him. Anyone can learn to do it on the Internet. It's easier than you think. I had a client whose wife melted down his collection of antique gold coins in a divorce case."

"Ouch! That must've hurt. What did she do with the gold?"

"Believe it or not, she sold the small ingot to a jeweler. By the time I figured out what she'd done, everything had been broken down and remade into costume jewelry. The coins were gone as was their unique value. She gave my client the check the jeweler gave her, but he cried like a baby. As far as she was concerned, his love for those coins had ruined her life, so she was just returning the favor. Sad to say, when love turns to hate, nothing's too cruel."

"Could she do that? Could she sell gold that way? I didn't think the general population was allowed to own bullion," he said, finishing his beer.

"Up until forty years ago, you would've been right, but the law changed, and there's no limit on it now. What she did was morally wrong, but he chose not to pursue the matter."

"I doubt Chester knew enough about computers to figure out where to find the information, but the kids helping him out would all have been computer savvy." He popped the tab on two more cans of beer and handed her one. "Tony Bronson, the oldest one of them, is a science whiz. If anyone could refine the gold, it would be him. So, given what I've told you, how much trouble are those kids in?"

"To be honest, I don't think you really have anything. The evidence you've told me about is circumstantial at best. While the art supplies could belong to … Kyle, is it?" she asked, sipping her beer.

He nodded. "The boy's really good. I've got some of his work for sale at the emporium, and the kid's only fourteen."

"You'll have to point them out to me. Maybe I'll buy one for my apartment in Santa Fe."

"I will, and it'll come with free hanging service." He wiggled his eyebrows.

"You're a nut." She shook her head and smirked. "No fair distracting me during my opening arguments. Where was I? Oh yes. The art supplies—they could be his, or they could be Chester's. Can you say for sure the man wasn't an artist, too? Maybe he's the one who taught the kid to paint."

"That's a stretch, but I get the point."

"Even if we accept the art supplies were Kyle's, it doesn't necessarily follow that the rest of the stuff was his, especially the mescal. Take the can of gasoline for example. You believe that links them to your four previous arson cases, but that's not what I see. If those boys were helping Chester, and he had some kind of mining operation going on, he would need a small generator at the very least. The kids could easily be the ones refilling it for him. The other fires may have been started with gasoline, but even if that jerry can is plastered with their fingerprints, you don't have anything linking the boys to those arsons. The fire at Chester's wasn't set that way—you said so yourself. Unless you've got something else—an eye witness, footprints that match shoes, anything that directly connects them to the crime—the gasoline can won't be enough to make any of the arson charges stick, even if the art supplies are Kyle's."

"What about the anti-freeze? There was a container half-full in the shed. It's the poison that was used."

"Ethylene glycol," she said, shaking her head. "It's probably the most popular poison out there these days. It only takes thirty milliliters of the concentrate to kill an adult. If their prints are on that, it could be damning, but all engines, even small ones like on a compressor or a portable generator, use coolant. Since none of the treasure was taken, you really don't have much of a motive. If the point was to steal from him, why not do it? You can't assume there was other stuff more easily accessible that they took, and even if you decide to go that way, you'd need to have the stolen goods in your possession, which you don't."

"We haven't looked for any other treasure or gold," he admitted. "I could ask Hal to get a warrant—"

"On what grounds? Guilt by association? Just because they helped him doesn't mean they helped themselves. If you do find more, can you prove Chester didn't share his booty with his minions? A finder's fee of some sort? Even if there is anti-freeze in the bottles of mescal you found, it doesn't mean they put it there. In fact, a good defense lawyer could argue someone left the bottles there, hoping the kids would drink them and die. Then, it might look as if Chester had accidently poisoned his own batch of homemade hooch. Some people cut the booze because it's too strong. If he used water, and there was still some anti-freeze in the container..."

Cole reached over and kissed her, not a long loving kiss, but a quick one that warmed her inside. "Damn you're good. If I ever get in trouble with the law, I want you on my side. I'll speak to Hal in the morning. For the record, I was playing devil's advocate here. Neither one of us think the kids are good for this, but we needed to be sure. Elmore Gunderson, the local prosecutor, will want to see heads roll. He'll make Hal's life miserable until someone's arrested."

"Gunderson would be an idiot to try to charge those kids with what you have. I realize teenage boys are smart, but something's off about all this. I know the fire at Chester's was different from the others, but the timing implies it could be related in some way, and if it is, it's too organized, too sophisticated for boys that age. Have these kids been in trouble before?" she asked, leaning against him.

He put his arm around her and pulled her close.

"No, nothing. They range in age from fourteen to sixteen, and they're all straight A students."

She frowned. "If they are involved, and that's a big 'if' in my book, someone else is pulling the strings. In my opinion, based on what you've told me, I doubt whoever killed Chester knew about the gold and the rest of that treasure, but if Chester did find Peralta's mine, and those boys were with him all the time, they must know about it, and people would kill for that. You said one of them is sixteen?"

"Not yet. His birthday's in December."

"I see. Well, that means none of them can legally file a claim for the mine, and if Chester filed one, they won't get a cent. Even if he doesn't have a will, the state will try to find his heirs. If those boys want anything out of this, they would have to go to the mine, take whatever they could, and hide it. The best you could do is charge them with claim jumping and theft. It might make them look like suspects for the murder, but—" She stopped talking as a new thought came to her. "Listen. Maybe the boys *were* stealing from Chester. A few of these nuggets would go a long way toward defraying the cost of their education. All they need is an adult they can trust to sell it for them—maybe one of the parents. Dad mentioned people had seen lights on the mountain on Monday night. I didn't see them, but what if it was Chester's kids helping themselves to some of the loot? If they were using flashlights or lanterns like yours, I'm sure that light was visible for miles. If that mine is as rich as legend claims, Chester might not have noticed a few nuggets missing here or there. Hal should question the parents."

Cole shook his head and stared down at the blanket.

Casey cocked her head to the side. What was he hiding now?

"What do you know that I don't?"

"I saw those lights, Casey, he admitted sheepishly. "So did Chester. He claimed there were aliens in the desert, but I know the truth. While I don't know *who* it was, I do know *what* it was, and it couldn't have been the kids."

"How can you be that sure?" she asked, her gut telling her there was more to this, possibly another one of his secrets in play. She hated riddles.

"Because I know exactly what was responsible for those lights," he answered, his voice filled with remorse. He huffed out a breath. "We were still at Table Rock. You were asleep in my arms when I heard the sounds of engines. I turned off the light and saw them moving on the mountain, as if I were looking at ATV's or other small vehicles. Then, some of them rose up into the air. The lights I saw belonged to a helicopter. It's why I woke you up. Our light was probably visible for miles, and I was terrified someone would come to investigate."

"And you chose not to tell me we might be in danger?" she

cried, her voice rising on the last four words. She sat up abruptly as the truth struck her. "You *lied* to me. I heard those engines, and you dismissed them, made me feel as if I'd imagined them."

She was so angry she trembled, hurt more deeply than she could've imagined. She wrapped her arms around her middle, trying to protect herself from this latest blow. So far it had been a hell of a day. How much worse could it get?

"Is there anything else about Monday night you didn't tell me?" As her mother always said, lying by omission was still lying.

"I heard a big cat's cry," Cole stated awkwardly. "It could've been the puma—"

"And you kept *that* to yourself?" she shrieked, interrupting him. Furious, she stood, the items in her lap tumbling unnoticed to the blanket. "How dare you assume I didn't need to know that?" She shuddered in her fury as the reality of his omission sunk in. "I almost died because you didn't mention that animal. If you'd told me about it, I would've been smart enough to stay out of the wilderness."

"Do you think I didn't realize that when I was searching for you?" he pleaded. "If anything had happened to you..." He hung his head.

"I suppose that gunshot wasn't someone poaching deer, either," she said, swallowing the lump in her throat. She was upset and angry, but it was more than that. He'd disappointed her, proving she'd made another error in judgment when it came to the men she should trust.

"It could've been. I was guessing, but I thought it was someone after the cat," he said defensively. "You were spooked, and there seemed no reason to add to your fear. When Hal told me about the body at Weaver's Needle, I thought it might've been the gunshot we heard, but the timing's off. The guy was shot in the back, his head moved about thirty feet away, but he's been dead a week, maybe longer."

She shivered, barely able to suppress her pain and wrapped

her arms more tightly around herself.

"The Apache curse?"

He nodded. "But unless the spirits are armed now…"

"I see. Someone's trying to mess with your head and the investigation. Is there anything else you haven't told me? Any other secrets you want to share?"

He reddened, started to speak, but shook his head.

"Fine. I assume these kids don't have a gun? Your prosecutor won't try to pin this on them?" She had to focus on the case, not her breaking heart. It might not seem like a big deal to someone else, but to her, it was. He'd made an arbitrary decision, one that had almost cost her her life.

"I doubt he will, but Chester had a hunting rifle."

"You want to blame a dead man for that murder?" she asked, her voice heavy with sarcasm, but she was in pain and wanted to lash back at him in any way she could. "Convenient, but hard as hell to prove. Believe it or not, someone's going to ask for a motive."

"Damn it, Casey, work with me here. You're putting words in my mouth, and I don't like it one damn bit. I'm sorry I didn't mention the helicopter and the cat, but, I thought I was doing the right thing by not telling you. You were so scared—"

"You thought wrong. If there's one thing I can't abide from a man, it's dishonesty, and withholding information is just another way men lie, and from what I've learned tonight, you've perfected the art." She shook her head. "What the hell is happening in this town? Set a bunch of fires, frame a group of kids, poison an old man and burn his body, shoot and decapitate another? What's next? It has to be a hell of an encore he or she has planned. By the way, do you know the name of the dead man or is that another secret you don't plan to share?"

"It wasn't part of the information I was authorized to give you," he admitted.

"Fine." She shook her head slowly, reaction setting in. She was suddenly bone-weary as if she'd been the one who hadn't slept last night. "It isn't any of my business anyway. I want to go home now."

"Damn it, Casey," he said, his frustration clear. "I said I was sorry. If I could go back and do it again, I would do things differently. I made a mistake—an error in judgment for God's sake. Haven't you ever made one? Last night, you didn't tell your mother and father about getting lost in the desert and being stalked by that cat. Why? Because you knew it would upset them. How was what I did any different?"

Casey felt the color drain from her face when Cole's accusation hit the mark, and cold filled her, bringing with it unbearable pain.

"I never said I was perfect," she spat the words, both angry and humiliated. "I've made several mistakes in my life, and I won't deny it. Coming home and getting involved with you seems to be another one. You're right about my withholding information from my parents, but you don't understand. I want to go. Please take me home."

"Trent Gibbs." His voice was low, filled with defeat. "The man they found at the base of Weaver's Needle was Trent Gibbs, who incidentally is the nephew of Leon Turner, the man whose bones we found a few months ago."

"The guy I went to school with?" She felt her stomach cramp. If one of them was involved in this, you could bet your ass the other two weren't that far behind. In the past, one had never done anything without the others. They'd been the ones watching Rick and her that night.

"Yes." Cole sighed. "You might as well hear it all, because, whether Hal agrees or not, I'm convinced everything is connected."

When he finished talking, she shook her head, intrigued in spite of herself. She was still annoyed with him for lying to her, but not quite as upset as she'd been. There was no way she'd forgive him for what he'd done, but she could almost understand why he'd done it. No one liked to be reminded they'd committed the same sin. When it came right down to it, she'd lied by omission far more than he had, and last night hadn't been the first time.

"Wow. That's one hell of a mess. So, Leon was blackmailing someone. If Chester went to investigate his aliens on Tuesday and whoever's involved saw him that's a hell of a motive for murder. I ran into Eddy Ramos on my way to collect my bike today. The guy went on about how Minerva's losing it, and he was forced to move in with her for her own good. I know there's no proof Eddy and Rick Harvey were involved with Trent's death, but my gut says those two would know what he was doing out there. In years past, Trent never did anything without those two by his side. Eddy said he was going to be with them in Vegas, so he can't know the man's dead."

"Good point. I'm not sure if those three are as close as they used to be, but Trent worked for Skansen Mining, and Eddy is the CEO. Rick Harvey's a greedy son of a bitch with a drinking problem who likes to gamble, and his son is one of the boys I mentioned. There was a hell of a fight at the Country Club at New Year's, and he accused Kristal of foisting someone else's brat on him, since that 'artsy-fartsy kid' as he called him, couldn't possibly be his son. If Rick somehow found out about Chester's mine, he would have a hell of a good motive, too, especially if he thought he was entitled to some of that gold."

Casey took a deep breath, refusing to dwell on the possibility she might have to face Rick, but prayed it wouldn't happen. All Cole and Hal wanted was legal advice. If any of this got to court, Horace would be doing the job the same way he had for the last forty years.

"I would watch that mountain and those boys, not because I think they're guilty, but they may know too much. If you're right and they can identify the location of the mesa in the photograph, then they're a danger to the men bringing in drugs. As far as the gold goes, once that's made public, the chances are those boys could lead anyone to it. Since I've never considered Rick to be honest and upstanding, I wouldn't put anything past him. Once a schmuck, always a schmuck. Using his kid to get rich is probably right up his alley."

Cole chuckled. "If anything happens to that kid ... Kristal may not be mother of the year, but she's very protective of that boy and she has one hell of a temper. You should've seen the way she clocked Rick at New Year's. Hal talked him out of pressing charges, but as far as I was concerned, he'd earned that punch."

"From what I've heard, she must have the patience of a saint to stay with him."

"Not patience, desperation. Rick's father insisted she sign a pre-nuptial agreement before they got married. If she walks out on him, she's got nothing."

"Nice. He can do whatever he wants, and she has to grin and bear it. I can almost feel sorry for her. Now, if you don't mind, I'm really tired and would like to go."

CHAPTER EIGHTEEN

Cole bent to pick up the items on the blanket and stuffed them back into the leather pouch. If she wanted to go home, there was no way he could keep her here, but he hated the idea of ending the night this way. Maybe she was right and a relationship between them was a mistake. Reluctantly, he collected the empties and put them in the cooler while she folded the blanket.

Once they reached the SUV, he started the engine. Unlike Monday night, the silence between them was oppressive. If she was angry with him for withholding the information about the puma and the helicopter, she was going to be furious when she discovered the truth about CJ Coleson. How the hell had he gotten himself into this mess?

Earlier tonight, when she'd asked if he had any more secrets, he'd almost come clean, but he'd been afraid it would complicate matters. Complicate? That was the understatement of the century. When she did find out, all hell would break loose.

Sighing, he let his mind wander back to the discussion they'd had before she'd gotten angry with him. Talking to her had been an eye opener. Casey had put the information together so well and so quickly. What would it be like to have her collaborate on a novel? Would she see the intricate details in the story that he sometimes missed and his beta readers found? Doing so could shave days, maybe even weeks, off the editing time and the necessary rewrites. Neither he nor Hal had considered the possibility the boys might be in danger, and now that she'd brought it up, it made sense. He and Hal had thought about it, but they hadn't seen the big picture; she had.

"Do you think Chester has a will?"

"I don't know. Up until today, I wouldn't have thought he had anything worth inheriting," he said, grateful she was speaking to him again, even if it was about the case.

"Did he have any family?"

"Not as far as I know. As I recall, he had an older brother who died in Viet Nam. They read his name at the service on Veterans' Day."

"Well, the state will search high and low to find family, no matter how remote it is. If they don't, everything will 'escheat' into one of the state's coffers. Maybe the kids can somehow convince the heirs to give them something, but money does strange things to people. One thing is for sure. Whoever's responsible for the helicopter has to be found and stopped. The last thing you want is for Fortune to become a drug depot."

"You're right. When Horace gets back, I'll check on a will." He swallowed. Maybe it was time to grovel a little more. She didn't sound as angry as she had. "Thanks for letting me pick your brain, and I'm really sorry about keeping that information from you."

"What's done is done. Just don't ever do it again."

There was a fatal resignation to her tone he disliked, and as for doing it again, hell, he was way beyond that.

"Let's forget about us and focus on those boys," she said. "You've got a stone-cold killer on your hands, one who could well be gunning for those kids. As far as a connection between these crimes and CJ Coleson's books, yeah, I can see some resemblances, but the motives are different, and none of the crimes in his books were connected the way these seem to be. Plus, you have two very different issues here: Chester's gold and the drugs. CJ's novels may all revolve around Prospect and Tate Silvers, but they aren't dependent one on the other. If CJ's afraid he'll get blamed for any of this, you can tell him to relax. It's probably just coincidental. While I hate putting anything down to that, sometimes, it's all you have."

"I keep thinking about what you said concerning the boys' safety. Maybe we should consider some kind of protective custody," he said, hoping to keep her talking. She seemed fine as long as they focused on the case.

"I agree." Her voice lacked the bite it had earlier.

He relaxed. Maybe she would forgive him after all.

"You'll have to consider how much information you want to put out there," she said. "If you let it be known that Chester struck it rich, you're courting disaster. The town's full of strangers here for Gold Rush Days. If they find out about the gold, it's going to cause all kinds of problems. And there's something else to keep in mind. Whoever killed Leon to protect himself won't hesitate to do it again. If those drugs are from one of the big Mexican cartels, they've got hired killers on the payroll who wouldn't even blink at any of this. They may have killed Chester, and who knows, maybe Trent found something in his uncle's stuff that led him to them. As unlikely as it may seem right now, Chester could've told someone about the mine. I'm going to go out on a limb and say Mr. Stone knows, and possibly Minerva. Why else would he have gone to see her? If someone knew he'd struck it rich, they could well want to keep the gold for themselves and those boys would definitely be in their way."

"True, and what you said just made me think of something else. Those fires we've had were all in the direct line of sight of that part of the mountain where I saw the helicopter." He hated to bring that up again, but now that the thought had come to him, he needed to hear it out loud to judge its merits. "I just assumed I was looking at the old, abandoned Skansen mines, but I could've been facing public land and other mining claims. When those houses were on fire, between the smoke and the flames, no one would've noticed anything going on up there."

"That's for sure, not that you had a lot of people watching, but it would definitely guarantee they didn't see anything else. Why was Monday different? People noticed them that night."

"Because there was no fire, and we had that unexpected meteor shower. We had that storm on Tuesday. Maybe the bad weather forced them to move up their schedule?"

"It's possible. When was the first fire?" she asked, her voice filling with interest once more.

"There was a fire about a year ago that we didn't connect to the recent ones since we know someone was camping nearby and didn't extinguish their campfire—"

"Wait. Did you say a year ago? Isn't that when the medical examiner said Leon fell?"

"You're right. Let's assume the fire theory holds, we had one in April, May, June, July and August, if you count Chester's place, all of them early in the week, but near the end of the month. It could be a regularly scheduled drop. Leon may well have died the night of that first fire if he'd gone back to wherever he'd seen that helicopter looking for more blackmail material. It's impossible to identify the individuals in the pictures we have."

"It's a good theory, but why wait nine months between the first one and the second one?" she challenged. "I don't think the fires are in any way connected to the drugs. You have no proof the helicopter was there those nights. No. Someone else is burning down those houses and once you find the people responsible, it'll all make sense. I suggest you focus on who stands to gain from the acquisition or sale of that land."

Before he could answer her, his volunteer firefighter beeper went off, and he pulled onto the side of the road.

"What was that? Why are we stopping?" she asked, a hint of nervousness in her voice.

She wanted honesty? She would get it.

"That was my volunteer firefighter beeper. I need to see where the fire is."

He pulled it out of his jeans and read the message, exhaling a sigh of relief.

"Well?" she asked nervously.

"It isn't another fire. There's a single car accident just this side of town. We aren't going to be able to get to your place without passing it. I'm sorry."

"No, that's fine. I understand."

Cole checked his mirrors and pulled back onto the road, worried that what they were about to see could be upsetting. They didn't usually call in the fire department for an accident unless the injuries were serious.

"It shouldn't be much farther. I can tell you I'm glad it isn't another fire. Most of the guys are still worn out from last night, and a tired firefighter can get hurt."

Casey didn't answer. Instead, she wrapped her arms around herself as if she were cold.

He turned down the AC.

Within minutes, the flares along the road indicated they'd reached the site of the accident. One of the town's police vehicles was parked across the road, a heavy rope attached to the tow bar beneath it. Whoever had responded to the call had closed off the road in both directions.

"Stay in the car. I know you might like to get a closer look, but you'll only be in the way. I'll come and check on you when I can. I don't know if you want to call your mother or not. It's after ten, and we could be here a while. You can try to sleep if you want to. The blanket's just on the seat if you get cold."

"I'll be fine, Cole. Go do what you have to do," she said and smiled weakly. "Be careful."

He wanted to kiss her, assure himself things between them were okay, but he doubted she would welcome the gesture here and now. Instead, he nodded and ran over to the engine where the boys were gearing up as they arrived. He had a job to do first, and then he'd try to figure out how to tell her the truth about CJ Coleson without completely destroying any chance they had at happiness.

"Where's Noah?" Cole asked as soon as he reached the fire engine.

"The chief's in Phoenix. Won't be back until tomorrow. Looks like you're wearing the white helmet tonight," Jason, Rita's husband, said. "I'm glad you made it. Otherwise, I would've had to, and I hate making the tough decisions." Even though they were all volunteers, they'd established a pecking order some years ago. Someone had to be in charge.

"All right then. Let's get this done," he said, adrenalin chasing his fatigue away.

After getting into his protective clothing, Cole hurried over to the police car parked about twenty feet away. "What have we got?" he asked Ramon, not seeing a vehicle on the road. "Don't tell me this is a hoax."

Hal stepped around the Jeep, brushing the dirt from his pants and jacket. "No, not a hoax. I wish it was. Ramon called me as soon as the 9 1 1 call came in. Christ, Cole, we've got the whole thing on tape. I listened to it twice on the way out here—heard her screams." He let out a deep, shaky breath. "Never want to hear anything like that again. It's Horace Stone and his wife. He called in a large, black SUV following them from Apache Junction. The vehicle was getting closer, behaving erratically. Horace assumed the driver was drunk, but I don't think so. This was intentional. I've been down there. The ambulance from Apache Junction is on its way, but I don't know if they'll get here fast enough ... I've called the ADPS station in Phoenix, asking them to have their officers on the lookout for a damaged, black SUV. It's all I can do without more information," he uttered the words bitterly, his anger barely under control. "The vehicle could've turned back or continued east. Hell, he might've even turned off into the wilderness or along one of the mining roads."

Cole gritted his teeth. Horace Stone was more than the town's lawyer. He was a close, personal friend, and knew the truth about CJ Coleson. If Casey's assumptions were correct, the lawyer might know who was at the bottom of this, and if this accident had been intentional, then someone didn't want the old man talking. Since according to Sylvia no one but Horace took care of Chester, he could easily take whatever information he had to the grave.

"What was he doing out here?"

"He was on his way back because of Chester's death. Sylvia called him, and he cut his vacation short. When I talked to him earlier tonight, he just said he had to take care of things. He sounded upset, but wouldn't say anything else. I just figured he took the news hard."

Cole followed Hal to the place where the car had gone off the road, down an embankment at least eight to ten feet deep. If someone had been following Horace, then they knew he was on his way back. How? Had Sylvia mentioned it to anyone? Cole stared at the tires. If Horace hadn't made that 9 1 1 call, it could've been days before anyone noticed the vehicle.

The forty-year old sedan, a collector's piece that had been Horace's pride and joy, sat on its roof. Even this high up, Cole could smell the gasoline leaking from the ruptured tank. Whoever had forced it off the road and down the embankment had probably expected the old automobile to blow up the way cars did in Hollywood movies, but such explosions rarely occurred in real life. Given the fumes surrounding the vehicle, it would only take a spark to turn it into a burning death trap. The biggest danger at the moment, the one the Stones and Hal faced, was the one caused by direct inhalation of the gasoline fumes which could result in carbon monoxide poisoning and damage to the nose, throat, and lungs.

Wide awake now, Cole reached out and grabbed Hal's shoulder. "Wait. You can't go down there without a mask and tank. Jason," he called, "we've got gasoline leaking pretty badly. Get the suppression powder and a couple of oxygen units for down there and one for Hal. We'll need backboards and collars, but I don't know if we can get them out on our own. That's an old roof and may not hold up too well. The ambulance is on the way."

"Got it."

As soon as Hal was masked, he and Cole descended the rope to the car. The ground was soft and mucky, and thanks to last night's rain, the mud sucked at Cole's boots, slowing his steps.

"Horace, can you hear me?" he asked, bending down to talk to the lawyer partially hanging by his seatbelt inside the overturned vehicle.

The windows had shattered when the car had rolled, and now the roof seemed to be compressing from the additional weight it supported. How many times had he suggested Horace trade his car for something newer, but the man was an antique car buff and wouldn't hear of it. The only concession he'd made had been installing top-notch seat belts for the front seats as mandated by state law.

Stepping back a few feet, he yelled up the embankment. "I need something to reinforce the roof." He turned to Hal. "Stay here and don't touch the vehicle. The body of the car could collapse on them at any minute. My men know what to do."

Not waiting for an answer, Cole turned back to the car and checked Horace's carotid pulse. It was strong and steady, but there was a substantial amount of blood on his clothes. While most of it was probably from the cut on his face, Cole couldn't dismiss the possibility of another open wound or internal injuries. The lawyer opened one eye, the other swollen shut no doubt from the impact with the door frame.

"Clara ... How's Clara?" he whispered, his eye closing once more.

"Stay with me, Horace." Cole placed one of the oxygen masks Jason had given him over the man's mouth and nose. "You need this right now. Jason's going to look after you while I take care of Clara. Just breathe normally."

Cole let Jason attend to the injured man, and moving around the car, he reached into the vehicle, found Clara's pulse, but it was thready. Given that her seatbelt had torn, she'd fallen onto the roof, and now lay in a mixture of mud and her own blood. Hopefully, there was more mud than blood, and she wasn't on the verge of hypovolemic shock. It would be impossible to know for sure until they could properly assess her injuries.

He did the best he could to fit her with an oxygen mask, and relief filled him when he heard the wail of an ambulance approaching, getting louder by the second, and stopping abruptly as it arrived.

"We need to get the body of the car off the roof so the paramedics can do their jobs. Has the gasoline been covered?" he asked.

"Yes," Jason said, "and the guys are on their way with the saw and the suppression blankets."

Thirty tense minutes later, Horace had been released from his seatbelt, and the body of the car cut away from the roof, pulled back like the lid on a tin of sardines. The paramedics strapped Clara to the stretcher and motioned for the firefighters to hoist it out of the mud. Jason and Cole stabilized Horace and waited beside the now unconscious man. As soon as the metal cable reached them, he turned to Jason.

"Let's do this," he answered, knowing more was at stake than his fellow firefighter could possibly imagine.

Fifteen minutes later, the second ambulance left, taking Horace to Apache Junction. Exhaustion weighing heavily on him now that the job was finished, Cole removed his equipment and stored it in the truck. In the morning, he would go to the police station, and explain everything Casey had told him. Hal would be relieved to know the evidence they had probably wouldn't be enough to act on, but Gunderson was such an ass he might insist on it. Without a lawyer in town, the boys would get sent to Phoenix, and everyone knew a lot of bad things could happen in juvenile hall. There had to be something they could do to prevent that. If Horace Stone died, those boys were the only ones who knew the truth.

The scream of the metal winch pulling the vehicle out of the mud echoed loudly in the late night silence, reminding him that, until they had a suspect and a motive for these crimes, no one was safe.

Following the others who'd arrived at the scene by truck or car, Cole had almost reached his SUV when Hal stepped over to him.

"Cole, I know this is the last thing you want to hear after the two days we've had, but I need you at the station in the morning," the police chief said, running his hand through his hair before replacing his worn Stetson. He'd never looked so old and tired. His eyes were puffy, his forehead wrinkled in concern, and his lips pursed. It was as if he carried the weight of the world on his shoulders.

Cole could identify with that since he felt much the same way. "Sure, I'll be there, say around eight? I've got Casey in the car. I need to get her home and then get some sleep."

"I know, but we've got to talk," Hal continued, his voice betraying his disquiet. "The techs should have an ID on those prints from the Morris place, and Leon's landlady is meeting with the sketch artist in the morning. I'll have them go through Trent's apartment with a fine-toothed comb. But we've got a problem. Those kids didn't do this. None of them drive." He held up what looked like a cigarette package with a partially burned book of matches attached to it. "Hansen found this near the back of the wreckage when he attached the hoist. We were only a few minutes behind the accident. The sirens probably scared the perps away before they could finish the job. Lucky for Horace and Clara, this landed in a puddle of water not gasoline. Why the hell would someone want to kill Horace Stone?"

"Because of what he knows about Chester," Cole answered, quickly filling him in on the conversation he'd had with Casey, omitting the argument and her accusations. That was a personal matter as was the truth about CJ Coleson.

"According to Clay, that fire last night started with a lit cigarette dropped onto an old couch. Something's been bothering me ever since Clay took me through the fire sequence and I just realized what it is. I've never seen Chester smoke. I don't know why I didn't realize that earlier. Could be whoever did that, did this."

"By God, you're right," Hal said, shaking his head. "He used to, but it's been years since I've seen him light up."

"You've got to talk to those boys."

Hal's frown deepened. "Son of a bitch! Someone's made sure I can't. I made arrangements to see them at the station at half-past ten, but without a lawyer ... I can ask the parents to waive their rights to an attorney, but..." He shrugged. "Maybe if I can convince them the boys are in danger, they'll let me talk to them off the record."

"It's a possibility. If my son was in danger, I would move heaven and earth to keep him safe. We have to find a way to protect them, at least until we can talk to Horace and get to the bottom of this."

"I agree. I'll have to think of something. Take Casey to her parents' house and then go home and get some sleep. I'll see you around eight. I'm going to have Hansen go over the car tonight and get those paint scrapings to the lab as soon as possible. By then I should have the prognosis on Horace and the information about the prints and the mescal—not that any of that information will make much difference based on what Casey said, but you never know. If any of this hits the fan, we're going to need more help this weekend."

"I'll see you in the morning," Cole said and yawned.

Cole left Hal and covered the distance to his vehicle quickly. Casey was asleep on the front seat, the blanket draped over her. She woke as soon as he opened the door.

"Is it true? Does that car belong to Horace Stone?"

Knowing better than to lie to her again, he nodded.

"He and Clara are in bad shape, but still alive. This was deliberate, Casey. Horace made a 9 1 1 call. If he hadn't, they'd both be dead by now. I think you're right, and if you are, those boys are definitely targets."

"My God. Whoever's behind this has to be getting

desperate."

"I know. Hal spoke to Horace. They were on their way back because of Chester's death. He definitely knows something, but damned if I can figure out what it is. My brain's fried."

Casey rubbed the sleep out of her eyes.

"So is mine. What's Hal going to do?"

"He's hoping to get permission to talk to the kids. Before we go off halfcocked, we need to know what they do know. It could be something, or we might just be whistling into the wind. We want to show them the pictures Leon had in his safety deposit box. If they recognize the mesa, maybe they can take us there."

"You could set a trap."

He nodded. "We could station someone there to watch for signs of activity, and maybe track the chopper."

"And if they don't know where it is?"

"Then we need to know what they can tell us about the gold. Either way, I think they could be in trouble."

"I agree," she said, her voice filled with concern. "Do you have any idea where we could stash them until this is all cleared up?"

He chewed his lower lip, knowing he was about to dig himself into an even bigger hole, but it couldn't be helped.

"CJ Coleson has a cabin on Apache Lake. It's isolated, and he sometimes goes there to work on his books or to relax."

She frowned. "That must be where you meet with him, not in Fortune. No wonder he knows so much about this area. Is he there now?"

"No, but I know where he keeps the keys. The place has four bedrooms. We could take the boys there. Maybe ask their parents to help watch them since I've got to work."

"You want to entrust Rick Harvey with his son's safety? He could be right in the middle of this. I forgot to mention Eddy had a nasty case of post-nasal drip when I saw him, but I doubt he had a cold. He and the other two were suspected of doing drugs back in high school, but if they were, they were good at hiding the signs." Although both drunk and high would explain but not excuse Rick's behavior that night.

"You think he might be using?"

She nodded. "I'd bet the farm on it. And giving his supplier a safe place to land might get him a deal on the product. I'd like to have my investigator dig into the five men—Leon, Trent, Chester, Eddy, and Rick. He's discreet, and the best damn gumshoe there is."

"I suppose it can't hurt, but you should run it by Hal first. He's in charge, not me. As far as Rick goes, he's rarely around on the weekends, and I'm sure Kristal would be only too glad to keep the secret if her son's life depended on it. I know you've got issues with Kristal and Rick, but Kyle's a great kid. You know what they say: you can choose your friends, but you can't choose your relatives. Now, we've got to get out of here. I'm bushed, and I'm sure you are, too. We both need sleep."

He put the car in gear and joined the line of vehicles moving away from the accident scene. Somehow he would have to tell her the truth about CJ Coleson, but damned if he knew how to do it without destroying the tenuous relationship they had.

Pulling into her driveway, he stopped the SUV, and she opened the door, jumping out of the vehicle quickly. He lowered his window.

"Casey, are we going to be okay?"

She stopped and turned toward him. "I honestly don't know. I need to think about this. Any relationship between us would be a tough one since you're here, and I'll be in Santa Fe. At the moment, I feel a little raw. You withheld vital information from me and lied about those engine sounds I heard—maybe not lied exactly. It was more like you made fun of it, but the end product is the same. You deceived me. I had time to think about what you did while you rescued Horace and Clara. While I still don't like what you did, I can understand why you think you needed to do it. The most important aspect of a relationship for me is trust, and I'm not sure we have that. Goodnight, Cole. I'll call Hal in the morning. I really think Ryan would be a big help here."

She turned around and climbed the stairs, never looking back.

Cole pulled back onto the road, feeling more depressed than ever. Mom had warned him women didn't like being lied to, but he'd done it with the best intentions, hadn't he? He'd wanted to protect her and not scare her.

And what do they say about good intentions? his conscience asked.

"The road to hell is paved with them," Cole answered, his voice echoing in the vehicle. "And once she discovers I'm CJ Coleson ... This is not going to end well, and it's all my fault."

CHAPTER NINETEEN

Disheartened, Casey unlocked the door, punched in the code, and then reset the system after she was inside and the door was locked again. It was well past midnight, and everyone was in bed. She wished she could talk to someone about the way she felt right now, but that would mean waking Randy, and she had to be at work in the morning.

As quietly as she could, Casey climbed the stairs to her room, got undressed, and dropped into bed, hoping to get a few hours of sleep. She tossed and turned, recalling the argument she'd had with Cole. While she was sure he hadn't meant to hurt her, it didn't make the pain she felt any easier to bear. She'd foolishly set herself up for a fall, believing Cole was different, a man who wouldn't lie to hurt, but in the end, he had.

The memories she'd revisited in the desert the previous night haunted her sleep, and it was still pitch dark when she sat up, tears running down her cheeks once more. Since no one was clamoring to get into the room, she couldn't have cried out, and that was a good thing.

Repressed memories. How many times had psychiatrists used that term to explain someone's behavior? She might not be a frightened virgin any longer, but that night had damaged her in ways even she hadn't understood until now. No matter whom she'd dated, she'd always been able to find fault with them, something that guaranteed she wouldn't have to open her heart and trust them. Rick had lied to her, pretended to like her, presumed she would enjoy his despicable attention, when all he'd wanted to do was humiliate her. Tonight, she'd seen Cole do the same thing. He'd lied to her, presumed he knew what was best for her. He'd humiliated her in his own way by reminding her of her own short-comings. How could they ever have a relationship if she couldn't trust him? If she was always waiting for him to deceive her, or hurt her in some way? Turning over, she buried her face in the pillow and cried herself to sleep.

It was just after eight when she headed down the stairs, the slight throbbing at her temples a vivid reminder of the unsettled night she'd had. Knowing she needed to call Hal, she procrastinated, not in the mood to talk to anyone yet. There was always a possibility Cole might answer the phone at the police station. Maybe after a jolt of caffeine she would be able to hear his voice, but at this moment, she was too disconcerted to consider it.

The few hours of sleep she'd gotten had been filled with contradictory images and dreams. After the nightmare, she'd relived their argument, but instead of it ending as it had, thanks to her conscience, he'd presented a litany of all the lies of omission she'd told over the last fifteen years, leaving her guilt-ridden and more conflicted than ever.

"Morning, Dad. Hi, Jaxon," she said, trying to sound cheery. Reaching for a mug and the carafe of coffee, she poured herself a cup. "Where's Mom?"

"Gone to deliver the last of Sunday's costumes, and then she's joining her friends at Minerva Skansen's. Ms. Minerva is all broken up about Chester's death, and they've gone to cheer her up as well as box the last of the items she wants to donate to the town as part of the Skansen Legacy. Maria claims there are all kinds of treasures in those boxes including some artwork worth thousands. I can't see greedy little Eddy being any too happy about that."

"I saw him yesterday," she said and frowned. "The last thing I would call him is 'little' Eddy. He claimed the house was a mess, a hoarder's paradise."

Her father chuckled. "Your mother said something similar. I guess the attic was crammed to the rafters. It's amazing how much stuff one accumulates during a lifetime, and since she has several generations of stuff in there with her…"

"It would look like hoarding to someone with no appreciation for the past."

"Or someone who wants to discredit her. I was talking to Juan at the barbershop, and he was saying Eddy tells anyone who'll listen that his aunt is losing her marbles. No one believes him, but you know, say it often enough and people will start to wonder about her."

"Ms. Minerva lost her marbles? I can give her some of mine," Jaxon said. "I got doubles."

Casey chuckled. "That's nice of you, but these are different marbles."

He shrugged and went back to eating.

"I feel sorry for her," her father said. "She's been alone for years, obeying her father's wishes. Your mother and I saw her sitting near the band shell with Chester a couple of weeks ago, and we thought she might be spending her golden years with the man she loved, but it doesn't look that way now."

"Cole mentioned Ms. Skansen and Chester had been engaged at one time."

"They were. They'd both gone to school in Phoenix and had fallen in love. Most people don't remember Chester had a degree in history. He asked Minerva to marry him and she agreed, but when they went to see her father, he was furious. His only daughter wasn't going to marry some penniless teacher. His word was law, and a tearful Minerva sent Chester away. He promised he'd come back for her when he'd met her father's challenge. I don't think they ever spoke to one another after that. I know your mother and I were surprised when we saw them together."

"But why? Mr. Skansen died before I was born."

"I know," he said and nodded, "but even in death, Minerva wouldn't disobey her father, and Chester was too stubborn to walk away from a challenge. He probably would've made good money teaching, but he was determined to find the gold he needed to claim her heart. I doubt he found it, but as we get older, we realize that we don't have as much time as we thought we did. It changes us. I'm glad they started seeing one another again, but now, she'll be in more pain than ever. Life's too short to put love and happiness on hold. You look tired. Late night?"

"Yeah. There was an accident on the highway, and Cole got called in to help." She added cream and sugar to her coffee and drank deeply, his words about Minerva and Chester preying on her mind. Such a tragedy, especially now when Chester had found the gold he needed to win her hand.

He nodded, his mouth compressed. "I heard about it on the news this morning," he said, his voice betraying his anxiety. "It must've been a bad one if the called in the fire department. They haven't released the names of those involved."

"Yeah, the car went off the road into a ditch. I stayed in the SUV while the firefighters got them out," she answered, realizing she was lying by omission once more. Maybe she needed to rethink this moral high ground of hers before the quicksand engulfed her, and like Ms. Minerva she would be left with only a few bittersweet memories in her old age. She would have to apologize to Cole for losing her temper last night, but humble pie wasn't one of her favorites.

She turned to Jaxon. "Did you sleep well?"

The child nodded, as he spooned cereal into his mouth. "And I had no bad dreams."

"That's good. No one likes bad dreams," she agreed, wishing her sleep had been as uneventful.

"Have they handed out the agenda for Sunday's activities yet?" she asked, wanting to avoid discussing the accident, Chester, Minerva, and anything else that had her feeling sad and unsettled. Talking about the big day and thinking about that gorgeous costume would lift her spirits.

"Yes. It's printed in this week's edition of the *Fortune Examiner*. The mayor will make his usual welcome speech and give the microphone to Minerva. I'm assuming she'll go through with her special announcement about all the stuff the women have been moving from her place to the town museum—you know, one of those surprises everyone knows already. There will only be two speeches this year. Talk about a bonus. Your mother has three pies in the contest. She placed second last year to Hal Rankin's wife and is sure she can take first this time around. There'll be the usual games and races for the kids, and we'll have some gold panning, courtesy of Skansen Mining who've donated a scoop of dirt pulled out of *Lucky Seven*. Then, we'll have the picnic basket auction. Randy's refused to put one in—what about you? I'm sure Cole would bid on it," he said and winked.

"I'm not sure I'll do that. I've never been too keen on that aspect of the celebration. You never know who might bid on the basket just to get free legal advice."

Her father frowned. "Did you and Cole have an argument?" he asked.

"Not exactly an argument," she admitted, "more like a reality check. I mean as a couple, we're a bit of a stretch, especially since I won't be living in Fortune, and he came back specifically to live here." But her heart wanted them to be a couple, even if her brain insisted otherwise.

The doorbell rang.

Saved by the bell.

"I'll get it." She hurried from the kitchen, grateful to whoever was at the door. The last thing she wanted to do was discuss Cole with her father. "Coming," she called, raising her voice.

Her heart leapt into her throat when she opened the front door, stunned to see Cole standing there, dressed in his police uniform, looking tired still, but so handsome and desirable that she ached. Clenching her fists to keep from reaching out to him, she turned her attention to the man beside him.

Given the number of stars on the epaulettes of his uniform, this man had to be the chief of police. While he was almost as tall as Cole, and had to outweigh him by forty pounds of solid muscle, he had steel-gray hair and a prominent chin. CJ Coleson must've used him as the model for Tate Silvers. This man didn't look like he would take crap from anyone. She could picture him swaggering down the main street, gun belt strapped to his legs, ready to defend whoever needed him. He removed his Stetson and mirrored sunglasses and smiled at her.

"Ms. Stevens, I'm Hal Rankin, Fortune's chief of police. Can we come in? I need to talk to you and would rather not do it on the veranda."

"Of course." She'd given Cole all of the answers he could possibly need last night, so unless something else had happened, why were they here? "I was just going to call you. I don't know if Cole mentioned it, but I think my investigator would be a big help here. You have too many unanswered questions." She stepped aside to let them into the vestibule.

"He told me, and I think it's a good idea. The department has money to pay for his services, too."

She nodded. Ryan might be able to give them a starting point. There was no one better at digging up the kind of information people liked to hide. If Eddy was into drugs, he would find out. She didn't know how he did it, but he never ceased to amaze her.

"I'll contact him as soon as I can. Was there something else?" she asked, when he didn't appear ready to leave.

Cole played with the brim of his Stetson and looked guilty as sin. She frowned. What had he done now?

"I need your help," Hal said, pulling her attention away from Cole. "This won't take long, I promise."

"Who is it, honey?" her father called from the kitchen.

"Chief Rankin and Cole, Dad," she answered, knowing it would probably bring him into the living room, and she was right.

Jaxon followed behind his grandfather and raced over to Cole. "I watched the whole movie. From now on it's my favorite."

Her father chuckled. "Those little guys have deposed Batman, and believe me that's quite a feat."

"I'll bet," Cole said. "Heroes aren't easy to replace."

He glanced at her, and she looked away.

Her father examined the two men and scowled. "Jaxon, why don't you go up to your room and watch it again while we talk?"

"Can I take some cookies up, too?" the child asked eagerly.

"Only two."

The boy ran into the kitchen, and then seconds later raced up the stairs.

"He's probably got more than two, but that'll keep him busy for a while. Now, what can we do for you today?" Her dad stood next to her. "Judging by the look on your faces, it's serious. Come into the living room. Maria and Randy won't be back for at least a couple more hours."

"I'll get some coffee," Casey said, wanting to get away from Cole if only for a minute. Part of her longed to reach out to him, soothe his furrowed brow, and feel his arms around her, but her common sense told her giving in to that need would only hurt them both. Trust and honesty were the cornerstone of any relationship. During the night, one thing had become clear to her. Until she could tell him the real reason why she couldn't stay in Fortune, there could be no future for them.

Ten minutes later, Casey entered the living room, carrying a tray with coffee, mugs, cream and sugar, and a plateful of chocolate chip cookies. With her emotions firmly under control she assumed the lawyer persona that came to her rescue in difficult situations like these. The three men stood by the fireplace admiring the family pictures on the mantel.

Cole hurried over to take the heavily laden tray from her and placed it on the coffee table.

"Thank you," she said softly, pulling back quickly when his

fingers touched hers, sending a torrent of need cascading through her. Why couldn't her body understand what her brain told it?

Hal's voice pulled her back before she could humiliate herself by throwing herself into Cole's arms.

"You're the spitting image of your Irish grandmother," he said, "but from what my wife tells me, you don't have her temper. The whole town's talking about how well you handled Kristal Harvey the other day. When Rick's on a tear—and that happens more and more lately—she's insufferable. My daughter Ella's a psychiatric nurse and claims being a bitch is Kristal's coping mechanism. If it is, I would say she's coping quite nicely. If you can keep calm around that woman, you must be a hell of an opponent in court."

"I've been told I'm good at what I do. I seem to be able to sift through the bullshit and get to the truth," she answered curtly, but felt her cheeks heat at her father's frown.

Way to go, Casey. The man's just being friendly. No need to bite his head off. Especially when he wasn't the one to blame for her foul mood.

"How do you take your coffee, Chief Rankin?" she asked, hoping she sounded friendlier.

"Black, thanks, and call me Hal. There's no need for formalities here."

She poured the dark brew into one of the mugs and handed it to him, automatically fixing Cole's and her father's before offering them their mugs.

Hal dropped his Stetson onto the chair behind him and reached for a cookie on the tray.

"Let's sit down," he said, before taking a bite. "I'm on the clock here. Casey, you know how serious the accident was last night."

"You know who was involved? Why didn't you say so?" her father scolded.

"Because it wasn't my call," she said, defending her own lie of omission.

"I see," her dad answered, but the censure in his eyes remained.

He dropped onto the couch beside her. Cole sat across from them, and while sitting had been Hal's suggestion, he stood.

"How are they?" she asked.

Hal shook his head and swallowed his cookie before taking a mouthful of coffee.

"Alive, but in serious condition." His face mirrored his concern. "The AJPD are providing around the clock security."

"Isn't that a bit unusual?" her father asked.

Hal paced. "It is, but in this case, it's necessary. Austin, what I'm about to say is confidential. If I thought I could ask you to leave us right now, I would, but knowing you as I do, you would undoubtedly stay close enough to hear everything anyway."

"Probably," her father admitted and shrugged. "My house, my rules. You have my word I won't say anything. Now, what the hell's going on?"

Hal explained about the accident. "I spoke to the hospital. Horace's spleen was damaged and had to be removed. His heart stopped during surgery, but they brought him back. Unfortunately for us, they're keeping him heavily sedated for a few days, so we won't be able to talk to him until Monday at the earliest. Clara has a broken arm and some severely bruised ribs. She was cut up pretty badly, but she's holding her own. She'll be sore for a while, but it isn't anything they can't treat."

"My God," her father said, his face a mask of horror. "This has to be a mistake. Are you saying someone deliberately tried to kill Horace?"

"I am, and believe me, that fact scares the daylights out of me. Horace is the heart and soul of this town," Hal stated. "For the past forty years, he's handled every legal aspect of the lives of most of the citizens of Fortune. He's drawn wills, created business and company contracts, negotiated settlements, looked after house purchases and land transfers, handled mining claims and patents—you name it. He's also the lawyer I call if I have a detainee who requests one. Without him, this town is in a hell of a fix." He stepped over and stood in front of her. "I understand Horace was looking for a partner, and offered that position to you."

"That's right, but I said no," she answered, annoyed that Cole would mention something she'd confided in him during a private conversation. No wonder he looked nervous. This was the second time he'd betrayed her trust.

"I'm aware of that, but I'm asking for your help. I want you to reconsider and take over from Horace."

Casey choked on a mouthful of coffee, and stared at him.

"No way. I'm not staying here for the rest of my life," she said belligerently.

"I'm not asking you to," Hal snapped back. "I'm sorry. I need you to step into Horace's shoes, only as long as it takes to get him back on his feet and get this mess settled." He ran his hand through his hair and huffed out a frustrated breath. "If the idea was to deprive the town of a lawyer, your presence will change that. I'm hoping whoever's behind this will panic and make a mistake—force his hand, if you will. Without a lawyer available, I'm in a hell of a mess. I can't question any suspects. Hell, I can't even talk to those kids, and you know I have to do that. If Gunderson decides to charge them, and we don't have a lawyer available here, they'll get sent to Phoenix. If you're right, they won't make it there."

She nodded, subdued by Hal's passion and what he was saying. "You can't be sure of that. You're talking collusion between your prosecutor and whoever's behind all this."

"Until I know who's behind this, I'm not dismissing anyone."

Casey frowned. "Fine. Due process guarantees the accused the right to representation. While I can probably help you out with new cases, I can't touch Horace's clients without his permission. Cole mentioned those kids had been in to see him with Chester ... Until I can be sure he doesn't represent them in some way, as far-fetched as that may sound, it would be a violation of ethics." She shrugged her shoulders.

"I understand, but Horace did ask you to reconsider your refusal, right?" Hal asked tenaciously. He was like a dog with a bone, unwilling to let this go.

She nodded, not certain she knew where Hal was going with this, but fairly certain she wasn't going to like it.

"Then, I'm going to assume that if you said yes, he would welcome you on board. It wouldn't be a reach to think he would be happy to have your help right now, especially if his clients were involved, and I consider that his permission. Since this is an emergency, Judge Ambrose agrees with my assessment. Jethro is more than satisfied with your credentials and will accept you as Horace's replacement in all matters until Horace can say otherwise. That speaks to the intent if not the word of the law."

If the judge was satisfied with the legality of the matter, who was she to argue? Besides, after she'd learned about her dad's health, she'd considered staying here a couple of weeks longer. Hadn't she thought about offering her services? This might just mean staying longer than she'd expected to, but the odds were Horace wouldn't be out of commission for more than six weeks. Could she do it? Could she be around Cole that long and hold firm to her decision?

"I'm not saying I'll do it, but if I did, what would you like me to do first?"

"I need to talk to those boys, find out what they know, and then put them into protective custody in case you're right and they're in danger. I understand you and Cole have discussed this and have come up with a possible solution."

"We have. He suggested moving the kids and some of their parents to a secure location out of town. In most cases, parents can be as protective as any rent-a-cops we might hire. If we needed to bring in muscle, I can think of a couple of marines who could help."

Hal nodded. "If push comes to shove, we may need them.

I'll be damned if anyone else in this town is going to die. These cases remind me of the maze puzzles I used to do as a kid. I never had trouble figuring them out. I've got six paths leading to my perp, and I can only go so far on each before I hit a brick wall.

"Six paths? I assume that's an analogy for the crimes? Why six?" her dad asked.

"Three deaths, the fires, the attempted murder, and the three boys who may be targets. I'm convinced everything is related—I just don't know how. Come Monday, I need to talk to Eddy Ramos and Rick Harvey about Trent Gibb's death, but apparently they're both out of town this weekend."

"Trent Gibbs is dead?" her father interrupted once more. "He called me to see if the university was interested in acquiring a rare nineteenth century edition of the Dramatic Works of William Shakespeare that belonged to his uncle. I suppose with Leon dead … He wanted to meet on Friday, but since Casey was coming home, I put him off to next week."

"Now, that's interesting," Hal commented, one eyebrow raised in question. "When did he call?"

"About a week ago, maybe a few days more. Why does that matter?"

"Because at that time, we didn't have a positive identification of Leon's remains, and the only way he could know his uncle was dead was if he was involved in it," Cole answered, speaking for the first time. His brow was furrowed, making him look even more tired. "What would that book be worth?"

"If it was in the shape he said it was, he could get at least twelve thousand dollars for it. I wondered why Leon had hung onto it after the mine closed, but if they'd been a family heirloom—those are the last things you sell."

Casey thought of the land her father sold to cover the cost of her education, and guilt flooded her once more.

"We learned yesterday that Trent and a friend had been using his uncle's apartment, and were possibly embezzling from the old man's account as well. Selling off Leon's property without his knowledge would be tricky unless he knew he would never get caught," Hal said, his lips pursed.

"Or figured he could convince his uncle not to press charges, but I see what you mean. How did Trent die?" her father asked, his face furrowed with concern.

Casey noted how red he was. If Mom were here, she would be furious that they'd involved him like this.

"He was shot in the back about a week ago," Hal answered, "and then decapitated. I figure it's someone playing with that Apache curse, but I can't dismiss the idea Trent might've gotten himself in trouble over gambling debts. Some Mexican cartels have been known to decapitate their victims. If it hadn't been for those hikers who were forced to go around some fallen rock, thanks to Monday's quakes, the body would still be out there feeding the animals."

"That's terrible," her father said, his voice barely a whisper.

Casey bit her lip. Maybe they needed to move this conversation downtown sooner rather than later. She knew her father could keep a secret, but how much was Hal willing to let him know?

CHAPTER TWENTY

Cole saw the questioning look on Casey's face and knew she had reservations about what Hal was about to share, but her father had just given them a lead, as slight as it might be. If Trent was selling off Leon's belongings, then they might have a better timeline for Leon's murder.

Hal ran his hand through his hair. "A good chunk of police work involves examining evidence and theorizing about it. Sometimes those theories pan out; at other times, they don't, and you have to go back to the beginning and reexamine what you have. In this case, whoever's behind this has us all running after our tails. I'm convinced everything is connected. Greed is the most powerful motive of all. If Chester wasn't killed for the gold, he was killed because he knew something that was even more valuable than those rocks were."

"Gold? What gold?" Austin asked, his face redder than ever. "I feel like Rip Van Winkle—as if I've been asleep for years while my world changed."

Cole didn't miss the concern on Casey's face. Was her father ill? Hal didn't seem to notice anything wrong.

"Austin, you can't breathe a word of this. Chester struck it rich," Hal said. "There was more than one hundred thousand dollars' worth of gold at his place."

"So that's why he and Minerva were together. Well, I'll be

damned."

"Dad, calm down, please? You need to relax," Casey begged. "As Hal said, Chester found gold—lots of gold—somewhere on Superstition Mountain. Maybe he struck a new vein, but given the other objects they found at his place, he may have found Peralta's mine."

"You've got to be kidding me," he said and shook his head. "And just like those who've found it before, he didn't live to enjoy it. There's a hell of a curse on that mine. More than one hundred and fifty years later, it's as strong as ever."

"I don't believe an ancient curse had anything to do with this," Hal stated, his jaw stuck out stubbornly. "Someone murdered Chester and tried to kill Horace and Clara. We think it's the same person. We just need to figure out who and why. If it wasn't for Chester's gold, something I believe Horace knew all about, then it has to do with what's been happening on the mountain and—"

"Are you saying Chester's death wasn't an accident?" Austin interrupted once more, his color fading to a pasty white.

Casey reached for his hand and tried to calm him again, and Cole wished he could do the same for her. The pulse at the base of her throat throbbed visibly.

"That's exactly what I'm saying," Hal said. "Chester was poisoned, and then the house was set afire to cover the original crime. I'll know more after Hal talks to the boys. That's why I need Casey's help. Whoever killed that old man may be responsible for those mysterious lights on the mountain."

"My God!" Casey jumped up and wrung her hands. "Monsters with red eyes in the desert. I just put it together. When did Jaxon start having trouble sleeping at night?"

"About fifteen months ago. What does this have to do with that?" Her father's confusion was genuine and matched the looks on Hal's face and no doubt his own.

"What are you talking about, Casey?" he asked.

"Jaxon's developed this intense fear of the dark. You saw the way he clung to Randy on the veranda last night. Mom was telling me that if he wakes up during the night, they have a hell of a time getting him back to sleep. His window faces south, and he claims there are red-eyed monsters on the mountain. He's seen the helicopter. I'm sure of it. That's the only thing that makes sense."

"What helicopter? What the hell's going on? Can someone please start at the beginning?"

Hal nodded. "Why not? Maybe if we go through it, step by step, we'll find something we've missed. A little over a year ago, we had a fire out on the old Skansen mine road..." Hal related all of the events in chronological order ending with Horace's accident last night. "We have to get to the bottom of this before someone else dies. It's like an elaborate variation on a game of *Clue*—Leon, on Superstition Mountain, with a push, Trent, on Weaver's Needle, with a gun, Chester, in his bedroom, with poison. Hell, last night, we almost had Horace and Clara, on the Apache Trail, with a car. And God alone knows how the fires fit in, but those helicopters have to be behind some, if not all our troubles. So, I'll ask you again. Will you help us out, Casey? I know it's a lot to ask—"

"No, she won't," her father interjected. "I'm sorry, Hal, but I've been listening to everything you've both said as well as to what you haven't. I may want my daughter to come home, but not now—not like this. Whoever's behind this may have killed three people and tried to kill Horace, and you want Casey to step into his shoes, where she could easily become the next target. I won't let you place her in danger."

"Austin, listen to me. Hal and I had this argument earlier. Do you think I want to endanger her? Of course not, but I can't think of any other way to deal with this right now. I won't leave her side. People won't have a problem with that once word gets out that we're a couple. She's been seen going into the emporium at least twice, and Mom's told at least a dozen people she was at the house Tuesday night. I'm sorry, Casey, but you know how the grapevine works."

She nodded, but she didn't look happy about it.

"People can add in this town," Hal continued. "While one and one sometimes ends up three, we can use that to our advantage. Cole will be camping out here in your living room at night. If I could send you, Maria, Jaxon, and Randy some place safe, I would, but considering what weekend this is, if you four aren't here, it would tip our hand. We can't have the bastard skipping town for a while and coming back later. It has to end now."

"I won't let anything happen to her. You have my word on that," Cole added. He would protect her with his life if he had to.

"Dad, this is my decision," Casey said, staring her father in the eye until he nodded, anything but pleased. She turned to Hal. "When do you need me to start?"

"In an hour. I arranged for the boys to be at the station by ten-thirty," he said. "We'll tell the families Horace is on extended vacation. No point in putting him and Clara in any more danger."

"I'll be there. One more thing. I won't endanger my family, which means I won't stay here. If Cole is going to be my bodyguard, then you need to find me a safe place to stay for as long as this drags on, and a way to salvage my reputation when you do. The last thing I want is the people of this town commenting on my lack of morals."

"Don't be ridiculous, Casey. This is your home," Austin said. "We've got an alarm system, and if Cole's on the couch—"

"Dad, think about it," she interrupted, sounding more confident. "Mom and Randy can't know about any of this right now. How long do you think we could keep this from them if Cole never left my side? Even the world's most ardent fiancé leaves to go home at night."

Her father nodded, not happy with her decision, but understanding it.

Cole stood, the germ of an idea taking root in his mind. "I'm really sorry about involving you in this, Casey, but I *will* keep you safe. You have my word on it, and whether you believe it or not, my word is my bond. As far as a way to protect your reputation, you've just nailed it. Since we're supposed to be a couple, let's go one step farther and tell people we're engaged."

His eyes pleaded with her to go along with him. This could solve a lot of their problems if she gave it a chance.

"Are you frigging nuts?" she exclaimed. "Engaged after five days? No one will believe that." Her shocked voice dropped to a mere whisper.

Her stunned reaction didn't do a hell of a lot for his self-esteem, but Cole was sure he could make this work to his advantage.

Hal chuckled. "I wouldn't be too sure about that. Old Cole here hasn't had a date with anyone since he moved back to Fortune, and yet he's been with you three days in a row. You, on the other hand, haven't been home in fifteen years. You were both at school in Texas. He leaves for parts unknown on a regular basis. Who's to say he hasn't gone to see you? People believe what they want to believe. A dying man in the desert imagines he sees water. Even though it's really sand, he tries to drink it. I've seen it before, and no doubt I'll see it again."

Cole reached for her hand and noted the way she trembled. "Casey, I know how you feel about lying, but think of this as a sting operation. If there were any other way we could lure the killer out, we would. We need to catch whoever's behind this, but we have to keep you safe. It's the twenty-first century. Lots of engaged couples move in together, even in Fortune."

"He's right," Hal said. "My daughter Ella lives with her fiancé, and no one's made any negative comments—not even Heidi or Kristal. Ella and Joel will be married next spring. It's a good, believable cover."

"Mom and Randy won't buy it. Neither will your parents," she argued.

"My parents may be easier to convince than you think," Cole admitted, knowing she wasn't going to like what he had to say. "They saw us together Tuesday night, and yesterday I told them I was looking for a house. The agent at Apache Trail Realty will attest to that. If I gave Mom the least bit of encouragement, she would be over here in a flash asking to help pick out linens and china patterns. I was supposed to see the house tomorrow, but we can both go and see it later this afternoon."

"And as far as your mother and Randy go, leave them to me," Austin said, obviously on board with the idea. "If you're determined to put yourself in harm's way. I can keep your mother off your back. We have to go into Phoenix this afternoon, and Randy and Jaxon are coming with us. I was supposed to ask you to come along, but I'll use the time to explain about you and Cole. Your mother already knows there's something going on between you ... I'm no CJ Coleson," he said and winked, "but I've got a good imagination, too. Cole, if anything happens to her..."

"Understood," he answered, his cheeks burning. What had Austin meant by that wink?

"I feel as if I'm one of those rodeo calves being herded into a pen with no escape but the chute once it open," Casey said, her cheeks red. "I've always abhorred lies, and here you're expecting me to propagate a whopper. Saying it is bad enough, but living it? When this is over, people I care about are going to be hurt, and there won't be a damn thing I can do about it."

"But three boys may get to grow up healthy and happy and more lives will be spared," Hal said. "I know the ends don't always justify the means, but in this case, they have to. I'm sorry, Casey. If there were any other way..."

"Fine. I'll see you in an hour, and we can work out the details," she answered resigned.

"I *will* keep you safe," Cole repeated his earlier pledge. "I'll see you at the station."

She nodded, but didn't say another word. He wished he could take her into his arms and tell her everything was going to be fine, but he couldn't offer her that assurance. They didn't know what they were up against, and until they did, he wouldn't lie to her again.

"I'll show you out," Austin said.

"Thanks, Austin," Hal said. "I know I can count on your discretion, and we will keep her safe."

Cole shook Austin's hand.

"I'm entrusting you with my greatest treasure," Austin said. "She's worth more to me and Maria than a dozen gold mines."

"I know."

Cole turned and followed Hal out to the squad car, knowing this was one responsibility he would take to heart.

* * * *

Casey sat on the sofa, too overwhelmed to stand. What the hell had just happened? Not only would she be facing Kristal again, she might have to face Rick, and she'd agreed to do so pretending to be Horace's partner and Cole's fiancée, living with him until this was over. Her head was reeling. If was as if she were caught in a tsunami on a surfboard. All she could do was hold on and pray she would come out of it alive. While part of her wanted to jump on her Harley and ride away as fast as she could, another part knew it was time to face her demons.

"I can't change your mind about this, can I?" her father asked, coming back into the room.

"I don't see that I have any choice, Dad. If I can help Hal stop a serial killer—and that's what this person is if he or she is responsible for all the deaths—then it's not only my duty but my obligation to do so." She stood, pacing as Hal had. "What I don't want is for you to worry, especially now."

"I'm tougher than I look, baby, and so are you. I've always believed you couldn't go wrong in life if you followed your heart. That advice has served me well, and it hasn't let me down yet. Do I want you in a killer's sites, hell no, but I know you have to do what's right, and if anyone can protect you, it's Cole."

"I know that, Daddy. He's a good man." He might've lied

to her, but he'd done so with the purest of intentions. "I've always tried to do the right thing, but suddenly to do that I have to give up my integrity and live a lie. Do you really think people will believe we're engaged?"

"I do, but I don't believe it's all a fabrication—the engagement, maybe—but I saw the way Cole was looking at you earlier. There's chemistry between you, baby, and you can deny it to yourself as much as you want to, but it's there. Family lore claims Grandma Maureen had the sight. Who knows, maybe I inherited her gift, but I'm convinced everything will work out the way it should. Earlier, you said you and Cole had a reality check. I'm going to assume he disappointed you somehow. Girl, if I had a nickel for every time someone had let me down, I would be a rich man. No one's perfect, Casey. Not me, not you, not Cole. Now, since you're determined to do this, we need to get a move on. I've got to work on the story I'll spin for your mother. Maybe I'll just follow that line Hal started about you two getting together in Texas. Lord knows you've been closed-mouthed about your private life."

"Thanks, Dad. On the plus side, this makes one of my decisions much easier. I want to be around until I'm sure you're on the mend. Now, I can do that and help those kids at the same time."

"How's your boss going to be about this?"

"Honestly, I'm not sure, but I intend to ask for a temporary leave of absence. I've never asked for any favors before." She bit her lip. "Let's hope he's in an understanding mood. I'll tell him as much of the truth as I can. That should help." She shrugged. "I'd better get a move on. If it's okay, I'll use the old sedan Randy was using before I bought her the van. It'll look better than my showing up at the police station on my Harley."

He chuckled and nodded. "Yeah, your mother will be happier with that, though I have to admit, you were a sight in that tight black leather and boots. What will you do afterwards?"

"I'll come back once Cole and I have a place to live and get my stuff. If you and Mom are gone, I can avoid the inquisition. Then, I'm going to Horace Stone's office. The more I know about what's been happening in this town, the easier it will be to do my job. I'll call his secretary first and tell her I've accepted Horace's offer. If we tell Mom and Randy that I've reconsidered because of Cole's proposal, it should make them both too happy to worry about anything else—at least until after your surgery. Cole and I will discuss this, but I think you're right. Hal's lie is the most plausible one—better than some hokey 'love at first sight' scenario." She huffed out a deep breath. "I'd better get changed."

"Give your mom a call tonight. She'll need to gush and blubber, but if you don't she'll be suspicious."

Casey nodded, turned, and went upstairs, praying she could pull this off. Not only was she the world's worst liar, she was its lousiest actor.

When she'd gone into law, it had been with the intention of making a real difference in the lives of innocent people, and she had a chance to do that here. It was time to open the closet and shake out the skeletons and spider webs, but if this was going to work, she had to put on her happy face, not just her lawyer persona.

The engagement might be a lie, but it had to be a believable one. When they were alone, things would be as normal between them as they could be, and that meant convincing her body that her brain and not her confused heart had the right idea. That crazy biological clock of hers had to be reset. In public, things would be different. They would act like a couple in love, with all the touchy-feely, kissy-kissy that implied. While that might be hard, the difficult role would be the one she would play when she confronted Rick—and she would have to, sooner or later— and pretend what had happened between them never had.

Being sexually assaulted was a crime, but like so many victims, she'd run away in shame. Over the years, she'd helped other women to confront their attackers. Now, it was her turn. Rick Harvey was going to see she wasn't the scared little girl she'd been. If he was involved in this on any level, she would make him pay, and if he wasn't? Well then, he'd better not piss her off. Since there was no statute of limitation on aggravated sexual assault, she could threaten to charge him. The fact was, she would never go through with it because it would mean telling everyone, including Cole, what a fool she'd been, but Rick wouldn't know that.

"Get a move on, Casey. It's show time." The words echoed in her room, spurring her to action.

* * * *

Cole sat next to Hal, staring straight ahead, but seeing nothing as his mind tried to process what had just happened. Pretending he and Casey were engaged was going to be hard, not because it wouldn't be believable, but because he would have a hell of a time keeping his hands off her. The minute she'd said the words, he knew that was how they could make this work. Alone with her, he would have time to get to know her and figure out the best way to introduce the fact that he was CJ Coleson. Right now, that lie of omission stood between them, bigger than Superstition Mountain itself. If he wanted this relationship, including the pseudo engagement, to be real, then he had to be patient.

While she'd brought up the idea of an engagement, even if it had been in jest, he'd been surprised she'd consented to go along with it. As Hal had said, it was a good cover story, and people often believed what they wanted to even when it made little sense. Maybe news of their engagement would be enough to keep everyone's mind off Chester's death until they could figure this out. The one person they really needed to convince was the killer because Cole was determined to keep her safe. But what if they'd misread the situation? Would Casey be in even more danger?

"What if we're mistaken about everything that's happened, and it's all a desert deception like the mirages people claim to see?" he asked when Hal pulled the Jeep into the parking area behind the police station. "I can't stop thinking we're not seeing

271

the big picture here. All we have to connect these crimes is a motive we've created in our own minds. It's conjecture—like a writer making the clues fit so that the novel moves along smoothly—but this isn't a novel, and God knows how many people are dead or will die before we get to the bottom of it. What if blackmail isn't the reason behind all this? Think about it. Whoever killed Chester might well have been after the mine and didn't realize that gold was under him. That could be why he left it behind. We could be looking for three separate killers."

"God almighty, Cole. Things are complicated enough without having you second-guess every damn thing. Police work is based on evidence and theories, and right now, we've got a viable one. Let's run with it and see where it leads. If after we talk to the boys, things don't add up, then we'll go back to the drawing board and start again. I wish to hell we could talk to Horace. Hansen sent over the man's briefcase. It was in the trunk and reeks of gasoline, but if we're lucky, there may be something in it that can help us. I'll have to bust the lock, but I don't want to do it until Casey's there. We need to focus on the evidence we have and shove supposition in a drawer for now. The facts are simple. Someone's woven an elaborate subterfuge around these crimes, and we're trapped in a web of conflicting and confusing lies, half-truths, and suppositions. Those kids have spent the better part of the last year with Chester. They have to know something, even if they don't realize they do. By the way, where do you and Casey plan to stash them?"

"CJ Coleson has a cottage on Apache Lake—"

"Cut the crap, for Christ's sake," Hal exclaimed, his voice filled with frustration. "I've suspected for a while that you're CJ Coleson, and your analogy about a novel just clinched it. I've got too much on my plate to be worrying about your secret identity right now. Based on what Austin said, he knows the truth, too."

Cole was about to deny it, but stopped. He'd seen the look on Austin's face even if Casey hadn't. Maybe it was best to get this out in the open.

"You may be an incredible writer, but you aren't Superman. I don't know why you think you have to keep everyone in the dark about who you are, but that's your decision," Hal continued, getting out of the vehicle. "When I was recapping everything that's happened, one thing struck me. Why the hell would Trent have been over by Weaver's Needle? That's a good ten miles from everything that's happened. Since examining that crime scene now that it's been contaminated would be pointless, we need to re-think some of this. We're only guessing Chester was poisoned in the house. He could've died on the mountain and been relocated there. Even Leon could have been pushed or have fallen elsewhere and been moved. The problem is, because every crime scene was tainted in some way, we can't prove they died where they did, and we can't assume they didn't. So, with that in mind, it looks like someone may be trying to being your books into play. Why?"

"To throw a monkey wrench in the investigation," Cole said, convinced he was right. "If the killer knows I'm CJ Coleson, then he also knows I'm a cop. By using my novels, he's throwing the investigation off balance, and if he's moved the corpses to fit the books, then we have no idea where our murders actually happened." He cocked his head to the side. "How long have you suspected the truth about me?"

"Close to four years. At first I thought it was just coincidence, but then, I would read something familiar—it could be a turn of phrase you used, a situation that was all too similar to something that had happened recently, and it all fell into place. Once I'd figured it out, I couldn't imagine why I hadn't realized it sooner. Tate Silvers could be my physical clone, but he thinks like you do."

"You're not upset about it?" Cole asked, his eyebrows raised in surprise.

"Upset because you chose me as a role model for your fictional sheriff? Why would I be? Tate Silvers may be fictitious, but he's a mighty fine man. He's got integrity, and I try to live up to him in as many ways as I can. Melba saw it first by the way." He chuckled. "If anything, she's tickled pink about all this, but disappointed she hasn't made it into a book." He shook his head. "This is probably why you keep your identity a secret—to stop people like me from making suggestions about your next one. Still, if you could work a character like hers into a book, she would be thrilled."

"I'll definitely think about it," Cole said, grateful his friend was as understanding as he was.

Would Casey feel the same way when she found out? Somehow he didn't think knowing she'd inspired his newest heroine would be enough to atone for the lie.

"How many others know?" he asked, curious now that the information was out in the open.

"Can't say for sure, but I'll bet the ladies in her book club suspect it. I'm certain Rita knows, too. This morning she said it was a good thing we had Tate Silvers on the job, and I don't think she meant me." He unlocked the back door to the station and stepped inside.

Feeling like a fool, Cole followed him into the station, astonished by what Hal was saying. Had he made a big deal out of nothing? It certainly looked that way.

CHAPTER TWENTY-ONE

"And that's pretty much all I know, Ryan," Casey summed up everything that had happened, the phone pressed to the side of her face so she wouldn't have to speak too loudly. Jaxon was in the next room, but the child had excellent hearing. "I need you to find me something that ties all these people together somehow and explains why three of them ended up dead."

"Sounds like you've had one hell of a week, Red. You're convinced the kids aren't behind it?" Ryan asked, his usual skepticism evident in his voice.

"Not the kids themselves, no, but since I don't know all the parties involved, I'm not dismissing the rest of the families. As strange as it sounds, my gut tells me we're missing something and finding that elusive piece that pulls everything together is your forte. That's why we need your magic. Chief Rankin assures me the town will pay your full fee, so I'm not asking for something pro bono. Find me the common threads I need to get to the bottom of this before someone else dies."

"You do realize that their innocence could all be an act?" Ryan continued, seemingly unwilling to let the kids off the hook.

"I know," she admitted, acknowledging his concern, "and if you find proof they're implicated, I will make sure they get exactly what's coming to them. As I told you, I don't know all the parents, but the ones I do know aren't the best." And that was an understatement. Rick as a father and Kristal as a mother would be less than ideal for any kid, especially one with an artistic side. "Since those boys have been with Chester all summer long, they've been everywhere on that mountain just like he has. If Hal's right and this is all about blackmail and drugs, they should recognize that drop off point. If it's about Chester's treasure, and someone is trying to steal it, then they know where it is, and because of that, they may be in danger. There's a reason someone tried to kill Mr. Stone. He knows something and my instincts say they do, too."

"Okay, it's your call, and your senses, when it comes to guilt or innocence, have never been wrong, but be careful. You know how I feel about loose ends, and it sounds as if you've got a hell of a lot of them, starting with those mysterious fires."

"You're right," she agreed, nodding her head even though he couldn't see her. "We'll be stashing the kids and some of their parents at a lakeside cabin belonging to CJ Coleson, the author. He really values his privacy, so they should be safe there. If I think we need back-up, I'll let you know. It could be a second honeymoon."

"Right, one with chaperones." Ryan chuckled. "I wouldn't have any trouble behaving myself, but I don't know about Sally. She's a wild one."

Casey giggled. "As if…"

"What are the names of the people you want me to look up and how far back to you want me to go?"

"Let's make it fifteen years."

"From when you left home? Interesting. By the way, how long do you plan to be away?"

"I've sent Mr. Hinckley a request for a six-week leave of absence, explaining about my dad's health and the fact that with Mr. Stone away, the police chief has asked for my help with a case. He'll either grant it or fire me."

"And if he fires you?"

"Then I'll be looking for work in six weeks' time," she

admitted, hoping it wouldn't come to that. "You might have to put me up for a while."

"I can work on my harem. Maybe you'll decide to stay," he said, his voice taking on a serious tone.

"I can't see that happening."

"You didn't see this coming either."

She swallowed. No, she hadn't seen this crime spree nor the way she would react to Cole, and that was another problem.

"So, what are the names you want me to check?"

"Leon Turner, Chester Morris, Trent Gibbs, Eddy Ramos, and Rick Harvey. If I think of anyone else, I'll let you know."

"I'll do a search on the area, too, see if anyone's looking to pick up land cheap. All of this will take me a few days, but I should have something for you by Sunday. Where do you want me to send it?"

"Hard copies can go to the Fortune Police Department, you can look up the address. You can send me an email. I've got my laptop and it's secure. I'll use my cell phone as a Wi-Fi hot spot, and if you need to talk to me, call my cellphone. It won't be on all the time, but I'll check it a few times a day. If you come across anything that's life and death, call Hal Rankin at the station."

"Red, you realize if whoever is doing this knows you're stepping into the lawyer's shoes, you could be in danger," Ryan said, all of his customary humor gone.

"I've thought of that, which is why I need you to FAX my gun permit to Fortune's police department. I'll ask Hal for a handgun." She explained about the Cole-bodyguard-engagement lie, too. "I can't believe people will fall for it, but my dad feels better knowing I'm not in this alone."

"I do, too. Having someone on your six is always a good thing, but be careful. You have a tendency to jump in before testing the waters. As far as the gun goes, good idea. I'll send him your last qualifying scores, too. Be careful. If someone hurts my favorite red head, I might just have to come down there myself and beat the shit out of them."

Casey chuckled. "I'll talk to you Sunday. Thanks, Ryan, you're the best."

"I know." He hung up, and she shook her head.

Ending the call, she sighed. Two tasks accomplished, but they were the easy one. She headed into the bathroom to fix her makeup. If there was ever a time for war paint as Ryan called it, it was now.

* * * *

Cole followed Hal into the break room and helped himself to a cup of coffee. The pot was full which meant it couldn't be more than an hour old since he'd grabbed the last cup before going out to see Casey.

"Melba's made it her goal to pick out as many people as she can from each book," Hal said. "She claims Pete and Chester are in them—actually when I told her Chester was dead, she reminded me of the similarities before you did. I've recognized Heidi and Rick. Come to think of it, that gambler in *Rattlesnake* must've been Trent. Other than requests to be put into a novel, why don't you want people to know you're CJ Coleson?" He opened the side door to his office and went inside, by-passing Rita at the front desk.

Closing the door behind him, Cole shook his head. "This is the last conversation I expected to have with you today. Why didn't I tell anyone? I guess I was afraid people would laugh if I told them I'd written a book and created characters based on them—either that or run me out of town on a rail. I never expected *Fool's Gold* to sell like it did, and then when *Rattlesnake* took off ... I didn't want people treating Cole Warner any differently. I eased my conscience by having Horace make generous donations to various civic projects in CJ's name. I didn't want my fictional life to destroy my real one. Do you know I've had women send me their underwear?"

He chewed his lower lip, remembering Casey did the same thing when she was worried or upset ... something else they had in common.

"Can you imagine what life would be like if people showed up at the station or the emporium looking for CJ Coleson? We've got enough crazies coming through town with gold fever. We don't need that, too, especially not now, but maybe that's the point of all this. If enough people see the similarities between the crimes and the books, he might think it would force me to reveal myself. Doing that might detract from what's happening and give the killer or killers the time they need to finish whatever they're doing." Cole pursed his lips and took off his Stetson, praying it wouldn't come to that.

"Underwear? Seriously?" Hal chuckled. "You're exaggerating. It can't be that bad."

"Believe me, it is. You can't imagine what a phenomenon Tate Silvers is. I certainly never expected it. Once those movies come out, it'll only get worse. My publisher had to hire a person just to look after all my fan mail, website, and all the rest of it. I get marriage proposals as well as other propositions—you name it. I've turned down hundreds of requests for personal appearances." He sighed. "But that's not the worst of it. One of the authors with my publisher had issues with a stalker a few years ago—a real *Fatal Attraction* kind of thing, but without any encouragement from him. She tried to kill his wife so they could be together. I don't want that, Hal. I don't want my family endangered because someone confuses my fictional life with my real one. I want to be able to walk down the streets of my home town without being bushwhacked by crazed fans. The people of Fortune probably have the right to know. I mean they aren't unhinged, but it would only take one slip…"

Hal removed his hat. "Yeah, I can see where that might be a hell of a problem, especially if someone thought I *was* Tate Silvers." He hung the Stetson on the rack by the door and moved behind his desk. "Melba wouldn't take kindly to that. Well, your secret's safe with me, and I'm sure the locals who think they know are keeping quiet for reasons of their own. Hell, if Heidi Slocum can keep her mouth shut about it … but if you have any other ideas about this, don't hesitate to share them."

Cole groaned. "I wish I did. The fact is I'm not a nineteenth century lawman, Hal, just a guy with an imagination and a story to tell. Unlike real life, everything always works out in my books. I have a plot line, and I follow it. I wish to hell we had one now."

"Maybe that's how we should look at this," Hal said, dropping into his chair, his lips pursed and his forehead wrinkled. "If someone is using your books to cover up their crimes, it might give us a way to get ahead of them."

"You mean plot out what we have as if I were writing the story?" he asked, his mind already processing the idea.

"Why not? What have we got to lose?"

"I don't know. That's not the way I work, but it's as good an idea as any."

"I was no great shakes in English class, but I remember that writing process the teachers were always drilling into us … not the write, edit, and rewrite part, but the stuff about plot development. In every book you've got the same elements—setting, characters, a timeline, a catalyst or inciting incident, and then your rising action, climax, and falling action, right?

"Yeah. Everything has to connect smoothly, and nothing can fall by the wayside and be forgotten."

"I'm pretty damn sure this is still rising action. We haven't gotten to the climax yet—hell, we don't even know what it's going to be—but what if we can predict it based on what we know?"

"That's a pretty big leap, but you're on. It'll be like writing those damn synopses my publishers demand. I'll get to work on it as soon as we finish with the boys, but you left something out. The key is going to be figuring out goal and motivation," Cole said, reality hitting him in the face making him cringe. "Damn! I'm going to have to tell Casey the truth, and she's going to rip me a new one. She was furious last night when she learned about the helicopter. She was asleep in my arms when it happened, and I chose not to tell her about it."

"Let me guess," Hal said, shaking his head. "You didn't mention the cat either, which is why she ended up in the desert Tuesday night."

"I didn't want to scare her," Cole admitted, shrugging his shoulders and feeling like a fool. "Believe me, when she was out there by herself, I went to hell and back regretting that decision."

"You may have quite the imagination when you write, but you don't know much about women, do you? I suggest roses and a bottle of fine wine after you get back from the opening ceremonies of Gold Rush Days tonight. Since you're supposed to be engaged, I'd go over to Harry's and pick out a suitable ring for the occasion, too. When she's in a mellow frame of mind, then you can tell her. I'm not a matchmaker, but I can see there's definitely something between you. She'll be pissed for a while, but if you do it right, she'll forgive you."

"I hope to hell you know what you're talking about, Rankin. Listen, you're right about one thing. I'd better get to the jeweler's and then call Apache Trail Realty. When I get back, Casey should be here. But mark my words, the fewer people who know about the gold, the better. Assuming Casey will still talk to me when she knows the truth, I can ask her to help me plot out the case as you've suggested. Sometimes, it's easier to see the connections that way, but it'll also show us where stuff just doesn't go together. She's got a quick mind and is damn good at adding things up. What we need is a motive, and once we have that, we'll find our main characters."

Hal chuckled. "Motive's easy—greed—but you're on your own as to who, why, and for what. Maybe that gumshoe of hers will find something we haven't. I have to go through proper channels, but they have backdoors into everything. I need to call Apache Junction PD and find out if they've gotten anything from the surveillance video at Leon's apartment or from the sketch artist. If Trent left that apartment with his friend, where did that bastard go? Then I'll call the hospital. Get back as soon as you can. I want you here when I question the boys."

Cole smiled and nodded. He would take Hal's advice and with a little luck, Casey would take the news as well as Hal did.

And pigs fly, his conscience said.

* * * *

Dressed in a floral skirt and coordinating blouse she'd borrowed from her sister's closet, Casey parked in front of the police station. Taking a deep breath, she exited the car and climbed the two steps to the antique wooden door. Never having gone inside the place, she wondered if it would be like all the stations she'd been in, or if she'd be stepping back in time. Entering the building, she was surprised to see it was a little of both.

A receptionist, wearing the same uniform she'd seen on Hal and Cole this morning, sat in what at first glance appeared to be an old jail cell, but after a second look, was actually a security barrier, preventing someone from walking into the depths of the stationhouse unannounced. On the left, the name plate on the door identified the room behind it as Chief of Police Hal Rankin's office. The walls were sand colored. Across from the chief's office, portraits of all of Fortune's past police chiefs hung next to a map of the town and the surrounding area including the lakes to the north and Superstition Mountain to the south. Oak benches lined the wall under the photographs. A large potted saguaro cactus stood in the corner. Next to Hal's door, a corkboard was almost completely covered in wanted posters—some dating back to the eighteen hundreds, others no more than a few days old.

"May I help you?" the woman asked without looking up from her paperwork.

"Yes, I'm Casey Stevens," she answered, grateful her voice didn't sound as anxious as she felt. "I'm supposed to meet Chief Rankin at ten-thirty."

The woman's head popped up as if she were a bobble-head

doll.

"Hello, welcome back to Fortune, Casey. I don't know if you remember me. Rita Sanchez. I married Jason Hynes. Congratulations. The chief told me about you and Cole. That sly dog. I should've guessed he had a special lady tucked away somewhere. He isn't back yet, but Hal and the others are waiting for you in one of the interview rooms. If you'll come this way?"

A buzzer sounded, and the gate separating the receptionist from the inner sanctum of the station swung open.

"Thanks. It's been an interesting courtship," she lied, "but, it's time. Is everyone here?"

"All of the boys and three of the parents. Joey Pearson only has a mother and Tony Bronson just has his dad, but that Rick Harvey is off somewhere as usual. If you ask me, Kristal should dump that ass. Her life and disposition would no doubt improve if she did."

Casey nodded. If there was anything that could make a person mean-tempered, it was living with a snake in the grass like Rick. Raising a child on her own, with little to no financial aid, would be difficult. Randy was proof of that, and she had a loving family to help her.

"They're right in here." Rita knocked on the door and opened it. "Ms. Stevens is here, chief."

Casey took a deep breath before following Rita inside. Closing the door behind her, she pasted a false smile on her face and turned to gaze around the small room. Three adults sat at the table, their faces displaying fear and confusion. In the far corner, the three boys were having a whispered discussion.

"Thanks for coming, Ms. Stevens." He turned to the receptionist standing beside her. "You can go back to your desk, Rita. I'll call you if I need anything, and when Cole arrives, send him in."

"Yes, sir," Rita answered and nodded before leaving the room.

Hal smiled at her. "Horace apologizes for having to put you

to work so quickly, Casey, but with him and Clara in LA, he can't get back in time to help us out."

"That's okay, Hal. I would've started Monday, but I don't have anything pressing to do, and since I'm going to be sticking around…"

The boys had moved back to the table, their eyes shining with unshed tears. Had she looked that young and vulnerable at that age?

Kristal Harvey sat at the far end of the table, away from the others as if she'd purposely isolated herself, but she was a far cry from the person Casey had met only two days ago. Not only was she not berating her, the woman looked old, defeated, as if life had struck her down one too many times. Tears had left her with smeared makeup, but she didn't seem to care. Her son Kyle stood beside her. The boy was small for his age and bore absolutely no resemblance to his father, something that would make this much easier on Casey. He was scrawny, and so fair that his eyebrows were almost invisible on his sallow complexion, his face blending into his white-blond hair. His eyes, the most unusual shade of aquamarine she'd ever seen, gave him a mystical look, reminding her of the changelings she'd read about as a child. In his right hand, he gripped a blue asthma inhaler. This teen looked like a strong wind would blow him over. She could well imagine how a delicate son like this would've been a bitter disappointment to his athletic father. Her heart went out to the boy whose health problems would've made him an easy target for bullies. Like wolves, they always went after the weak and vulnerable. He reached out to his mother in an attempt to comfort her.

"Casey," Hal said, taking charge of the situation. "Let me introduce you. You know Kristal Harvey. This is her son Kyle. Over here, we have Joey Pearson and his father Matt, and lastly, this is Tony Bronson, and his mother Evelyn, but people call her Evie. Ms. Stevens has accepted Horace Stone's offer of partnership and in his absence will be handling the town's legal matters."

Matt Pearson, a large man with dark auburn hair and strong features, frowned, his face turning red as his temper rose. "Hal, why do we need a lawyer here? I thought you just wanted to talk to the boys about Chester Morris. Is something else going on?" The accent in his voice betrayed his Scottish ancestry.

Casey's gaze fell on the boy at his side. The teenager with the copper skin of his Apache ancestors and his father's piercing blue-green eyes reminded her of a young Richard Harris in the movie, *A Man Called Horse*. Joey Pearson had reddish blond hair worn long and tied back in a ponytail. Whereas Kyle was slight, Joey was well-muscled, but his mixed ancestry could've made him a target for the bullies as well. Beads of sweat dotted his forehead, and he wrung his hands. The boy was terrified, but doing the best he could to hide his fear from the others.

"Not at the moment, Matt, but there's a possibility that Elmore Gunderson may want to bring charges against them. That's why Casey's here to make sure their rights are protected, but the real reason I wanted you all to come in is because I think your sons are in danger."

"Danger? From whom? Why?" Evie Bronson asked, reaching out to grip her son's hand.

The woman, with cappuccino skin and dark eyes, had worry etched in the lines of her face. Like Matt Pearson, Evie wasn't someone Casey remembered, no doubt having moved to Fortune at some point in the last fifteen years. There was a wariness to her, as if this wasn't the first time she'd faced danger. While Evie was trying to look brave, she trembled, ready to collapse at any moment. Life had worn her down, and it wouldn't take much to finish the job.

Her son, the eldest of the three boys, had slightly lighter skin then hers, but his eyes, so dark the irises and pupils blended together, were haunted. Of average height, he carried at least thirty extra pounds, weight that would've made him the ideal target for the fat jokes that had assailed her in school. Cole had mentioned the boy was a science whiz who could've smelted Chester's gold.

Hardened criminals? Murderers? Hardly. Her gut told her these were three frightened children who were grieving the loss of a friend.

"Evie, I don't want to scare you, but we suspect your boys may know something that could get them noticed by the wrong people," Hal said, speaking calmly, trying to convey the sense that everything was under control, something Casey knew wasn't remotely true.

"I don't understand," she said, her voice filled with fear. "What 'wrong' people. This is Fortune. I moved here after the 'wrong' people cost me my husband, Hal. I left my family, my friends, and my life in New York to avoid 'wrong' people. Are you telling me they've found me anyway?"

"I'm sure these aren't the people you ran from," Hal said, furrowing his brow even more.

Casey knew he wanted to ask questions, but this wasn't the time nor the place.

"Mrs. Bronson, let's not get ahead of ourselves. We have some photographs we would like the boys to look at. Let's see how that goes before we push any panic buttons," Casey said, injecting every ounce of control and calm into her voice she could manage. If the boys didn't recognize the plateau, the only other questions they had were about the gold and the artifacts. "Chief Rankin, if you please?"

Hal nodded and handed each boy a copy of the photograph, one that showed not only the helicopter, but a good chunk of the landscape and Weaver's Needle in the distance.

"You boys must've traveled all over that mountain with Chester. Have you ever seen any place that resembles this?"

"Before we answer your question, there's something you need to know, chief," Joey Pearson said, standing. "The guys and I have talked about it, and we'll answer all of your questions, but if it's okay with you, I'll do most of the talking. Kyle's kind of shy and Tony stutters when he gets nervous." He paused and licked his lower lip. "For the past six months, Mr. Stone has been our lawyer, looking after our affairs, as he calls it." He smiled shyly, his eyes filled with the worry he was trying to hide. "I guess that means you're our lawyer, too, Ms. Stevens—I mean if you work for Mr. Stone, you would learn all this from him if he were here."

"With, not for," she corrected, too surprised by what he'd said to think of something more appropriate to say. "We're partners, so yes I would. Whatever you told him is as confidential with me as it is with him. I've got a lot of questions for you, but can you answer the chief's question first?"

He nodded and the three boys rose and moved back into the corner to huddle. After five minutes that felt like an eternity, they came back to the table and sat down once more.

"We've never seen or heard a helicopter there, but this mesa is one of the places we cross on our way to our camp. It's about an hour up the mountain going our way, but you can get to it from the wilderness trails. That path is steeper and harder on the horses, but it can be done. It's popular with tourists on ATVs and dirt bikes."

"How can you be so sure?" Casey asked, playing devil's advocate as Cole had put it. "I mean, don't all mesas look alike?"

Joey chuckled. "Most of the time they do, but do you see that black rock sticking straight up? It looks like a miniature Weaver's Needle. We called it Chester's Arrow because it points the way to the hidden path we take to our camp. That's our resting place. There's a small spring you can't see in the picture. It's a good place to water the horses and the mules. There's a mean old ram who likes to hang around there with his ewes in the spring, so we're extra careful not to annoy him then."

"Have you ever seen anyone else there," Hal asked, trying hard to hide his excitement.

"Not in a long time," Joey answered, puckering his brow. "Last year, we met a friend of Chester's camping there. I think his name was Leon. They yakked for a couple of hours, long enough for me to find an old canteen, which was hidden in the brush. Kyle made some sketches."

Kyle nodded. "I turned a couple into watercolors. You remember, Mom. Mr. Gibbs bought one of them."

"Trent Gibbs?" Casey asked, biting her lower lip to hide her excitement. Kyle might just have connected Trent to the helicopter's landing place. Why else would he buy the boy's painting?

"Yes, ma'am," he answered shyly, his pale face turning pink.

Kristal's sorrow was replaced by anger. "His father insisted he give it to him even though Trent didn't have the money on him to pay for it. Did he ever pay you?"

Kyle shook his head, and looked down at the table.

Casey met Hal's gaze and nodded.

"Can you boys find this mesa?" Hal asked, the excitement on his face replaced by worry.

Joey nodded. "Yes sir. We have to cross it to get to the trail that leads to our camp and the CJKT Discovery. That's what we thought you wanted to ask us about now that Chester's dead."

Evie stood. "You've got your answer now give me mine. Is my son in danger?

Casey took a deep breath. "I think so, and we have a plan to keep them safe until we can figure out who's behind everything."

Matt reached for the photograph in his son's hand and examined it.

"The men in this picture are removing bags from the helicopter," Matt said, his brogue more pronounced than it had been. "Are there drugs in them?"

"We can't be sure," Hal said, "but we think so."

Matt's face lost its ruddiness. "Are you saying drug dealers might be after my boy?"

"Possibly, but we have a plan to keep them and you safe."

"Us," Kristal shrieked. "Are you saying some drug dealer has targeted us and our kids? Why?"

"We suspect they may have been responsible for the recent deaths that have happened in Fortune."

"May? May?" Evie rose, her hands shaking. "Either they did or they didn't. If I've got to cut and run again, I want to know why."

"Please be patient just a little longer, Mrs. Bronson," Casey said, trying to soothe the woman. "Our intention is to find these men and stop them before they hurt anyone else. You aren't going to have to leave Fortune, but it might be safer if you did until we get this straightened out. We have a place picked out for you, and we'll see that your employer doesn't hold your absence against you."

"That sounds a lot like the crap the DA fed us before Joe was killed," she said. "They couldn't protect him. What makes you think you can do any better?"

Hal stepped in front of Casey. "Evie, give us a chance to explain and you'll see. Now, Joey, you say you cross this plateau to get to the CJKT Discovery. What exactly is that?"

Suspicion filled Casey. Whatever the boys and Chester had found couldn't be a mine or he would've come right out and said it.

"It's a cave full of treasure," he said calmly, "and it's legally ours. Mr. Stone drew up all the contracts and Chester signed them."

"Treasure?" Kristal, Matt and Evie cried as one.

"Stuff like this?" Hal asked dumping the small bag Cole had shown her last night. The four objects she recognized fell onto the table.

Joey nodded. "Yes, sir. Those come from the Discovery, but there were a lot more things in that bag. He'd brought it in to show Mr. Stone."

"Son," Hal said. "Why don't you start at the beginning?"

The boy looked at her for confirmation and she nodded.

"Go ahead. You aren't in any trouble. The more we know about what's going on, the easier it'll be to protect everything."

CHAPTER TWENTY-TWO

Cole stuffed the small, black velvet-covered jeweler's box into his pants' pocket. Picking out the ring had taken far longer than he'd expected it to, but even though the engagement was a sham, he wanted it to be perfect. He'd been torn between the oval sapphire and the ring he'd finally selected. The square-cut emerald surrounded by sixteen diamonds, set in a gold band, was just right for her. Seventeen stones—one for every year she hadn't been a part of his life. He chuckled. That had to be his writer's imagination at work. He'd guessed the size, basing it on his memory of the feel of her hand in his, and Trudy, the sales' clerk, assured him that it could be resized overnight if necessary.

He still found it hard to believe how easily everyone accepted the news of his engagement. Hal was right. People were romantics at heart, and since his no dating policy had been a frequent topic of conversation, finding out he had a girl and was about to get married was most people's idea of a happy ending. Besides, people would much rather focus on good news than bad. Once the truth about everything came out, he would probably have to leave Fortune for a while, but it couldn't be helped.

"She's going to love this," Trudy said, placing the credit card slip on the counter for him to sign. I knew there had to be someone special in your life," Trudy gushed. "It doesn't surprise me it's Casey. You were sweet on her back then. My mother still talks about the night you beat my brother Travis out of that pink bear I wanted."

Cole felt his cheeks heat. "Well…" He shrugged.

"I can't wait to read about the wedding. It's going to be the best one yet."

"Pardon?" Cole asked, feeling the blood leave his face as the tourist beside him glanced up.

Trudy reddened and smiled at him uncomfortably. "You know … in the *Examiner*. I'm sure all the details will be there. Did you want me to set the matching wedding bands aside?"

Cole let out the breath he'd unconsciously been holding, well aware that Trudy hadn't been talking about the newspaper. She knew, but she'd caught herself before blurting in out in front of a stranger.

"Yes, please put them aside," he answered and smiled at the woman watching him.

"We haven't set the date, but once the size is settled, I'll pick them up." He didn't know what he'd do with wedding bands once this was over, but not buying them might make people question the engagement.

"I've got a gorgeous emerald and diamond necklace and earrings set that match the ring beautifully if you ever wanted to give her a special birthday or Christmas present," Trudy added and winked.

Cole nodded. "I'll keep that in mind." Tipping his Stetson to the woman, he left the store and headed to the station.

On his way to the jeweler's, he'd stopped by Apache Trail Realty and had been given the keys and the code to the security system at the house on the edge of town, as well as the instructions on how to change the code. He'd also handed the realtor a twenty-five thousand dollar check. If the house met with his expectations, he would buy it for the asking price. No one else was looking at the place right now, so the man, a newcomer to Fortune who didn't shop at the emporium, had accepted his proposition—after making sure the check was good, of course.

Stepping into the station, he nodded to Ramon.

"How's your wife doing?" he asked, knowing the pregnancy had been hard on her.

"As big as a house and ornery as a wet hen," he chuckled, "but everything's good with the baby, and she's only got another six weeks to go."

"Fallon was miserable during her first pregnancy, too, but once the baby was here, to hear her talk, you would think it had been a piece of cake."

Ramon shook his head. "I hope you're right. I'm off to an early lunch and then I'm taking her into Apache Junction for an appointment. She's decided she wants to know the baby's sex after all. If it's a boy, she wants to name him Tate." He laughed. "Tate Ramon Hernandez. It does have an unusual ring to it. I'll see you later."

Cole nodded. "I hope everything goes well." It looked as if Ramon knew the truth, too.

He walked over to the desk where Rita had just hung up the phone.

"Where are they?" he asked, still stunned by the fact people knew his identity and took it in stride.

"Interview room three," Rita answered and smiled. "They got started about ten minutes ago. Congratulations, by the way. She's a sweetheart. I didn't really know her at school, but you two make a lovely couple. Now I know why you wormed out of all those blind dates I tried to set up for you." She moved her head forward and whispered. "The chief said you went to get a ring? Can I see it?"

Cole shrugged, not sure what the etiquette was in situations like these, and pulled the box out of his pocket.

Rita reached for the small case and flipped it open.

"Holy guacamole!" she whispered. "That's gorgeous and must've cost you an arm and a leg."

"Not quite." He chuckled, shaking his arms at her before reaching for the ring, tucking it into his pocket once more. "I'd better get in there."

Rita pressed the button, allowing the gate to swing open.

"I'm looking forward to all the details," she said. "I'm sure I'm not the only one."

Knowing she probably knew the truth about CJ Coleson, he shrugged.

"Maybe. Nothing's carved in stone yet."

Rita burst out laughing. "Well, think about it. Women love reading about weddings."

Cole walked down the hall to the interview room and opened the door. No one was talking. In fact, it looked as if they were shell-shocked.

"Sorry I'm late," he said, closing the door behind him. "What did I miss?"

His arrival seemed to rouse everyone.

"Glad you made it back," Hal said, "The boys not only know where the mesa is, they can take you there. I'm thinking first thing tomorrow morning. I have to stick around because of the celebration, but the sooner we know where that place is, the better I'll like it."

Cole nodded and went to stand next to Casey.

"Joey was just explaining something to us," she said, pointing to the items on the table.

He noticed the bright color in her cheeks and the way the pulse in her throat throbbed.

"Go ahead, Joey. Sorry I interrupted."

The boy nodded. "No problem, sir. Kyle, Tony, and I have been friends for a long time, ever since we moved here when I was little. The other kids liked to pick on us because we're different, and so we formed a gang of our own—strength in numbers, you know? Once we were old enough, Dad taught us all to ride, and we spent a lot of time hanging around the base of Superstition Mountain. We weren't allowed to climb it without an adult. A couple of years ago, after a storm, we were looking for unusual rocks that might've washed down the mountain and saw Chester fighting with his mules. It looked like he was trying to get them to walk straight into the cliff, but once we got closer, we saw the cleft in the rock and offered to help him get to wherever he was going." He glanced at his father and shrugged. "We were dying to go into the mountains, and he was an adult..."

Joey described how their friendship had developed. After getting permission from each of their parents, Chester had taken them under his wing and taught them how to snare rabbits, which cacti could be used for water, food, or medicine, and how to see the subtle differences in the desert landscape others missed. He also taught them all about the myths and legends of the mountain, how to dry pan for gold after a storm, and always shared the proceeds of whatever they found. In exchange, they did the grunt work for him. The money Chester gave them allowed the boys to help out at home, and in Kyle's case, to buy art supplies which his father refused to pay for.

"Kyle's mom bought him some last year, but when his dad found out—well, it wasn't good."

Casey looked over at Kristal and saw the tears crawling down her cheeks. The last thing she would've taken her for, based on what Cole had said last night, was an abused woman, but maybe Rick hadn't taken his rage out on her. The boy beside her seemed to have shrunk in size.

"Last year, we started camping out overnight on the mountain. That's where we were when the earthquake struck. You remember, Dad, you were so mad because I didn't answer my phone when you called."

His father nodded. "I wasna mad, Joey, I was worried."

"Cell service isn't always reliable in the mountains," Cole agreed. "So you were there during the earthquake. That must've been scary."

"It was, but Chester believed I was a link to the Apache spirits, and they would protect us. In the morning, everything seemed normal, but when we went back into the mine Chester was working, the oldest claim he'd ever filed, the mine entrance was blocked by boulders. Since we'd gotten a little gold out of there, Chester decided we should see if we could dig it out. It took weeks, but eventually, we moved enough rock out of the way to make a new entrance and braced it. Chester went in first—he always did to make sure it was safe, and that's when he found it."

"Found what?" Kristal asked as rapt as the rest of them.

"There was an opening in the wall on the left side and what looked like a cave beyond it. We enlarged the opening and Kyle volunteered to stick his head inside and look around. There wouldn't be much point in digging the wall out if there was nothing there but an air pocket in the rock. He flashed the light around and jumped back so quickly he knocked me down. That space is a room a bit bigger than this one. There are half a dozen skeletons inside—some of donkeys, others of men with and without armor."

"My God," Kristal whispered and squeezed her son's hand. "You must've been terrified. I would've been."

He nodded. "I was, but Chester said we had nothing to fear from the dead. It was the living who could hurt us."

Cole ran his hand through his hair. As Casey had pointed out the previous night, the historical significance of such a find would be incredible.

"What did you do next?" he asked.

"We worked at the opening for a few weeks and once it was big enough for Chester to get through, we went inside. At first, Chester thought they were Spanish *conquistadors* and slaves from Coronado's expedition who'd sheltered in the cave during a storm or something, and an earthquake like the one we'd had a few months earlier had sealed them inside, but then he saw the coins and noticed the arrowheads. He thought we'd found some of Peralta's men who tried to hide from the Apache."

"So the gold *is* from Peralta's mine," Casey said, the awe in her voice hard to miss.

Cole shook his head. After all these years? This was too fantastic to believe, a story begging to be told, and who better to do that than CJ Coleson?

"That's what he said. We've been collecting stuff and cataloguing it. Kyle's drawn most of the artifacts—that's what Chester called them. That cave's like a scene out of that *John Carter* movie. There are cave drawings on one of the walls—not petroglyphs—real paintings way older than the glyphs elsewhere on the mountain."

"What kind of paintings?" Cole asked, marveling at what could be one of the greatest finds in United States' history.

"Animals," Kyle answered softly, his voice barely above a whisper. "Cavemen hunting. I've seen similar paintings in my art books. They disappear into the back wall of the cave. Chester thought there might've been another one behind it, but the walls were too thick to try to get through. We would need more powerful drills, but they could destroy everything." He lowered his eyes again, embarrassed to have spoken up.

"There are chests full of coins, silver and turquoise jewelry, even some made of copper, and leather bags filled with gold nuggets. Chester thought the cave might've been a storage room of some kind but the cave in that had sealed them inside had done so on two sides. We collected some of the stuff—gold and silver coins dated in the early 1800s, some jewelry and a rosary—but we didn't take anything off the bodies—and a couple of the bags of gold. After that, we used rocks and boulders to close up the outside opening and moved our camp back to another one of Chester's claims. If anyone asked, he would say the gold came from that one. We weren't going to say anything about the rest of the stuff until Mr. Stone made some inquiries."

"You found a fortune and didn't say anything," Evie asked her son, the stunned look on her face mirrored on the face of the other two parents.

"Mom, I couldn't. I told you. We swore an oath," Tony said, as if that explained everything. "Where did you think the money I gave you came from? Each month, Chester would bring a few nuggets into Mr. Stone's office and have him sell them. Then, he would divide the money among us." The boy looked at his mother. "We weren't trying to pull a fast one, honest, but Chester said if anyone found out about the cave they would rob it rather than preserve it, and we couldn't have that. That cave is their grave. Those men deserve to be treated with respect, but the right people needed to know it was there so they could study it."

"It's okay, you did the right thing," Evie said and smiled. "You're an honorable man, just like your dad. If he were here, he would be as proud of you as I am."

The boy hugged his mother.

"Chester said there were rules about removing artifacts, but the gold was different," Joey spoke up again. "Since he'd patented all his claims, what he found above the ground was his as well as what might be buried."

Cole looked around the room, gauging the reactions of all those present. Kristal was no longer crying, her face a mixture of relief and awe. Matt's face had lost its angry scowl, and he sat there, mouth agape, too stunned to speak. Cole could appreciate that. For the first time in his life, he was lost for words, trying to get his head around the scope of this historical find. If this was indeed Peralta's mine, someone would be set for life.

Joey licked his lips. "I heard that Chester died in the fire because he was drunk. I know what people think, but it isn't true. After we found the cave, Chester stopped drinking because he said when he was drunk, he might let something slip that could ruin it for all of us. Now that he'd found the gold, he would finally have everything he wanted."

"Are you sure about that?" Cole asked.

"Yes, sir. He was really excited about it."

"No, I mean are you certain he stopped drinking the home-made mescal?"

"Positive. At least two of us stayed on the mountain with him for almost a month. Since it was summer we didn't have school, and … all of our folks are really busy. We rotated so we would all be home some and could pick up supplies. I guess they were just glad to have us out of their hair and by then they were used to us 'working for Chester.' It was really hard on him—he had sweats and saw things that weren't there—but we took care of him. We helped him dismantle the still and poured out all the mescal he had left. Chester hasn't had a drink of that poison, as he called it, in almost a year now."

Cole looked at Hal, who nodded.

"You boys should know Chester didn't die in that fire. He was poisoned, and someone wants us to think he ingested it in his mescal, but if he wasn't drinking anymore, that means he didn't get it from the bottles even though the ones we found in the shed near your art supplies had the poison in them."

Kyle frowned. "What shed?" he asked.

"The one near the old Morris place," Hal answered, his gaze meeting Cole's. "We found a box of used oil pastels, some drawing paper and other things in there. Your prints are on the pastels, but everything else was wiped clean."

"Oh God. The man was murdered and someone's trying to say my Kyle did it?" Kristal whispered.

Kyle's breathing grew shallow and he reached for his inhaler.

"I didn't do it, Mom," he swore, his breathing rapid in his distress.

"It's okay, Kyle," Casey said. "No one believes you did. Hal, can you go get that box of pastels?"

He nodded and left the room.

Cole smiled. "Did Chester ever use gasoline or anti-freeze?" he asked.

"Yeah. We lugged an old compressor up the mountain last year so we could have some brighter light to work with. The thing overheated all the time, but we haven't used it in months. It's up at the camp. Tony rigged up solar panels for power. Is this why you think Mr. Gunderson might arrest us? He thinks we killed Chester for the treasure? But that makes no sense. It's ours. Mr. Stone has all the paperwork."

Hal came in with a box, opened it, and removed the items inside.

Kyle reached for the sketchbook and stopped. "Do I need to put on gloves?"

"That would be best, son," he said, handing him a pair.

The boy put on the gloves and then reached for the sketch pad.

"Mom, this is the stuff I thought I'd lost—you know the stuff I had with me when we went to Canyon Lake." He held the paper up sideways. "See? You can see the impressions of the boat I drew for that little girl. I was sure I'd brought them home, but ... Dad really lit into me." He looked up at Hal. "These are mine, sir, but I don't know how they got into that shed." The boys breathing was rapid, and he used his inhaler.

"What about this lock?" Cole asked.

Joey tried to open the lock with his combination, but it wouldn't budge, Tony did the same, but the lock didn't open.

"Let me try something," he said. He used a different combination, nodding when the lock opened. He looked up, his face full of confusion.

"If someone is trying to frame us, it's someone we see every day, someone who knows us. This is my old lock. It was sticking so I took it off my locker and took it home. I was going to have Dad have a look at it, but it disappeared out of the truck when we stopped for groceries on the way back to the ranch. I had to buy a new one."

"When was that?"

"April, maybe?"

I see," Cole said. Whoever was behind this had put a lot of thought into it. The first fire was in April. The presence of the empty jerry can was probably meant to implicate the kids in those, too, but as he'd learned from Casey, the circumstantial evidence was too flimsy to hold any weight. What it did do was keep them chasing their tails. "What about the rest of this stuff?"

"I've never seen any of it except Chester's tool box," Tony said. "The gas can we used was an old metal one. Maybe Chester used this one to refill ours. As far as the anti-freeze goes, we had a different brand. Is that the poison they used? I'm hoping to go into chemistry someday. If whoever's behind this knows us well enough to plant Kyle's art supplies and Joey's lock, then he knows I know all about the chemical properties of ethylene glycol. As far as the toolbox goes, that's where Chester hid the artifacts, but he didn't keep it in that shed; he carried it with him all the time. I don't understand why it would be in there. The last time I saw it was Monday morning when we met at Mr. Stone's office. I suppose we're in big trouble, aren't we?" His forehead was creased with worry making him look older than his years.

"No," Casey said, "but I think we need to make sure you stay that way. Cole, why don't you explain about the cabin?"

He nodded. "My good friend CJ Coleson has a cottage on Apache Lake. It's isolated and has four bedrooms. We want you six to go and stay there for a few days until we figure this out. Matt, I know you need to make arrangements for the ranch, and Evie you'll have to get a leave of absence from work. Hal can talk to Doc Creighton."

"That's not necessary unless this goes longer than two weeks. I start vacation tomorrow. I was hoping to head to my sister's in Utah."

"Let me think about that," Hal said. "Until we know what we're up against, it's best to keep you together, but as soon as I think it's safe, we'll let you go."

Cole turned to Kristal, the one unknown who could ruin everything. As much as Rick might be her husband, there was no way he could be told any of this, especially not before Hal questioned him about Trent. "Kristal, can you spin something Rick will believe?"

"I don't give a rat's ass whether he believes it or not," she said, a little of her old bravado back in place. "He's in Vegas with Eddy and Trent. They're supposed to be meeting some friends from college."

Cole glanced at Hal who shook his head slightly, just enough for Cole to see and understand not to say anything.

They hadn't mentioned Trent or Leon's death and it was best to keep it that way.

"If he bothers to call, I'll tell him I'm taking Kyle to Phoenix for a while. I've done it before, so he shouldn't care."

"I can take you all to the lake after supper," Cole said, satisfied that everything would work out. "That'll give you time to pack, but we'll need the boys here early tomorrow to show us that plateau and the discovery."

"Why don't we all stay at the ranch tonight?" Matt asked. "I've three good, strong men there, former marines who served with my wife. "I'll tell them that animal's been spotted near the house and put someone on guard duty. I've got foals and my best mares in the pasture nearest the house. Ye can leave early in the morning and I can convince my men we're all going to Phoenix, but leave them on alert. Ye can take us to the cottage when you get back from the mountain. No point in making that trek twice and possibly being noticed. My men would certainly wonder." His brogue was as strong as his stress level.

"Good point," Hal said. "But Casey and Cole can't be seen as being too buddy-buddy with you. Besides, they have to attend the opening ceremonies tonight. I assume you'll go with them, Casey?"

She nodded reluctantly.

"Okay," Hal smiled. "What time do you want to meet in the morning?"

"Around seven," Joey suggested. "It's about a five hour round trip.

"Seven it is," Cole said, looking at Casey for confirmation.

She nodded once more.

"I'll be right back," Hal said as he and the families filed out.

"You don't look too thrilled about tomorrow," he said, watching Casey bag the treasure and collect the evidence. "I know you don't want to spend any more time in public with me than you have to, but I can't leave you alone. I promised your father I would keep you safe, and I won't break my word."

"It isn't that. I haven't been on a horse since Ginger died,"

301

she admitted, putting the pouch inside the box with the other items and pushing it across the table to him.

He chuckled. "Don't worry, it's like riding a bike. You never forget."

He reached over and grabbed the special tape used to seal the boxes, taped it shut, and initialed the tape where the lid and the bottom met.

Hal came back into the room carrying a plastic evidence bag with a soft-sided briefcase inside.

"Casey, I wanted to give you this. It stinks to high heaven, but it belongs to Horace. Hansen took it out of the trunk last night." He took out a penknife and popped the lock. "I'll let you go through it. Might be a good idea to make photocopies rather than work with the originals. Some may be ruined, but hopefully you'll find something of use. I've got to get to the morgue and then the rangers need me to stop over and sign for the body. They sent it directly to Doc Creighton yesterday, but you know how the higher ups get when the paperwork isn't done right. I'm expecting that sketch from Apache Junction, too. It's almost noon. Why don't you two get some lunch, and we'll meet later?"

Cole nodded. "Sounds like a plan."

Hal left the room.

"How does pizza for lunch sound?" he asked.

"It's fine. I'm starving, so I can probably eat a couple of pieces. I can look at this later." She slipped Horace's briefcase back into the plastic evidence bag.

"I'll lock it all up and be right back." He moved toward the door.

"Wait," she said. "I spoke to Sylvia Langston, Horace Stone's secretary. The office is closed from twelve-thirty until one-thirty. If you don't mind, after we eat, we can pick up my stuff at home, and you can drop me there. I assume I have a place to call home somewhere?"

He nodded. "I've got a house you can use for as long as you need it."

"The place you mentioned earlier that you'd looked at yesterday?" she asked curiously, her head cocked to one side.

"I *heard* about it yesterday, but all I've seen are photographs. The realtor says it's partially furnished, but I'm sure you'll want to pick up some stuff before you move in."

"You might want to rephrase that. I'll be staying there with you because I have to until the case is over, but I'm definitely not moving in."

"Bad choice of words," he said, noting her annoyance. "I picked up the key and the security code earlier before I came in for the interview."

"Good. I told Sylvia I'd decided to accept Horace's offer, and she seemed thrilled but clearly not sure how much she could tell me. I said I'd drop over around two. Let's hope she won't be a problem."

"We'll have Hal talk to her if she is. She should probably know the truth, but I'm not dropping you anywhere. You're stuck with me. Now that you're officially Horace's partner, your safety is my concern. We can stop by my place so I can pack a bag, and when you're finished we can go out to the house. We have a few hours until the opening ceremonies, but before we leave here, there's something else I need to give you."

He reached into his pocket and pulled out the ring box. "Every fiancée needs a ring. Consider it window dressing for the part." He handed her the small velvet-covered box.

"Is this necessary?" She stared down at the box as if he were offering her one of the creepy crawlies she detested.

"Hal thinks it is. It was his idea. Any good cover story is in the details. I don't know about you, but I'm pretty damn sure whoever's behind this is local. How else would he know enough about the boys to frame them that way? The last thing we need is for people to suspect this is all an act."

"Fine," she huffed out and reached for the box. Reluctantly, she opened it, her breath catching audibly when she saw the ring.

"Oh my God, Cole. This is the most beautiful thing I've

ever seen. It's incredible, but it seems sacrilegious to use it in a sting like this." She blinked her eyes quickly.

He'd seen Fallon do that when she tried not to cry.

"Try it on," he said softly.

Nodding, she took it out of the box and slipped in onto her ring finger.

"It's a perfect fit," she said her face displaying her amazement. "How did you know the size?"

"I didn't."

"I hope you can bring it back when this is over."

He smiled. "I'm sure I can," he said, knowing he wouldn't. That ring belonged on her finger, and letting her keep it, no strings attached, was the least he could do for the mess he'd put her in. "I'm sorry I told Hal about Mr. Stone's offer. I know you told me that in confidence, but…"

"It's okay. I was annoyed, but you did the right thing. After meeting those kids, there's no way I could let them be railroaded. Evie's obviously had a brush with the mob or some street gangs. She left everything to come here and keep her son safe. The least I can do is make sure she doesn't have to run again."

She stood on tiptoe and kissed his cheek. "Thank you. I'm sorry I got so angry last night. I guess I over-reacted, but I've always had issues with trust and honesty. Maybe we can start over and be friends again."

"If that's what you're offering I'll take it," he said, knowing that once she knew the truth, he might not even have that much. "Come on. Next stop, Louis's Pizzeria, and then it's on to your place so you can pack."

CHAPTER TWENTY-THREE

An hour later, full after the pizza and salad she'd eaten, Casey packed her suitcase. Louis's hadn't been crowded, but the news of their engagement had spread like wildfire, and they'd fielded a barrage of questions—none about the hoax itself, but mostly about how they'd managed to keep the relationship a secret. Half a dozen women she barely remembered had salivated over her ring, a couple of them giving her less than friendly glances quickly masked. Thank God Cole had had ready answers because she'd felt lost in the wilderness all over again. She chuckled as she grabbed the pink teddy bear off her bed. He was probably as creative a storyteller as his friend CJ.

After collecting her toiletries and laptop, she placed them all inside her backpack. Looking around the room to make sure she hadn't forgotten anything, she added a couple of family photographs, a picture of Jaxon, and *Black Widow* to her loot. She would need to borrow more dress clothes from Randy, something she'd never been able to do given their difference in size years ago. Maybe after the weekend, she could ask her mother to whip her up a dress or two. She shook her head. Cole's crack about moving in might not have been that far off the mark.

Looking down at her hand, she examined the ring on her finger. She'd always loved emeralds and if she'd been asked to pick out the perfect ring, she was fairly certain it would've been similar to this one. One of the few hobbies she'd indulged in over the years was the study of crystals, and she didn't dismiss their power. Emeralds had always been her favorite stones, and she had a few small ones in her jewelry case at home—nothing as pure and beautiful as this one. According to the experts, emeralds were called the "stones of successful love" because they targeted the heart, nurturing it. They symbolized hope and were said to reveal truth, justice, compassion, and harmony. Unfortunately, it was window dressing in a huge lie right now. She wished things could be different, but if wishes were horses, she'd have the largest herd in Arizona.

Swiping at her tears, annoyed with herself for letting the situation get to her like this, she went into the bathroom, washed her face, and reapplied her makeup. Unless she was working, she didn't bother with it, limiting herself to moisturizer, lip gloss, and mascara, but she wanted to make a good impression on Sylvia, and the more polished she looked, the better. Grabbing her purse, suitcase, and backpack, she went downstairs. Being with Cole wasn't the worst part of this charade, but it would be difficult spending so much time with him and not giving in to her body's needs. Damn biological clock. Who needed one of those anyway?

Cole stood in the living room near the fireplace, looking at the photograph of Grandma Maureen, much as he had earlier when Hal had been with him.

"She had a hell of a temper," Casey said going over to join him.

"She was gorgeous. You could be her clone," he answered, his voice filled with admiration that made her antsy. She disliked compliments. They always brought back Rick's words when he'd asked her to accompany him that night. Pretty words from pretty boys meant nothing.

"Apparently," she admitted grudgingly. "I have more than my share of her temperament, even if Hal doesn't think so. I fly off the handle and overreact at times, as you well know, but then, when I come to my senses, I feel like an ass and swear not to do it again."

"Hey, you aren't the only one guilty of rash behavior. Did she have trust issues, too?"

Casey felt her cheeks heat. "Not like mine," she conceded. "In fact, she was a mail-order bride, so she must've had more faith in her fellow human beings than I do."

"By that you mean men, don't you?"

She shrugged. No point in denying the obvious.

"Let's just say my track record hasn't been the greatest. She's really my great-great-great-grandmother," she went on, trying to smooth over the uncomfortable moment. "We've always just called her Grandma Maureen. I carry her name, but we're alike in other ways, too. Her skin was as fair as mine, and she'd coat her face with a paste she made to prevent sunburn when she was out riding. According to everything I've been told, like me, she loved to ride. My great-great-great-grandfather bought her a strawberry roan just after they were married. He claimed the animal's color matched her hair. When Dad gave me a roan of my own, I named her Ginger, after Grandma Maureen's favorite horse. When Ginger died, it broke me."

"Dad mentioned your horse had an accident. What happened?"

"It's a long story, and it always makes me sad to tell it," she answered, not wanting to dwell on that now. "Maybe someday I'll tell you all about Casey's folly, but not today." She glanced at her watch. "It's almost two. Let's get back to town so I can go and see Horace's secretary."

"Have you got everything?"

"I do. I'll come by for my costume on Saturday. I don't want it to get all wrinkled."

"What kind of costume is it? Some sexy saloon girl outfit?" he asked, wiggling his eyebrows.

She forced herself not to laugh. "Hardly. Do I look like the saloon girl type to you?" She put her hand up to stop him from speaking. "Don't answer that." She chewed her lower lip. "I'm afraid Mom's going to want to gush all over you, and if we don't let her, she'll get suspicious. I'll make sure she understands you didn't jilt me when this is over."

Cole didn't answer, but nodded.

Heading back into town, Casey was grateful he'd let the matter of Ginger's death drop. It would be impossible to explain that without mentioning her horrific experience with Rick, something she wasn't ready to share. She closed her eyes against the brightness of the afternoon sun, preferring silence to awkward conversation.

"We're here," Cole said, his voice rousing her.

"I'm so sorry," she apologized. "I don't usually fall asleep during the day, but I didn't get much sleep last night."

"That's okay. You didn't snore, and I only took two pictures of the drool slipping down your chin." He laughed.

"Cole Walker Junior, you better not have," she admonished, imagining an unflattering picture posted on the Internet for everyone to see.

"I was joking. You look like an angel when you're asleep. Not even a drop of drool."

"That's good to know, but I'll try not to keep falling asleep on you. This is the second time I have. You might get a complex."

He chuckled. "I'll try not to take offense. Ready to get out?"

"Yes. Let's get this over with. Hopefully, she can shed some light on Chester's visit on Monday. The boys weren't in with them the whole time. I want to go back to the station and have a look at Horace's papers and see if there's anything in them that might help."

Opening the door, she stepped out onto the street and up onto the boardwalk. The words, Horace Stone, Attorney at Law, were stenciled in black on the window. She stepped closer, attempting to peer inside, but the blinds were drawn.

"It must be like the bat cave in there with the blinds closed like that."

"I see Jaxon's rubbed off on you," he said and chuckled.

"What do you mean?" she asked distracted, still trying to see inside the office.

"Those superhero references are only the beginning. Soon you'll be craving all things related to larger than life characters."

"You can be such an idiot." She laughed.

"You wound me." He held his hand over his heart. "As far as the blinds go, some people don't like the distraction that others walking by create."

"That's true." She turned back to him. "My office in Santa Fe is on the sixth floor. I leave the blinds up all the time. If anyone did walk by, it would be more than a little distracting."

"It would be at that," he agreed and chuckled.

She huffed out a breath. "It's hotter than hell out here. Let's get inside and meet the intrepid Ms. Langston. I sure hope the AC is working." But when she tried the door, it was locked.

"What's wrong?"

"The door's locked. I don't understand. She should be here. I told her I was coming." Casey knocked loudly, but no one answered.

"Maybe she was delayed over lunch, or she's got headphones on, transcribing notes. I've seen her do that."

Casey snorted. "I hate it when this happens. If she is working on something, she should still hear the knocking. Those headphones aren't usually powerful enough to block off other sound. She's not here. People need to learn punctuality is important. I would've expected a lawyer's secretary to know that." She pulled her cellphone out of her purse. "She gave me her cell number. Let me call and see how long she'll be. Maybe we can go to the station first, and I can arrange to see her later." After dialing the number, she waited, listening as it rang.

She heard the faint sound of an answering ring coming from inside the office.

"What are the odds someone is calling the office at the exact moment you're calling her phone?" Cole asked, tipping up his hat.

"If she's in there, why isn't she answering?" Casey chewed the inside of her lip, feeling guilty for her less than charitable thoughts. "Do you think something may have happened to her?"

"I don't know. Get in the car. We'll go around back and see if her car's there. Maybe she forgot her cell when she went out or doesn't realize the front door is locked. All of the buildings on this section of the street share a lot out back. It's where I park when I come to see Horace."

"Horace is your lawyer?" she asked, surprised not to have realized that. As the only lawyer in town, Horace would be just about everyone's lawyer.

"Yes. He looks after all of my affairs, including the emporium."

Cole started the car and drove around the block to the laneway off Peralta that led into the courtyard behind the buildings.

"Stay here," he said, parking the car in front of the door with a sign similar to the one in the front window. "I'll make sure everything's all right."

"Not on your life," she answered. "You may be in charge of my safety for now, but you don't make my decisions. If Sylvia is sick or has fallen, she may need both of us. So, are you going to stand there with your mouth open, or are we going inside?"

Cole stared at her as if she'd grown another head.

He nodded. "Yes ma'am. After all, you're in charge."

She swallowed. That was right, and when she saw Rick, she would need to remember that.

Quickly getting out of the vehicle, Casey hurried to get to the door at the same time as he did. Moving ahead of her, he reached for the doorknob, but the door swung open.

"That's not good," she said softly, the butterflies in her gut taking flight.

"Stay here," he said.

"No."

Before he could stop her, she stepped past him into the

office, determined to get to the bottom of things. If the woman were sick or injured, then she needed help, but if she was just blowing her off … that needed to be fixed.

"Oh my God," she wheezed out the words on a shaky breath, staring at the destruction in front of her. It looked as if a tornado had gone through the office. Papers, books, and files were strewn all over the place, glass bowls, lamps, mirrors, and picture frames shattered. The computer monitor from the secretary's desk was on the floor, the screen smashed. From the pile of ashes in the center of the room, documents had been burned as well. She bent to move a magazine rack out of the way.

"Stop! Don't touch anything," Cole said, pulling out his cellphone. Dialing quickly, he waited for someone to answer.

"Where's Sylvia?" she asked, unable to subdue her anxiety.

He shrugged, but she could see the unease matching hers in his eyes.

Hopefully, the woman wasn't back from lunch yet. Her car was still in the lot.

"Rita, it's Cole. I'm at…"

While Cole spoke to the dispatcher, Casey moved around the room, anxious to see if the computer itself was still there. The paper files would take hours to organize. She didn't envy Sylvia the task. A forensic expert like Ryan might be able to recover some of the data if whoever had done this had tried to erase it from the hard drive, but he wasn't here, and there was no way she could send this to him. Careful not to touch anything, she stepped around the desk and cried out.

The body lying there had to be Sylvia Langston. She was on her side on the oak floor next to the overturned chair as if she'd tipped it with her when she'd fallen. The woman looked like a crumpled marionette, her once pristine white blouse now red, her light hair matted with blood and God alone knew what else. At least two dozen yellow roses were splattered atop her, along with pieces of white ceramic, shards from the broken vase probably used to strike her. A small white card lay face up on the floor near her hand, the words, "Happy anniversary, Sylvia, love Buck" was the last straw.

Turning away from the gruesome sight, tears blinding her, her stomach roiling, Casey covered her mouth and ran back to Cole, paying no attention to what she trod on.

"Hang on, Rita," Cole said into his phone, and reached for her. "What is it Casey? What did you find?"

The anxious concern in his eyes was her undoing, and the tears flowed harder. She couldn't speak, only pointed behind her.

Cole followed her pointing hand.

Letting go of her, he walked over to the desk.

"Damn," he said, his voice filled with anger and regret. He stooped behind the desk, and then stood again.

Casey's stomach roiled, and she swallowed the bitter taste of bile and pizza, covering her mouth and nose at the stench, something she hadn't noticed until she'd gotten closer to the body.

Cole came back to her, took her into his arms and turned her head into his shoulder. His heart pounded beneath her ear.

"Rita, connect me with Hal," he ordered into the phone, his words rumbling in his chest. "I don't care if POTUS is the one on the line with him, I need to talk to him right now." He moved Casey slightly away from him and looked down at her, his eyes filled with sorrow and an emotion she couldn't identify in her duress. "Are you okay?"

She shook her head, unable to speak, too afraid to open her mouth.

"It looks like she was hit on the head, probably with that flower vase near the body."

"Who?" It was the only word she could manage.

"It could be whoever delivered the flowers—we'll check on that first—but it could also be someone who just picked up the vase because it was handy. Either way, it was someone she knew, someone she trusted since he came at her from behind and given the way her desk is oriented, that would be hard for a stranger to do. It looks as if Hal has another murder for his game of *Clue*—Sylvia, in the office, with a vase."

"Why?" she asked, choking on her tears.

"I don't know, but my guess is this has something to do with Horace. Whoever did this was looking for something specific, and if they did find it, they've burned it. Hal," he said, into his phone. "I need you to get over to Horace Stone's office. I'm sorry to be the one to tell you this, but Sylvia's dead and the place has been trashed." He listened for a minute before turning to her.

"When did you talk to Sylvia?"

"Ten." Monosyllabic answers seemed to be all she could give.

"Sometime between ten this morning and now. Yeah. We won't touch a thing." He hung up the phone.

"I—" She pushed away from him, her hands clamping her mouth shut, and raced back the way they'd come. She'd barely made it outside before she vomited into a trash can beside the door, unable to keep down the contents in her stomach any longer. The undigested pizza she'd had for lunch smelled almost as vile as it had near the corpse. After a half dozen more bouts, the last two no more than dry heaves, she stood upright, embarrassed by what had happened.

"Here," Cole handed her a tissue and a bottle of water. It was warm, having sat in the car most of the day, but it helped the burning in her throat and took away the taste of the vomit.

"I may never be able to have pizza again," she said, swiping at the tears crawling down her cheeks. "I'm sorry. I'm not used to..." She gestured to the office.

"My first time, I puked all over my partner and contaminated the crime scene. So I take it this was your first?"

She nodded. "I've seen lots of crime scene photos, but I didn't know about the smell."

"It could've been a lot worse. When a person dies, all the muscles relax including the bowels and the bladder. It isn't pleasant, but as hard as it is to believe, after you've seen a few, you get used to it. She's only been dead a couple of hours so decomposition hasn't really started and the office was cold. Whoever killed her probably turned up the AC to minimize the odors while he searched the office."

"The scorch mark on the floor ... Why didn't the building catch fire?"

"My guess is he didn't want it to. Looks like he stamped out the ashes once the papers had burned. It was an extremely dangerous thing to do, but there's an excellent print over there. The techs should be able to tell us the size and the brand of the shoe, although, it looks like a man's dress shoe to me—harder to trace. He was probably hoping no one would discover her until the weekend was over. There's a sign over there that said the office would be closed from today until Monday. She was probably planning to put it in the window when she left. Whoever did this is likely to be the same person who ran Horace off the road. Otherwise, they couldn't be sure Horace wouldn't be in."

"What about the other staff?" she asked, grateful she could speak again.

"Carmen Esperenza works part-time as a paralegal, but she's on maternity leave. She had a baby a month ago. I'll have Hal call her in. If we're lucky, she may be able to tell us what's missing. I didn't see the computer when I looked."

She nodded. "Neither did I. It's possible the killer took it with him." She licked her lips. "If you don't mind, I'll sit in the car until Hal gets here."

"Good idea." Cole handed her the keys. "It's possible whoever did this didn't mean to kill her, but it's unlikely. If she'd survived, she would've been able to identify him. I'll go back in and check the offices, make sure we don't have any other bodies in there. Are you going to be okay?"

"I may never be okay again, Cole. What kind of monster does something like that?"

"A desperate one, but you can rest assured, we'll catch the son of a bitch and make him pay. Now lock the doors and don't come out until Hal gets here."

He turned and walked back into the office.

Despite the fact she was cold and clammy, Casey started the engine, letting the AC cool the overheated interior of the car, and leaned back in the seat, letting the tears fall.

The sound of the police siren in the distance forced her to swallow her distress, dry her tears, and turn off the engine. She waited until Hal pulled up beside her to get out of the vehicle, mindful of Cole's words that she could be a target, but he must've heard the sirens. He stepped out of the office as she shut the car door. Casey walked to his side. He reached for her hand, and she took it, drawing comfort from him.

"You must've broken a few speed records to get here so quickly," Cole said, as Hal joined them. "I thought you were over at the campground."

"I was, and I did—stopped at the lab, too. How are you feeling, Casey? You look a little green."

"I've been better. This is the first … you know." She hung her head, ashamed of what had happened.

"Got sick, did you? In there or out here?"

"She made it to the trash can. Didn't contaminate the scene," Cole answered for her.

"Don't feel badly, Casey," Hal said and smiled encouragingly. "Most people react that way the first time. This is Anna, our best forensic technician." He indicated the young woman who'd gotten out of the police car with him. "Doc's on his way with the coroner's wagon. I've sent Cletus over to check the house in case they didn't find what they were looking for here. Feel well enough to come back inside?"

"Is that really necessary?" She would rather walk on a bed of hot coals than go inside that office right now. Hell, she might have trouble convincing herself to go in there after the body was gone. "I don't mind waiting out here. I can lock myself in the car again," she offered, praying that would be acceptable.

"We don't really need you here," Hal said, nodding in understanding, his voice filled with compassion. "Cole, why don't you take her back to the station and set her up in the breakroom? She'll be safe there until you can pick her up later."

"Will do. Come on. I would take you to the house and let you rest, but Mom would want to know what the hell was going on, and you don't look ready to face that just yet. There's a shower at the station, and you can change into something casual. I think we can skip the opening of Gold Rush Days for tonight. Once word gets out that you found Sylvia's body, people won't expect us there."

"I would appreciate that," she said, thankful Hal and Cole had understood. That image of Sylvia was branded in her mind forever. "Honestly, the last thing I need or want right now is a corn dog and a roller coaster ride."

Cole put his arm around her shoulder and led her back to the car. He chuckled softly. "I can certainly understand that. How does chicken soup sound? Mom usually keeps some in the freezer. That stuff's guaranteed to cure just about anything."

"Perfect. You're definitely back in my good books," she said, meaning every word and trying to lighten the mood for her own peace of mind. She opened the car door, but before she could get in, Hal stepped out of the office, his face so red, he looked as if he might explode.

"I don't care who this son of a bitch is, but he's not going to kill anyone else. I'll cheer when they give him that lethal injection. He'll get more mercy than he's shown to Sylvia. I'd better call Buck. The poor guy needs to hear this from me, not the grapevine, and then I'll have to tell Melba. Damn it." He slammed his Stetson so hard against his leg that it slipped from his fingers and fell to the ground. His eyes filled with unshed tears. "Monday was their twenty-fifth wedding anniversary. I hate this part of the job." Reddening even more, he gazed at her and bent to pick up his hat. "I'm sorry, Casey. Sylvia was family. This is never easy, but when it's personal ... After Cole takes you back to the station I'll need him to come back here and stay with Anna in case the bastard comes back. If he does, Cole, shoot first, ask questions later. After I see Buck, I'll arrange for a crime scene clean-up crew from Apache Junction. The offices should be available to you by Tuesday."

Casey nodded. "That'll be fine," she said, hoping his crew could clean it up enough that she could forget what had happened here. "I understand. Thanks for letting me go." She smiled at Cole, hoping she looked braver than she felt. "We'd better get over there so you can get back."

An hour later, after showering and brushing her teeth for ten minutes, determined to get the foul taste out of her mouth even if she couldn't erase the image from her mind, Casey dressed in her denim crop pants and a plaid, sleeveless shirt, slipping on her flats. She sat down at the table in the lunch room, a cup of peppermint tea beside her. Spread out on the table in front of her were photocopies of all the documents found in Horace's briefcase. She'd managed to keep from getting sick again over the nauseating smell of gasoline as she'd made copies of the more than fifty pieces of paper and documents there, some handwritten in a scrawl she couldn't read. It looked like some form of shorthand, and with Sylvia dead, they might have to wait until Horace was awake to decipher it—if he could.

Once she'd made all the copies, she'd returned the briefcase to Rita who'd locked it in the evidence room once more. If the person who'd killed Sylvia had been after any of these, he wouldn't be happy to know they had them.

There were three separate files in the case, each labelled according to its contents. She set aside the files marked Minerva Skansen and Skansen Mining, and focused on the one labelled CJKT. Chester, Joey, Kyle, Tony—the first names of all those involved. She went through the documents meticulously, examining each one in detail, impressed with Horace's thoroughness.

Chester's will left his shares in the CJKT Discovery to the other members of the team as he'd called it. The trust agreement for the partnership was ironclad and guaranteed Rick Harvey wouldn't get his hands on his son's assets. Furthermore, contrary to what Cole thought, CJKT owned not only the mineral rights to several patented claims, it owned the land and the house that had once belonged to the Morris family. Chester had shared everything he owned with the boys, even claims dating back to the seventies. Among the documents was a proposed repair and renovations plan for the Morris house. Chester had every right to spend that night there, the documents having been signed and filed the afternoon of his death—possibly one of the things Horace had done before coming into *Cookies and Cream*.

Judging by what she'd found, it appeared Chester had planned to bring the items down from the mountain and turn his family home into a small museum to exhibit them, no doubt hoping to leave the bodies themselves in the cave undisturbed. Kyle had drawn the poignant scene, and it could easily be recreated by skilled craftsman. Perhaps archeologist could visit the site if only to try to identify these people. If the boys agreed, personal items, like the signet ring on the hand of one of the skeletons, could be returned to the families. While the Native American Graves Protection and Repatriation Act of 1990 wouldn't apply to those bodies, they did deserve some measure of respect.

The door opened and Casey looked up. Cole stood in the doorway.

"Are you ready to call it a day?" he asked.

"You're early," she said, her voice catching on the last word. "More than ready. I can finish looking through all this at the house. It's really so sad, Cole. He loved those kids and gave them everything."

"Did you find anything we can use?

"Yes. I've got Chester's will and all of the documents relating to the CJKT Discovery. Cole, the Morris house belonged to them. Horace filed the papers on Monday. Chester had every right to sleep in his own bed that night. It's really so sad."

"Come on. Let's get out of here. I've got supper in the car

and a bottle of red wine to wash it down with. We have a long day tomorrow."

Before she could finish, Hal stepped into the room.

"Cole, can I see you before you leave?" he asked. "It won't take long."

She smiled. "Go ahead. I'll finish getting my stuff together. Don't worry. I won't go anywhere."

CHAPTER TWENTY-FOUR

Cole followed Hal out of the breakroom and down the hall to his office. What could've happened that he didn't want to share with Casey?

"I meant to tell you how sorry I am about Sylvia," Cole said. "Have you got something new?"

Hal rubbed his eyes with the heels of his hands and turned back to him. He'd let down his guard, and without that mask in place, his face was haggard, his eyes heavy with sorrow and disillusionment.

The image of a broken Tate Silvers filled Cole's mind. Every man had a breaking point, and for Hal, this was it.

"Not another body, if that's what you mean," Hal answered, sighing heavily, "but the way things are going, it's only a matter of time before I do, and I hope to hell it isn't someone else I know. How's Casey holding up?"

"She seems okay. Horace's files have kept her occupied." Cole filled Hal in on what she'd told him.

"So, the boys have no motive—that's pretty much what we thought. The question is who stands to win if those kids somehow get blamed for this and the Slayer Rule comes into play?"

"I don't know," Cole admitted. "If they were convicted, they couldn't profit from the murder, but that would only apply to the fourth they would inherit from Chester since they each own a quarter of the CJKT Discovery. Maybe Chester has some long lost relative out there, but that person would have to know about the gold. I'm convinced the cave and its contents have nothing to do with Chester's death, but damned if I can figure out why anyone who knows those boys would want to frame them. Considering what we learned this morning, there's no doubt whoever's behind this, is someone who knows them well."

"Given the size of this town, that's still a lot of people, but with that in mind, we may have caught a break. Doc confirms Sylvia's time of death at between ten and ten-thirty. The cause of death is massive trauma to the back of the head. Whoever hit her did so with an incredible amount of force, and from the angle of the wound, the person was left-handed—good news I suppose since we can rule out all the right-handed people in town."

"I'm not so sure about that. While only 12 percent of the world's population is left handed, there's another 30 percent who switch hands during certain tasks. Look at Pete Rose and Mickey Mantle. There are even a few out there who are ambidextrous, doing everything with both hands equally well."

"Thanks for pissing on my parade. I didn't need that, but we can eliminate any of Horace's clients who are out of town. By the way, I sent Cletus over to the Stone house to have a look around and gave him Horace's keys." He chuckled bitterly and shook his head. "The damn fool forgot to call the security company and set off the alarm. It scared the bejesus out of him, but Clancy over at *Total Protection* turned it off and reset it remotely after he left. The good news is no one's been in the house. The bad news is we don't know if that was because they found what they were looking for at the office or simply haven't had the time to go there. Since Horace and Clara live in Mesa Park, there's always someone around, and a daytime break-in would be noticed. I've put some of the undercover AJPD officers I'd scheduled to work the fair for Gold Rush Days over there. If the killer is planning to break in there tonight, we'll catch him red-handed."

"So, in the meantime, we're back to square one?"

"It looks that way."

Cole huffed out a breath. Unless Casey's friend found something in his search, it didn't look as if they were going to get any breaks on this case. Glancing back at his friend, his frown deepened.

"Something else is bothering you, Hal" he said. "What is it?"

"I'm afraid it really isn't anything you can fix," Hal admitted, leaning against his desk. "I have to figure this out on my own. Maybe it's time for me to get out of this game. Sylvia was Melba's cousin, and we were close. Knowing I don't have any idea who's responsible for her murder makes me feel helpless, and it isn't a feeling I enjoy. Informing Buck his wife was dead was one of the hardest things I've ever done, and yet telling Melba was even worse. I'm too old for this shit."

"Nobody's ready to deal with this crap, but if you ask the people of this town, hands down they'll say you have their confidence. We will catch this son of a bitch. He'll make a mistake, you'll see. They always do, and if he thinks he's gotten away with this, which he will, given how little information is in this week's *Examiner*, he's going to get sloppy. What are you going to do now?"

"I honestly don't know," Hal said. "In all my years as a lawman, I've never had to deal with a murder case, and now I have three, with no concrete motive for any of them, plus all the rest of the stuff happening this weekend. Hell, you've got more experience with this than I do."

"I won't deny that. I saw my share of murders in Dallas, but every one of them was different. There's no magic formula for solving one, but maybe we're looking at this the wrong way."

"What other way can we look at it, for Christ's sake? We've talked it to death as it is, looking for a clue."

"Basically the first death took place over a year ago. Let's assume for the moment that the fires have nothing to do with the deaths. What if something changed, something that forced the killer's hand? Since three of the deaths and the attempted murder have all taken place within the last week or so, what if we factor Gold Rush Days into the equation?"

Hal stepped around his desk and sat down. "It's a new angle. You're thinking there's something about this year's celebration that's critical to whatever's going on?"

"Maybe. It's the two hundredth anniversary of the founding of this town. I know we're primarily celebrating the gold strike, but the stagecoach stop was here long before that. If the drug drop is the key, we'll have thousands of tourists, more than we normally get, who could spread the stuff across the country in days."

"It's a thought," Hal said, perking up. "There isn't anything to stop them from moving drugs anywhere they wanted to. Hell, they could bring in people who could just mix with the rest of the tourists. We have no proof those men we saw unloading the stuff didn't come in on the chopper, too. It would be ideal."

"That means there could be more deliveries this weekend," Cole said. "I just hope they don't come with more fires. We'll need to make sure we're well off that mountain before dusk. The last thing I want to do is put Casey or those boys in the killer's sights."

Hal nodded. "Finding the guy who was staying with Trent in Leon's apartment is critical. They promised me the sketch days ago, but the woman's memory and her eyesight just aren't panning out. Since we know Trent won't be going back, AJPD have sent in their techs. They've found lots of prints. Now, it's just a matter of separating them and hoping they're in the system. The building had no security cameras, but they're trying to get footage from anything in the area. They figure if they can find Trent in the footage, the man may be with him. It's a long shot, but it's all we have. While I would like to solve Sylvia's murder first, I'll take any win I can."

"I agree. Did the ADPS have any luck finding that SUV?"

"No. That damn vehicle has vanished. As soon as Eddy and Rick get back, I'll contact them since I need a formal identification for Trent. I doubt his ex-wife wants to come here from Wichita to do it, even if she is looking at a big insurance payout since his kids are the beneficiaries. Rick would know who might do questionable repairs on a car—hell, knowing him, Harvey Motors might even do it. The staff is constantly changing over there."

Cole laughed. "Would you want to work for Rick?"

"Point taken," Hal said and chuckled. "Maybe when this is over I'll sic immigration on him. His father wasn't above hiring paperless employees—the cheaper the better. If that man had been any tighter, he would've squeaked, but I shouldn't speak ill of the dead. As Joey said earlier, the dead can't hurt you, it's the living you have to worry about."

"Okay. Maybe Casey's friend will come up with something. She's got him looking into all of the dead as well as Eddy Ramos and Rick Harvey. If Trent was into something that got him killed, the chances are they know what it is. In the meantime, I'll concentrate on plotting the crime as you suggested and then making a list of everyone I can think of who would know the boys well enough to frame them like that. We know Trent bought a painting, and someone was able to get close enough to steal the lock and the art supplies. Since Tony won the chemistry prize at the science fair, his picture and his ability was all over the *Examiner*. I'll see what else I can get out of the boys tomorrow."

"While you're at it, add smoking into the mix. Chances are whoever killed Chester and forced Horace off the road is a smoker. There aren't as many around as there used to be. Are you going to tell Casey about CJ Coleson?"

"I don't have any choice. I'm convinced whoever is behind this knows it and has read my books. I can't come clean until I tell her. It's time everyone in Fortune knew the truth. Some people may be pissed at me, and I've got a feeling the killer is counting on that, but he isn't calling the shots any longer. We are."

Hal opened his desk drawer and took out the key for the armory.

"I got a request to provide her with a gun. All her permits are in order, and her last qualifying scores were the best I've seen in a long time, better than mine actually. We'll get her one before you leave. There are a few accessories she could use, too. Normally the last thing I want on a case is an armed civilian, but damned if I know how to do this otherwise, and while you're there to watch her back, knowing she can defend herself if she has to, makes me feel a little better. Maybe I'll throw in one of the new concealable vest. I bought three different sizes when I was ordering Rita's. Now, let's get back there before she gets too worried."

Cole followed Hal back to the lunchroom. Casey sat there absorbed in the paper she was reading. She looked up.

"What is that?" Hal asked. "You looked as if you were trying to memorize it."

"It wouldn't do me much good. It's all gobbledygook, but it does affect Minerva and Skansen Mining. I think it's a variation on some sort of old-style shorthand. Other than those two names, the rest of it might as well be hieroglyphics. Have a look."

She handed Hal the page and Cole looked over Hal's shoulder to see it for himself.

"My mother was a secretary. Looking at this, I'd say it's a personalized variation of Gregg shorthand. Since the strokes are all the same thickness, it can't be Pitman."

She chuckled. "The things you know, Cole Warner, never cease to amaze me."

He shrugged. "I tried to learn it in Dallas. I had a few quirks to mine, too, but it did make taking notes when interviewing a suspect easier. If Horace can't decipher it, I can ask Mom to give it a try—that is if it's okay with Horace."

Casey nodded. "If he doesn't object, it can't hurt. The document's useless as it is, and it could be important in the end."

"Okay then," Hal rubbed his hands together as if he were trying to warm them over a fire. "All your permits have arrived, so let's see if we can find you a weapon to use. If you can shoot, you might as well be armed. I know it's only after four, but you've had a hell of a day—we all have. If I need you before Saturday, I'll call."

Casey added the documents to her backpack.

"I can carry that for you," Cole said, picking up her soft-sided suitcase.

"Thanks." She handed him the backpack and picked up her purse.

"My own weapon is a Colt Wiley Clapp Lightweight Commander pistol. Have you got anything that comes close to that?"

"As a matter of fact, I've got one of those and a belly band as well as thigh and ankle holsters for it. Ammunition won't be a problem either, but I want you to see if one of the vests will fit you."

Casey frowned. "A vest? In this heat? I'll melt."

"Better to melt than die," Hal answered stubbornly.

Cole relaxed when she didn't argue.

Once Casey had her weapon, Cole led the way out to the parking area behind the station. She handed over the keys to her car.

"You should drive," she said. "You know where we're going. I just want to get there, drop into bed, and forget today even happened."

"Sounds like a plan, but first we need to stop for groceries. I don't want to deprive you of your morning coffee, and then we need to talk."

"About what?" she asked her voice wary, her eyes shadowed.

"The case and stuff."

She nodded, fastened her seatbelt, and leaned back in the seat.

It looked as if she had her emotions under control, but looks, like the desert, could be deceiving. As much as the timing sucked, he had to tell her the truth about CJ Coleson tonight. Maybe he should make sure she wasn't armed when he did.

Twenty minutes later, two sleeping bags, two pillows, and three bags of groceries on the seat behind them—primarily rabbit food as far as he was concerned—Cole drove Casey's sedan along the Apache Trail. He glanced at her sitting beside him. She stared straight ahead, a deep frown marring her forehead, but even that didn't detract from her beauty. She hadn't spoken much since they'd left the station, and her silence concerned him. This wasn't the quick-witted woman he knew. No doubt she was still suffering from the shock of finding Sylvia.

The late afternoon sun reflected off the tarmac making him squint in spite of the sunglasses he wore.

"In two hundred feet, turn left," the mechanical voice on the GPS instructed.

"She sounds about as friendly as you look right now. If you keep glaring at the road like that, you'll hurt your eyes," he said. "You should be wearing those sunglasses of yours."

"Sorry. I didn't mean to look menacing or unfriendly. You're right about the sunglasses," she conceded, "but they're packed in something. I'll find them when I unpack later—that is if I have anywhere to keep things."

"The realtor did say the house was partially furnished. You looked miles away. Penny for your thoughts?"

"I doubt they're worth that much. I'm trying to make sense of it all. Tell me about Matt and Evie."

He smiled. "Contrary to what you may think, I'm not on Fortune's grapevine. I haven't had time to really get to know them, but Matt's a horse breeder who specializes in animals for dude ranches. He bought the land and started his business after his wife died. Dad calls him the horse whisperer. A couple of years ago, a wild mare and her filly got separated from their herd and ended up in his. How he got those animals into his stable is still a mystery, but he did, and they've both provided him with excellent, trainable offspring. His wife, a marine he met while serving in Afghanistan, was from the San Carlos Apache Reservation, but she died shortly after Joey was born. He's a hard worker, keeps to himself. I know very little about Evie. She works as a personal support worker at the Riveredge Retirement Home. She came to Fortune from the east coast, New York I guess, about the same time as Matt. No one knows anything about Tony's father, but judging from what she said he must've been killed trying to do the right thing. Neither one of them have ever mentioned him until today. I see Evie and Matt when they come into the emporium."

"Are they CJ Coleson fans?" she asked.

"I don't think so," he said, and concentrated on the road. "Not everyone is, you know. Evie usually comes in once a week for a copy of the *New York Times*, and a few of the women's magazines I carry. Matt's into sci-fi and anything to do with horses."

She unpinned her hair and let it fall around her face, rubbing the sore spot. "I probably look like Medusa, but I haven't worn my hair up like this in weeks, and it's giving me a headache."

"You look fine. For what it's worth, I like it down like that—but it doesn't look like snakes—more like tongues of fire. I do know my mythology."

"There you go saying those things again. I told you, I don't need them."

"You're an enigma. I haven't known tons of women, but you're the first one who refuses to accept a compliment."

"Because I know it's bullshit most of the time."

He frowned but didn't argue with her, since he knew there was truth to what she said. Flattery wasn't always honest. It could be used as a tool to manipulate people, especially those who were young and impressionable. So who had used it on

Casey and why?

"I looked up maps to the Peralta and Lost Dutchman mines online earlier," she said, changing the subject. Do you realize thousands of people comb these mountains looking for those mines each year? Imagine what the odds were against Chester and the boys finding that particular cave. Even Joey knows how fantastic it sounds. He likened it to one of Edgar Rice Burroughs's novels."

"Maybe Burroughs stumbled onto something similar when he wrote *John Carter* and the mysterious tales of Barsoom. That book was written in the early twentieth century. People were still finding donkey skeletons with baskets of gold nuggets back then," he suggested. "We're not talking a portal to Mars here, but the gold is tangible as are the artifacts. You saw them. I'm not blowing smoke here, Casey. This is real."

She pursed her lips. "I know, and it's possible people may have died because of it." She shivered. "We're overlooking something. I know it in my gut, but damned if I can figure out what it is. My dad says the town owns the land where the houses burned down—well other than the Skansen properties. Is that right?"

"It is. All of them were confiscated for back taxes. Those houses were built for the men who oversaw the mines. Once the mines closed, most of the employees just walked away. I suppose a developer could come in and buy the land, but it's still in the Tonto National Forest, so there are restrictions on its uses. Without the Skansen land, I doubt anyone would really be interested, and Minerva won't sell that land no matter how worthless those mines are. She's convinced they're part of her legacy."

"I don't see Eddy feeling that way. As I recall, even back then, he ran through money as if it was sand, and if he can convince enough people that Minerva is demented..."

"He could wrest control of Skansen Mining from her. Eddy's got huge alimony payments to make each month, and as much as he'd gladly sell off that land for some extra cash, as long as Minerva's in charge, he's shit out of luck. She may be over seventy, but that woman is in excellent health. I see her out walking her cat at least once a day."

"Walking her cat? Seriously?"

"Yes. She has this big old marmalade cat named Peaches. That animal means the world to her. He's got to be at least twenty years old."

Casey shook her head. "I don't remember her walking a cat. Living out of town as I did, I didn't spend a lot of time in your neighborhood. How much farther?"

"In one hundred feet, turn left. You have reached your destination."

Casey chuckled. "And here I thought it was a computer. I didn't know she answered questions."

"I think that was just a coincidence, but it was kind of spooky." He pretended to shiver.

She giggled nervously.

He turned as instructed and stopped in front of a majestic wrought iron gate depicting the mountains in the distance.

"What do you think?" he asked, hoping she would be as fascinated with the house as he'd been after seeing the pictures. "I've only seen photographs, but it reminds me of the area around Table Rock. There's a pool and hot tub out back, and it comes with three fenced acres bordering the Superstition Mountain Wilderness and a top-of-the-line security system. I know you may not be too fond of the desert right now, but you shouldn't let one bad experience ruin it for you."

"You're right. My second night in the desert is best left forgotten, but nothing can spoil the memories I have of the first night." She smiled warmly. "If these gates are anything to go by, the house must be magnificent. How does it open?"

"The realtor gave me a code and the instructions on how to change it from inside the house. Here goes nothing. Open Sesame," he said in a bad imitation of Ali Baba from the Disney movie she's seen years ago. The gates remained closed.

"Don't give up your day job."

Cole shrugged, punched in the numbers, and watched as the gates slowly swung open.

"I may not be much of a magician, but that works. They should shut as soon as we've driven through."

He put the car in gear and drove ahead, moving less than ten feet before the gates started to close.

"Impressive," she said. "Maybe we should keep the boys here. We'd all sleep better with that."

"We could," he agreed reluctantly. He was looking forward to spending time alone with her. "Keeping the boys here would be counterproductive. We'll be coming and going. The last thing we want is for someone shadowing you to see them."

She shook her head. "You make it sound like there's a gang involved. Let me delude myself that there's no one watching my every move, nor will there be. This isn't the Wild West, nor is it a CJ Coleson novel, although, if it was, he'd know exactly what was going to happen next."

Cole burst out laughing. "I happen to know half the time, he doesn't know what's going to come next either."

She scrunched up her face, blew out a breath, and then chuckled. "Please, just because you know my hero's flaws, don't tell me his secrets. I want to keep worshipping from afar for a while longer."

Cole's stomach cramped. Maybe he should just tell her now and be done with it.

"Who else has the code to the gate?" she asked, and the moment was lost.

"The realtor has the one I used, but once we get to the house, I'll change it and reset it."

He drove around a curve in the road.

Casey gasped. "Oh, Cole! It's beautiful ... a hacienda straight out of *Zorro*. Does it have a stable, too?"

"No stable, but it wouldn't be hard to add one. There's a three-car garage around back—lots of place for our Harleys as well as a car."

"How on earth did you find it? No one's going to believe

this is my new home. I couldn't afford it no matter how much I'd saved, especially not after I'd supposedly just bought into Horace's practice. And the owner's okay with letting us use it like this?"

"The house is for sale. The real estate company is letting us use it for now until a sale goes through. Don't forget, it's supposed to be *our* house, as in the two of us. I'm not exactly a pauper. There's an underground sprinkler system to maintain the grass and plants, although most of them are common enough in this area. We're close to a small tributary of the Salt River. The management company has kept everything in tip-top shape."

"Well, it's incredible. So how *did* you find this particular place?"

He reddened. "You seemed to have issues with my living arrangements, so I thought I would find a place of my own. I went to see the realtor yesterday, saw pictures of the place, and fell in love with it."

Casey stared at him, her eyes the size of quarters, emotions racing across her face faster than he could identify them.

"Can you afford a place like this? I mean it's gorgeous, but it must cost an arm and a leg."

Cole chewed on his lip, not wanting to lie again. He'd need a steam shovel to fill the hole he'd already dug.

"I came into a chunk of money last year. The price of the house fits my budget." He'd gotten a seven-figure royalty check for the movie rights to his books.

"What did you do? Win Powerball?"

He shrugged his answer and smiled. "Ready to see inside?"

"Absolutely."

He smiled. "Your wish is my command."

CHAPTER TWENTY-FIVE

Casey berated herself for her nosiness. When it came right down to it, Cole's finances were his business and none of hers.

Removing the key from the pocket of his uniform jacket, he got out of the car and led her up the three steps to the stone veranda. After unlocking the door, he stepped inside to silence the alarm with the second code he'd been given, and turned to her.

"Yesterday, when I imagined bringing you here, I saw myself carrying you over the threshold, kissing you breathless, and then making love on a blanket in front of that beautiful stone fireplace, but none of that is going to happen, is it?"

She shook her head, regret pooling in her stomach.

"Cole, we agreed to take it slow, remember? I'm not saying that scenario of yours will never happen, but … That's the best I can do."

He might not have any more secrets, but she did. Until she could be 100 percent honest with him, it would have to be enough for them both.

"Now, let's have a good look at this gorgeous house."

"Right this way."

He climbed the circular staircase on the right, and she followed in his wake, oohing and aahing as they moved from room to room. There were four bedrooms, two of which were furnished. The master bedroom had the biggest bed Casey had ever seen, with matching dressers, a vanity table, and its own fireplace. The en suite bathroom was huge, complete with a double multi-headed shower and a Jacuzzi tub built for two. The other bedroom also had a private bathroom and held a queen-sized bed and matching dressers.

"What do you think?" he asked after they'd returned to the main floor.

"I'm speechless. It's incredible. I don't see how anyone wouldn't love it here. If I could imagine the perfect house, this would be it. And that view ... You were right. The angle's off a little, but it's similar to the one from Table Rock. If there are any lights up there tonight, we'll see them." She stepped over to the breakfast island in the kitchen.

"If you're expecting gourmet meals, you're out of luck. The cooking gene isn't as strong in me as it is in my mother and sister. I'm great at nuking frozen food, or perhaps you'd like to use that fancy grill?" She pointed to the deck off the lanai. In addition to the gas grill, there was a beautiful wrought iron, glass topped table with at least a dozen chairs. "I do make a mean salad."

"I hope so. We bought enough greens to feed an army. Tonight we've got soup and sandwiches, courtesy of Mom."

"And I'm not sure how much of that I'll manage."

"We don't have to eat for a while. Why don't we check if the hot tub is operational? If it is, you can have a relaxing soak before we eat."

"That sounds heavenly. I've got a swimsuit in my bag. You take the big bedroom, and I'll use the other one."

Cole was outside and back inside within seconds. "Everything is good. I'll get the stuff from the car. If you put away the groceries, I'll take the luggage upstairs."

"Deal."

Two hours later, refreshed from her soak followed by a swim, Casey sat in the lanai talking on the phone to her mother. She'd described finding Sylvia's body and knew her mother understood the severity of the situation.

"I will, Mom. You have my word. I'll come by Saturday evening to get my dress," Casey said into the phone, grateful her mother couldn't see how red her cheeks were. She could feel them flaming, and if Randy had been anywhere near her, she would've see the falsehood for what it was. Hopefully by Saturday, she would have herself under better control.

"Plan on staying for supper," her mother answered sniffling, her tears not only from happiness but from sorrow and fear. Sylvia had been an old, dear friend. "We've got more to celebrate this weekend than Gold Rush Days, even if terrible things have happened. It's almost as if this town is cursed, just like the mountains. I need to remind myself that good always wins in the end, but this week's events have shaken my faith. Your engagement is the best news I've gotten in months. You aren't using that death machine, are you?"

"My Harley's going to stay right where it is for now, and Cole and I will travel together in the sedan, you have my word on that."

"I still think it's odd that Horace chose to go on vacation this week of all weeks. You could use his help getting organized." Her mother's indignation replaced her distress.

"I told you. He'd made the plans beforehand. No one expected any of this, especially not Cole's proposal and my decision to accept his offer. I encouraged him to go. It's been years since he and Clara have had a vacation. You did mention you and Dad want to travel ... It's only going to be for a couple of weeks. It'll give me a chance to get my bearings." The lies were slipping off her tongue too easily, and she hated herself for it, but the truth might mean more deaths.

"What about your apartment and your things?"

"I'll instruct the realtor in Santa Fe to put it up for sale. It'll show better furnished and clean. Look, I have to go. After the day I've had, I want supper and an early night. I love you."

"I love you, too. Be careful. I want grandchildren, but I don't want you waddling up the aisle."

"Mom!" Casey's cheeks were on fire.

Her mother chuckled. "Have you set a date yet?"

"No. We've only been engaged one day. Give me time."

"Well, a Thanksgiving wedding would be lovely, and Fallon would be home. Just saying. You've been cooking this up for years. What's the point of waiting any longer?"

"Mom," the warning note in Casey's voice said it all.

"I know. Give our love to Cole, and Casey, I'm really happy you've decided to come home."

"Me, too, Mom. I'll see you Saturday." Casey swallowed the lump in her throat. When the truth came out, and it was time to return to Santa Fe for real, hearts would be broken, but that was the price she would have to pay for doing the right thing now. She just hoped they would be able to forgive her. She doubted she would ever be able to forgive herself for hurting them all once more.

Casey ended the call and stared out into the desert. Dad must be a hell of a storyteller since Mom and Randy had accepted the news so easily. Of course, having Noella and Senior gushing about it, as well as Rita who'd told just about everyone in town, had added to its authenticity. When they'd stopped at the Warner house to pick up something Cole had forgotten, she'd wanted to crawl under a rock and hide, but her distress, attributed to finding Sylvia and not to perpetuating lies, made it easy for them to escape quickly.

It seemed her world revolved around deceit these days—so much so that even she didn't know what was true, what was conjecture, and what was false. At least, she and Cole were almost being honest with one another. The only thing standing between them was her real reason for refusing to come back to Fortune, and that truth wasn't one she expected to share—that was assuming Rick didn't say something, but he wouldn't brag about committing a crime, would he?

Of course, it he was part of that macho mind set, the locker room mentality that excused almost any boorish behavior, he might not even realize it was a crime. Maybe he'd been too drunk to remember. She shivered and shook her head. This wasn't the time to worry about that. She had more than enough to concern her.

Swiping at her own tears, she stared at the setting sun bathing everything from the Superstition Mountain in the distance to the water in the pool beside her a vivid golden red. The temperature was now in the high seventies, and the sky was clear, promising another hot day tomorrow. It was quiet, too quiet, and that unsettled her. Back in the day when home had been an isolated ranch, there were always sounds of some sort—cattle lowing, chickens clucking, birds, insects—but now, nothing and that filled her with dread. Tomorrow was going to be hard on her. Superstition Mountain might look inviting, but it wasn't.

Stepping into the house, she walked back to the empty living room and looked at the half dozen watercolors Cole had brought with him from the emporium. She recognized Weaver's Needle, the old Skansen homestead, no doubt drawn before the fire, pictures of the typical Sonoran Desert landscape, one she was certain depicted the part of the wilderness where she'd gotten lost. There was one view with Weaver's Needle in the distance that was at an angle she would never have thought possible. It was as if Kyle had drawn it from the heart of the mountain.

She stretched her tight shoulders. The loaded Colt rested in the belly band under her shirt. On the one hand, she felt safe, knowing she was armed. On the other, she wished it wasn't necessary, but memories of Sylvia forced her to accept that it was.

"How about I heat up that soup for us now?" Cole asked, coming back downstairs to join her at her private art showing. "You really should eat, and like I told you, Mom's chicken soup cures everything. There are chicken sandwiches and slices of apple pie for dessert."

"You're right," she conceded. "I don't know that I can do the food justice, but I'll probably feel better after I eat. Maybe if

I walk away from these for a bit, I'll be able to tell which ones are familiar and which ones I've convinced myself I've seen before. This one in particular bothers me."

"I've never seen that one before. It wasn't one I had up on the wall. He brought it in a couple of weeks ago," Cole said, picking up the twelve by fourteen canvas. "Judging from the shadows, it's as if he's in the interior of the mountain in some kind of crater. If the chopper had landed there, I wouldn't have seen it."

"Is it possible it's near their cave?"

"If it is, we're certainly not going to sell it." He pulled out his phone and took a picture of the painting. "We can look for those rocks tomorrow. They remind me of those inuksuit—you know the Inuit rock statues denoting safe passage. Hikers are building them all over the place these days to mark their paths."

"Yeah. I was reading something not too long ago that claims they're becoming a nuisance at some UNESCO sites, and that signs have been posted prohibiting them. Leave it to people to overdo something and ruin it for everyone." She set down the painting she'd been examining, just as her stomach grumbled loudly.

"I would say that's my cue to feed you," Cole said and chuckled.

"My body knows better than my brain does," she conceded, refusing to give in to what else her body wanted that she intended to deny it.

Following him into the kitchen, she sat on an oak stool at the center island which doubled as a breakfast bar, and watched him put the container of soup in the microwave.

"I see you cook like I do," she said and laughed softly. There was a familiar intimacy to the scene she'd fantasized years ago, when she'd imagined that she and Cole might fall in love someday, but that had been a lonely teenaged girl's dream. The reality was, she would never be able to give her heart to any man until she could trust them, and while her heart said she could trust Cole, her brain refused to listen. They could be friends, nothing more. He turned back from the stove, forcing her to push the sad thought to the back of her mind.

"Tonight, I do, but one of these days, I'll grill you a steak that will melt in your mouth."

"Well, you do make good coffee," she admitted, hoping her tone was as lighthearted as his had been, "so I'll take your word on it."

"How did the call with your mother go?" he asked. "I wasn't eavesdropping. I heard the phone ring on my way in."

"She's thrilled about all this—you, me, the partnership— but devastated about Sylvia and what she now see as a curse on the town as well as the mountains. I'm beginning to feel the same way. I've always maintained that honesty is the best policy and right now, I couldn't be more dishonest if I tried."

Cole reddened slightly and chuckled uncomfortably. "You shouldn't feel that way. Look at the big picture. The truth right now could get you, me, and those boys killed."

Casey nodded, knowing he was probably correct, but that didn't make it right. When they caught the killer, a good defense attorney could use all the half-truths they'd come up with to create reasonable doubt in the mind of a jury. If she were the one prosecuting the case, she would make damn sure she had a solid confession and a mountain of irrefutable evidence. Whoever had killed Leon, Trent, Chester, and Sylvia deserved to burn in hell.

Cole ladled the soup into bowls and placed a plate of sandwiches on the counter between them, next to a sleeve of crackers.

"Thank you," she said, reaching for a soda biscuit. "I can't remember the last time a man made me dinner."

"I would be happy to make you any meal you wanted," he answered huskily.

"Let's not go there tonight, Cole," she pleaded, her body quite willing to go that route even if her common sense said it would only make things worse. "I can't deal with us and everything else right now."

He nodded, but took her free hand in his.

"Fine—for now—but we will have to talk later."

Reluctantly, pulling her hand away, she picked up the spoon and started to eat. They ate in silence, each wrapped in private thoughts. Once they'd finished their meal, Cole seemed to pull even deeper inside himself, and Casey was afraid she'd made a calculated error. This stoicism wouldn't help.

"Coffee?" he asked as he collected the dirty dishes.

"Yes, please."

The serious way he'd asked had her as antsy as she'd been on the deck earlier.

Moments later, he carried two cups of coffee back to the table with him and placed a package she hadn't noticed on the breakfast bar in front of her.

"Cream and sugar, just the way you like it."

"Thanks." She took a mouthful of the hot brew. "What's this?" she asked, unable to deny her curiosity.

"I brought you a present."

"What's the occasion?" Most people looked happier when they handed out gifts.

"None. Open it, and then we'll talk," he said, sighing heavily.

"About what?" she asked confused, hoping he wasn't going to make it about them.

"You'll know when you open the package."

Despite her mixed feelings, Casey smiled weakly as she carefully unwrapped the gift, revealing a copy of the anthology CJ Coleson had released to family and friends, the book Cole had started reading to her Monday night.

She smiled. "Thank you. I promise it won't put me to sleep again."

"Look inside the front cover," he instructed.

Opening the book of short stories, she saw what he meant. This was the real gift—the one thing she'd asked him for on the day they'd met.

"For Casey, the woman I hope will always be my greatest

fan, CJ Coleson," she read aloud before squealing with joy much as Jaxon had several times yesterday. She placed the book on the counter, stood and reached over to kiss him on the cheek. "This is the best gift I've ever gotten, and a real pick-me-up considering the day it's been. Thank you."

Expecting him to stand and take her in his arms, she was surprised when he didn't and stared down at the counter instead. Reluctantly, she backed away from him and sat down once more, cradling the book to her chest, worry making the acid in her stomach bubble and churn threatening to return the soup as it had the pizza.

"How did you manage to get this so quickly?" she asked, bewildered by his odd behavior. She knew the case was bothering him—hell, it was eating at all of them—"Are you afraid I'm going to ask to meet CJ in person now?" She chuckled nervously. "Don't worry. I'll give it a couple of weeks."

The fact that he wasn't answering scared her, and she chewed on her lower lip, anxiously waiting for him to speak.

He sat there silently, one hand running through his hair, clearly struggling with something.

"Cole—"

"You've already met him, Casey," he said softly. "I'm CJ Coleson. It's *my* pen name. I created Tate Silvers, Prospect, and all the rest of it." The words rushed out of his mouth.

Casey felt as if she'd been slapped.

He reached for her hands. "Say something," he begged.

"I don't believe you," she whispered, tears clogging her throat. Cole might have lied to her about the helicopter and the cat's cry, but he'd done it with the best of intentions. This ... he would not have lied about something like this.

"It's the truth, Casey. I've spent the better part of five years keeping my identity secret—or at least I thought it was secret. I didn't set out to deceive you."

At the sincerity in his words, she wanted to weep. Her heart ached. The words, "just like the others," screamed in her brain.

Here she'd almost been ready to give him another chance and now this. She pulled her hands away, stood, put the book on the breakfast bar, and went out onto the lanai, staring out at the deck lit by solar lights now that it was dark.

"Why?" The only word she could think of split the heavy silence.

"To protect myself. A friend of mine worked as an acquisitions editor in Dallas. He knew I wanted to write and encouraged me to do so. I started with that anthology, and while he would've published it, I felt it lacked something. When I came home to Fortune, it was as if my inspiration came to life. I went to work for Hal Rankin, and Tate Silvers was born. You said my novels were like coming home. You must've recognized Heidi Slocum in Elvira Meddler. If you spent enough time here, you would be able to see those who've inspired some of my other characters, too. Fortune is my muse." He shook his head. "At first, I didn't want anyone to know I'd written a book because I didn't want to be the town joke. Then Tate Silvers took off, and it was too late to tell people without having them thinking I was either lying or bragging. Hal knows the truth as do my parents and Horace Stone who's my lawyer and negotiated the movie rights' contracts."

"That's where you got the money to buy this house." He'd said he'd come into money last year and hadn't explained where. Her heart hurt. She wanted to run away and hide, but stood there, hearing him but not listening to his words. She forced herself to concentrate.

"You should see the bags and bags of fan mail I get," he went on. "I needed my identity to remain a secret if I wanted any peace. Now that I've had time to think about it, I realize that may have been a big mistake. While I might've been protecting myself, someone else figured out who I am, and may have used my books to complicate this case. I never actually lied to you, you know. I just let you think I was two people instead of one."

There was desperation in his voice, but she was numb

inside. At least, for all intents and purposes, the pain had gone. Logically, she could see his explanation made perfect sense. My God! How dumb could she be? Of course he hadn't lied. The answer was right there in his name. CJ Coleson—Cole Junior Cole's son.

"You may not have lied to me in the strict definition of the word, but you haven't been honest either. I can see why you wouldn't tell me the truth that first day in the store, but you've had ample opportunity to do so since then. That night you took me to Table Rock, when you rescued me from the puma, last night by the lake when I mentioned asking CJ for help. I specifically asked you if you had any more secrets. No wonder your father looked at me as if I were three bricks short of a load. You may not have lied, but you implied a lie, and to me, it's the same thing."

"Is it?" he challenged. "If I were writing a biography for a book jacket, it would say exactly what I told you. 'CJ Coleson was born in Arizona with the desert in his blood. He attended the University of Texas at El Paso and worked in Dallas until giving up his job to become an author. Community minded, he does all that he can for his home town and the people who inspire him.' Not lying, Casey, prevaricating. As a lawyer, you know people tell half-truths all the time. You've done it at least twice that I know of since you've been home. This isn't like last night. The only thing I withheld from you was that CJ Coleson is my alter ego. I'm sorry for not telling you sooner, but like you, I'm a very private person."

"So why tell me now?" she challenged. "Did you think I hadn't had enough bad news today?"

"Naïvely, I assumed you might get a kick out of realizing you know the man you claimed was your favorite author, but since we've had enough lies between us, it was Hal's suggestion. You heard him yourself. We're pulling a CJ Coleson to figure this out. He wants me to plot what we have as if it were a novel and see if I can get the various pieces to fit. I don't know if it will work, but we have to try something before whoever's behind this gets whatever it is he's after."

She frowned. "If Hal hadn't brought up this idea, would you have told me the truth?"

He ran his hand through his hair. "Yes, but maybe not right away, and certainly not like this. I know you're hurt and angry, but if you think about it, it's not that bad."

"Not that bad? Really?" She fought to tamp down the bitterness in her voice. She couldn't let him see how devastated she was. "Why did Hal want you to tell me now?" she challenged.

"He thinks you can help me with this. Your ideas last night were bang on. Casey, you told me the other day that you liked to keep things to yourself, well, so do I. That day we met, you called me the Howard Hughes of authors, and you're right, but CJ is part of me, and I don't want any secrets between us. I know it's been a rough few days, but I'm hoping there can still be an 'us' when this is over. The last thing I wanted to do was hurt you."

"But you did hurt me—more than you can possibly understand," she said, that sense of betrayal she'd felt time and again nipping at her. Another man, another liar. "I'm going up to my room to unpack. I can see the wisdom in plotting out the crimes, but right now, I don't think I would be of much use. It's been a hell of a day. Give me some time to think." She chuckled, but had to blink to hold back the tears. "I thought getting to meet my favorite author would be a huge thrill, but now all I feel is disillusioned."

"Think about this, please … Haven't you ever bent the truth around strangers to protect your privacy? I care about you, Casey, more than I've ever cared about another woman in my entire life." The sorrow in his voice increased the pain she felt.

"Just let me deal with this in my own way, please?" she begged. "We need to be able to work together on this case. I'm not angry—yes, I am—there's no point in prevaricating as you said, but not for the obvious reason. This is really all my fault. Getting involved with you the way I did was a mistake. I knew it, but I did it anyway. Now, we'll both pay the price." She stood. "I'll see you in the morning. It's been a long discouraging day. Goodnight."

She stood, took the books he'd given her, and climbed the stairs to her room, feeling his gaze following her all the way up the staircase. It would take an eternity to get over this pain, but better to end it now than to go on lying to herself that they could make it work. Entering her room, she closed the door, and threw herself down on the bed, sobbing into the pillow, knowing it muffled the sounds she made. When she had cried herself out, she got up, unpacked her cases, and put her belongings away. Her heart ached as it never had before, but she would get over it—she had to. Unfortunately, there was nowhere to run, nowhere to hide this time.

She'd always known CJ Coleson had disliked publicity. If she'd realized Cole was her favorite author when she'd met him again, how would that have affected the way she'd responded to him? It wouldn't have. The man drew her, and as hurt and angry as she was, she couldn't deny he still did. Sighing, she admitted the truth to herself. Not divulging his identity to her hadn't been a personal slight, it had been a survival mechanism. The more she thought about it, the more she realized it was exactly what she would've done in Cole's place, needing to keep normalcy in her life. She would have to apologize in the morning. Where their relationship might go from here was anyone's guess.

Glancing at the folder of photocopies she'd brought home with her, she realized she should take some time to go through them, but she was too heart-sore to give them more than a cursory glance. The papers relating to Minerva Skansen were a combination of land title papers and the gibberish short-hand that was either Sylvia's or Horace's. There was a copy of her will among the papers, but as for the rest of them … She wouldn't be able to make sense of this without Horace's or Minerva's help. She'd bring the documents with her on Saturday when she dropped in on Minerva.

She yawned. Right now, what she needed to do was get what little sleep she could. Getting into her pajamas, she brushed her teeth, and climbed into bed. Tomorrow was going to be another long, difficult day.

CHAPTER TWENTY-SIX

The sound of the alarm woke Cole from a restless sleep. It was five-thirty, and they needed to get up and get going. Pulling on his jeans, he left the room to wake Casey.

He hoped she'd had a better night than he had—what little of it there'd been. When she'd left him, he'd opted to stay downstairs and had spent a couple of hours making that outline Hal had suggested. He'd listed all the facts they had in a quasi-chronological order, even adding the earthquake now that it had taken on new significance, and the cigarette smoker, but every time he tried to connect the events, that binding agent, which would make the pieces all come together and hold up in court, was missing. All they had were theories, and unproven, those ideas were worth nothing. Time and again, he'd wanted to climb those stairs and apologize for being an ass among other things, and beg her to come and help him, but she'd asked him to leave her alone, and so he had.

When he'd finally decided to try and get some sleep, there'd been no light coming from under her door, and the house had been deathly quiet. He'd gone into his room and gotten into bed, but sleep had been slow coming, and he was more tired today than he'd been yesterday. While he felt as if he'd lost a piece of himself—the best part—the most he could hope for this morning would be some measure of civility.

He knocked on the door. "Casey?" he called loudly. "It's time to get up."

"I'm awake," she answered, her voice muffled. "What time is it?"

"Almost a quarter to six. We have to be at the Pearson ranch within the hour if we expect to leave at seven. I'll shower and then make coffee. See you downstairs."

He heard her groan and smothered a chuckle. Not a morning person. He would file that tidbit away for future reference—if they ever had a future.

"Make that coffee strong."

"Will do."

Fifteen minutes later, he stood at the counter waiting for the coffee to perk.

"God, it isn't even light out," Casey commented, stepping into the kitchen.

"And that's a good thing." Like him, she wore jeans, boots and a long-sleeved cotton shirt. She would be warm, but at least she wouldn't burn. "We'll be comfortable for a few hours. I assume you've got stuff for your face? The sun will be up soon, and the weatherman's calling for a hundred degrees again today. Joey said it takes almost three hours to get to the cave. He claims he can break the ride up a bit, but when it comes down to it, that's a lot of time in the saddle for both of us. While I ride horses as well as my Harley, I don't do it on a regular basis."

"I haven't been on a horse in a long time, but to answer your question, I've slathered on the sunscreen, and have more in my pouch. While I have my sunglasses today, I forgot to pack a hat. I hope to borrow one from Matt," she said and yawned. "About last night—"

"Let's not go there right now," Cole said. "You have every right to be furious with me, but in time I hope you'll forgive me. I know you believe we can't make 'us' work, but I'm not ready to give up yet."

The percolator gave that familiar whoosh that indicated the

brew was ready.

"Coffee's up." He reached into the cupboard and pulled out two mugs. "Do you want something to eat?"

"Yes, please. Give me a yogurt, and one of those bananas." She chewed her lip. "I just want to apologize for overreacting last night, and then I'll let this go. You have every right to your privacy, and if people knew who you really were, then they might treat you differently. I can see why you would want to keep your identity to yourself. I can only imagine what a flood of paparazzi and avid fans would do to your life. As far as *we* go, I think we work well together and we can be friends, but as for the rest of it, let's put that on hold for now. There's probably a reason why we didn't come together years ago, and while I can't deny we have great chemistry, maybe some things just aren't meant to be. When this case is over, I'll be returning to my life in Santa Fe, and you're staying here where your muse is. I can respect and understand that, I don't see anything changing it."

"But you aren't telling me to give up, either." He smiled at her. It was an opening, not a big one, but any chink in the wall she'd built between them was a welcome one. "I told you the other night, I'm not going to let geography get in the way."

She shrugged. "Suit yourself." Rubbing her eyes, she yawned again. "I had the strangest dream last night. I felt as if I was on some bizarre carnival ride with the bed rolling and shaking."

"You weren't dreaming. There was an earthquake just after midnight. According to the Internet, it wasn't a big one—3.2 on the Richter scale. The epicenter was near Sonora, Mexico. We'll probably have a few more aftershocks in the next couple of days."

Chuckling, she shook her head. "I should've realized it was something like that. Last year, I spent three weeks in Sacramento. There were several minor tremors while I was there. They felt a lot like a freight train passing. I have gaps in my memory when it comes to living in Fortune, but I don't recall earthquakes when I was growing up."

"That's because the ones we normally get barely shake the pictures on the wall, but we aren't as far from the San Andreas Fault as people think. The quake we had last year—the one the boys claim revealed the cave—measured 5.3. A couple of people got hurt. At one point, we thought that might've been why Leon fell, and we still can't dismiss that. It was the strongest one we've had in this region since 1887."

"Well, as long as they stay small ... I'm not ready for Arizona to become beach front property. Hal has enough on his hands without something like that."

Forty-five minutes later, Cole drove through the gates of the Pearson ranch. The sun was slowly rising, the horizon bathed in pink. A large dog, at least part collie given his coloring, barked a welcome and came over to the sedan.

Cole opened the car door, allowed the dog to smell him and watched as Casey did the same, rubbing the dog between the ears, sending his tail wagging.

The door opened and Kristal came out. Cole almost didn't recognize her. She wore jeans and a baggy T-shirt. Her hair was pulled back into a ponytail, and for the first time in the five years since he'd been back, her face was devoid of makeup. She looked tired, but weren't they all?

"Good morning," she said, more in command of herself than she'd been yesterday. "Clover, come here, girl." She patted her leg calling the animal to her. "Matt wants her inside when you leave. He doesn't want her following Joey."

"Where's everyone else?" Cole asked.

"Matt's in the barn, saddling your horses. Evie's inside making lunch for you. We talked about this last night, and if we could, we'd all go with you, but since I'm not much of a horsewoman and Evie's never ridden, five to six hours on a horse would probably kill us both." She chuckled. "Look at me caring about someone other than myself. Will wonders never cease?"

Cole frowned, not sure whether to believe this transformation or not. From Casey's raised eyebrows, she

350

wasn't sure either.

"It's going to be hot and uncomfortable up there, and for someone who doesn't ride at all, it would be hell. Staying put is a good choice."

"Yeah, well what can I say? Suddenly I'm Miss Congeniality, worrying about others." She shook her head. "I've made a career of being Queen Bitch and everyone knows it. Unfortunately, it's almost cost me my son." She sighed. "Rick called my cellphone last night to tell me he was on a hot streak and staying in Vegas until Saturday. Apparently he and Eddy have met up with old friends. No doubt he's got a woman with him, and I don't care anymore. Rick was looking for Trent— why he thought I'd know where that jerk was is beyond me— but apparently he was supposed to show up at the casino and bring Rick some money he owed him. Some lucky streak if he's counting on anything from Trent to support it. That asshole never pays his debts. He still owes Kyle fifty bucks for that watercolor he bought."

"A watercolor of what?" Casey asked, chewing her lip as if she expected Kristal not to answer her.

Cole scowled. Whatever history she and Kristal had wasn't good. Kyle had mentioned he'd made drawings the day he'd been at the site he'd recognized from the photos in Leon's safety deposit box.

"Just some interesting rocks. I thought it was Weaver's Needle, but it wasn't big enough. Trent just had to have it— some boloney about fond memories of the place as a kid. Kyle didn't want to sell it, but then Rick got into it with him, and the next thing I knew Trent left with the painting, promising Kyle the money. That was a month ago."

"Maybe he gave the money to Rick. Did it look like this?" Cole asked, showing her the photograph he'd taken of that watercolor last night.

"And of course he gambled it away. That makes sense. Rick doesn't care whose money he loses." She reached for the phone and scrutinized the photo. "Maybe a little, but the one Trent wanted was from a different perspective. You could see part of Weaver's Needle in it, or at least some tall thin rock that looked like it." She returned the cellphone.

"Thanks."

It was possible Rick had called fishing for information, knowing Trent was dead and trying to give himself an alibi, but the man just wasn't that smart. More than likely, he had no idea what was going on, unless Trent had told him the real reason he'd wanted the painting, but unfortunately Cole had no idea what that might be.

"I don't know why I put up with him and all his loser friends for so long."

"You were in love," Cole offered. "Sometimes things don't go the way we planned." The way things were between him and Casey was a good example of that.

"Well, I've had enough. When this is over," Kristal continued, "I'm filing for divorce. In the meantime, I didn't tell him anything that had happened. I just said I was going out of town for a little rest and relaxation of my own, and that Kyle was spending the weekend with Tony and Joey. I figured that made more sense in case he decided to go to Phoenix looking for me. If he goes bust, he's going to need more money. He's blown through most of my inheritance, but I've managed to squirrel away a few dollars, and if there's anything to this treasure Kyle's been telling me about, we should be able to manage on our own. Hell, I've got enough evidence of Rick's cheating on me, I should be able to blow the pre-nup out of the water and get child support at least."

"I can appreciate that," he said.

"Thanks. I have my moments of lucidity." She turned to Casey. "I know you have no reason to like me or trust me, especially after everything I did to you, but I want to make amends." She took a deep breath. "Some of the things I've said to you, I can never take back or fix, but thank you for what you're doing for my son. You were always smarter than I was. I guess you're a better person that I'll ever be, too. For what it's worth, I had nothing to do with that night." She shrugged. "I would say I was sorry, but we both know what that's worth."

Cole frowned wondering what she'd done to Casey whose face was now as pink as the sunrise.

"I don't have a hat," Casey said softly, not commenting on anything the woman had said, but reaching for the olive branch Kristal was offering. "I didn't pack one. Do you think Matt might have an extra one?"

Kristal shook her head. "Not to worry, I brought two. You're welcome to use one of mine. Let me get it." She turned on her heel and entered the house.

"Who is that woman and what has she done with the real Kristal Harvey?" Cole asked, repeating what Casey had said about her mother on Tuesday night, trying to lighten the tense atmosphere. He would love to know what had happened the night she'd mentioned.

Casey giggled nervously, but he could see the tears shining in her eyes.

"Abducted by Chester's aliens, perhaps?"

Cole chuckled. "Maybe, but whatever's responsible, it's an improvement."

"I'm sure once the danger's over, she'll be her old miserable self again. I hope Horace is back when she decides to file for that divorce. Here's Matt."

The big man, dressed in jeans and a plaid shirt, led two horses out of the barn, a light red chestnut and a strawberry roan.

"Good morning. I saddled these two for you. Ms. Stevens, Kristal said you're a good rider. Scarlett here is nice and tame, and one of the more sure-footed animals I have, while Geronimo," he indicated the chestnut, "is equally well behaved. If you want to get up on her, I'll adjust the stirrups for you. Since we're almost the same height, Cole, Geronimo should be fine the way he is."

"Please call me Casey," she said, smiling at Matt and admiring the roan. "We're all in this together, right?"

Cole reached for her horse's reins, and held the animal still while Matt helped her mount.

"I've given you a rifle, Cole, just in case you run into something up there. Joey and Tony each have one, too. They're decent shots. Chester taught them. Since that old puma Hal mentioned might still be in the area, it's better to be safe than sorry. As far as supplies go, you've each got two full canteens of water."

The door opened and Evie came out. She handed Cole a large paper bag.

"There should be enough in there for the five of you—sandwiches, cookies, and some fruit," she said. "Tony took apples and carrots for the horses." She stepped over to Matt. "I separated the energy bars and juice as you asked." She handed him a small bag. He placed the contents in one of Casey's saddlebags.

"Thanks, Evie," Casey said. "I didn't have much to eat, so I'll probably be hungry before lunch."

"This is much appreciated." Cole placed the lunch bag into one of the saddle bags. "We'll be back before supper."

Matt finished adjusting Casey's stirrups. "How does that feel?"

"It's good thanks," she answered.

He nodded. "Then, I'll check on the boys. If you'll excuse me." He walked back to the barn.

"She reminds you of Ginger, doesn't she?' Cole asked, mounting his horse.

She nodded and swallowed. "She's the same color and size. I loved that animal ... I haven't been on a horse since that night."

"You'll be fine. Is that the night Kristal mentioned?"

Casey paled and nodded.

"They say it's like riding a bike."

Before he could say anything else, the stable doors opened once more and the boys came out, leading their horses. Evie moved over to Tony, pulling him into a fierce hug.

"Where's Mom?" Kyle asked, looking around anxiously. "I want to say goodbye before we leave."

"I'm right here, sweetie," Kristal came down the steps from the house carrying two cowboy hats. She held them up to Casey. "Take your pick."

Casey reached for the natural straw one. "Thank you."

Kristal nodded, put on the white Stetson, and walked over to her son.

"It looks like you're ready," Matt said, mounting his black stallion. "I'll escort you as far as the base of the mountain and make sure no one's following. The women will stay inside until I get back. One of my men will stay with them."

"Good work." Cole turned to the boys. "We're only going to be gone for the day. No long goodbyes."

The boys chuckled and mounted their horses.

"Okay. You guys know the way. Lead on."

"Yes, sir," Joey nodded. Kyle moved to ride next to Tony, followed by Cole and Casey. Matt brought up the rear.

Kristal and Evie, both teary-eyed, stepped up onto the veranda and waved.

Expecting the boys to go along the road, he was surprised to see them head behind the barn and travel cross-country. He'd expected to go into the wilderness, and climb the mountain that way, somehow staying near Skansen land. He wouldn't have seen those lights if the chopper had been on this side of the mountain.

The morning air was crisp and clean, and no one spoke as they rode closer and closer to Superstition Mountain, the horses moving at a steady canter. Ahead of them, the crag seemed thrust out of the earth, its cliffs, dikes, and necks, the remnants of ancient volcanic activity from more than twenty million years ago, daring the elements to beat it down. From this level, with the sun shining on it, the rocky slopes were a kaleidoscope of color thanks to tuffs and lichen-covered rocks set in the center of desert with its majestic saguaros and other succulents.

"Are we still on your land, Matt?" Cole asked, as the shrubs and trees increased in number the closer they moved to the mountain itself.

"Yes. The very edge of it. Higher up, you're on public land. Joey told me last night that Chester had a few claims not too far from here, but most of what's theirs is farther inside the range. We're riding into the *bajada*, the slope area. The soil here is primarily gravel and sand. Because of that, rainwater and runoff soak into it easily, allowing more of the woody plants to take hold. Over there, you can see some jojoba and that's white-thorn acacia."

"For someone who wasn't born here, you know a lot about it, don't you?"

"Aye. Our first Christmas together, my wife gave me a book about the mountain and the desert. I loved the place before I ever saw it. It seems that even though she's gone, I feel close to her here. Joey's always going on about the Apache spirits, something else he learned from Chester. He's convinced his warrior mother is with them, watching over us. I know it makes no sense, but I like to believe he's right."

Cole nodded, only too aware of the hold the desert and these mountains could have on a man. He glanced at Casey riding beside him, noting the serene look on her face.

"How are you doing?" he asked.

She smiled, the first genuine one he'd seen since she'd said goodnight to Jaxon Wednesday night.

"Wonderful. I forgot how it feels to ride, to be one with the horse. The Harley's great, but it isn't really the same, is it?"

"No, it's not," he admitted, understanding how she felt. "Although you may not feel that way after six hours in the saddle today." He would talk to Matt about buying a couple of horses after this was over. As much as he loved his Harley, she was right. There was lots of room to build a stable near the house, and while three fenced acres didn't seem like much, there were miles and miles of public land where they could ride. He refused to believe that house wouldn't be her home someday.

Half an hour later, the boys stopped their horses near

rugged land that climbed steadily up the side of the mountain. Foothill Palo Verde shared the space with boulders, mesquite and fairy duster with its bi-pinnate leaves and flattened bean pods not yet ready to harvest. There wasn't a definite path that Cole could see. It was possible they needed to move farther west. Cole pulled out his compass. They were still east of the wilderness and Table Rock.

"This is as far as I go," Matt said. "I'll hang around here for a while pretending to mend those fences," he pointed to an area behind them. "Once I'm sure no one's followed you, I'll go back."

"Be careful," Cole replied. "These people aren't in this for kicks. They may have killed four times to protect their secrets. They won't stop now."

"Four? That would be three more than ye've shared," he said, his brogue showing his concern more clearly that his words did. "I knew you weren't telling us everything. Just as well. The ladies are upset as it is. Take care of our sons. We'll have dinner and beer on ice when you get back."

Matt moved his horse closer to his son, spoke to him quietly, and then rode back along the trail they'd traveled.

"Mr. Warner," Joey said, coming up to stand beside him.

"Call me Cole. What is it?"

"We'll be climbing the mountain now. The path isn't too steep, but it's not very wide, so we'll need to travel single-file. It widens in places, narrows in others, but don't worry, it's never too small to get through. We'll get to that mesa you wanted to see in about an hour, and we can get down and rest there. It's about halfway to our camp."

"What path? I don't see anything that looks like a traveled trail."

Joey chuckled. "That's because you can't see if from here. We're going to head toward those trees, the acacia ones, near that clump of boulders."

Cole shook his head. "How did you guys find this? I know you say it's there, but I can't see it."

"When we were younger, we used to play at the base of the mountain and go along the ATV tracks, but we never went very far up. Dad didn't want us trespassing on the Skansen property. One day, we were on our way to our usual trail when we saw Chester fighting with two loaded mules. It looked like he was trying to get them to walk right into the rock. We couldn't understand why until we got closer and saw the opening."

"If Chester negotiated this path with a pair of mules, so can we. Lead the way."

The horses, now moving in single file, with him in last position, walked past the rocky outcropping. The pebbled ground underfoot rolled loosely beneath the horses' hooves, but didn't appear to have been used recently. After a few more twists and turns, a path, the rock worn smooth in the center from what must've been centuries of wear, appeared. The trail, no more than four feet wide, basically a cleft in the rock, led directly into the heart of the mountains.

"Are you sure this is safe?" he called to Joey.

The boy turned in his saddle. "Yup. Chester said it was one of the original Apache trails."

Pursing his lips, Cole nodded and noticed Casey was moving much slower than necessary. He trotted closer to her.

"What's wrong? Sore already?"

She turned to him, her face almost as green as it had been yesterday.

"No. It's nothing," she answered, trying to look calm and failing miserably.

"Bullshit. You look scared to death."

Pulling in a shaky breath, she attempted to smile. "I'm not exactly claustrophobic, but I really don't like small, tight places. At home, I usually take the stairs rather than the elevator."

"You said your office was on the sixth floor. That's quite a climb."

"I'm used to it." She shuddered. "The walls feel like they're closing in on me."

He smiled. "They really aren't. According to Joey, this is an ancient trail. If it's been here this long, it isn't going anywhere. Look at the walls. See how smooth they are?"

"Yeah." Reaching over, she brushed her hand along the rock.

"They're made of welded tuff, breccia, granite, basalt, and some conglomerate rocks. Mixed in with all this are mica, various colors of quartz, calcite, malachite, and of course, copper and gold. This chasm was most likely carved by a river eons ago. It's like a miniature Grand Canyon. Don't think of anything else. Look on the bright side. As long as we travel in here, we won't get sunburned."

"Ever the optimist, aren't you?" she asked, smiling weakly.

He shrugged. "I try. Feeling better?"

"Yes, thanks."

Cole followed closely behind Casey, pointing out an interesting rock formation here and there. Where he could, he rode beside her, telling her everything he knew about the rock and the mountains. Despite the fact they were climbing, other than that sensation, he had no way to orient himself since the rock walls rose at least twenty feet above them. He checked his compass, noting they were traveling southwest. He took comfort in the fact that, while he night not know exactly where he was, no one else did either.

The walls grew substantially narrower, his legs almost brushing the stone. Unable to walk beside her, he worried about Casey. The walls were indeed closing in. He was beginning to get antsy himself when her surprised gasp startled him. They'd stepped onto a plateau at least forty feet wide and just as long. They were much higher up the mountain than he'd expected to be, which meant the Skansen property had to be below them. Dismounting, careful to stay well away from the edge of the cliff, he used the binoculars he brought with him to identify landmarks in the distance. To his far left was Weaver's Needle, which meant the Superstition Mountain Wilderness was in front of him. He scanned the horizon, but not surprised when he couldn't identify Table Rock. From up here, it wouldn't stand out against the desert floor any more than other rocks did.

Putting down the binoculars, he examined the mesa.

"Those are the rocks you noticed in the photograph," Casey said, coming to stand beside him. "It looks like there's a trail leading down from here. I'm no expert, but something's used it recently."

Cole walked over to the edge of the mesa and stepped down onto the trail.

"You're right." He reached for something white caught on the branches of a thorny bush. "This looks like a chunk of raw wool. There's a ram who likes to hang around here, but I'd say ATVs went down there not too long ago. It must be a hell of a rough ride."

"We went down that way once," Tony said. "The path snakes side to side, but it's really hard on the horses. Chester talked about getting a couple of ATVs, but he wasn't sure they could make it from our base to the cave. The path gets narrower in places."

"Why would they use that trail?" Casey asked. "The one we used would be wide enough for ATVs I'm sure—well, it would be tight at the end, but..."

Tony chuckled. "They probably don't know it's there. Unless you do, from this angle you can't see it at all, and since the walls are so high, it gets darker in there than it does here, so by late afternoon, there's nothing to indicate it even exists. Watch. Kyle," he called. "Show them the way back."

Kyle nodded and walked back the way they'd come, disappearing into the rock wall itself.

Casey gasped. "That's incredible."

Within seconds, he walked out, seeming to come straight out of the rock.

"That's amazing," Cole agreed. "Let's have a look around and see if we can find any trace of that chopper or the ATVs."

With Tony by his side, Cole examined the mesa. Thanks to the hard-packed dirt and rock, the only prints he could see where faint impressions from their boots and the horses' hooves. It was as if someone had swept the plateau clean. The strong wind and the rain they'd had on Tuesday night might have done it.

Joey walked to the far side of the mesa and stepped behind some rocks.

"Where's he going?" Cole asked.

Tony reddened. "He probably needs to go. There's a lady here…"

"Enough said."

"How high up are we?" Casey asked, coming to stand beside him and handing them each an energy bar.

Cole reached for the canteen she held. He drank deeply. "I'd say we're up over two thousand feet. The Skansen mines are roughly a hundred feet below us and over to the north a bit. The campground is over that way about five or six miles. That trail could be popular with hikers, but once they got up here, they'd probably rest awhile and head back down. Even if they saw that cleft in the rock, I doubt they'd go in. The rangers warn them to avoid such places. A lot of them are dead ends, and popular nesting areas for rattlers as well as wild cats. He looked around. "Come to think of it, where the hell do we go from here? We can't ride up that slope. It's far too steep and covered with chain-fruit cholla. The only place I've seen this much of the stuff is over on the Goldfield Mountains."

"This way," Kyle said. "Chester's friend tried to mine a little over there," he indicated the far said of the mesa where Joey had gone. "He dug a pit, hoping to tunnel down to the mines below to find the gold in them that the company couldn't extract since it was in the ceiling of the mine, but he must've given up. We haven't seen him in almost a year and the pit's no deeper. We pulled a dead ewe out of there a few months ago, really stunk. Usually the cats get at them or the coyotes, but they probably couldn't get down to it. After we got it out, we took it partway down the trail over there and left her for the scavengers. Next time we came back, there was nothing left but a few bones. Chester built a wooden cover for it so no other animals would fall in."

Cole nodded and stepped away, moving in the direction Joey had, stopping just past the outcropping. He held up his hand as if he were holding a cellphone, trying to take a photograph. No doubt the man Kyle had mentioned was Leon. If he'd been mining up here when the helicopter had landed the first time, he could've taken those pictures. The angle was right. He must've recognized someone—the person responsible for the money in his safety deposit box.

"I found this," Joey said, coming from behind and startling him. The boy held out a twig with an empty pack of Mexican cigarettes dangling at the end of it. "It looks like someone left a clue after all. It wasn't here the last time we were."

Cole reached for the twig and walked back to the others.

"Here," Casey handed him a small pack of tissues. "What's that?"

Wrapping the package in the tissue, he put it inside the empty saddle bag on Casey's horse. "Hopefully, it's evidence of that helicopter and we'll find some useable prints on it."

"Are you ready to go on?" Joey asked.

"On where? I don't see any place to go," Casey said.

Kyle chuckled. "Over there. This is where I was when I drew the sketch for the painting Mr. Gibbs bought." He indicated the thin basalt rock at least ten feet tall. "We call it Chester's arrow. We'll stop again when we get to our base camp. We can have lunch before we go onto the cave."

He mounted his horse, and Joey and Tony followed suit.

"Better get up," Cole said. "I'm not leaving you behind, and the boys want to move on." He laced his fingers to give her a step up.

"Thank you." Once atop the horse, she cocked her head to the side. "Is it just me or do you feel like you've fallen down Alice's magic rabbit hole?"

He took another drink of water before handing her the canteen. "I'd say that sums it up nicely."

CHAPTER TWENTY-SEVEN

A little more than an hour later, after following a tunnel-like trail that tested her mettle in more ways than one, Casey gaped in amazement. In her mute terror, had she fainted? Was she hallucinating? The sun had yet to reach the bottom of the valley, and the temperature was cooler than she'd expected—no more than seventy degrees. She was in a lush green bowl, at least fifty feet in diameter, the scenery different from anything she'd ever seen in the Superstitions. She blinked her eyes, trying to convince herself that the fantastic vista before her was real.

Most of the vegetation consisted of chaparral—dense shrubs and trees less than six feet tall. Among them, she recognized creosote bushes, fire adapted by nature to regrow quickly. Near the pond, small oak trees grew in abundance. It was as if she'd stepped into Eden. To the east, the face of the mountain, a bare ragged cliff, rose steeply, tilting toward the west as it went higher up, almost as if it were trying to hide and shelter them. To the left and right of her, the two slopes were not as steep and were peppered with pines and junipers, as well as other small bushes. The truly magnificent sight was right in front of her. The stone wall no more than five feet high, looked like a fancy fence edged in scalloped lace. Astride her horse, she could see over the delicate-looking barrier, observing the typical desert landscape in the distance. To the south, she could make out Weaver's Needle rising skyward, looking more like a finger pointing at heaven than ever.

"How are you doing? That was a little nerve-racking even for me," Cole said, helping her down off her horse.

She chuckled. "I went way passed that. When we went through the enclosed section, I had to close my eyes. It's a good thing Scarlett knew what to do. It wasn't easy, but this is incredible, well worth the heebie-jeebies I felt. Are we in a crater?" she asked.

"It's possible," Cole answered. "It's like an oasis in the desert, only it's in the dead center of the mountains, hundreds of feet up."

"It's too incredible for words. They've got everything they need, probably the most beautiful camping place I've ever seen, but it doesn't look like any of the mines I've ever visited. We've been going down for quite some time now. At first, I thought I was imagining it, but I felt it in the horse's gait." She led Scarlett over to the small pond fed by a stream pouring out of the rock wall. "If you told me this was here, I wouldn't believe you."

"You wouldn't be the only one. There are still many sections of these mountains that haven't been explored. It reminds me of a book I read at university called *Lost Horizon*. The hero finds a mythical magic place in the mountains of Tibet called Shangri-La."

"Ms. Stevens," Kyle stood beside her. "Our mine's back behind those bushes. We're still at least half an hour from the Discovery, but we can rest here for a while. If you want to follow us, we'll show you around."

"What about the horses?"

"Just leave them. They won't go anywhere."

"Matt told me the horses are all trained to ground tie. It comes in handy around these parts where there's nothing to tie them to," Cole said. "There's enough grass to keep them satisfied."

She nodded and dropped Scarlett's reins. "After you, Kyle."

Cole put out his hand to stop her. "Wait. Are you armed?"

he whispered.

She nodded.

"If you see so much as a cockroach that doesn't belong here, shoot it. We don't know what we're going to find. Trent wanted that painting for a reason, and I find it hard to believe it was art appreciation."

"I know. Can you imagine what a greedy son of a bitch like him could do to a place like this?" Stepping closer to Kyle, noting Joey and Tony were nowhere in sight. She smiled. "We're ready now."

Casey, with Cole at her back, his presence far more comforting than she wanted it to be, followed the boy around the rocks and along the path, past an outcropping, barely wide enough for a man to pass. Rounding the next bend, she stopped as the main wall of the crater melted away, revealing the interior of the Superstitions, a breathtaking view she doubted few people had ever seen.

"Kyle, why haven't you drawn this? It's magnificent."

"I wanted to," the boy said, "but Chester didn't want the world to know this place existed. He thought if people knew it was here, they'd want to see it, and in time, they would destroy it."

Cole nodded. "He was probably right."

Casey smiled. "But it feels wrong to deprive the world of this beauty. If you ever change your mind, I would love one."

Kyle smiled shyly. "I didn't say I won't paint it someday, but when I do, I'll make it look magical enough that no one will believe it can be real, except those of us who've been here." He pursed his lips. "We aren't going to be able to come back, are we?"

"Not for the foreseeable future," she said. "Once word of the Discovery gets out, and it will since I can't imagine how we could keep it quiet, especially if you decide to follow through with Chester's plans, people will try to follow you any time you go into the mountains."

"And they won't necessarily be the best kind of people.

That's a fact of life," Cole added.

The boy took a long look at the vista in front of him, nodded, and then turned to Cole.

"You've got a cellphone with you, don't you?"

"I do," Cole answered, and handed it to the boy.

Kyle took several pictures and then held out the phone to Cole. "I'd appreciate it if you would print those for me."

Nodding, he reached for his phone and put it away.

Since the path was wider here, Casey glanced at Cole walking beside her, noting the way he scanned the ground as he walked, no doubt looking for scat. Just because humans hadn't found this place didn't mean animals hadn't. On cue, a rabbit crossed the path ahead of Kyle. Food and water could easily attract hungry predators like the puma she'd seen the other night. He probably wouldn't have any trouble finding his way up here.

"Ever see any big animals in this area?" Cole asked as if he could read her mind.

"We've seen a few deer and there's a couple of wild horses who come down to drink, but mostly it's been rabbits and noisy birds."

The path gave way to a small clearing. Over on the left, pressed close to the escarpment, she spotted a shack that could serve as shelter from the weather as well as a place to keep equipment.

"Is that your base camp?" she indicated the shack.

"No. There's not much in there," Kyle answered. "It's a decoy in case anyone finds this place. We keep most of our stuff in the mine itself."

"Where is this mine?" Cole looked around, his forehead creased in confusion.

"Over there." Kyle pointed to where Tony and Joey stood in front of some chaparral. Once they were closer, the boys brushed the bushes aside to reveal a small opening in the rock wall, reinforced with wooden two by fours.

"How the hell did you ever find that?" Cole asked.

"Chester found it years ago and transplanted the bushes to hide the entrance," Joey answered. "He was really smart." The boy choked up on the last words and looked away.

Cole reached for her hand.

"Ready to go down the rabbit hole, Alice?" he asked.

"I thought I already had. Are you sure whatever's in there is large enough to hold all of us?" She tried to remember how many liters of air a person needed to be able to breathe in order to stay alive. It was something like seven or eight a minute, assuming you were doing nothing. The way her heart was beating, she would need twice that much.

"Don't worry, Casey," Kyle said, laughing softly. "It's bigger than it looks."

She nodded, not in the least bit reassured.

Cole squeezed her hand. "I won't let anything happen to you."

The sincerity in his words warmed her and chased away some of her fear.

Joey went first, and within seconds, light emanated from the dark hole.

"You've got power in there," she said, awed by the fact they'd managed such a feat. "You're right, Cole. We are in Wonderland."

"Those lights are motion sensitive," Tony explained. "They come on when you cross that threshold, but we can turn them off anytime we want to with a switch. Once we flip it, we've got ten minutes until everything goes dark."

"Impressive. After you, Alice." Cole released her hand.

She took a deep, calming breath and followed Kyle inside.

"This is unbelievable. I thought it would be musty and full of bats and stuff."

The cavern, about fifteen feet in diameter was lit by four spotlights, rendering the small room as bright as the outdoors. On one side, mining equipment was stacked neatly next to camping equipment. A small, rectangular box about three feet high stood against the wall by itself.

"Is that a mini-fridge?" she asked, having trouble believing what she saw.

"Yeah," Tony said. "With solar power, it can run all the time. We turn it off when we leave, but we can keep food in it when we camp. There's an electric hot plate over there, too."

"How did you get it here?"

"On the back of one of Chester's mules," Tony answered.

"Where are the mules? We didn't find any animals near the Morris house."

"They stay at the livery stable and get rented out when we don't need them. Chester split the money he made for their rental with Mr. Johnson to cover their keep."

"Who did all this?" she indicated the lights.

"I did," Tony admitted. "I read about solar panels on the Internet and convinced Chester to try it. The collector panel is up higher and faces west. You can't see it unless you know it's there. The rocks are all black, and so is the panel. It's way better than the smelly, noisy, old generator we had. It's in that lean-to if you want to check it for any reason. The anti-freeze is in there, too."

"You said Chester mined part of this cave?" Cole asked. "It looks centuries old."

"It is. He figured the Apache might have used it long ago. Maybe a medicine man had come here to communicate with the spirits. There was a fire pit over near the door, but Chester filled it in when he first discovered the place. He found some gold here—not enough to make him rich or anything—but he was convinced there was more." Joey led them to the far end of the cave where the wall had been dug out in places. "Since we've been coming here, we've found a little gold ourselves. Most of it is in the white bags over there. It's not as rich as what we found in the other cave, but it's worth something. It kept us going until we started selling Discovery gold."

"Wasn't Chester afraid of getting robbed? Getting the claim jumped? I mean you were three boys and an old man." Casey tried not to make her comment sound judgmental, but it did.

"We were always armed," Tony added, "but in all the time we've been here, the only other person we ever saw was his friend. He was supposed to meet us down below the week after the earthquake, but he never showed up. He talked about moving away. Chester got the impression he'd won some money." The boy shrugged, picked up a LED lantern, and moved over to the side, shifting some old crates out of the way, revealing a metal box half buried in the stone floor of the cave. "We kept the stuff from the CJKT Discovery in here."

The strongbox was closed, a heavy u-shaped combination lock securing it.

"There are ten bags of nuggets in here, as well as a bag of coins and jewelry like the stuff you showed us yesterday, and the last of Kyle's sketches. We were planning to visit the cave and bring up another load once Mr. Stone looked into something for Chester—I don't know exactly, but it had to do with the artifacts."

"Can you open it?" Casey asked, not sure Chester would've shared the combination with the boys. Could the business Horace had attended to have been the reason he'd been forced off the road? It was possible.

Tony nodded. "Anyone of us can."

He opened the lock and raised the lid. Ten small leather bags similar to the one Cole had found in Chester's mattress sat in the box.

"Do you realize how much that may be worth?" she asked. At the current price of gold, the boys were looking at almost a million dollars.

"Not exactly, but each bag weighs about five pounds, and the nuggets are really high in quality," Tony admitted.

"So far we've only emptied one bag," Joey said. "Chester felt we would attract less attention that way until we got all the details sorted."

"There's a lot more gold in the cave where the bodies are," Tony volunteered. "More than three hundred bags. Chester said the gold belonged to the Apache spirits, and they would let us have whatever we needed for our future, but we couldn't have it all, and if we got greedy, we wouldn't live to enjoy it. Do you think the treasure is why Chester was killed?"

"It's possible. Someone might've found out Mr. Stone was selling gold for him, but since the gold and the other things were left there, I don't think the person who killed Chester knew about this. There has to be another reason," Cole answered.

"Why would they want to frame us then? If they knew about the gold, I could understand, since getting us out of the way would clear the field for them, but why else?"

"Maybe because of the painting Mr. Gibbs bought from you," Casey suggested.

"So you think it could be the people in the photograph you showed us? The ones with the helicopter" Kyle asked.

"Maybe. I'm sure they didn't think anyone knew where they landed."

"Who took that picture?" Tony asked.

"We think it might've been Leon, Chester's friend," Casey answered, knowing there was no point in keeping the information from them.

"He's dead, too, isn't he?" Joey asked, his eyes wide, showing his fear.

She nodded. "He died about a year ago."

"How many times have you been to the Discovery?" Cole asked, hefting one of the bags of gold, trying to change the conversation before the boys asked questions they couldn't answer.

"About a dozen times," Joey answered, relief evident in his face. He didn't want to talk about this anymore either. "Kyle has been drawing the interior of the cave while Joey and I were cataloguing the coins and other treasures. Chester examined the skeletons themselves, looking for clues as to how they died. He figured they'd suffocated when the cave in had sealed them in and they'd been too weak from their injuries to dig their way out. He brought some of the sketches to show Mr. Stone on

Monday."

Those had to be the ones she'd found in the file.

Cole glanced at his watch. "It's almost eleven. I suggest we eat now and then we can take a ride down to the CJKT Discovery. When we come back, we can gather whatever you want from the cave and seal it off. By the way, how do you keep the animals out?"

"We close the door," Kyle answered. It's just chicken wire and boards, but it seems to work."

Casey giggled at the look on Kyle's face that clearly said 'what else would we do?' "How far is the Discovery from here?"

"About forty minutes, but it's slow-going since we're going up again and it's pretty steep," Tony explained. "Coming back is easier. The trail's in a narrow ravine, and it gets dark early here. We need to head back home by three at the latest."

"Good enough. I don't know about you guys, but I'm starving," Cole said.

"Me, too," Casey agreed, and she was. All the fresh air and excitement had sharpened her appetite. "Let's get the food from the saddle bag. Once we're done eating, we'll move on. I can't wait to see what surprises you've got for me next."

* * * *

More than an hour later, Cole helped the boys move the last of the rocks they'd used to hide the entrance to the cave they'd discovered after the earthquake. The LED lantern they'd brought with them illuminated the old mine where they stood, but he could hear scurrying in the darkness that had to indicate rodents and reptiles moving around out of sight. He hoped none of the furry or scaly creatures showed themselves. A scream in here would echo loudly enough to hurt anyone's ears.

"That should be big enough," Tony said, after they moved most of the loose boulders out of the way.

"We've talked about it and decided to take two more bags

of gold each," Kyle said, seeming more mature than before. "If you take two each as well, that means we'll have taken a hundred and ten pounds of gold from here. That should be enough for our futures for now. We'll wait to see what Mr. Stone wants to do about the rest of it. We want to honor Chester's wishes, but we need to be sure the wrong people don't get their hands on it. People like my father and his friends would ruin it for everyone."

Cole nodded. The boy had his father pegged, and if one of those friends was Eddy, their greed would indeed destroy everything. At least he wouldn't have to worry about Trent, but the men in the helicopters were another story. A hundred pounds of gold was probably worth close to two million dollars, and that was motive enough to change anyone. If Kyle was right and there were more than three hundred five-pound bags in that cave, it was certainly motive for murder. As it was, the money divided three ways, would cover their education and a lot more. Properly invested, it would grow nicely, assuring them all a good future. Casey said the trust was unbreakable. For Kyle's sake, he hoped she was right.

"Who wants to go in first?" he asked.

"I will," Joey said. "I did the last time. Chester said the spirits preferred it that way."

"I never realized how superstitious Chester was," he whispered into Casey's ear.

"Lots of people are," she said softly. "When you're in a place like this, there's a feeling to it ... I know it sounds kind of crazy, but I swear I can feel eyes watching me. I used to get that feeling years ago when I would ride Ginger out into the foothills on our ranch. Dad said it was probably him with his binoculars, but I was convinced it was the spirits."

"Did they scare you?"

"Strangely enough, no. I always felt they were watching out for me."

Tony and Kyle followed Joey into the cave. Casey hesitated, obviously reluctant to enter another small space.

"Are you okay?" he asked as soon as he was beside her.

"I guess so, but stay close to me, okay? I've been in more tight quarters today than in the past twenty years," she said nervously.

"Like glue." He reached for her trembling hand. "Let me go first and then you can come in after. He entered the room and then pulled her quivering body inside, holding her next to him. "Open your eyes, Alice. Have a look at the CJKT Discovery"

Cole turned her toward the glow of the lantern and sucked in a breath himself as she gasped in wonder. The rock walls were smooth, almost polished and unlike any rock he'd seen in the mountains elsewhere. If he hadn't known better, he would've sworn it had been made by some kind of tool. As the boys had mentioned, the walls were covered in cave paintings. The last time he'd seen anything like them had been when he'd visited the Lascaux Caves in France. The drawings were almost identical to the Paleolithic cave paintings he'd seen there. How was that even possible?

"My God," Casey whispered, the reverence in her voice reflecting the way he felt. "These drawings have to be thousands of years old. They're beautiful."

He continued his perusal of the cave and its contents. He counted six human bodies and four that must've been mules. Near the mules, eight incredibly well preserved baskets leaned against the wall. Joey bent over the first basket and handed the small pouches to Tony who placed them on the ground at his feet.

With Casey by his side, Cole examined the cave, snapping pictures on his cellphone camera. While Joey and Tony attended to the gold nuggets, carrying the bags out to the horses and securing them in the saddle bags, Kyle collected some of the coins and jewelry from the small chest next to the skeleton he'd called the captain. Judging by the armor and the signet ring, the man would've been an officer of some sort.

"Ms. Stevens?" Kyle asked, coming up to stand beside them. "We would like you to have something special from here." He held open a small chest. "It's to thank you for believing in us."

"You don't have to do that," she said.

"I know but we talked about it and want you to choose something for yourself. Chester took a ring he said was for a special friend. I hope she got it. It wasn't in the stuff you showed us at the police station."

Casey looked up at him for advice. He nodded.

"Consider it a retainer."

She smiled, scanned the items, and chose a half-inch wide copper bracelet. It was engraved with curlicues, small lines, and dots, beautiful in its workmanship and simplicity. Knowing it had to be more than two hundred years old amazed her and had her thinking of Vaca's rattle.

"Thank you. I'll cherish it always."

"We need to get going," Joey said. "We've loaded the gold and the other things we want. It's after one and we need to wall up this up again before we go. That'll take another half-hour. We want to be back at the ranch before dark."

They had almost finished closing up the opening in the wall when the earth rolled under his feet.

"Cole, did you feel that?" she asked, her voice tinged with concern she was trying to hide.

"I did. It's probably just an aftershock from last night's tremor." He did his best to sound confident.

The boys looked at one another nervously, but continued piling up the rocks to fill the gap.

When the ground moved again, harder this time, he tossed aside the rock he'd been holding.

"That's it. It isn't an aftershock, it's another quake," he cried loudly. "We need to get the hell out of here."

Debris showered down on them, filling the cave with dust. He squinted and saw Tony grab Kyle and follow Joey out into the open. Cole held Casey tightly to him, trying to shield her from the falling dust with his body as he pulled her outside. The dust was even heavier there, the horses stamping and snorting in their distress.

"Is everyone okay?" he yelled. His voice barely audible over the sound of the rumbling earth.

"We're fine," Tony and Joey answered loudly.

Kyle coughed.

"Get to your horse and hold onto it," Joey said. "They splay their legs for stability. Chester had us do that the last time."

The ground bucked and rolled again, small rocks rained down on them. Cole pulled Casey into him, trapping her between her horse and his, fighting to retain his footing, knowing he had to if he didn't want to get trampled.

He leaned down so that Casey could hear his voice. "I'm sorry about involving you in this," he said.

"It wasn't your fault," she cried back. "I made the decision to come."

Unable to stop himself, aware they might all be dead in minutes, his mouth claimed hers, with a hunger he knew he would never be able to satisfy. His tongue pressed softly against her lips, until she opened to him, taking him inside her as she had that night that seemed an eternity ago. The kiss was one of passion and desperation, pouring everything he had into what could be his final act, his final breath. Casey didn't pull away. Instead she clung to him, returning his ardor as only she could. If they were going to die, it would be like this joined together for eternity.

A roar as loud as a dozen freight trains all going by at the same time sounded and the earth shook so hard, even the horses whinnied with nervousness, but they clung to one another, lips locked, and he prayed it wouldn't end this way. And then, just as quickly as it had started, it was over. The silence was deafening. Dust continued to shower down on them, covering everything in a fine powder. Within seconds, it stopped. Kyle coughed.

Cole broke the kiss. Tears slipped down Casey's cheeks, and she stepped away from him, still holding her saddle with one hand.

"I need to see if Kyle's okay," she said, licking her bruised lips.

"I'm not going to apologize," he said.

"Don't." She lifted her hand to his cheek. "I'm not sorry you did. If I was going to die, I was quite happy to do so in your arms. Now, let me check the boys." She stepped away from him toward Kyle and gasped. "It's gone. It's all gone!"

"What's gone?" Cole asked turning toward her and inhaling sharply.

"Everything."

They stood on a small plateau, barely ten feet wide, surrounded on three sides by emptiness. Where the cavern had stood only minutes ago was a vast abyss, the far wall a series of strata bent into tightly reversing folds, similar to those he'd seen along Fish Creek, one of the three tributaries of the Salt River that ran through the mountains.

Casey stood beside him, her face, hair and clothes covered in fine dust, trembling. He reached for her and pulled her close. He looked over her head. The trail they'd come up seemed intact, and he prayed it was, because if it wasn't they were all going to die here.

"Chester was right. He said the spirits would let us have what we needed and keep the rest," Joey said.

Cole swallowed. "As I recall, those spirits have issues with anyone living to enjoy their booty. Let's hope we're the exception to the rule and that path we came down is still there."

"You mean we could be trapped here?" Casey asked, her voice edged with panic. "There's no other way out of here." She indicated the gorge surrounding them.

"If that path is blocked, I'll dig us a new one with my bare hands. We'll get out. Don't worry." He bent his head to capture her lips once more. "You and I have unfinished business. I said I would take care of you. I'm not about to stop now."

She smiled weakly, tears brimming her eyes, and nodded.

"Mount up and let's get out of here."

Contrary to his fears, the trail they'd followed down had hardly been disturbed, a few loose rocks here and there, the only thing to show anything out of the ordinary had happened. By the time they got to the cavern, had it not been for the dirt and dust covering them all, he could well believe he'd imagined it all. But the bags of gold in their saddlebags were all too real.

"Let's get what we need from the mine and then get the hell out of here. I'm not going to wait for an aftershock."

CHAPTER TWENTY-EIGHT

Casey heaved a sigh of relief when her horse stepped out of the crevasse into the *bajada* once more. The sun was low on the horizon, so low in fact that many sections of the trail had been crossed in the dark, something that had increased her nervousness. Cole had done his best to keep her distracted by discussing what they would do next.

Having survived the earthquake, Casey was inclined to believe Leon might well have fallen, especially if he were anywhere near the edge of the plateau when it had hit. Without Cole and Scarlett to steady her, she would've lost her footing for sure.

The CJKT Discovery was gone, eliminating one potential source of danger for the boys, but they were no closer to finding any of the killers or whoever was trying to frame the kids. They did know the location of the helicopter's landing place and might even have one of the men's fingerprints, but unless they were in the system ... As soon as they got back to the house, Cole would call Hal and the two men would contact the DEA and Homeland Security. It wasn't much, but it was a checkmark in the solved column.

Once they'd reached the camp, they'd worked to remove as much of the dirt from themselves and their horses as they could. Kyle's breathing problems had increased with the amount of dust in the air, and while he'd used his inhaler, Casey insisted he do nothing more than sit and rest. The boy had fallen asleep on the grass near the stream and she'd watched over him—not that there was any danger there—but it had given her time to think.

Her life had changed today, and no matter what happened next, there was no going back. From now on, her future included Cole. For how long was still a mystery, but she wouldn't deny how important he was to her. Did she love him? Possibly, but she now had the opportunity to explore whatever it was that made her heart beat faster when he was around.

Cole, Joey, and Tony had gone into the cave to collect the bags of gold as well as personal items the boys wanted, including more than a dozen sketches Kyle had made. Since they wouldn't be returning to the area for some time, at least not until whoever was behind the helicopter had been arrested, they'd secured the cave and removed a number of items that had been important to Chester, which they divided among themselves. They'd given her a framed photograph of a young Chester and Minerva Skansen, when she'd identified the woman in the picture, and wanted her to return it to Minerva.

Hopefully, the woman would want to meet the boys, but she knew only too well that people dealt with grief differently. The near-death experience had made her see a lot of things about herself in a new light. Life was too unpredictable to spend it nursing her shame and pain over something that had happened fifteen years ago and couldn't be changed. She'd been given a second chance with Cole, and if what she felt was love, she wouldn't cast it aside the way Minerva had. She'd tell him about Rick and the events of that night. It was time to get rid of all the skeletons in the closet. Judging by what Kristal had said this morning, people knew what had happened, and no one had publicized it. Maybe life in Fortune hadn't been as bad as she thought it had, and if that was the case, did she really want to leave her family and Cole to go back to Santa Fe?

By the time they were ready to head back home and she'd

roused Kyle, whose breathing was almost back to normal, it had been well after four. The sun no longer lit the crater, and they'd needed the flashlights when they'd entered the trail. Without a doubt, those had been the longest two and a half hours of her life. By mutual agreement, they stopped no more than ten minutes when they'd reached the halfway point, just long enough to appreciate the warmth of the sun once more. The helicopter pad as Cole had christened the mesa, didn't appear damaged by the quake, but he maintained everyone had to stay well away from the edge just in case.

"How are you holding up, Alice?"

She shook her head. "After everything that's happened, I'm not sure how I am. It's a shame the cavern is gone. It was an incredible archeological find, but maybe the spirits aren't ready to share their secrets yet. I've been thinking. What if Peralta's mine or the Lost Dutchman were near that cave? It could've vanished in a quake just like the cave did. It's still there. Maybe hundreds of feet deeper than it was. Who knows, maybe it will resurface someday."

Cole smiled. "Maybe it will. Don't tell anyone, but I think you just hit on the next CJ Coleson plot. If you want, we can take a break here. We're less than half an hour from the ranch. That trek down was a hard one."

"It was, and while going through the dark areas had my heart beating a mile a minute, I think I was more frightened on the way up," she said and chuckled ruefully. "But, I just want to get home and soak away some of this soreness. I'm tender in places I didn't even know could hurt. This day may have cured me of my claustrophobic tendencies. I may even manage to ride elevators once in a while. One thing is certain, the next time I decide to take a seven-hour ride, I'll use the Harley."

Cole laughed. "I'm sure if you did it often enough, your body would get used to it. If you like, I can give you a rub down when we get back to the house," he said and winked at her. "I'm sure Matt has some liniment we can have."

She chuckled. "Eau de horse liniment, this year's

provocative new scent. There you go saying those wildly romantic things again. How soon before we can go home? I'm looking forward to that hot tub and a glass of that wine you bought yesterday. Then I'm going to bed. Did you happen to pack any silk sheets?"

Cole choked on the air he'd breathed in, the look of stunned surprise on his face priceless.

"If I'd had any indication…"

She giggled. "That's okay. Next time," she said and reached over to caress his cheek. "Tonight, I'm too sore to fully appreciate your charms. I'll settle for cuddling in a sleeping bag."

"Maybe we can move it out onto the deck for a while. I promise to sweep it thoroughly and make sure there isn't a spider or scorpion in sight. There's supposed to be a full moon. It should be as spectacular as those meteorites were."

"Offering me the moon? You smooth talker, you. Sounds very tempting, but I can't promise I won't fall asleep on you."

Laughing, Cole removed his hat and swept it in front of her, bowing in the saddle. "You can sleep in my arms any time you want to. If it hadn't been for that helicopter, I would gladly have stayed there with you all night."

"And risked my mother's wrath?"

"Sure, besides, she likes me—feeds me chocolate cake." He wiggled his eyebrows before leaning over to kiss her.

He pulled away suddenly and swore. "Damn! We can't go straight home. Matt's expecting us to stay for supper." He looked like someone had stolen his favorite treat. "He's going to want a full report. We'll have to give them all one. It's too bad Hal isn't here. It would save us having to repeat it all tomorrow."

"I'm just glad my parents had no idea I was on the mountain."

"I hadn't thought of that." He pulled out his phone. "There's no signal here."

"I'm sure Mom will be frantic when she can't reach me.

Even if I had a signal, it wouldn't help. I left my phone charging back at the house. As far as being alone goes, we've waited this long, a few more hours will just make the anticipation all that much sweeter. Don't forget, after supper we still have to take them to the cottage. I'm looking forward to seeing that place."

Sighing heavily, he nodded. "I would've shown it to you on Wednesday night, but then the fire happened, and Chester died. I'd forgotten about needing to take them there, although they may be quite safe for another night on the ranch. Did you see that man on the porch this morning? No one's going to mess with him."

"You may be right. Maybe we can wait and move them tomorrow. Now, let's get going. The boys aren't too impressed with this delay." She indicated them waiting on their horses about twenty feet away. "I'm sure Matt, Evie, and Kristal are worried. We're much later than we expected."

Galloping at a faster pace than they had all day, they rode toward the ranch. As soon as they entered the paddock closest to the house, Clover came racing across it, barking an excited welcome. When they reached the barn, Matt stood waiting with two of his men ready to take the horses. The boys dismounted, told the men to wait, and Joey moved into his father's arms. Kyle and Tony ran to their mothers. The boys had said very little about the quake, but like her, they must've been terrified. Lost in Cole's kiss, she hadn't even thought of them. She tried to imagine how Randy would feel if one of those two boys had been Jaxon.

Dismounting slowly, praying her tired body wouldn't disgrace her, Casey patted Scarlett before handing the rains to the behemoth who'd been on the porch this morning. Cole was right, with that guy around, everyone would be quite safe right where they were.

"I called you after the quake," Matt said to Cole, one arm protectively around his son. "It was as strong as the one last year. I was afraid you might've been hurt. It was all I could do to convince Evie and Kristal to wait and not send my hands out looking for you."

Casey glanced over at the mothers and sons, both mothers crying and fussing over them.

"I tried to call, but couldn't get a signal. I won't say I wasn't scared," Cole said, acknowledging the fear they'd all felt, "but Joey knew what to do. We may all be a little dirty, but we're safe and sound. You've got every reason to be proud of him."

"I am," Matt said. "I always have been. His mother would be, too."

"It's gone, Dad," Joey said, moving out of his father's arms. He stepped back to his horse and began removing the items in the saddle bags. Kyle and Tony did the same.

"What's gone?"

"The Discovery. The ground opened up and swallowed it. That whole section of mountain disappeared into the earth as soon as we stepped out of it. It was as if the spirits were waiting until we were all safe and then hid the cave away once more. Maybe in a hundred years, someone else will find it. The path from our camp to it now ends on a small mesa surrounded by canyon at least fifty feet deep. When it's safe to go up again, I want to show you our mining camp. Cole took pictures, but when you see it for yourself, you'll understand why I loved it so much. Maybe we could all go camping there someday. You could even search for gold. We've got three bags of it from the mine, but Chester was sure there was more. What we were able to get from the Discovery is all we'll ever have."

Matt smiled at his son. "Don't worry about it. We got each other and that's more important than any gold or artifacts. We've managed on our own this long, and we'll continue to do so. The ranch provides us with a decent living. You'll get into the finest school in the land, even if I have to sell everything to pay your way. We'll be fine, as will the others."

Joey laughed. "That's not what I meant. We didn't come away empty handed." He pointed to the contents of the saddle bags, now all piled on the ground. "We brought down twenty bags of gold, and there's another one in the evidence locker.

That works out to seven bags each, more than six hundred thousand dollars at today's prices. Properly invested, we should be fine. The coins and jewelry we can sell, and some things, like the rosary, we can donate to a museum. We may even go ahead and build one of our own. It's what Chester wanted to do. We've got pictures and sketches of everything that was there."

Matt stared at his son and shook his head in amazement. "Casey will know how the trust works and what can be done. I'm sure she'll do what's best for you all. Now, I need a wee dram of whiskey to celebrate your safe return. Will you join me?" he asked Cole.

Cole looked at her, and she shook her head. "Go ahead. The only thing I want is some cold water and a place to clean up a bit before we eat. "I'm starving."

A chorus of "so are we" filled the air.

"That's good because Evie made enough food to feed an army," Kristal said, coming over to stand beside her. Casey reached up to take the dust encased hat off her head.

"I'm not sure all the dust will come out of it. It's probably ruined," she said apologetically. "I'll replace it as soon as I can."

"Don't worry about it. Kyle was telling me about the tremor and how well you looked after him. In your place, I would've screamed bloody murder and probably brought down the rest of the mountain on us. I can never repay you for what you've done. You've reminded me of what it means to be a mother, and you've secured his future and kept him out of jail. I can get a straw hat anywhere. Someone like you in my life and Kyle's isn't something I deserve, I certainly didn't do anything to earn it, but I hope we can be friends. Lord knows I made your life miserable back then, and so did Rick, and for that I am truly sorry." She swiped at her tears. "I can get you some ice water while they have their celebratory drink. While I didn't pack a lot of clothes, I'm sure between us, Evie and I can find you something to wear if you want to get out of those and have a shower. The men will take care of the horses once the boys finish emptying those saddle bags. Come on. I'll show you to the bathroom."

Casey swallowed awkwardly. The last thing she would ever have expected was kindness and consideration from Kristal. Maybe this new Kristal wouldn't last, but Casey held out her hand, accepting the offer of friendship.

"Thank you," she answered, her voice clogged with emotion. "I can't wait to feel clean again."

Smiling at Cole, she followed Kristal into the house. Today had been full of surprises, and the night was young. Maybe, like Alice, she hadn't come out of that rabbit hole yet.

* * * *

Cole sat on the sofa, his arm around Casey. They'd just watched the slide show of the photographs he'd taken in the cave and on the mountain.

"I can see why you want to go back to that campsite," Matt said. "It's incredible. If I hadn't seen these pictures, I wouldn't have believed a spot like that existed in those mountains."

"Chester wanted to build a house there," Tony said. "He claimed he'd have everything he needed. Once we found the gold, he wanted to build it more than ever, but Mr. Stone wasn't sure he would be allowed to. Do you think we could take his ashes up there and scatter them on the wind?"

"I don't see why not," Casey answered. "As his heirs, you make that decision, but right now, we have a more pressing one. Are you ready to go to the cottage? It's only an hour away, but Cole and I are pretty beat, and looking at those two, they're done in."

Matt chuckled. The two younger boys were asleep—Kyle on the floor at his mother's feet and Joey in a chair.

"If it's acceptable to you," Matt said, "we would prefer to stay here. We're well away from the town, and no one knows Kristal and Evie and their boys are here. While you were gone, we arranged to have someone stay in their homes to make it look like they were still there. I thought about what you'd said

385

and if someone was determined to frame them, I didn't want them to go looking for the women and the boys."

"It's a great idea. Who did you get?" Cole asked, realizing he should've considered someone might be watching the houses in town.

"I called my father-in-law, and he sent some women from the reservation. Don't worry, they can take care of themselves. I have extra men here, and can get more simply by calling him. This place is as safe as Fort Knox. Besides with all that gold in my safe, I don't feel right leaving. We won't broadcast our presence, and we'll not leave the ranch without your say-so. There's a fenced pool out back and plenty of food."

"If that's what you think is best," Cole said, well aware that the extra manpower could come in handy if push came to shove. "The cottage is there if you change your mind. Now, I think I'd better get Casey back before she falls asleep on us all and I have to carry her."

Casey chuckled. "You make that sound like an imposition. I'm not that fat anymore."

"You never were, really. I mean, we made you feel far worse than you deserved to. I think one of the things I was most jealous of was that you were pretty and didn't have to work at it, and of course, you were so smart—scary smart—just like you, Cole," Kristal said. "I envy you. You've got each other and lots of happy years ahead, while all I foresee is a bitter divorce from a man who never really wanted me. The joke is, I don't think I wanted him either. I just didn't want anyone else to have him because he was supposed to be the best." She shook her head. "Be careful what you ask for. I'd better get him to bed."

Matt stood. "I think we should all get some rest. Will we be seeing you tomorrow?"

"Probably not. Casey and I have a few things to do during the day, including putting in an appearance at the fair, and then we're going to her parents' house for dinner."

"I don't suppose we can go to the Sunday event, can we?"

Kristal asked.

Casey smiled. "I know what it means to be a member of Fortune's founding families. Let me talk it over with Hal and Cole, and we'll see. No one would dare try something in a place as public as that. Will Rick be back?"

There was something in the way she said the name that convinced Cole she wouldn't be upset if he wasn't.

"Maybe, but Gold Rush Days were never his thing. Let me know if we can go. I have a new dress your mother made me that I'd love to wear, and I think it's time I mended a few more fences. Goodnight."

After a round of hugs and goodnights, Cole led Casey back to the sedan.

"Are you okay?" he asked.

"Yeah, but I never thought I would see the day when Kristal and I could be civil to one another, let alone be friends."

"I take it she treated you pretty badly in school. You never said anything. If you had, I would've come to your defense," he stated. He might not have been as confident back then as he was now, but if he'd known someone was hurting her, he would've done whatever it took to put an end to it.

"Thanks. You know, it's funny. All these years I had this image of myself as downtrodden, treated miserably and yet, that's not how most people saw me. Ella Rankin thought I was this great, strong, independent risk-taker who simply ignored Heidi and Kristal and did whatever I wanted to do. They couldn't have been more wrong. I spent those years seeing myself as this big fat blob. I had body image problems, even in university. When Ryan and I were a couple, he used to get so angry at me for starving myself. Even now, I worry about overeating and gaining weight."

He did his best to ignore what she'd said about Ryan. It was obvious the two of them were still close.

"I never thought of you as fat. In my books, you were just about perfect—you still are."

"There you go again saying sweet things. That low self-esteem is only part of the reason I have trouble believing people who compliment me. For years, I did my best to efface myself in crowds, staying out of the limelight. The only time I would stand out and speak up was when I was in court or working to help someone. I love being a lawyer, especially when I can see justice done, like I can on this case." She yawned.

"I'm sorry it was hard on you. So I guess you and Ryan are still close?" he tried not to let his jealousy show.

"We are. He and his wife Sally are the only real friends I have."

"Ryan's married?"

"Yes, for five years now. Ryan and I dated for a while, but we decided we were better friends than lovers and opted to keep it that way. I actually introduced him to Sally. I met her when she moved into the condo next to mine. They live there now." She sighed. "Contrary to the way I behave when I'm with you, I tend to shy away from physical situations. I haven't had a lot of experience, so when we decide to take the next step, I hope you won't be disappointed. I had a bad experience fifteen years ago, and it's made it really hard for me to trust people."

"I have a feeling we'll be terrific." He reached for her hand and squeezed it gently. "That bad experience, did that happen on the night Kristal mentioned?"

"Yes, but let's wait until we get back to the house. The story's a long, sad one, and you have to focus on your driving."

Cole chuckled. "I do, but I would much rather concentrate on you. That being said, we should be near the turn off."

Ten minutes later, Cole pulled up to the gate, punched in the code and drove up to the house. He parked in the garage and opened her door. He helped her out of the car and pulled her against him.

"You don't have to tell me anything until you're ready. I'm not going anywhere. Today has been a hell of a day. Let's just go inside and relax," he said, shutting the car door and locking it. He led her to the door that opened into the kitchen, unlocked it with the code he'd reprogrammed it with last night, and closed it behind them. "I'll get the wine, and we can sit on the deck and watch the moon."

Casey smiled at him. "You're a very special man, Cole Warner."

She stood on tiptoe and kissed him. He was just about to take the kiss deeper when his firefighter beeper went off. He'd left it on the kitchen counter this morning since he wouldn't have been able to answer it on the mountain.

"Talk about bad timing. Let me make a call. Maybe Noah won't need me."

"Cole, if you've got to go, go. I'm sure I can just lock myself in until you get back. Besides, I'm armed, remember?"

Looking at the address on the beeper, he frowned. "I think you're going to want to come with me," he said. "The fire's at the Skansen house."

"Minerva's house?"

"Yes. And I don't think it's a coincidence. The fact Eddy's in Vegas seems damn convenient." He picked up his cellphone and dialed Noah for details.

"Noah, it's Cole. I just got in. How bad is it?"

"Pete Putnam changed his mind about going to the barn dance tonight and was walking his dog when he saw smoke coming from the back of Ms. Skansen's house. He called 9 1 1. He used to be one of us and knows a lot about fire. Said it was small, in the incipient stage, located at the back of the house. I sent a few of the boys over, but Jason just called. He says it's growing faster than it should. I've called for backup from Apache Junction. If this gets out of control, we might lose the whole block. That rain Tuesday night wasn't enough to ease the drought."

"I'm on my way."

Within twenty minutes, Cole pulled up to the curb, half a block from the Skansen House, almost directly in front of his own home. His mother and father were on the veranda, their faces proclaiming their horror.

"Mom, keep Casey with you. I have to go."

"No, I'm coming with you," she said. "Once I'm sure Minerva is safe, I'll come back here I promise."

He pulled her to him, kissed her soundly. "You will come right back."

"I will. Promise." Pulling away slightly, she crossed her heart.

Releasing her, Cole reached for her, and hand in hand, they ran down the street.

"Cole," his mother shouted after him. "Please be careful."

"Wait over there while I gear up," he said as he stepped over to the truck where other firefighters were getting dressed or listening to Noah for instructions. Less than five minutes later, he was back by her side.

"Let's check on Minerva together. Once you know she's safe, you'll go back to Mom and dad. I'll feel better if I know you're away from all this. We still don't know who the bad guys are, and this fire seems too damn convenient for me."

Together they hurried over to where Ms. Skansen was sitting in a lawn chair. The firefighter paramedic with her seemed to be having trouble with her.

"Jason, this is Casey Stevens. What's the problem?"

"She won't let me touch her," he said softly. "She's babbling, and keeps saying 'he's inside' but I know Eddy went to Vegas."

"She knows me. Let me try," he said. "She knows Casey, too."

Casey was near Minerva trying to calm her, but it didn't seem to be working. The elderly woman was more agitated than he'd ever seen her. She was crying, wringing her hands, and staring at the house, trying to get up, but unable to. If he didn't know better, he would say she was high or drunk. Watching the only home you'd ever known burn would be hard on anyone, but this wasn't what he would've expected from the woman he knew so well.

Jason handed him the blood pressure cuff. "The ambulance is on its way. I'll go help the others. Do what you can."

Cole bent down beside her. "Ms. Skansen, it's Cole Walker." He raised his face shield. "I know this is upsetting, but I need to check you out. Can you tell me what happened?"

She blinked at him as if he were a stranger. Had she had a stroke?

"I can tell you what happened, Cole," Pete interrupted. He held Bullet in his arms. The poor dog was terrified. "I know what these old frame houses are like—tinder boxes. I knew Minerva had to be in there. Some fool said he'd seen her leave, but she never goes out at night."

"Who told you she was gone?"

Pete looked around. "I don't see him. He wasn't a local, probably one of the tourists in town for the celebration. Seemed to be in a hell of a hurry to get away from the place. Before he left, he said he'd seen three boys running away from the house, just before I came around the corner. He described one of them as a small kid with white hair. Sounds to me like Kyle Harvey. Damn shame. I guess the apple didn't fall far from the tree after all. I heard someone else said those kids had probably set all the fires, including the one that had killed Chester. Probably doing drugs. It's just not right."

"Do me a favor," Cole said. "Don't repeat that rumor. It's a lie. Casey and I had supper tonight with Kristal and Kyle as well as Tony and Evie Bronson, and Matt and Joey Pearson. We left them less than an hour ago. There's no way those kids got from where they are to here. It would take a teleportation device to accomplish that."

Pete nodded. "I didn't see them myself, but he was talking pretty loudly. I'm sure others heard him. That rumor will be all over town by morning. It's a good thing they'll have an alibi. You'll need Clay here for sure. I'd stake my life if those kids didn't set this fire someone else did. For the record, I had a hell of a time waking her up and getting her out of the house. I swear she didn't know me, still doesn't. She keeps mumbling about peaches and Chester."

"How did you get her out?"

"The front door was unlocked, and I let myself in. Good thing she didn't lock it, but it's a stupid thing to do to go to bed and leave the doors unlocked. This town isn't the place it used to be. The fire alarm was blaring, and she was sound asleep, out cold. I practically had to carry her out, and she's not a small woman. You know, I thought that nephew of hers was shooting his mouth off just to hear the sound of his own voice, but maybe Eddy's right and she's a danger to herself."

"Thanks, Pete. Why don't you take Bullet home? Your poor dog's about to have a coronary, and I'm sure your wife is worried. Casey and I will look after Minerva."

Casey had calmed the woman enough to strap on the blood pressure cuff while he'd been talking to Pete.

She looked up at him and frowned. "I didn't hear everything he said, but isn't it odd that particular rumor should be circulating this fast?" she asked.

"Yeah, and it's a damn good thing we have a bunch of people who can testify it isn't true."

CHAPTER TWENTY-NINE

Cole looked down at Ms. Minerva, every one of his senses telling him something was wrong. He'd known the woman for years, and as he'd told Casey she was physically fit and healthy. She most definitely didn't have trouble with her ears. So why hadn't she heard that alarm?

He bent down to speak to her, as he pumped the bulb to add air to the bladder of the sphygmomanometer Jason had given him. Tears moved down her cheeks, her eyes staring at the fire, but Cole doubted she could see anything.

"I'm sorry about your house, Ms. Minerva. We'll do whatever we can to save it, but you're safe, and that's what really matters. I heard Eddy was staying with you. We'll contact him to come back as soon as we can." He released the valve and watched the manometer. Her pressure was low—too low.

He reached for a flashlight from the kit Jason had left and noted her pupils were enlarged and didn't react to the light.

"Ms. Minerva," he shook her shoulder.

She blinked.

"Do you take medication to help you sleep?"

She blinked again as if she'd heard him but hadn't understood the question.

"What's wrong with her?" Casey asked. "I know this is frightening, but she's zoned out."

"She's either had a stroke or she's been drugged," Cole said, taking her pulse a second time. "This fire was set and someone didn't want her coming out of this alive. I can only think of one person who would feel that way."

"And conveniently he's out of town right now, but he can't be behind this. I know Eddy's always been a little out there, but that's his inheritance. The paintings and antiques inside that house are worth a fortune themselves."

Suddenly, Ms. Minerva grabbed his arm, the strength of her grip surprising him. "Peaches is still inside," she said, the words garbled by her tears, hard to understand. "Chester's gone. Don't let my Peaches die, too."

Cole turned to look at the burning building. While the fire was still in the growth stage, with all of the combustible materials inside the house, it was dangerous and unpredictable. The high ceilings might facilitate thermal layering where the potential for a deadly flashover could occur, possibly trapping, injuring, or killing anyone caught inside. If Peaches didn't get out of there before the fire was fully developed, the animal wouldn't stand a chance.

"What did she say, Cole? I couldn't hear her."

"She's worried about the house," he lied. "Can you go over to that box near the truck and get her a bottle of water?"

Casey nodded and hurried away.

Cole watched her go, knowing she would be angry when she realized what he was about to do, but having almost lost her and getting a second chance, he wasn't going to let someone else lose the only thing they had left. Minerva hadn't lost Chester, he'd been taken from her, and Cole had a sneaking suspicion whoever had killed the old man was behind this, too.

"Where was Peaches when you left the house?"

Minerva blinked rapidly.

"Ms. Minerva, there isn't much time. If you want me to rescue her, I've got to go now."

"Upstairs in my bedroom." Tears flowed freely down her pale cheeks.

Casey returned with the water bottle, opened it, and offered it to Minerva, who was shaking with reaction, unable to hold the bottle without help.

Cole pulled the emergency blanket out of the kit and draped it over the old woman's shoulders.

"Stay with her until the ambulance gets here," he said. "Tell them she's been heavily sedated. Don't let her fall asleep. Once the paramedics take over, go back to the house and wait with Mom and Dad until I come for you. If we can't put this fire out, we'll have to focus on saving the neighboring houses. It's going to be a long night. I have to go."

She frowned, about to argue with him, but he pulled up his mask, dropped his shield into place, and ran toward the house, turning on his oxygen as he did. He grabbed an axe from the truck, and headed into the building.

"Noah," he spoke into his radio, "there's someone upstairs. I'm on it."

"What the hell do you mean, Cole? Eddy's gone to Vegas," Noah's angry voice filled Cole's helmet as he ran toward the burning structure. "She was alone. Stay with the others, you fool!"

"I only need a few minutes," he answered. "I'll be careful."

Cole stepped inside the open front door and moved aside for one of the other firefighters to go out. He hadn't noticed the wind earlier, but now it blew debris across the rug in front of him.

Even without the smoke, the house was a mess, with boxes stacked high in the hall, reminding him of someone getting ready to move, or the hoarder's home in Dallas, where they'd gone in and found the man crushed to death by his own mess. The flames seemed to be concentrated at the back, probably in the kitchen. If the fire had started on the porch, as Pete had suggested, it could've spread there fast enough, and if an accelerant had been used, most likely gasoline once more, it would burn hot and fast. The problem was kitchens were often full of combustible materials that exacerbated the fire, ingredients that didn't always react well with water, among them liquid fuels like vegetable oil, or animal fats like bacon grease. There was always the chance an explosion could make matters worse.

Other than being filled with smoke, the front part of the house seemed unaffected, but that could be deceptive. Knowing fire could travel between the walls, the floors, and the ceilings, Cole knew enough to respect it and be careful. Glancing into the parlor, he saw that the paintings were missing. Had the men gotten them out this quickly? The one over the fireplace had been an original portrait of Hezekiah Skansen, painted by Samuel Morse, the inventor of the single-wire telegraph system. Mom had mentioned Minerva was donating items to the town museum, but he wouldn't have expected it to be something as valuable as that. In the dining room, the table was covered in boxes. Here, too, the paintings were missing, as was the Limoges china Minerva had prized. He'd been to a dinner party here last year when she'd explained how Hezekiah's wife had ordered it from France.

Leaving the others to save what they could, he headed toward the stairs. History would suffer and irreparable loss tonight. Aware that he didn't have time to waste, Cole climbed the oak staircase, checking each step as he did. The alarm continued to blare in the house, its shrill noise muted by his mask and helmet. While he didn't see any flames, it was smokier up here, and that set off warning bells in his mind. Smoke, like heat, rose, but there shouldn't be this much more of it up here unless something was smoldering. Maybe the fire hadn't started downstairs out back as Pete had claimed. The doors to the rooms were all closed except for one.

"Cole. Where are you?" Noah's voice came over the radio once more. "The guys are pulling stuff out of there, but I don't like the way this thing is behaving. Something's off. The roof's on fire and if the fire started downstairs, it shouldn't have moved up that fast. We've got hoses on the back, but it doesn't seem to be doing much good."

"I hear you. I'm upstairs now. There's a hell of a lot of smoke. Give me two minutes, that's all I need."

Cole looked down the hall, checked to see if smoke was coming from under or around any of those closed doors, but given the amount everywhere, it was impossible to tell. He let out a shaky breath. Minerva's bedroom was at the front of the house. He needed to find Peaches and get the hell out of here sooner rather than later. Obviously, Casey hadn't cornered the market on irrational, bone-headed behavior. If Mom was mad because he'd taken on a puma with a rock, she was going to skin him alive for this. He just prayed she would get the chance to.

* * * *

Casey watched Cole run toward the firetruck and prayed none of the firefighters would get hurt tonight, remembering what he'd said about tired men being more likely to get injured. She bit her lip nervously. If anything happened to him...

She turned back to Minerva. The old woman sat hunched over under the blanket, looking every one of her seventy-six years, her head down, her gaze focused on her hands. She'd stopped shivering, but she seemed so lost. Casey's heart went out to her.

"Ms. Minerva, I'm so sorry."

The woman looked up at her, her eyes puffy and red from crying, the only color in her pale face. "We were going to get married." She said so softly that Casey barely heard her with all the noise going on around them.

"I know," she answered, her voice filled with sorrow, blinking her eyes to keep her own tears back.

"Chester gave me a ring." She held up her hand.

Casey gasped. This was one of the rings from the Discovery. If he'd given it to her, it had been recently. Kyle had mentioned Chester had chosen a ring for someone special. She'd noticed the ring on Tuesday, but hadn't understood its significance.

"It's a beautiful ring," she said, her heart aching for the woman. "He must've loved you very much."

"I've loved him all my life. What a fool I've been."

Casey understood the woman's pain only too well. She herself had been about to toss Cole aside for pride. Thankfully, the Apache spirits and the earthquake had shown her the error of her ways.

Tears ran down Minerva's cheeks once more. "We were going to get married at Thanksgiving."

Casey stared at the woman. "Did Eddy know?"

"Eddy? Why yes. I told him the day Chester proposed. He was so happy for us."

Somehow Casey doubted that. If anything, Eddy would've seen the man as a threat to his inheritance. "When was that?"

But Minerva didn't answer, she was focused on the ring once more, no longer lucid, lost in a drug-induced world. Casey looked around anxiously, praying the paramedics would get here quickly. Not only was the woman's breathing shallow, she was shivering again.

Glancing over the crowd, Casey tried to spot Hal. He had to be here somewhere. If Eddy knew Minerva was getting married, that gave him a hell of a motive for wanting Chester dead. His aunt could well have changed her will in favor of her new husband, and if Eddy also knew about the gold, then he'd have a reason to frame the boys, too. The fact one of them was his best friend's son wouldn't bother him in the least.

She scanned the heavy crowd. More people had arrived since she'd gotten here with Cole. The street was covered with gawkers. Disasters drew the curious, and with the fair on only a few blocks away, no doubt someone had seen and smelled the thick black smoke clogging the air. Wrinkling her nose at the acrid scent, she coughed.

"It's those old asphalt shingles," Noella said, coming to stand beside her. "God knows what's in them. They were manufactured long before we knew about the danger they posed."

"They certainly stink," she agreed. "Have you seen Hal?"

"No, but I'm sure he's here. Melba was telling me about all the boxes they brought down from the attic. All that stuff won't make it any easier for the firefighters. Such a shame. I hope they can salvage some of it."

"I'm sure they'll do their best," Casey answered, unable to hide the anxiety in her voice. She turned back to the house, hoping to spot Cole among the men, but dressed as they were, it was impossible to tell them apart from here. Some of the firefighters were manning the large hoses, wetting down the neighboring houses. The second truck, the one from Apache Junction, concentrated their streams on the back of the house, but if anything the flames stubbornly seemed to grow larger. The roar reminded her of the earthquake this afternoon and she shuddered.

The firefighters carrying stuff out of the house moved more quickly as if they knew they would never save enough. She watched one fireman go back inside after the others had come out, and breathed easier when he returned, carrying one end of an antique sofa, another man she hadn't seen go in helping him. How many were still in there?

The danger involved in this job hit her hard, forcing her to recall the huge number of firefighters who had died on 9-11 as well as those who'd been injured in the line of duty. Not only was Cole risking his life in there, he did it every time they called without considering the cost. How could she ever have believed he lacked integrity?

"Minerva, are you all right?" Noella asked, drawing Casey's attention back to her charge.

"Peaches is still inside in my bedroom, Noella," she said.

Casey relaxed. The woman had recognized her neighbor and seemed a little more with it now. Maybe the drugs were wearing off.

"Cole went to get her for me. Such a nice boy."

Casey's heart stopped beating and she barely registered Noella's gasp. She spun around and gaped at the structure, more of it ablaze than before. Why wasn't the water helping?

The fireman she'd seen enter the building alone hadn't been the one who'd come out with the sofa. That's why Cole had left her here so suddenly. Moving toward the engine where the fire captain stood, she could tell from his posture that he was angry.

"Cole, you knucklehead," the captain shouted into the radio. "I'm pulling the men out. Get your ass down here now. A damn fool cat's life isn't worth yours."

Cole must've answered, but she couldn't hear what he'd said.

"Damn fool!" The captain said before shouting another order. "Burgess, pour as much water as you can on the front of the building. Cole's still inside looking for a cat."

"Will do, Captain, but this fire's not acting right. There's something. The Apache Junction firefighters have gone to cut a hole in the roof. We need to control the venting."

The captain moved away out of range and Casey couldn't hear anything else, but one thing was clear. Cole was inside that house and from the look on his captain's face, he was in danger. She looked back at Minerva and realized the truth. Her life wouldn't be worth living without Cole in it.

* * * *

Since the fire hadn't started in the bedroom, there was a good chance Pete's arrival followed by all the smoke and commotion had scared Peaches, and she'd stayed put, hiding under the furniture. The floor at cat-level would be reasonably clear, and there wouldn't be a danger of serious smoke inhalation for the small animal, but every second he spent looking for her was one second less they had to escape.

Unlike the main area downstairs, the hallway upstairs was almost clear, with only a few stacked boxes here and there ready to go. What struck him were the bare spots on the wall where paintings had been removed. It was highly unlikely any of the men had come up here and removed them, so who had?

Minerva might be donating items to the town museum, but all the paintings off the walls? Eddy couldn't have been happy about that.

Finding Minerva's bedroom was easy enough. He knew it was the larger one at the front of the house, and surprisingly, the only one with an open door. Maybe he was wrong and the men had checked the upstairs, closing the doors to each room once they confirmed it was empty. That was standard procedure. So why hadn't they closed this one?

Cole stopped, turned off the oxygen for a second, and took off his face mask. The fire was quiet, too quiet. Crouching low, he called out to Peaches, hoping he would spot the animal quickly, but because of the heavy smoke and its unmistakable chemical scent, he masked up again. Examining the room looking for a likely hiding place, he noted the open drawers. Unless Minerva was a bigger slob than he'd been as a teenager, someone had searched the place, and whoever it was had known Minerva hadn't been likely to wake up while he did. Could the fire have been caused by a robbery gone bad? Stepping over to the dressing table, he opened the built in jewelry box. It was empty. It was possible Minerva kept her jewels in a safe elsewhere in the house, but he doubted it.

A loud roar told him the fire had jumped up a notch, and he prayed it would stay down until he found the animal and got out. Given the thick blackness of the smoke, time was of the essence, and if it got much worse, he could get disoriented and never find his way back. Only two things burned that color—polystyrene from foam plastic packaging and tires—it was a damn good bet Minerva didn't have tires in the house, but she had tons of other stuff, and he'd sent over several boxes of packing peanuts last week when Melba had asked for them.

After checking under the covers and under the bed, he scanned the room. Where would a cat hide? The closet door was closed, so it was a safe bet the animal wasn't in there. He began to move the furniture away from the wall, hoping that the tabby had hidden behind them. Jackpot! Peaches was behind the chaise by the window. The angry, frightened cat hissed at him, but Cole caught her just as she was about to bolt, and with the cat tightly secured in his arm, he turned toward the door and hurried into the hall. At the far end of the landing, flames licked at the walls and ceiling, and he prayed the staircase was still manageable.

"Cole, for God's sake, we can't stop it. Water's not helping. Apache Junction's on the way with a foamer. The building's almost fully engaged. Get your sorry ass out of there now!" Noah yelled.

The words chilled him. He'd almost died once today, and here he was pushing his luck again. He wasn't going to tempt fate any longer.

"On my way, captain."

As he moved along the rug to the top of the stairs, he noted there appeared to be fewer flames now than there had been moments ago and that scared him. If oxygen were introduced into the area now, a backdraft would occur, and he'd be a goner for sure. Moving quickly toward the staircase and down it, he discovered the front door had shut. He would have only a second or two to get the door open and get out. After that, the fire, fueled by fresh oxygen would roar and destroy whatever was left in its path.

A crack split the air. He looked up as pieces of the ceiling rained down on him. Tossing his axe on the ground, he tucked the cat more closely into his body, thrust his arm up to protect his face mask, and threw himself headfirst through the door. The inferno whooshed behind him and more of the ceiling rained down. Two firefighters ran over to him and pulled his half-prone body out of the way. Once they were clear, one of them helped him stand.

Cole looked down at a slightly singed and definitely upset Peaches. He handed the cat to one of the firefighters.

"Give her to Minerva, will you?"

"You're one lucky bastard." He recognized Jason's voice. "Noah's going to tear you a new one for pulling a stunt like that. You can write about shit like this, but don't ever do anything like that again. The paramedics just got here."

"Cole," Noah's voice shouted in his ears. "You crazy son of a bitch. If you ever pull another stunt like that, I'll kick your ass from here to kingdom come."

Cole chuckled. "Don't worry, I won't. Give me five, and I'll get on the hose." He removed his mask and face shield and had just taken off his helmet when a body barreled into him, almost knocking him off his feet, pummeling his chest with her fists, crying heavily, and screaming at him.

"Whoa! Whoa!" he yelled. Reaching out, he tried to grab Casey who was intent on using him as a punching bag. Damn, she was mad. He'd expected anger, but not this deranged fury. Tears streamed down her face as she continued to cry and yell incoherently at him. Her eyes were puffy and swollen, her face red and blotchy, and she was blubbering all kinds of nonsense. She'd never looked more beautiful.

"Calm down, honey. What's your problem?" he asked.

She stopped hitting him and stood back, her hands fisted in rage.

"What's my problem?" she shrieked. "You're my problem. You could have been killed, you idiot."

Shaking in her fury, she reminded him of an enraged cartoon character. Her hair was wild, the red tresses glowing in the light from the flames, making them seem on fire, too. The only thing missing was the smoke coming out of her ears. If she hadn't look so terrified, he might have laughed, but unwilling to risk anymore of her wrath, he decided against it.

"How dare you put yourself in danger like that?" she spat at him, pounding him in the chest again to emphasize her words.

"I was doing my job, Casey." He kept his voice calm and grabbed her hands to stop the abuse, but she pulled them away and backed up, hugging herself instead.

"No, you weren't. You put yourself in danger when you didn't need to. I heard the other firefighters—I heard the captain yelling at you to get out. What you did was stupid and reckless … We both almost died this afternoon, but we were together. Did you think of that when you went into that house? Did you think how I'd feel if you died? Losing you would destroy me."

Cole stopped moving and gawked at her, a stunned look on his face. Had she meant what he thought he'd heard?

CHAPTER THIRTY

Casey stared at him, trying to hold onto her rage, but the adrenaline surge that had driven her to react so violently and blurt out her feelings like that had waned. The emotional turmoil of the day had taken its toll. He stood there, mouth agape, staring at her like the dummy he was. How dare he endanger himself like that? Of course the cat was important to Minerva, but not more important than he was.

His face was covered in soot, his beautiful brown eyes wide and staring. He looked like he'd been poleaxed. The longer he stood there gasping like a fish out of water, the more uncomfortable she felt. While she'd expected some kind of reaction to her words, stunned mutism hadn't been it. Maybe she'd been wrong. Perhaps she'd misunderstood when he said he wanted them to have a future together.

Crushed, she prepared to walk away and salvage whatever shreds of her dignity remained before she gave way to tears and crumbled to the ground in anguish. He gently took her arm preventing her from leaving.

Pulling her toward him, his face deadly serious, he looked down at her. Gently, his large hands, now missing his gloves, cupped her face raising her chin, and he gazed into the eyes. "I'm sorry I scared you. I didn't realize just how risky it was to go in after Peaches." The emotion in his eyes made her heart soar. "I don't know what I'd do if I lost you either."

He bent his head, and heedless of the crowd surrounding them, claimed her lips briefly before releasing her. She wasn't ready to let him go. Her mouth met his once more. The smell of the smoke mixed with his spicy sent intensified the desperation and urgency in the kiss. Knowing she could have lost him and never again have felt the ecstasy of being in his arms, the touch of his lips on hers, his tongue dancing with hers, she acknowledged what she'd suspected from the moment he'd kissed her in the desert. She needed this man the same way she needed air to breathe. He was her other half, her soulmate.

They would find a way to make this work. Once she told him about Rick, there would be no more secrets. Cole slowly pulled his mouth away, his eyes glowing with happiness.

"Sorry to intrude," Jason said, coming up beside them. "There about to take Peaches and Minerva to the hospital. It'll probably be the one and only time a cat rides in an ambulance and don't ask me what'll happen when she gets to the hospital, but she wants to talk to you."

Cole nodded, releasing her, and they walked over to the ambulance hand in hand.

The old lady stroked the purring cat, and if Casey could purr, she would, too.

"I know you put yourself in danger to save her," Minerva said, more in control of herself now. "Chester gave her to me almost twenty years ago when he found a little gold. He was convinced that would be the big one, and we could finally be together, but he didn't have any luck. I told him it didn't matter, but he could be as stubborn as my father. Then, six months ago, he came back and gave me this ring and this." She held up the cat's head so they could see her collar.

Casey gawked. Attached to the cat's collar was a gold nugget.

"We both made mistakes. I should've married him back when he first asked me. Even if my father had disinherited me, we would've managed, but I was a coward, lacking my sister's spirit, ever the obedient daughter, and look where that's left me—a lonely, miserable old lady with nothing but a cat." She turned to Casey. "Don't make the same mistake I did. Follow your heart." Tears slipped down her cheeks.

"When you're feeling better," Casey said, "I have some young people I want you to meet. They spent a lot of time with Chester and would love to share their stories with you."

"I'll look forward to it. And Cole, thank you again."

"Don't mention it, Ms. Minerva. I'm glad I was able to find her."

"We've got to take her now," the paramedic said. "The vet's going to meet us at the hospital."

Cole turned back to Casey. "I have to get back and help."

"I know," she said, "but no more putting yourself in danger like that."

"Cole Walker Junior, as I live and breathe, if you ever do anything stupid like that again, I will turn you over my knee, and don't you think you're too big for me to do it!" Noella yelled, rushing up to her son. "When Minerva told me you'd gone into that house after Peaches, I almost had a heart attack. I can't imagine how Casey felt. What were you thinking?"

"That no one deserves to lose everything they love. Casey's already given me hell about it, so you can back down. I didn't realize how erratic and dangerous the fire was, but I'm safe, Peaches is safe, and that's really all that matters. Nobody deserves to lose someone they love, not if it can be helped."

The scowl on his mother's face gradually eased and turned into a smile as she looked at Casey in Cole's arms. "I'm glad you two found each other, but it won't stop me from worrying your sorry butt if you ever do something like this again. I thought you'd agreed not to do anything stupid after the rock and the puma."

Cole chuckled. "What can I say? I'm a sucker for a damsel in distress, especially if she's a feisty redhead."

Casey pivoted to look back at the house. The structure was engulfed in flames. The roof had collapsed on itself. The men

407

manning the hoses aimed water onto the fire, and while it appeared they had it contained, the blaze would burn for hours.

"This was arson, wasn't it?" she asked.

"It looks like it. I'll bet my bottom dollar, that fire started in more than one location. As much as I'd like to stand here and hold you for the rest of the night, I have to get back to work. I promise not to do anything reckless, but it's almost eleven. You should go home and get some sleep. Have you got your phone?"

She nodded. "I grabbed it before we left the house."

"Good. I'll call you later when I get a break." He bent his head and kissed her again, before slowly pulling away. "Remind me to pick up silk sheets on the way home."

"I will." Reluctantly, she let him go, and he walked toward the fire engine and almost immediately relieved one of the guys holding the hose.

"Are you coming back to the house with me?" Noella asked.

"In a bit. I really need to find Hal and talk to him. You go. I'll be along as soon as I do."

Noella nodded. "I'll have the whiskey waiting. We both need a drink after that stunt."

Casey chuckled. "We certainly do. I'll see you shortly."

She watched Noella walk along the sidewalk and stop to chat with people she knew. Turning around, Casey scanned the crowd looking for Hal. She spotted his squad car pull to the curb and saw him get out. He wasn't wearing his hat the way he usually did. He probably removed it to drive. She was halfway to him when movement across the street caught her eye.

Two men stood near the veranda of the house, their bodies partially hidden by the bushes growing there. They were both dressed in black, with what looked like hoods pulled up over their heads. With the fire blazing, it was anything but cold here. Why the strange outfits? One man moved away slightly and something about the one remaining struck a chord with her. Those slouched shoulders and bulging belly were familiar. He struck a match and brought it up to his face to light a cigarette, momentarily revealing his profile. She would recognize that silhouette anywhere. She'd seen it fifteen years ago. Eddy Skansen. He was supposed to be at a business meeting in Vegas. What the hell was he doing here? And why was he skulking around like a coyote at a garbage dump?

Despite her dislike for the man, without giving the matter any thought, her curiosity spurred her to action. Casey moved through the crowd and crossed the street, hurrying toward him. The other man had vanished, but Eddy stood there, as cocky as ever, the oversized sweater's hood camouflaging his identity.

"I thought it was you, Eddy," she said, hoping her tone was friendly and not judgmental. "What are you doing here? Why didn't you come over and help with Minerva? She's very upset. They've taken her into Apache Junction."

"Isn't it beautiful?" he asked as if he hadn't heard a word she'd said. Relaxed, he leaned against the veranda, his face rapt, his left hand tucked into his pants' pocket, the remains of a joint she'd mistaken for a cigarette dangling from his right.

"What are you talking about? The fire?"

He sniffled. His eyes were glassy, the pupils dilated. He watched the flames dance across the street, an expression close to euphoria on his face.

"It's different every time, you know. You have to listen to it. Sometimes it crackles, at others it sizzles, and now and then, it even pops."

"You make it sound like breakfast cereal. I never really thought of it that way." She enjoyed a fire on a chilly night or out camping, but when someone was as high as he obviously was, reality was skewed. "That *was* your home, you know."

He sneered, and focused on her. "Never *my* home, Casey. My father wasn't good enough for the Lord Almighty Hosea Skansen. He disowned his own daughter. That uppity aunt of mine, my mother's only sister, was no better, and it broke my mother's heart. Now, I've broken hers." He chuckled. "Karma's a bitch."

"I didn't realize there had been family problems," she said, hoping to calm him, trying to remember what had happened to Eddy's parents. They'd died when he was young. He hadn't moved in with Minerva until high school.

He blinked and turned back to the burning structure. He sniffed the smoky air. "Don't you love the aroma of burning wood and the caustic scents produced by the lethal chemicals we surround ourselves with? And the color. How can anyone not adore the constant shifting of the multifaceted flames, their tones dependent on whatever they devour? It's wonderful to watch."

"You know a lot about fire, don't you?" Could he be the arsonist? Looking down, she noticed the bulge in his black jeans. He was sexually aroused by the flames. When she'd seen him Wednesday morning, he'd looked pretty rough. She'd assumed he'd been at the casino. What if he'd spent Tuesday night watching the Morris house burn? She shivered in spite of the heat and glanced back to see if Hal had come back to his vehicle. Coming over to Eddy like this might not have been her smartest move. "Tell me about fire." As long as he was engrossed in the flames, he seemed docile enough.

He smiled. "Look at the building. The combusted gases burn a soft blue that produce the most heat. Organic material blazes hot and white, but once it's consumed, the flames turn yellow and then shift to orange and finally red. Beyond the redness, the non-combusted carbon particles rise, the soot, visible as smoke—sometimes black, sometimes gray, sometimes brown, but rarely white, despite what the church says when the Conclave of Cardinals elect a new pope." He chuckled at his own joke.

The hairs on the back of her neck stood on end. He wasn't only high, he was insane. Why hadn't anyone noticed it before? She'd always thought him odd, scary weird, but deranged? How had he hidden that so well?

"Fire is an avenger meeting out justice," he finished.

"Justice?" She thought of the character in one of Cole's

books, the one who'd died like Chester had. "Why did Chester deserve that kind of justice?"

His face darkened in anger, his eyes so cold they chilled her to the bone. "He was going to take away what's mine, what should've been mine all along."

"What should've been yours?" she asked, certain she already knew. Not only had Eddy set the fires, all of them, he'd poisoned Chester.

"My heritage. He asked Aunt Minerva to marry him, and the old bitch said yes. I couldn't let that happen. For years she made me beg like a dog to be part of what was by rights mine. My mother was the elder daughter. When my parents died, instead of nurturing and sheltering me like she should've, she said I was sick and sent me away. But I wasn't the one who was sick, she was. It took a long time to convince them to let me come back, and when I did, I had to be so careful. She watched my every move, but I found ways around her, convinced her I'd changed. The mountain and the desert hold many secrets, Casey."

She shuddered, unwilling to think about what he meant. Somehow she knew it would be a thousand times worse than torturing frogs. "If you were worried about your inheritance, why destroy it?"

He laughed. "This house? I hated the place. Fire's my mistress and she deserved a gift, so I gave her one. She's a beautiful dancer writhing and gyrating just for me. She's alive and makes me feel alive, too. Look at them." He indicated all the people who milled around. "They're as much in her thrall as I am, but they don't control her. I do. As a boy, I played with it, studied it, learned its secrets, experimented with it, and honed my ability to control it, until at last, I mastered it. There are lots of ways to release its energy—slowly like a python slithering and coiling itself around a branch, waiting for its unsuspecting victim to come within range before crushing the life from it, or quickly, striking like a cobra and claiming its prey swiftly and smoothly. Each method brings its own level of satisfaction."

He turned to her, his face now devoid of emotion, not even acknowledging the inferno raging behind her. He drew deeply on the joint, closed his eyes and slowly exhaled.

"It's really too bad you recognized me. Too many people in this damn town need to mind their own business." He pulled his hand out of his pocket and cupped her cheek.

Casey shuddered and stepped back.

"I heard you took Horace Stone up on his offer of partnership. That's a shame."

"How would you know that?" She frowned. The notice would be in Saturday's *Fortune Examiner.*

"Nothing happens around here that I don't know. Sylvia was thrilled. Couldn't wait to tell me how you would help Horace with all his clients."

"You! You killed Sylvia!" she shouted the words, but they were drowned out by the roar of the fire as more of the house collapsed in on itself.

"Not me, Casey," he said, his voice bland as if he were discussing the weather. "Because you accepted that offer and were going over to see her, I had to improvise. When it comes right down to it, you and your refusal to stay out of my business, killed her. I knew you were going to be trouble when I saw you the other day. I'd hoped I could seduce you over to my side, but then..."

Casey felt her cheeks heat and trembled. Coming over here hadn't been a bright idea. She glanced around, but still couldn't see Hal. If she cried for help, would anyone hear her over the noise?

"I'm not involved in your life, nor do I want to be," she answered, injecting as much disgust into her voice as she could, remembering that she wasn't a helpless little girl. She was armed for heaven's sake, and as doped up as he was, he might be overconfident, as his confession was showing, and he could become aggressive, but normally coordination was impaired as was judgment.

"Unfortunately for you, that's not true, but it won't be for much longer. By accepting Horace's offer, you blundered into my business, and Sylvia knew too much. She was going to show you Horace's files, and there were things there nobody needs to see. I burned them and destroyed her computer. Everything is gone."

She thought of the documents in the evidence locker. She'd concentrated on the CJKT Discovery. What if the other two files held some of the information he'd destroyed—those shorthand notes could be rough copies.

"Horace knows what's supposed to be in those files. You won't get away with any of this," she said, her voice filled with bravado as she looked around nervously, wishing she'd approached Hal first. "You just confessed to arson and murder. I'm not going to let you walk away."

"Still so naïve? I thought you would've learned a thing or two, but maybe not. I'm going to enjoy teaching you. As far as Horace goes, he won't be around much longer. You thought putting a police guard on his door would help, but my associates have deep pockets and a long reach. They'll take care of my aunt, too. So many people in this town need to learn to stay out of my business."

Horrified, she looked at the man she'd known for years and saw a monster—not a monster, a sociopath. She lifted the edge of her blouse and pulled out her gun. "I'm taking you over to the sheriff."

He laughed. "Oh please, I never knew you were a comedian."

"There's nothing funny about this, and when you come down from your coke high you'll realize you've reached the end of the line." She swallowed nervously and fought to keep her hand from shaking. "People are dead."

"And that would be my problem because?" he asked, finishing his joint. "It's a damn shame I can't stay and watch the rest of this, but someone else may come over and stick their nose in my business." He dropped the butt onto the grass and ground it into the earth until nothing remained. "We're done here."

"Yes, we are. Now, put your hands up. I'm taking you—"

Pain ripped through her head, and everything went black.

* * * *

Cole removed his filthy gear, shoved it into the truck with all the others, and waved as he walked away. Bryce would get everything cleaned up and put to rights. He was the only member of the squad paid by the town since someone had to make sure they were ready to go from one fire to the next. The town council was actually considering hiring a few full-time firefighters because of the recent arsons. They could assist with search and rescue, too.

It was light out, just after six according to his watch. When he'd been given a short break around three, he'd wanted to call Casey, but had opted not to in case she was sleeping. She'd been exhausted when they'd come down off the mountain and while his rescue of Peaches might've given her an adrenalin boost, once she relaxed, the tiredness would've come back full force. It was like a sugar rush followed by the inevitable crash.

The volunteer firefighters, with assistance from the Apache Junction Fire Department, battled the blaze all night, and hadn't been able to save the house, but they had stopped the fire from claiming any more of the neighborhood. The closest buildings would all have suffered smoke and fire damage, but that could be repaired. Of all the arsons, this one had been the most destructive. Minerva's home was a blackened, smoldering ruin, which would have to be demolished as soon as possible. A replacement squad from Apache Junction had arrived half an hour ago, and they would monitor the building until they were sure the fire was dead. They'd already had a couple of flare ups. It would be at least a day or two before Clay could walk through what was left of the place.

He glanced at the handful of onlookers who remained, grateful Casey had taken his advice and gone to his parents' house. While he'd love to see her face right now, knowing she might be asleep in his bed pleased him, and he wouldn't mind cuddling for a few hours. She hadn't said she loved him, but her words had been the next best thing. With a little luck, she would be willing to keep that ring now. If she was open to deepening their relationship, then maybe she would want to make it a permanent one.

If she didn't want to live in Fortune, that was fine by him, although he would miss working with Hal and the volunteer firefighters he considered friends. The important part was that he and Casey would be together. CJ Coleson could write anywhere, and now that he realized his secret wasn't one, would it really matter? They could spend their weeks at her condo in Santa Fe and weekends and holidays at the house on the edge of the desert or at his cottage on Apache Lake. A small chopper could cut the commute in half. He hadn't mentioned he was a qualified helicopter pilot and would surprise her with that as soon as he could. Arizona by air was an incredible sight.

Yawning, he turned down the sidewalk and stopped next to the police car. Hal stood there, looking as tired as Cole felt.

"Not planning to get any sleep tonight?" Cole asked.

"Look around you. It's morning. I was waiting to talk to you before I go by the station, and then head home to grab two or three hours' sleep. Melba and Rina stayed at Buck's last night, helping him with the kids. Their youngest is only ten. This is still Gold Rush Days, and despite the excitement of the past twenty-four hours, people are going to be up and at'em, celebrating again when the rides open at noon. Some of the town's regulars will be concerned about Minerva, but to a lot of the people here this weekend, she was just a lonely, old maid. Most of them don't know or care about the people we'll be burying next week."

"That's a little cynical even coming from you. Rough night?"

"Rough week, and while my night was frustrating, it wasn't as rough as yours. Retirement is more appealing by the second.

Those pick pockets are back, and I must've had ten calls from irate citizens who were robbed. Then there was a knockdown, drag out fight at the saloon, but by the time I got there, the troublemakers had run off. There has to be a few hundred dollars' worth of damage. I should be able to spot some of them today. They won't all have walked away without a scratch."

Cole chuckled. "You can't arrest every person you see with bruised knuckles or a black eye."

"Try me," Hal answered belligerently. "I was on my way here when I got called to an accident not too far from where Horace ran off the road. Some guy lost control of his truck and flipped it into the ditch. He's alive, but barely—smelled like he'd had one too many at the bar and might've been one of my brawlers. When he recovers, assuming he does, he'll be looking at DWI charges for sure. The paramedic drew blood for me."

"Will it hold up in court?"

"Maybe, maybe not, but the poor bastard wasn't in any shape to give his consent. They'll take more at the hospital anyway. That's what held up your ambulance. He needed the first one. I felt badly about it too, especially when I heard Minerva was in bad shape when Pete carried her out."

"Yeah. I'm convinced she was drugged, but by the time the paramedics got here, most of it had worn off. You know, she's damn lucky. If Pete hadn't been walking by, she wouldn't have made it."

"Drugged? Are you sure? The poor thing has to be heartbroken. She and Chester had been estranged for years, and to get him back only to lose him like that ... Maybe she needed something to sleep? Melba mentioned she didn't seem like herself yesterday morning when they moved out the last of the items she was donating to the town."

"I thought so myself until I went inside." He frowned. "If the stuff she was donating was already out of the house, what's with all boxes left inside?"

Hal shook his head. "Damned if I know, but some of them were earmarked for charity. A company from Phoenix was scheduled to pick it all up on Monday. I guess they can save themselves the gas now. The ladies spent days cleaning out the attic and basement." He shook his head. "Given what happened tonight, that was a waste of time and elbow grease. Minerva mentioned she was thinking of moving out and letting the town have the house and whatever was in it she didn't need. Of course, that was probably grief talking."

"Eddy wouldn't like that. But we may have another problem. Like I said, she was drugged, and I think it was done to facilitate a robbery, one committed by someone who knew her routine, had access to her, and knew she'd be alone tonight. The most likely suspects are her servants. So the questions are, who's been looking after her and where are they? Half the town was at the fire tonight, but I didn't see anyone worried about her, or her well-being."

Hal frowned. "Minerva's long-time housekeeper retired last spring and moved to Florida. That's about the time Eddy moved in. He arranged for an Apache Junction housecleaning service to look after the house, and there's someone who cooks for her each day, but the man leaves late afternoon, leaving them to serve themselves at night. Minerva didn't like the arrangement, but she told Melba it was only temporary. You know, if she was drugged, that man would have had ample opportunity to put something in her food. Melba met him once and said he looked more like a thug than a gourmet chef, but apparently his food was excellent. It would have to be to meet fussy Eddy's tastes. I'll look into it later today. Are you sure the place was robbed?"

"I have to check with the others on the squad to be absolutely certain, but I would swear it was. All the paintings were missing from the rooms I passed when I was looking for that damn cat. Someone had tossed her bedroom, and the jewelry box in her dressing table was empty. Now the guys could've removed some of the paintings downstairs, but no one would go through her drawers like that."

Hal nodded. "Good thing Eddy isn't around because he

417

would be the prime suspect. He's the only one who stands to gain from this in any way."

"I agree. Minerva will get a huge insurance payout since they weren't able to save much, and when she dies, it'll all be his. Casey mentioned he seemed a little high when she saw him on Wednesday. If his money's not only feeding his exes and his gambling habit, he might need to get creative to find more. She suspected he might even be helping whoever's bringing in the drugs for a personal discount."

"That's an interesting angle. Eddy made damn sure just about everybody knew he was out of town this weekend. He may not have done it himself, but he could've facilitated it. If he's involved, it could be insurance fraud as well as arson and perhaps even attempted murder, but how would I prove it?"

"We have to find the chef. If Eddy put him up to this, he's the one who drugged Minerva."

Hal nodded. "There's no honor among thieves. If we can find the man, we can make him a deal. Eddy will have an alibi, but if we get a confession, it won't matter. The problem now is how do we prove it? Given the level of destruction, we don't know what was taken and what was destroyed."

"I'll bet the insurance company has a pretty comprehensive list. Maybe if we watch the black market, we'll see some of those paintings show up."

"Could be," Hal said and rubbed the stubble on his chin. "I've got a friend at the FBI's fraud division. I'll give him a call when we get that list. You're pretty smart, even if you are half asleep."

"Thanks." Cole chuckled.

"I'll be interested in what Clay has to say about this fire. By the way, I heard about your valiant rescue of Peaches. For the record, that cat may have nine lives, but you don't." He ran his hand through his hair, looked around for his Stetson.

"To top it all off, my hat's missing, and it was my favorite one." He huffed out a breath. "I've fielded a number of calls from people who claim three kids were seen near the house just before the fire started, one of them, Kyle Harvey. The grapevine's running with this, and the story's growing by leaps and bounds. Gunderson's going to be all over me like a cheap suit."

Cole gritted his teeth. "If I get my hands on whoever's behind this ... The boys have a rock-solid alibi. We didn't get down from the mountain until after six. Casey and I had supper with them all at the Pearson ranch—that's a good ten miles away from here. Six other men, three of them his hands, another three, muscle from Matt's father-in-law, can attest to that, too. When we left just after nine, Kyle and Joey were sound asleep, and Tony was halfway there. Sounds like we need to put someone on damage control. It's like putting toothpaste back into the tube, once it's out, it's out for good. By the way, was there much damage from the quake?"

"Not as much as you would think, given how close the epicenter was. The news placed it about fifteen miles into the Superstitions—measured 6.2. We had a couple of downed trees and powerlines, and there are a few more cracks to fill in the road, but no major structural damage and no injuries. There were some frightened people caught on the rides when it happened—a few who may not get back on them for the rest of their lives. They shut everything down for a couple of hours while they ran safety protocols. One of the kids on the Ferris wheel had a panic attack, but the medic calmed her down once they got her off. I can't imagine anything more frightening than being on that with the ground shaking. How bad was it in the mountains?"

"Probably worse than it would've been on that ride. Scared the daylights out of us. 6.2? That's all?" Cole shook his head in disbelief. "From the way it felt, I would've expected 7.5 at least. We were right on top of it. By the way, the Discovery is gone. That whole section of the mountain was swallowed up in the earthquake. If we'd been in the desert, I would've called it a sinkhole, but the way it went down ... it was as if the earth had turned into quicksand. There's a brand new canyon where it used to be, but I'll tell you all about it later." He yawned. "I need to get back to Casey."

"Yes, you do, but it's a damn shame about that cave. It would've been one hell of a historical find. Before you go, you're sure this was arson? Eddy was telling everyone that Minerva was getting forgetful—leaving the stove on, letting the kettle boil dry, lighting candles and leaving them. That's why he claims he moved in with her."

"Damn convenient of him to be away tonight then," he spat the words, his voice filled with his disgust. "If I had to guess, Clay will find evidence of that as well as gasoline implicating the boys. I was in there, Hal. That fire had more than one point of ignition, and like I said, someone removed a hell of a lot of valuables. Pete did see a stranger who told him no one was home and mentioned seeing the boys. Maybe we need to hook him up with a sketch artist. He's one of the most observant people I know." He reached into his pocket and pulled out the Mexican cigarette package he'd placed in a plastic bag earlier. "In the meantime, you'll want to run this as soon as you can. We found it on that mesa where the helicopter lands. Maybe we'll get lucky with the prints."

"I'll get it to the lab on my way to the station and put a rush on it. I almost forgot to tell you. We got a hit on the prints from Trent's apartment. They belong to Jose Alvarez. He's got a rap sheet as long as your arm. He's associated with the Mendosa Syndicate out of Vegas, who in turn do business for the Acuna cartel. The Apache Junction police have an APB out on him."

"A syndicate and a cartel working together? That doesn't sound good for Fortune. Anything in that file make him a candidate for Trent's murder?" He yawned. "Sorry, I'm bushed."

"Nothing in particular, but he could've graduated from aggravated assault to murder. It wouldn't be the first time, and for someone like him, it wouldn't be much of a leap. If Trent tried to screw the syndicate in any way, putting a bullet in his back and decapitating him as a warning to others, is definitely something they would do. What doesn't make sense is leaving him out there. Can you manage with four hours of sleep?"

"If that's all I can have, I'll take it. I know you're short-handed. I'll leave Casey with Mom and Dad and be in by eleven. She's armed, so she should be safe enough there."

Hal nodded. "I agree. Besides, you two have to make an appearance at the fair in spite of everything that's happened. I'll see you later."

"You know, if whatever Trent did had anything to do with the cartel, leaving him near Weaver's Needle makes sense. That used to be called the Finger of God. Fitting place for punishment."

CHAPTER THIRTY-ONE

Cole yawned again, waved at Hal, and walked the half block to the house. His mother was asleep on the porch swing, the bottle of whiskey and two glasses on the table in front of her. It didn't look as if the glasses had been used. He leaned down to shake her shoulder and wake her.

"Mom, why didn't you go to bed? Sitting here with a bottle of booze is going to scandalize the neighbors." He chuckled.

Noella looked at him blinking her eyes owlishly. "I was waiting for you and Casey. I must've fallen asleep."

Cole's blood ran cold. "What do you mean? Casey's here. She came home with you."

"She may be in the house, but she didn't come home *with* me. I left her just after I left you. She needed to talk to Hal about something." His mother's brow furrowed and her eyes filled with worry. "I expected her at any minute, but…"

Cole ran into the house and checked every room, waking his father in the process. Not finding Casey, he ran outside once more to the car. Her purse was on the seat where she'd left it, but the car was still locked, and she wasn't in it.

He pulled out his cellphone, knowing hers was in the pocket of her pants. It rang and rang, but no one answered. When voice mail kicked in, he hung up and dialed Hal.

"What is it, Cole?" Hal's voice sounded tinny as it came

across the line.

"Did you talk to Casey tonight?" he asked, unable to hide his panic.

"No. I didn't even see her. I assumed you'd left her at the house."

"I didn't. Knowing the fire was at Minerva's she came with me. The last time Mom saw her, she was going to talk to you." He turned to his mother. "When did you see her last?"

"Right after you went back to the fire. When I got here, it was just after eleven. I sent your father to bed."

"No one's seen her since eleven. Hal that was seven hours ago. There's no way she left under her own steam. Someone took her and did it right under our noses." The enormity of his words flooded him. The woman he loved was missing, possibly in the hands of the man who'd tried to kill Horace and had succeeded in doing so with Sylvia. "The chances are whoever has her is responsible for everything that's happened."

"I'll meet you at the station," Hal said, the no-nonsense tone he'd always attributed to Tate Silvers loud in his voice. "Let's not assume the worse and go off halfcocked. Someone had to see her leave. She couldn't have vanished into thin air. Maybe she went home to her mother's house."

"How would she get there? She didn't take the car, and her Harley's still at her mother's place. She wouldn't have gotten in with anyone, and you know it. I'll be there as soon as I can."

Cole hung up. Beside him, his mother was crying into his father's shoulder.

"I shouldn't have left her. I didn't know there was any danger, but with Sylvia dead and the fire … This is my fault."

"No, Mom, it isn't," Cole answered, suddenly calm as adrenalin and his professionalism took over. If Casey was in trouble, she needed him alert and focused. "There may be a perfectly logical explanation as to where she is. Hal's right. We can't assume the worst." Not if he wanted to remain sane. "I'm going to go up and shower and then I'm going to the station. I know it's early, but Randy's at *Cookies and Cream* by seven each morning. I need you to call Casey's house to make sure she isn't there without arousing suspicion. Tell Randy or whoever answers the phone that I asked you to call because we might be late for supper. If Casey's there, leave a message to have her call me as soon as she can. God forbid she isn't there. Either way phone me right away. If I can't find her, I'll go over and break the news to Maria and Austin myself."

He just hoped to hell her parents or Randy had heard about the fire and had come into town, and then taken her home. Maybe she'd stopped by the house and seen his mother asleep and had chosen not to wake her, but leaving without telling anyone where she was going was a damn irresponsible thing to do—worse even than going off into the desert halfcocked.

His mother nodded, swiping at her tears.

"Is there anything I can do?" his father asked. "Austin's having heart surgery next week. I hope this won't make matters worse."

Cole nodded, licked his lips, and turned to go upstairs. "Pray, Dad," he said. "Pray for both of them."

Three hours later, Cole stood in the living room at the Stevens's house. They'd searched the area around the fire, but given the number of people there tonight, finding anything to point to Casey was hopeless. He'd called Jason and half a dozen of the other firefighters, and none of them had seen her after eleven. Burgess thought he'd seen her talking to someone across the street, but he couldn't be sure it had been her. He barely knew her, and the woman he saw had her back to him. He thought she might have red hair, but even that wasn't a given since the fire turned everything reddish-gold. Cole had crossed the street, checked the lawns, but he hadn't seen anything that pointed to Casey.

"I'm sorry. It was all my fault. I shouldn't have taken her with me, but…"

"Stop, Cole," Austin said. "This isn't your fault. Casey knew the danger going in."

"You knew about all this, and didn't tell me?" Maria asked,

shaking in her distress. "Austin Stevens how dare you keep something like this from me? After that heart business you swore you wouldn't."

"Maria, it wasn't Austin's choice. Hal swore him to secrecy," Cole said trying to remain calm when he was as torn up as they were. "I'm sorry about all of this. I love her, and I *will* find her. You have my word on it."

When he did, someone had better hold him back because if that person had hurt her, he would tear him apart and feed him to that puma himself. Without saying anything else, he grabbed his hat and headed out the door to the SUV.

* * * *

Groaning, Casey tried to move her stiff arms, but couldn't. Similarly, her legs wouldn't move apart and she couldn't straighten them. Her head pounded, and the smells surrounding her were nauseating. In addition to smoke, no doubt from the clothes she wore, there was gasoline as well as the unmistakable stench of ammonia and rotten meat.

Opening her eyes slowly, she examined what little she could see of her surroundings, trying to stay calm, knowing she was on the verge of a full-blown panic attack. She was lying on her stomach on a cot covered with heavy, plastic sheeting, from which emanated the vile aromas threatening to make her sick.

Turning onto her side, she took in her surroundings. A small, dimly-lit room, a shed perhaps, with unpainted wooden walls and ceiling. There was no window, and what little brightness there was filtered in through the cracks between the boards. Not a shed, a warehouse of some sort, and this was a glorified box, possibly a shipping container, used to store cargo or prisoners like herself. She held her breath, listening for the least little sound that might tell her where she was. Silence. No hum of machinery, no birds or insects. Exhaling, she swallowed awkwardly, her throat so dry it hurt.

How had she gotten here? She scrunched up her face trying

to dredge up the memories needed, increasing the pain in her head. Slowly the events from what had to be last night returned. Eddy Ramos. He'd killed Sylvia, and if he was to be believed, his associates would take care of Horace and Minerva, too. Who could be that powerful? Better yet, why would they want a madman on their side?

She swallowed nervously, remembering his reaction to the fire. He had to be the arsonist. While pyromania was an Impulse Control Disorder, there had been nothing impulsive in Eddy's setting the fire tonight. It had been well planned, and he'd been sexually aroused and gratified watching Minerva's home burn. He'd felt justified and seen it as retribution for the way he'd been treated.

Casey trembled. There was no way he would let her live; in fact, it was amazing she was still alive. He'd confessed to her and that made her a danger to him. Of course, he could plead insanity, and she would be the perfect witness to collaborate it. She frowned. Was that what all this was about? The ravings of a lunatic? But why? No one wanted to be confined to an asylum.

It was warm in here, the air hot and stale. Would enough of it filter through those cracks for her to breathe? Had Eddy brought her here, somewhere on the edge of the desert, just to let her suffocate or die of dehydration? Why not shoot her? It would be more merciful, but he'd never been the compassionate type.

"Probably pulled the wings off butterflies as a kid," she muttered and shook her head. This wasn't the time or place to dream up scenarios of torture, but the images of that frog pinned to the board, his heart pounding visibly as Eddy dissected it, wouldn't go away.

"Cassandra Maureen Stevens. When will you learn to act rather than react?" Talking aloud helped calm her. Normally she would pace, but since she was trussed up like a Thanksgiving turkey, that wasn't likely to happen.

She'd done it again, acted without thinking just like she had fifteen years ago, just as she had Tuesday night. It had been more than stupid of her to have approached Eddy like that. She'd suspected he might be involved based on what Minerva had told her, and the fact he was there and not in Vegas should've set off all those personal security bells and whistles Ryan had tried so hard to instill in her. But oh no! As he would put it, she'd leaped before she'd looked. She'd ignored that other man, and it had cost her big time.

"I will not panic. I will not fall apart." She repeated the mantra half a dozen times before she felt calm enough to examine the situation rationally.

She was in a warehouse of some sort, one that had to belong to the Skansen family, so perhaps it was an old building on one of the abandoned mining sites, although judging from the aromas, the place could've been a slaughter house. The stench reminded her of the odors surrounding Sylvia's body, and her stomach roiled.

"Don't you dare get sick," she admonished herself. "It smells bad enough without that."

Whoever had brought her here had to have used a vehicle. If the man and Eddy had tried to carry her any distance, someone would've noticed. It was light out, so by now Cole and Hal knew she was missing.

Physically, she was uncomfortable but basically unharmed. She probably had a lump the size of a grapefruit on her head, and her hands were tied so tightly behind her back they were threatening to pull her arms out of her shoulder sockets. Her knees and ankles were bound in much the same way, a rope or wire connecting her feet to her hands, making it impossible for her to straighten her legs and stand. Hogtied! The more she moved and tried to stretch, the more they cut into her wrists and ankles. It could've been worse.

A few months ago, she'd read about a naked body found in a motel room just outside of Henderson, Nevada. The woman's body had been covered with electrical burns, her hands tied behind her back, her feet tied together, and the loose end of the rope in a noose around her neck. According to the medical

427

examiner, the only way she would've been able to relieve the tension on her throat would've been to keep her neck, back, and legs arched. Eventually, she couldn't hold that position any longer and had slowly strangled. The police had no leads, but there were signs of vicious rape and abuse. The room had been cleaned, not so much as a hair left behind, and the rapist had used a condom—if he'd ejaculated. From the viciousness of the attack, it was possible the sexual sadist had been unable to achieve gratification in any semblance of a normal way.

She swallowed. Eddy was crazy, but was he capable of doing something like that? Fighting to hold back tears of helplessness, she swore not to go down without a fight. Cole would find her—he had to. She'd finally found a man to love, a father for those children she wanted, a chance for that elusive happily ever after, and she wasn't going to die like a javelina in a trap, baking in the desert sun. She just had to hold on. Later today or tomorrow, Ryan would call, and he was bound to have found something in Eddy's background. He never left a stone unturned, and while Eddy might've managed to fool the people at home, his craving for fire and whatever else rocked his boat would need an outlet. Once he knew she was missing, together with Cole, they would leave no stone unturned in their search.

The need to empty her bladder was worse than ever, but she would be damned if she'd pee herself and give Eddy the satisfaction of humiliating her that way. Sooner or later the bastard would come for her, and when he did he wouldn't find a simpering coward.

Seconds crawled by. Sweat beaded on her forehead and ran down her face. The room was brighter which meant the sun was higher, and it was getting harder and harder to breathe in the small room. She'd almost drifted off again when a door slammed, startling her.

"Hello?" she called out softly, her mouth and throat dry, her voice hoarse.

No answer. Had she imagined the sound? She didn't want to be alone here, wherever here was, but she was afraid of what might happen to her if she wasn't. The maniacal look in Eddy's eyes last night terrified her. By now, the effects of the cocaine or whatever he was on would've worn off, and that might not improve his disposition.

"Hello?" she tried again, a little louder this time, her fear escalating. She licked her dry lips. Her heart pounded, increasing the throbbing in her head. Wasn't solitary confinement a form of punishment?

"Is anyone out there?" she asked as loud as she could and was rewarded by the sound of heavy footsteps moving toward her.

The door to her makeshift prison opened admitting a stocky man with jet black hair and a thick mustache. He was dressed in black and armed, the weapon in his hand—her weapon or at least the one Hal had given her—pointed at her. The gush of cooler air was the most wonderful thing she'd ever felt, and she breathed deeply even if that air was tainted with the man's body odor.

He stepped over to the cot.

Casey kept her gaze fixed on the gun in his hand. The safety was off.

"I'm going to untie you," he said, his Mexican accent strong. "If you try to escape, I'll shoot you—not to kill, just to make you behave—he won't care if you have scars on your arms and legs as long as your face and torso are okay. When he finishes with you, the boss will auction you off. Maybe some sultan will want a redhead to add to his harem."

"I'd rather die." Casey said bravely, her gut filled with terror she would not show.

He laughed. "That's what they all say. And who knows, you might get lucky that way. Some do. Now, do you understand? I will hurt you if I have to."

"I understand," she said, fighting to keep calm, her fear multiplied by what he'd said. Cole would find her, but to do that she needed to stay alive and give him the time he needed. "I ... I have to go to the bathroom." Tears she couldn't hold in any longer slipped down her cheeks.

"Madre de Dios," he said, bending down to cut the plastic tie on her legs, the gun leveled at her thigh. "I hate blubbering women."

Between the seven hours in the saddle yesterday and being hogtied like this, the muscles in her back, butt, and legs screamed in agony, as she straightened them, but she swallowed the pain and let him yank her upright. If he hadn't been holding her, she would've collapsed as the blood ran into her feet, the pins and needles' feeling excruciating.

Turning her around roughly, he cut the tie at her wrists, the blood flowing painfully into her hands, her arms and shoulders aching from the strain. Black spots floated in front of her eyes, but she refused to give into the agony and fright.

"You shouldn't have pulled so hard. You cut yourself for nothing. This way." He half carried, half dragged her to a filthy washroom that stunk of urine and feces. "In there and no tricks. If you obey, I won't tie you up until we have to leave. Obedience is everything. Remember that. It may save you some painful lessons."

Casey entered the washroom, her bladder aching and felt a few seconds of discomfort bordering on agony before the urine flowed. He hadn't closed the door, but he wasn't paying attention to her.

Finished, she washed her hands and splashed water onto her face. She cupped her hands to drink, but the man's patience was at an end, and he pulled her roughly out of the washroom, dragging her back to the box, and shoving her onto the bed. He closed the door. Less than a minute later, he returned and thrust an open bottle of water at her.

"Here. Drink."

Casey reached for the bottle and drained it.

"Thank you. Where's Eddy?"

"You shouldn't be so anxious to see him again, chica. He's not always a nice man, and this morning, he's very angry. Things didn't work out the way they should've. Just hope he doesn't take his anger out on you." He laughed, the sound raising goosebumps on her skin. "The last woman who annoyed him didn't do so well."

He closed the door, locking her in once more.

Terrified at what he'd said, Casey listened carefully until she heard a distant door slam and an engine start.

Quickly, she stood and reached into the back pocket of her borrowed jeans. In the bathroom, she'd discovered her cellphone was still there. Pulling it out quickly, she turned it on, cringing at its musical tone, muting it as quickly as she could. The home screen appeared, indicating a power level of almost 80 percent, but her moment of glory vanished as the words "no signal" brought tears to her eyes once more. No wonder they hadn't taken her cellphone. It was useless.

Throwing herself down on the dirty cot, she cried until she had no tears left. Exhausted and overheated, she fell asleep.

* * * *

Cole parked the SUV behind the police station next to a red sedan from a rental car company in Phoenix and entered the building through the back door. He grabbed another cup of coffee in the breakroom, knowing he didn't need any more caffeine. Grateful the area was vacant, he sipped the bitter brew. They were at a dead end. Feeling like his life had hit rock bottom, he rapped on the side door to Hal's office.

"Come in," Hal called.

Stepping inside, Cole was surprised to see a man, his back to him, standing in front of the window. Whoever he was, it wasn't someone Cole recognized. He was built like a linebacker.

"I'm sorry," Cole said. "I didn't realize you were busy. I'll come back."

"No. Sit down before you fall down. How many cups is that?"

"I've lost count, but does it really matter?"

"It should." Hal ran his hand through his hair in frustration.

"I'm sorry, Cole. Do what you have to do." He indicated the stranger. "We've been waiting for you. Cole Warner, meet Ryan Meadows, Casey's private eye. He got in about twenty minutes ago."

The man turned around, walked over to him, and held out his hand. Well over six feet, the easiest way to describe him would be a well-oiled fighting machine, reminding him of Sylvester Stallone's *Rambo*. There wasn't an ounce of fat on the ex-marine's toned, muscular body, and dressed in a black T-shirt and jeans, he looked deadly, like a panther ready to pounce on its prey. He wore a shoulder holster, which he probably covered with the black, lightweight jacket hanging from the chair in front of Hal's desk, but Cole would bet a month's royalties that wasn't his only weapon. Ryan wasn't a pretty boy by any means, but his rugged features would appeal to a lot of women. His dark hair was cut short, and he had a neatly trimmed mustache. Like him, he'd missed his morning shave. His piercing blue eyes were filled with anger and something else—guilt?

Cole reached for the outstretched hand, taking in the tattoos running up the man's arms. His grip was as firm as Cole had expected. This wasn't someone he would want pissed off at him, and from the frown on his face, he was really pissed at someone.

"Pleased to meet you," he said. "Casey spoke highly of you, but I thought you were going to call. Did she know you were coming?" He fought to tamp down his jealousy. Going all caveman right now wouldn't help anybody. Casey and Ryan had been lovers, and married or not, the man was important to her.

"That was the plan, but after what I learned and confirmed, I realized she was in a hell of a lot more danger than any of you anticipated. When I couldn't get her on her phone last night or again this morning, I knew something was wrong. I flew into Phoenix as soon as I could get a flight. This is all on me. I'm the one who forced her to come home. Hal told me she's missing." The sound he made after the word was similar to the puma's angry growl.

So he blamed himself?

Get in line, buddy, there's enough of that going around for everyone.

"I just finished giving that news to her parents." Cole couldn't hide the dejection in his voice. "She's been gone at least eleven hours now. She could be anywhere, and we haven't got a snowball's chance in hell of finding her anytime soon. We don't know where she is or who has her."

"You're the one pretending to be her fiancé. Red mentioned it when she called me on Thursday. Does she know how you really feel?" Ryan asked. "It's written all over your face. She's the second most important woman in my life, and if you can make her happy, you've got my vote. Knowing how she felt about this place, I was surprised when she said she was going to stay. I was positive there was more to it then helping out a bunch of runny-nosed kids."

"We had a rough start, but things were looking up. She means more to be than life itself, and if anything happens to her because I let down my guard—"

"Jesus Christ, Cole, don't do this to yourself. You were fighting a fire. This isn't on you. If I'd been there ... She stayed behind to talk to me. I realized after your call that I didn't get to the fire until after eleven. I was tied up with that damn traffic accident."

"Stop." Ryan raised his voice. "Neither one of you is to blame for this. You couldn't watch her 100 percent of the time. I know Red. She's too damned independent for that. She's one of the 'where angels fear to tread' types. If I'd known what she was walking into, I would've done my best to stop her. Unfortunately, life likes to throw us curves. I figured it was about time she faced whatever the hell had sent her running away from this place. I was wrong."

"Where did you two meet?" Cole asked, curious to know how this man fit into Casey's life.

"She walked into a biker bar in Austin where I was tending bar, looking for a job. She was this cute little innocent with the most beautiful eyes I'd ever seen. When she gazed at me, with that scared, wounded animal look on her face, but defiant and determined as all get out, I knew I had to take care of her. I'd met people with body image and self-esteem problems, but I'd never met anyone as determined to put everything behind her and move on. It was almost two months before she told me she had family here. I got her a job waitressing for a buddy of mine who ran a little place near the university. While she got her law degree, I finished my training and got my license as a private investigator. When she took the job in Santa Fe, I went with her. If she decides to come back here, Sally and I will be right behind her, and I'll bet Wonder Woman comes, too."

"Wonder Woman?" Hal interrupted. "Who the hell is that?"

"Her personal assistant. It's basically a 'wherever thou goest, we'll follow' relationship. In our own way, we're family and very protective of her, whether she likes it or not. Casey has a bad habit. She's as naïve as they come. Don't get me wrong. Her innate goodness is one of her most endearing qualities, but it leaves her open to danger and pain. She's honest and actually expects everyone to be truthful, when in reality we all lie sooner or later and crush her hopes and dreams. When she perceives an injustice or something doesn't fit with what she believes, she jumps in with both feet without checking the water or considering the consequences of her actions. I've seen her go nose to nose with perps as big as I am. It's one of the things I love about her and right now, it's what scares me most."

Cole nodded, recalling Casey's flight into the desert, her anger when she realized he'd lied to her, and the way she'd set aside her own agenda to help those boys.

"Hal, my guess is that traffic accident was orchestrated to keep you and the ambulance away," Ryan continued. "My investigation says everything that's happened in this town is related to the Skansen family. If Casey specifically went looking for you, it had to be because she learned something about the case that couldn't wait. I've told her time and again to look before she leaps, but she has a Nosy Nelly quirk to her personality and when she needs to know something, she keeps digging until she's satisfied. For my money, Casey saw something no one else did and went to investigate it."

Cole frowned. All about the Skansen family? He doubted that, but he'd seen her curiosity in action for himself, and Ryan was right. If she saw something or someone who looked out of place, she would investigate.

"The fire gave us a hard time, and most of the squad were too busy to notice anything, but I spoke to the guys earlier, and one of them thought he saw Casey cross the street to talk to someone. He doesn't know her well, so he couldn't say it was her for certain. There were a lot of people watching that fire, although the majority of them were concentrated outside the cordon we erected. The house directly across from Minerva's was vacant. It has creosote bushes planted near the veranda, which could offer some cover even if there were lots of people milling around."

"Then, we need to examine that area and those bushes. That's probably where he grabbed her."

"I had a quick look but with so many people, how do you expect to find anything of value?"

"You forget Casey believes I'm the world's best gumshoe," he said. "I've never let her down, and I won't start now. She knows you're looking for her, and that I'm supposed to call today or tomorrow. While she may go off halfcocked, she's smart. Once she realizes what a mess she's in, she'll play it safe. Since she knows her kidnapper already, she'll be extra careful."

"How the hell do you know she knows her kidnapper?" Cole asked, unable to get his head around the idea that this guy could walk in and solve the case just like that.

"Because I know Red. As curious as she might be, she wouldn't have separated herself from the crowd for a stranger. She was looking for Hal for a reason. Who did she talk to?"

Cole chewed his lower lip. Hadn't he said she wouldn't go off with just anyone?

"Me, my mother, and Ms. Minerva. I didn't see her talk to anyone else."

"Damn. I didn't realize Ms. Skansen had been lucid enough to talk. I know who has her, and I wish to hell I didn't. It's that sick bastard Eddy Ramos," Ryan said, but he didn't look happy about it.

Cole's disappointment was a physical blow to his already exhausted body.

"That's impossible. Eddy went to Vegas for the weekend with Rick Harvey."

"You're right and you're wrong. He's *supposed* to be in Vegas with Trent Gibbs and Rick Harvey. We know why Gibbs didn't show, and when I looked into it, I learned Harvey and Ramos checked in on Wednesday afternoon, but he hasn't been seen since Wednesday night. I did a little extra digging. His key card hasn't been used either," Ryan said. "Eddy may have gone to Vegas. But he isn't there now."

"How do you know about the key card?" Hal asked, his forehead creased.

"Let's just say I know my way around computers."

"You hacked the hotel's security system." Cole said, impressed in spite of everything.

"I did, but I didn't stop there. I was able to get all kinds of information on Gibbs and Harvey—not exactly stellar individuals—but when I went to look into Ramos, it was a different story. In fact, there's an eight year gap in his life, and that made my Spidey senses tingle. Take a look at this." Ryan moved over and took out an envelope stuffed in the inside pocket of his jacket and dropped it on Hal's desk. "This was why I called Casey. You guys needed to know this. Ramos is a genius—"

"Genius? Eddy? You've got the wrong guy. He barely made it through school," Cole said, his nerves at the breaking point.

"Believe me, an IQ test showed him to have above average intelligence. He scored 160, the same as Stephen Hawking, and that makes him one of the most dangerous serial killers around.

At age seven, he was diagnosed with intermittent explosive disorder, antisocial personality disorder, psychopathy, which I discovered means an abnormal lack of empathy. One shrink went so far as to say, he showed every sign of potentially growing into a narcissistic megalomaniac with tendencies toward sexual sadism."

"And that monster has Casey?" Cole asked, dropping into a chair, praying Ryan was wrong.

CHAPTER THIRTY-TWO

Cole reached for the envelope on the desk, his hand shaking from fear and caffeine jitters.

"Jesus Christ," Hal said, raising his hands to hold his head. "If what you say about Eddy is true, why isn't he in an asylum? Why the hell would Minerva let him move in with her?"

"Because he's brilliant, and he's learned how to manipulate the people around him to get what he wants. He was only seven when he set fire to his parents' bed, dousing the sheets and blankets in gasoline while they slept, his three-month-old sister in the bed with them."

Hal jumped up more agitated than Cole had ever seen him.

"My God. I remember that. Her sister's ashes were interned in the family plot, but Hosea Skansen refused to have Ramos's ashes included. There was no mention of a baby. I knew they'd died in a fire, but I sure as hell didn't know Eddy had set it. Someone asked Minerva about the boy and she said he was being cared for by others. Most of us assumed it was family on his father's side. When Eddy came to live with her, he was almost fifteen. I figured whoever had been keeping him had died. Are you sure of your facts?"

"They're all in there," Ryan said. "Believe me no one wishes I was wrong more than me. Eddy admitted that he'd done it because his father had spanked him and sent him to bed without supper when he'd knocked over the baby's cradle. He calmly informed the doctor that the baby was ultimately to blame because she had taken what was his. He'd planned to only kill her, but her presence in their bed that night proved that his parents didn't love him anymore. If they didn't want him, he didn't want them. He showed no remorse for what he'd done."

"Why the hell did they ever let him out?" Hal asked.

"Because the juvenile justice system was, and still is, incapable of dealing with child killers," Ryan said, sitting in one of the chairs in front of Hal's desk. "He was committed to a juvenile psychiatric facility, where he received treatment. He responded to medication, and when he turned fourteen he was released. You'll see one of the psychiatrists voted against it. She was convinced Eddy had somehow used his intelligence and abilities—although she didn't say what those were—to gain access to the assessment tests. His answers were too perfect, and she believed he'd memorized the responses to each diagnostic tool to convince the doctors that he no longer posed a danger to himself or others. She described him as a ticking time bomb, believing it was only a matter of time before he would explode once more like he did the night he murdered his parents. From what I managed to learn, his aunt was getting married and that would be repeating the same set of circumstances that had caused him to blow in the first place."

"Minerva was getting married?" Hal asked. "The woman's over seventy-five years old."

"When I looked into Chester Morris, I found he'd applied for a marriage license. The names on the application are his and Minerva Skansen. I'd say, that qualifies, and he's gone boom!"

"What happened to the doctor who opposed his release?" Cole asked.

"Gas explosion in her condominium about a month after Eddy was released into a supervised group home. Twelve people were killed. It was ruled accidental. Six months after the accident, Eddy requested permission to move in with Minerva, and it was granted. In high school, everything points to a reasonably normal, yet somewhat mean kid. He had a few disciplinary notes in his file for bullying, but the complaints generally were ignored or dropped. He was suspended for a couple of days in his senior year when he used a live frog for dissection in science class. Incidentally, someone blew up the science lab not too long after that. The teacher was badly burned and retired. The cause of the explosion was attributed to a faulty Bunsen burner."

"Shit. I was working in Fortune when that happened. Melba and I were terrified until we found out the twins were fine. Clay looked into that. He figured someone had played with the burner, but he had no idea who. Ella complained that they were all forced to sit through a week of lectures on lab safety. You think he did that?"

"I do. Eddy would've known exactly how to sabotage that thing. When he went to college in Denver, Colorado, his scores were mediocre despite his intelligence. He got into drugs and hung out with a pretty rough crowd. One of the people he spent a lot of time with was Enrique Mendosa, now the head of the Mendosa Syndicate. They control half a dozen casinos in Vegas, places where Ramos, Harvey, and Gibbs spent a lot of time. He and Mendosa shared a propensity for the darker side of sex. Eddy was accused of sexually assaulting a co-ed, but managed to get himself off on a technicality. After he graduated, he started working for the company, but continued his close association with Mendosa. None of Eddy's ex-wives or girlfriends had anything good to say about him, except that he was into kinky sex, and when it got too rough, they bailed. Look, why don't you two have a look at the papers while I ask your officer to get me a list of all the properties owned by Skansen Mining."

"There are a number of abandoned places in the area, too. Have her list those as well," Hal said.

Ryan nodded. "Good thinking."

Cole watched Ryan walk out of the office and shook his head. "Cocky son of a bitch, isn't he?"

"Yeah, but I like him," Hal said. "By the way, the rangers caught that puma, and he'll be relocated to the Phoenix Zoo. It's either that or euthanasia. He won't be the tamest cat in the place, and it's not the best solution, but they figure he's too old to just relocate. He'd find his way back for sure. And that cigarette package you gave me had prints on it. They matched those we found in Leon Turner's apartment."

"That Alvarez guy you mentioned?"

"Yes, and Trent Gibbs."

"Damn. Well, if Trent was involved with that helicopter, he could well have pissed off the wrong people."

"It would explain a bullet in his back, that's for sure. Casey was right. Meadows is damn good at his job and could be just what this town needs right now."

Cole pursed his lips. If Ryan stayed here, it would mean Casey would, too, and that meant they would find her. He opened the envelope and pulled out the sheets of paper, the top one dated twenty-five years ago.

* * * *

Casey awoke soaked in perspiration, her clothes stuck to her body, her hair matted and wet. She put her hand up to the lump on the back of her head and felt the crustiness of dried blood. It was brighter inside her prison, which meant the sun was higher, and the temperature had to be well over ninety degrees. How long had she been here? Pulling out her phone, she looked at the time. The last time she'd seen Cole, he had mentioned it was almost eleven, so roughly twelve hours. If it was this hot now, what would it be like this afternoon?

She stood and paced. Eight paces from one wall to the next. Four paces from the cot to the door. Her heart pounded the way it did when she had to take an elevator. Come to think of it, her prison was almost the same size. Struggling to take a deep breath, she sighed. And here she'd believed yesterday had gotten rid of her claustrophobia. Right now, she swore the walls were closing in on her.

"The room is not shrinking," she muttered through gritted teeth, berating herself. "Get some backbone."

She walked back and forth, counting her steps as she did, to prove to herself that her jail cell was staying the same size. When she reached three hundred, she stopped. All she was doing was tiring herself and increasing her thirst. The man who'd locked her in here earlier had promised to return. Pacing like a rat in a cage worrying about air quality wouldn't solve anything. What she needed was a plan. Resuming her steps, she focused on the facts as she knew them.

Eddy Ramos was a deranged killer, and from what she'd seen on his face as he'd confessed his crimes, he didn't feel the least bit of remorse over what he'd done. If that was right, he was a sociopath, but a damn smart one. Somehow he'd hidden his true character from everyone, including Minerva. The question was how had he done it? At times, he would have to have been lucid, capable of working and behaving so normally that no one would see the evil in him. At others, something would trigger his mania, with its lust for fire, sadism, and God alone knew what else. Could it be the drugs he used? Were they like the potion in Robert Louis Stephenson's novel that turned Dr. Jekyll into Mr. Hyde? Everyone reacted differently to their chemical composition. One thing was certain, Eddy hated the Skansen family and everything it had done to him, but he craved its wealth and power.

She stopped moving when she heard an engine, followed by the sound of the distant door slamming, and footsteps heading her way—too many for just one man. Her heart raced, and she swallowed awkwardly, her throat as parched as it had been earlier.

Moments later the door opened, but instead of her jailor, Eddy smiled at her, looking every inch the well-put-together executive and CEO.

"Getting a little exercise I see. Good. I like my women toned and fit. They can play better and longer that way."

Turning, he walked away, leaving the door open.

While he might look normal, his words proved he was still delusional, and Casey's blood ran cold. He wasn't going to kill her. No, he had something far worse in mind.

"It's much cooler out here, and Jose's brought you some food. It isn't up to his usual standards, but unfortunately, he couldn't get into the kitchen this morning." He chuckled. "Now, be a good girl and come out and join us. I'm not in the mood to play yet. Too many loose ends to tie up first."

Casey didn't wait to be asked twice. The last thing she wanted to do was make him angry. Exiting her prison, she followed Eddy over to a small table and chairs where Jose was opening a bag from a popular Mexican fast food restaurant.

"Sit," Eddy ordered. "Eat. I don't particularly like the stuff, but Jose swears by it."

She reached for the cup of soda. The icy drink was nectar from the gods.

Eddy and Jose moved away and as she ate, she took in the rest of the warehouse, surprised by the number of cardboard and wooden boxes she could see. Some of them looked like art crates designed to protect valuable paintings during shipping. She'd assumed the place was abandoned. Glancing back at her prison, she realized it could be used to ship something, too. It would also make a hell of a coffin. That thought made her stomach queasy.

Eddy dropped onto the chair across from her, a smug look on his face. Pulling out a pack of Mexican cigarettes, he took one out and lit it, using a monogramed butane lighter.

Was that the same brand as the pack they'd found on the mesa?

"Well, counselor, aren't you curious?" he asked, taking a long drag after he'd spoken. "Last night you were full of questions. Cat got your tongue?"

He slowly blew out the smoke, reminding her of the Cheshire cat in *Alice in Wonderland*, but this was far more like a trip *Through the Looking Glass* where everything was skewed.

"Why did you do it, Eddy?" she probed, knowing she might be courting disaster by giving in to him, but her curiosity demanded answers. "Why destroy the house? It was full of antiques and priceless paintings among other things."

He laughed, the sound of it chilling her.

"I didn't realize you had such a short memory. That could be a problem since I despise repeating myself. I told you last night. That place meant nothing to me. Look around you. Jose dosed Minerva at lunch. The poor old dear fell face-first into her mashed potatoes. He carried her upstairs and put her to bed where the firefighters should've found her. I'll have to find a way to thank Pete Putnam for rescuing her. Maybe I'll poison that damn dog of his. If it hadn't been for that mangy mutt, he wouldn't have been out walking. Jose tried to send him away, but there were too many witnesses, so, he blurted the lie about the kids and left. There was a fifty-fifty chance the old bitch wouldn't wake up anyway."

Casey swallowed the unappetizing and odd-tasting cold burrito, not one of her favorite foods. Maybe she shouldn't encourage him to talk. He seemed to be getting worked up again. She'd thought his drugs would've worn off, but he'd obviously taken another hit, and like some megalomaniacs, he needed to hear himself brag and gloat about his achievements.

"Where was I? Ah, yes. Between us, we took anything of real value out of the house. It was actually quite easy since all those boxes and cartons were already there. I wasn't fast enough to get everything I wanted, as some of it had already been delivered to the museum, but I'll turn a tidy profit on what I have. Once the insurance company pays up and the ruins are gone, I'll build something far more suitable. Did you know my aunt was actually considering giving the house and everything in it to the town? Horace was in the process of rewriting her will. She was going to screw me again—the way her father did my parents. Well, enough was enough. If I can't have it, no one can."

"But you just said you didn't want it," Casey said confused.

"There's nothing that bitch has that I want." He laughed again, his madness more evident now.

"No, that's not quite true," he said petulantly, sounding more like a spoiled child than a man. "I want what should've been mine—the money, the power, and of course the gold. Everything that comes out of the Skansen mines is mine, and then there's the stuff Chester found. I was there when he explained it all to Minerva. Did you see the ring he gave her? And that nugget on that stupid cat's collar? She was going to marry him and what was his would be hers, and that would've been acceptable, but she wanted it to go the other way, too."

"Edward, you'll still work for the company, of course. After all, you are a Skansen, but Chester and I will run it together," he said, his voice mimicking Minerva's almost perfectly.

How many times had he impersonated his aunt? He could easily have fooled someone over the phone.

"You're very good at that," she said.

"I have a talent for voices," he admitted proudly. "Over the years I've done well as a ventriloquist, specializing in, shall we say unique, private performances. I can mimic anyone I want. Even you, Cassandra. I'm sure your parents will be relieved to know you've gone back to Santa Fe for a few days, but poor old Cole will be heartbroken to know you've decided Fortune just won't work for you. Such a shame. You looked so happy together."

The similarity between her voice and Eddy's stunned her and frightened her more than anything he'd said and done. If he called and convinced Cole she'd left, it would wound him, but would he believe it? Depending on what he said, it was a distinct possibility, but she had an ace up her sleeve. Eddy didn't know about Ryan, and Ryan would be calling later today or tomorrow. Sucking in a breath, she tried to look impressed rather than horrified.

"Wow. You are good. I'll bet you fool people all the time."

"I manage to do what's necessary," he said, reverting to his own voice. "It's a skill I acquired as a child. It helped me gain access to anything I wanted, including Fortune."

"So you know about the CJKT Discovery," she continued, wanting to keep him talking. "Isn't it amazing? All that history, but tell me, how will you find it now that Chester's dead?"

He laughed. "I've been working on this for months now, cultivating his trust. Last week, once I realized what the bitch was about to do, I phoned him pretending I was her, and arranged to meet him at Horace's just to verify everything before Minerva carried out her civic responsibilities as she called them. Apparently, she told him I had concerns that his discovery was really all a sham to steal my fortune. It was almost too easy. He drew me a map and had Horace show me some of Kyle's sketches. Then, I drove him back to his place because he wanted to measure something. I spiked his lemonade with anti-freeze. He didn't feel well, so I encouraged him to lie down. Next week, my men and I will go and clean out the place."

Oh no you won't.

Even if she didn't survive this, there was satisfaction in knowing he would never get his hands on Chester's treasure. The spirits had made sure of that.

"What about the boys? They own it now."

"Casey, please. Slayer's Law. They can't profit from their crimes, and they'll be prosecuted for that fire and all of the others as well as Chester's death. I have people fabricating the last of the evidence now. I had a friend with a helicopter fly over the town around nine last night. Infrared cameras verified Kyle and Kristal were in the house. It'll be her word against that of several concerned citizens that her son wasn't out gallivanting with his weirdo friends. What kind of boys choose to spend all their time with an old drunk?"

"But Chester wasn't drinking anymore," she said, coming to the man's defense.

"He wasn't drinking any less either," he laughed. "I'm sure by now, Doc Creighton has the full tox results back proving Chester was very, very drunk, poisoned by his own mescal. Once he passed out from the ethylene glycol, I gave him five injections, each one containing two ounces of one hundred proof mescal mixed with the poison. With the way his body was burnt, no one would find the needle marks between the toes."

Casey finished her drink and the second burrito and prayed the food wouldn't come back.

She'd never considered Eddy to be particularly smart, but the fact that he had thought everything through not only proved she'd been wrong, but was truly frightening. And if someone was fabricating the right evidence, Eddy's plan could well succeed. After all, if Cole didn't find her soon, she doubted she would be around to tell anyone the truth. "So what will happen now?"

"After I tie up loose ends, you and I will leave here. I have a special place, a playhouse of sorts, where I'll teach you how to be properly obedient, and when I tire of you, I'll pass you on to some of my acquaintances. They pay well for top quality merchandize trained properly. By then you won't care one way or another." He stubbed out his cigarette and lit another. "It's really all about money and what pleases me. The longer you do, the longer I'll keep you."

"But people will search for me," she said, allowing her fear to show through, knowing he would like that. Cole would've spoken to her family when he'd discovered her missing. Randy, Mom, and Dad had to be frantic, and knowing her dad's health was compromised made the sobs come faster.

"Maybe, maybe not. It all depends what story you'll tell or rather I'll tell pretending to be you. You haven't been home in fifteen years. No one will go looking for you, but did you know someone was looking for Evie Pearson, or rather Edythe Larson, as she used to be called? I must remember to let them know where she is. Once my associates see to it that Minerva and Horace take a turn for the worse, I'll produce the proper wills. Minerva is Chester's heir—I convinced him to add a codicil to his will. I destroyed a few things, but I left that document. Once she's dead, it'll be legally mine. By the time those boys get out of jail—if they survive that is—that cave won't have anything in it, but moldy old skeletons, and all that lovely rich gold will be mine. Do you know how much it's worth? Chester said there were almost four hundred five-to-six-pound bags of nuggets. That's almost forty million dollars. It might seem like chump change, when you consider the rest of the Skansen fortune, but those mines have investors who must be paid dividends. I saw the photograph Chester took of a cave drawing disappearing into the wall. With the proper equipment, I'll drill through it. Peralta's mine is behind that cave, and that'll mean millions and millions of dollars that will be all mine."

She'd love to tell him it wouldn't be, but that might not be the best course of action right now.

"Won't Rick be upset you're framing his son?"

"That buffoon? You know better than anyone what an ass he can be. He's convinced the brat isn't his in the first place, so with the right suggestion from me, he'll see it as his unfaithful wife getting what she deserves. Besides, I've got him under control. Once I fed his baser appetites, there was no going back. Mr. Harvey enjoys inflicting pain almost as much as I do, but he doesn't like fire. Oh well, one out of two isn't bad."

"So what happened with Trent? I thought he was your friend, too?"

"He got stupid." The petulance was back. "I caught him stealing from me, shorting the accounts and lining his own pockets with the difference, and I couldn't allow that. He'd lost more than he was supposed to at the casino a couple of months ago and had to make good out of his own pocket, but when I realized it was my money, I allowed my associates to deal with him. Now, he's part of the Superstition Mountain legends, just like that nosy old uncle of his, and before you ask, I didn't kill him. One of my associates got to him first. Still he did cost me fifty grand that I've yet to recover." He glanced at his Rolex. "I think that's it. Now that you know what a brilliant strategist I am, as much as I've enjoyed our chat, I have to go. I've got an appointment in Phoenix with someone from the Bureau of Land Management concerning the solar farms. Sadly, you need to go back into the box, but Jose will come by later tonight with more food. He'll leave you two bottles of water. Don't drink it all at once. You may have noticed you'll be in there and the washroom's in here. I won't be happy if you have an accident."

"What solar farms?" The longer she could keep him here, the longer it would be before he could call Cole pretending to be her.

"The ones I'm going to build with my associates. Now that Minerva's out of the picture so to speak, I can finally move ahead. The Ramos name will be revered around here far above that of Skansen Mining. Actually, I got the idea from your father. Isn't that ironic? Everyone is desperate to find alternative energy sources, and Arizona has plenty of sunshine. That land is useless for mining or ranching, but as a solar farm, it's worth millions. I enjoyed watching those old houses burn. I experimented with them, deciding whether they should burn quickly or slowly. It's all in the amount of accelerant you use and where you use it."

"I thought that land belonged to the town."

"One of my associates put a healthy bid on it last week, and the town council is salivating over it, too stupid to realize how valuable the land can be."

"The Bureau of Land Management won't let you cover that whole area with solar panels."

"You're not that naïve, Casey. Anybody can be bought if the price is right. I've already got most of the permits. Now, it's just a matter of greasing a few more palms." He stood. "I'm feeling rather generous right now. Jose, let her go to the bathroom before you lock her in."

Eddy came over and helped her up. She thought he was going to walk away, but instead he grabbed her and pulled her into his arms for a punishing kiss. It took everything in her not to fight back, but her instincts told her fighting would only make it worse. He shoved her away. "You have a lot to learn about pleasing me, but I'm not a cruel master—well, I am, but you'll learn to love it."

He shoved her into Jose's arms. "Be out here within ten minutes. See you later, Cassandra. Enjoy the rest of your day."

As soon as Jose closed the door on her wooden cage, Casey threw herself down on the cot. She'd heard Eddy mimic her voice. Mom and Dad would believe it was her and be heart-broken, Randy would never forgive her, and she had no doubt Eddy would say things to Cole that could never be unsaid. The situation seemed hopeless. Suddenly too tired to fight any longer, she turned on her side, and let the tears fall once more.

CHAPTER THIRTY-THREE

Cole's heart raced as the helicopter rose skyward. Skansen owned several buildings in the area, some still standing near where the ranch had been, the others on the mining property itself, nine of which were abandoned. Added to that, there were five other structures in the area near the ghost towns and other abandoned mines. One of them had served as a meatpacking plant until two years ago. Interestingly enough, it now belonged to a numbered company Ryan was still trying to track down. Cole had used it as the location for the ranch he'd created in *Rattlesnake.* They'd decided to look into every building, including that one. Hal and Cletus were checking out the places in town while he and Ryan had taken the search and rescue helicopter up to investigate the more remote locations.

At Ryan's insistence, they'd grabbed something to eat before going to have a second look at the house across the street from Minerva's and discovered someone had broken in through the back door. They'd found Casey's running shoes inside. Hal was having them checked for prints. Knowing Ryan had been right about where she'd been snatched did nothing to reassure him, but it did mean that if he was right about that, there was a good chance the rest of his intel would be correct, too. Her kidnappers had probably waited until most of the crowd had gone and just walked out with her. It was now after two. Casey had been missing for fifteen hours. In most missing persons' cases, the first forty-eight hours were critical. In this case, knowing the man who had her was insane, meant every single minute counted—every single one could be her last.

"What else did you learn when you hacked into wherever it was?" Cole asked, speaking into the radio attached to the helmets they wore, almost afraid to hear what Ryan had to say, but needing to get out of his own head before he drove himself crazy.

"I found out that all three of them were being watched by the FBI."

"Watched why?" he asked.

"When I got into the casino's security camera, I not only found Harvey who was losing big time at the craps' table, but a close friend who seemed to be watching him. According to my informant, the investigation's been going on for more than eighteen months. The three show up at the *Golden Slipper*, that's a Mendosa syndicate casino, at the end of each month, and Trent and Rick drop a small fortune there and in some of the casinos the syndicate manages. My informant said that Rick was down about a hundred large."

"That's a hell of a lot of money. I knew he and Trent gambled—they did back in school but it was penny-ante stuff, usually having something to do with school sports. They were warned a couple of times and threatened with expulsion."

"Well, they moved up the food chain. I had a look at his IRS record, and believe me, while that car business of his does incredibly well for a small town, he can't support the losses he continuously builds up. Strangely enough, he always manages to pay his chit at the end of the run. That's interesting, especially when two years ago, everything he and Gibbs owned was mortgaged to the hilt. The FBI believes the Acuna cartel is bankrolling them, getting them to use the money they get from drug sales to gamble in the syndicate's casinos who in turn support a number of the cartel's supposedly legitimate businesses her in the United States. It's the perfect way to move cash. They can't exactly walk in an open an account at a downtown bank. Those two are compulsive gamblers, and they get to play with someone else's money. The money comes in from Mexico, dirty as all get out and ends up in the casinos coffers nice and clean. They're also moving product in that way, and the only reason the FBI hasn't moved on them is because they can't figure out how the cartel gets their drugs and money to them. Not one of them has been across the border in months."

"Maybe they don't have to," Cole said and explained about the helicopter and the mesa near the first area they would check.

"That makes sense. I'll contact my buddy and the DEA as soon as I get a chance. They can stake out that plateau and catch them in the act. Harvey has two of Mendosa's enforcers on him. At first, I thought they were making sure he didn't leave, but this changes everything. Those goons must be his muscle; they're for his protection."

"The first place we'll search is below us," Cole said. "It would be a good location to stash her. There's a decent road in and out, and the company hasn't mined this particular area in at least fifty years. Leon Turner's body was discovered near here. We found money and photographs in his safety deposit box that point to blackmail."

"That fits with what I discovered. He was collecting antique coins and rare books, something he shouldn't have been able to afford given his declared income. About a year ago, he started selling instead. I figure whoever killed him is the one doing that."

"That would be Trent Gibbs, but we aren't sure he's the one who killed Leon. We think he was blackmailing whoever was involved with that helicopter and might have fallen, saving everyone the bother of killing him. On the left is that plateau I mentioned."

Cole pointed to the deserted area. He'd rarely flown over here which was why he'd never noticed it. Now that he had, he couldn't imagine how anyone could miss it, but landing there at night would be tricky.

Once Cole landed the chopper at the complex he and Hal had checked out the previous Sunday, he used bolt cutters to open each of the three buildings there, but the only thing they found was a family of rock squirrels who'd moved into one of the shacks. He and Ryan removed the plywood boards covering the mine entrance, disturbing an old black-tailed rattlesnake in the process. Luckily, Cole saw it before it could strike and tossed a stone at it. The angry reptile slithered deeper into the mine. Disappointed, they returned to the helicopter. Minutes later, it rose into the sky once more.

"That was a hell of a big snake," Ryan said. "I can take just about anything, but I hate snakes. One of the men in my unit stepped in a nest of pit vipers in Afghanistan. There was nothing they could do for him."

"Hell of a way to die," Cole said, grateful to Ryan for trying to keep his mind off the fact that Casey hadn't been where he'd hoped she would be. "We'll be at the next site in about five minutes. Snakebite's fairly common around here. Doc Creighton keeps quite a bit of anti-venom serum on hand. Each year, the rangers have to airlift some hikers who weren't careful. Most can survive as long as they get the serum in time. Last year, they found a guy who wasn't so lucky. Every now and then, we get these amateur prospectors looking for the Lost Dutchman or Peralta's mine, who go in unprepared for the reality of the mountains. Between 1900 and 2000, more than seventy men went into those mountains and vanished."

"I read about that when Casey told me she had to go home. Peralta's mine. Isn't that the thing Chester Morris and those boys found? Casey told me a bit when she called. I didn't believe those things really existed. I thought they were just legends like the headless bodies."

"Existed is the right word because what Chester found is gone." Cole described the CJKT Discovery and what had happened during the earthquake, omitting only the earth-shattering kiss he and Casey had shared. One he hoped he'd have the chance to repeat soon.

"I'll be damned," Ryan said, amazed by what he'd heard. "At least they got something out of it. Two million dollars is a nice chunk of change. I wouldn't mind having a look at some of those sketches. It's probably just as well. You wouldn't want those kids wandering out there alone."

"I agree. It isn't that the people in the Superstitions are at any higher a risk than anyone else, it's that some don't bother to make a safety plan before they go in there. You explained why the FBI's after Rick and Trent. I assume Gibbs double-crossed them, and they taught him a lesson, one to keep Harvey in line, too. Severing the head to make it fit with the legends was overkill."

"I can't say for sure, but that would be my guess," Ryan confirmed. "Nobody but the FBI and Rick seemed to miss him. Rick called his room more than a dozen times."

"I see. Here we are."

Once again, the helicopter descended, this time scattering a small herd of bighorn sheep, the ram, leading his ewes away to safety. As before, they searched each of the ramshackle buildings and the mine, but found nothing.

In the air once more, Cole pointed to the activity below as they flew over *Lucky Seven*. They'd agreed to leave those buildings for last since the odds Eddy would've taken her somewhere occupied were pretty slim.

"That's the last of Skansen's official holdings," Cole said almost two hours later after they'd checked the ninth one. "The only thing we have left is that slaughterhouse near Goldfield. If she's not there, he's already moved her out of the area. Would he take her to Vegas? I mean is he part of this gambling thing, too? Nothing in what I read in those papers said he would be." But they'd hinted at some of the kind of things he could well be involved in and just thinking that monster had Casey turned his stomach.

"If he is, he's upper management. Someone like him wouldn't take orders well. He prefers to give them. Among the characteristics of a narcissist in addition to having an overblown sense of self, is their belief that they're entitled to special treatment and obedience from others, something their willing to exploit for personal gain. It's all about their fantasies of power, success, intelligence, and attractiveness, which makes them feel superior to everyone, giving them a sense of godhood."

Cole chuckled bitterly. "That certainly describes Eddy."

"You know, when Casey asked me to look into these guys, the first thing that struck me was their ages. They would all have been in school with her. When I met her, she was really messed up. I suspected something had happened, but I couldn't get her to open up. The girl had serious intimacy and trust issues and when that happens it's usually because of some ham-fisted asshole. I started with Trent Gibbs, and although the guy was a first class jerk, his biggest problem was gambling. I talked to his wife, and as far as she's concerned, he still owes the shirt off his back. She's garnisheed his wages—something Eddy would've known about. That might've given him the leverage to get Trent involved with Mendosa and the Acuna cartel. He wasn't a good husband, drank too much and got nasty when he did. Just before she left him, he got really mean. She was afraid and took off, went home where her brothers would beat the living daylights out of him if he ever showed his face."

"I know something happened fifteen years ago that sent her away from here, something so bad she won't talk about it. Last night, she was going to tell me something about the night her horse died, but the fire put that on hold. If what you say is right, my money says whoever was responsible was Rick Harvey." Casey had mentioned Rick and Kristal specifically when she'd said she couldn't come back to Fortune.

"You could be right. He's been known to frequent some of the stranger sex clubs in the area, specifically Lady Helga's Dungeon. One of her girls almost died last year and she banned Rick from entering. But for my money, I wouldn't exclude Eddy. I'd say he was the one who introduced Rick to the pleasures of bondage and sexual sadism. He and Mendosa have similar tastes, and that's why the FBI's watching him. Among the Acuna's activities, they suspect they're involved in sex trafficking and Eddy's their contact. He likes his women submissive. Helga said he got off on fire and pain. She couldn't provide him with the right girls so he took his business elsewhere. We think the cartel gets him what he wants and they don't have to be willing. While they can't prove it yet, he looks good for that case in Henderson."

Cole swallowed. "You mean the woman found in the motel? The FBI sent that to every department. Are you saying Eddy's into that?"

"He is and has been for some time. They were able to identify the woman just last week. She was an illegal from a small town on the Yucatan Peninsula. The family said she disappeared on a school trip to Mexico City. They know those women are being brought to Vegas, but they can't figure out where he's keeping them, and when he doesn't need or want them, there's a hell of a lot of real estate where they can disappear."

The acid in Cole's stomach burned. He had to find Casey, and it had to be soon before that monster touched her.

Ten minutes later, Cole landed the chopper on the far side of the meatpacking plant. The gate surrounding the facility was closed and locked, but the chain looked like a new one.

"This is promising," Ryan said, using the bolt cutters. "Why put a new lock on a building no longer in use?"

"There was a new lock on the shed at the Morris house, too." Cole stopped. "Someone's been here recently." He pointed to the faint imprint of tires on the sand-covered driveway. He pulled out his gun and Ryan followed suit.

Moving stealthily, they approached the building, circled it to make sure there wasn't a car or anything else they hadn't noticed behind it. Satisfied no one was around outside, Cole tried the door. As he'd expected, it was locked. He took a deep breath. Perspiration trickled down his back, and beaded on his forehead and upper lip.

"I've got this," Ryan whispered. He bend down to be eyelevel with the lock and expertly picked it.

Cole opened the door. Hot air gushed out as he did. This building, like most of them designed for the same purpose, was intended to be air conditioned and as such had poor ventilation. The flat asphalt roof would draw the sun to it, working in much the same fashion as a solar panel, but instead of storing energy it would heat the area below it. He swallowed, hoping he was wrong and Casey wasn't in here because if she was, unless she had a fan and water, she could easily succumb to heat exhaustion.

Ryan whistled. "Looks like someone is using this place as a warehouse." He pointed to the boxes, cartons, and crates.

Cole walked over and opened the top box, revealing the Limoges china he'd last seen at Minerva's house.

"This is stuff from the Skansen house," he said, excitement making his heart beat faster. "If this stuff is here, Casey has to be. Casey!" he shouted, the same feelings he'd had that night in the desert coming back to him when she didn't answer. He called again, with the same result.

"This stuff isn't only from the Skansen house." Ryan indicated two large duffle bags. "There's got to be a fortune in pharmaceuticals in these."

Cole nodded and called again, panic filling him. She had to be here. Why wasn't she answering? He refused to consider she wasn't here because that meant they'd run out of places to search, and if she couldn't answer, then he couldn't face that either.

"Maybe she's gagged," Ryan said. "I know the place is in the middle of nowhere, but ... Let's tear this place apart." He held up the bag from the Mexican restaurant. "I found this in the trash. Lunch for one."

Cole checked each of the small rooms, but there was no sign she'd ever been there.

"Cole, over here," Ryan called. "This oversized crate has a door cut into it. It's locked, let me get at the lock."

Seconds later, he opened the door. "She's here," he cried, rushing inside with Cole on his heels.

Cole stopped, the sudden sensation of being gut-punched almost bringing him to his knees. Casey lay on a plastic-covered cot. She was almost as pale as the wet, white blouse she wore. The only color he could see were the red marks on her wrists where she'd been bound.

"Is she alive?" he asked, barely able to get the words passed his dry lips.

"Yes, but her pulse and respiration are weak. She's been drugged, and between that and the heat, she's in bad shape. We need to get her out of here fast." Ryan moved to pick her up and stopped. "Why don't you carry her?"

Cole bent to scoop Casey into his arms. He'd dreamed of doing so, but never under these conditions. As quickly as he could, he carried her to the helicopter, secured her into one of the back seats. While he did, Ryan closed up the building, leaving the boxes there, but taking the drugs with them. If someone came back before they could get officers in place, they didn't want that stuff getting back into the cartel's hands. As soon as Ryan was aboard the chopper, the helicopter rose and headed toward Apache Junction.

"We have her, Hal," he said into the radio, the fear he felt wouldn't leave his voice. "She's unconscious. Ryan thinks she's been drugged. We're taking her into Apache Junction. Contact the hospital. I'll be landing on their roof in about fifteen minutes."

"Where did you find her?" Hal asked, his voice sounding strange as if he found it hard to believe what Cole was saying. "Her mother called me an hour ago to tell me Casey had called and told her she couldn't do it and had taken a bus back to Santa Fe. Maria swears it was her. Apparently she called here looking for you, too."

"They must've forced her to make those calls, to buy time for him to get her farther away." And if she'd told him she was leaving, he might've believed her, but he'd have wanted a damn

SUSANNE MATTHEWS

good explanation for it. "She was at the meatpacking plant. There's a whole lot of stuff here that was taken from the Skansen house before the fire. I guess Eddy didn't want to lose everything. This makes me think he's good for it. There was also two of the bags we saw in those photographs that we've taken with us. Someone had brought her lunch, so my bet is they'll be going back to get her dinner. Get somebody out there to give them a warm welcome."

"Will do. I've got two dozen ADPS officers here, and I'm sending them there right away. We'll catch the bastard, and if he comes out of there in a box, I won't shed a tear," Hal said, the anger in his voice hard to miss.

"Neither will I. Can you call Casey's parents and mine? They must be upset about that call. Convince them it was made under duress. I know they're going to want to come to the hospital, but tell them to stay put. I'll call as soon as I know more.

* * * *

"Come on, Casey. Time to wake up," a woman said.

"Go away, and let me sleep," Casey mumbled.

"I think you've had more than enough of that," she answered causing Casey's eyes to fly open. The voice didn't belong to her mother or Randy.

Where the hell am I?

She wasn't in the crate any longer. They'd drugged her, probably in those damn burritos that had tasted worse than ever. It could've been in the water, even though she hadn't had a lot of it. Where had Eddy taken her? Cole would never find her now. Tears filled her eyes.

"Welcome back. Blood pressure's good," the nurse said, removing the cuff from her arm. A frown creased the woman's forehead. "Are you in pain?"

"Where am I?" she asked, her voice barely a whisper, her throat raw. The tears trickled down her cheeks.

460

"In the ER at Apache Junction Memorial. We pumped your stomach. Your throat is probably a little sore. Whoever drugged you doesn't know the first thing about body weight to drug ratio. He almost killed you. They brought you in about six hours ago."

The curtain parted, and Cole and Ryan entered, both of them looking as ragged as she felt.

"I didn't think I'd be able to keep you two out of here once you heard her voice." The nurse chuckled.

"No, ma'am." Cole moved closest to the stretcher and reached for her hand, bringing it to his lips. "You have no idea how happy I am to see those cat-eyes of yours. I thought I'd lost you."

"That's my cue to exit," Ryan said. "I'll give you a couple of minutes alone and call Hal with the good news"

"Wait," she said, swallowing the discomfort in her throat. "How did you get here?"

"I found that information you needed, and when I couldn't get you on the phone, I flew straight to Phoenix. Red, you know me. Best gumshoe in the universe. I couldn't let my favorite redhead down."

Ryan stepped through the opening in the curtains and closed them behind him, giving them as much privacy as possible considering the circumstances.

"I thought I would never see you again," Cole said softly as he bent his head and captured her lips.

Casey returned the kiss hungrily, desperately, pouring all of her pent up emotions into her response. When Cole ended the kiss and pulled away, his eyes shone with unshed tears.

"I was so afraid, but I knew you'd find me, just like you did in the desert." She touched the side of his face, his stubble rough against her palm. Tears filled her eyes and spilled down her cheeks. "I'm such a fool. When Minerva told me Eddy knew about Chester's plan to marry her, I suspected he had a motive to kill him. I went looking for Hal and saw Eddy across the street. It was beyond stupid of me to approach him. I should've gone home with your mother."

Her sobs intensified, as she realized once more how foolish she'd been. Cole sat on the edge of the bed and pulled her into his arms. The strong, steady beat of his heart reassured her. She was alive and they were together. Sniffling, she raised her head.

"How did you know where to find me?" she asked.

"I didn't. I wasn't even sure who had you. If it hadn't been for Ryan ... He was convinced Eddy had taken you, and it was just a matter of searching everything Skansen owned. Of course, we didn't realize the meatpacking plant was his until after we'd found you. The only reason I even thought of looking there was because I'd been out there when I researched *Rattlesnake*."

"Eddy's insane. He's responsible for all of it. He didn't kill Trent and Leon, but he knew about it, and he didn't even care. He did killed Chester and Sylvia himself. He's a monster." She wouldn't mention what he planned to do to her. Just thinking of what could've happened to her made her tender stomach roil.

"Shh!" Cole said. "You can fill in all the details later. Ryan showed up and told us about Eddy's past." He explained everything Ryan had told him, and the more he talked, the more horrified she was.

"Wait. He's going to have Horace and Minerva killed. He told me so."

"Ryan suspected as much. Before we went up in the chopper to look for you, he called the Apache Junction police department and made arrangements for Clara, Horace, and Minerva to be moved to another part of the hospital while making it look as if they were still in their assigned rooms. They caught Jose Alvarez sneaking into Horace's room with a syringe full of ethylene glycol. The man's singing the sweetest serenade in the hope of escaping the needle. Not sure he will, but if he does, he'll be spending the rest of his life in prison. The first thing he did was try to make a deal by telling us where you were. I think the guy was actually worried you might die if he couldn't get back to you."

"I would've I'm sure. Before whatever he gave me kicked

in, I was so warm and all he'd left me were two bottles of water." She shuddered, realizing how easily it would've been for her to die.

"Drugged water. It's a damn good thing you didn't drink both of them."

"What about Eddy? Have you caught him?"

"Not yet, but the FBI has set up a reception committee for him in Vegas. According to Jose, that's where he was headed after his meeting with the BLM officers about his great solar farm project. He needed to check out of his hotel and come back to Fortune, distraught over the loss of his home and his aunt's death. Rick and a few associates in Vegas were going to provide him with an alibi. I told you the man's a treasure trove. My only regret is that Eddy may never stand trial and get what he deserves."

"He's insane. You should've heard him bragging about how he killed Chester and Sylvia."

"Don't worry about that now. We'll get him and everyone else involved, and put an end to whatever this is once and for all. You're safe. That's all that matters to me."

He pulled her into his arms once more and his lips claimed hers.

"Can I come in?" Ryan asked, interrupting the kiss. "Don't stop on my account."

"Get over here, you," Casey said holding out her other hand to him, not letting go of Cole's.

"I've got some good news. The FBI have picked up Eddy and Rick. They managed to get them after they'd checked out of the hotel, so no one should be the wiser. According to Jose, there's supposed to be a drop off and pick-up tomorrow night. It seems you were on your way to a house Eddy maintains south of Sonora. Once they get the guys in the helicopter, the Mexican police will raid that place. By the way, your mother was really upset by that call."

"Oh God," Casey cried. "He said he was going to call. I'd hoped he hadn't had the time to do it. Call the FBI and tell them not to let him near a phone. I didn't make that call, Eddy did He's a mimic, one of the best I've ever heard." She snuggled deeper into Cole's arms. "He's insane, and far more dangerous than I could've imagined."

"I suspected that, but if he can mimic voices like that, he could get himself released. I'll make the call shortly, make sure they don't let him near a phone without someone on his six. You know, that could be how he managed to get out of the asylum in the first place. We'll tell you all about it tomorrow. Now, the nurse says we need to get out of here and let you rest," Ryan said. "I know Cole won't leave the place without you, so the two of us will be camping out in the waiting room. They'll let you go in the morning." He kissed her forehead and winked. "Two minutes, Cole. Red needs to rest."

"Red, I like it," Cole said. "Now. Try to get some rest. I'll fly you home tomorrow. I guess we can let Kristal know she can make it to the celebration after all."

"Wait. There's something I have to tell you. It'll take more than two minutes, so I hope that nurse is patient. After we left the Pearson ranch, I was supposed to tell you what happened the night Ginger died."

"Casey, you don't have to tell me, not unless you're ready to. It won't make a difference to the way I feel about you."

"I know, but I want there to be no secrets between us. Back in high school..." She talked about the bullying, the loneliness, the dreams and hopes, the thrill of her first date, and the way it had all gone so wrong. "After they released me from the hospital, it took me six weeks before I felt well enough to leave. All that time I hid at home. I wouldn't go out, terrified that someone would say something or that Eddy had taken photographs. A few of the kids called, but I had Mom make excuses. I didn't want to talk to anyone, and so I slunk away in shame and that's it. Now you know all about Cassandra's Folly. Your turn." Silent tears crawled down her cheeks.

Cole pulled her into his arms and held her. He didn't speak. Instead, he feathered kisses on her brown, her cheek, the side of her neck. After what seemed like an eternity, he tilted her chin so that she could see his face.

"Rick Harvey is very lucky I didn't know what he'd done to you because if I would've known, he would've been chewing his food on its way out for the rest of his life. I can't begin to imagine how humiliated and upset you were, but I do know you did nothing wrong. I have a sister. I understand how devastating what you went through could be, so what do you want to do?"

"Do I want to charge him? No, I think Kyle and Kristal had a rough enough road ahead of them without that to deal with. For years, I thought Kristal has set me up, but now that I know she didn't and he's going away for a long time—money laundering, possession with the intent to sell, racketeering, not to mention fraud and tax evasion, and possibly collusion in the Henderson murder and the sex trafficking ring—I think I can count myself lucky. I did give him a pretty good knee in the balls."

Cole chuckled. "That's my girl." He kissed her tenderly, the kiss full of promise. "Now, I've definitely overstayed my time. Get some rest. I'll see you in the morning."

* * * *

Casey stood next to Cole looking up at the band shell where her parents stood with his. Wearing the beautiful costume her mother had made her, she felt like a princess. Beside her stood Kristal and Kyle, and if anyone thought the sight of Casey and Kristal chatting and laughing as if they were old friends, was odd, no one said anything. Randy and Jaxon were with them too, as well as Drew Macintosh. It seemed Randy had decided to give Drew a second chance, too.

"And now, Minerva Skansen has an announcement," the mayor said. "I know I speak for all of you when I say how grateful all of us are to see her here today."

Ms. Minerva, wearing a green gingham dress and bonnet, one her mother had probably stayed up all night sewing, walked to the microphone. The woman had aged since Friday night, not surprising given everything she'd been through. She would be staying with Noella and Senior for the time being.

"Thank you, Mister Mayor." She let out a deep sigh picked up by the microphone. "When I arranged to speak today, I had planned to give you very different news. There comes a time when a person has to make a decision about their future. At my age I don't have that many days left, but I can't complain. So, I was going to leave you my home, but there isn't anything left there; however I understand a number of the treasures it contained were saved. It was Chester Morris's dream to turn his home into a museum to the Superstition Mountains and it is my intention to do whatever I can to facilitate that. I intend to replace my home with the Chester Morris Superstition Mountain Museum and will be allocating funds from Skansen Mining to maintain it in perpetuity. I will also be setting up a Chester Morris Scholarship at the high school in honor of a great man. Thank you."

Applause broke out with cheers until the guests left the stage and the band took their place.

Casey walked over to Minerva and hugged her. "I'm sure he would've loved this."

"We spent our whole lives apart," Minerva said, her voice filled with so much sorrow it made Casey's own heart ache. "I can only hope we'll get to spend eternity together. Remember what I told you. Follow your heart. Love is too precious a gift to waste."

Cole put his arms around her and pulled her close to him. "Let's get out of here. I think you've had enough excitement for the day," he whispered in her ear.

"I couldn't agree more. Are we going back to the house?"

"Not tonight. I've got something else to show you. It's okay, I told your parents we would be leaving early. It's time for us to have some quiet time alone."

Forty minutes later, Casey stared in awe at the simple yet elegant bedroom bathed in the soft glow of lamplight. Cole's cottage was decorated simply using Native American artifacts. Throughout the house she'd seen a number of original items including, rugs, decorative bowls, and ewers in Navajo, Hopi, and Apache styles. The paintings on the wall included some of Kyle's watercolors of the desert and Superstition Mountain. While all the rooms were gorgeous, this one was an absolute gem.

A stone fireplace, its hearth full of wood waiting for a match, took up most of the far wall. Beside it sat a full wood box. The focal point of the room was a king-sized bed covered by a beautifully woven blanket, its cream silk sheets shimmering invitingly. Near the patio doors leading out onto a deck that faced the lake, there was a small sofa, and a desk and chair. In the corner, a four-foot Saguaro cactus had been decorated with white miniature lights, giving the room a magical quality.

She turned into Cole's arms, her eyes awash in unshed happy tears.

"Cole, it's perfect. It's just perfect! I love it." She kissed him softly and felt him relax.

"When I bought this place, I wanted it to be as simple and yet authentic as I could make it. I needed a place where Tate Silvers could feel at home, a place where CJ's creative juices could stir, but most of all, a place where I could unwind and relax. Now, I want it to be a place where you can stay without any shadows of what happened to you creeping in to disturb your happiness."

She smiled. "That can't happen when you hold me like this. You rescue me from all the bad dreams. When I'm in your arms, I feel safe and protected. More than that. I feel whole."

"Our engagement was supposed to last until the case was over. Well, Rick and Jose are in prison in Phoenix and Eddy is locked in a secure room at the state psychiatric facility where he'll spend the rest of his life. He'll never stand trial for what he's done. There's no doubt in anyone's mind that he's insane. Minerva feels responsible, even though she isn't, and she'll see he gets the best care. The DEA have that mesa staked out for tomorrow's drop and as soon as that's done, thanks to Jose, they'll move on the rest of the information he provided. It's over. That being said, I don't want the engagement to end. I love you, Casey. I have since the first time I heard you talking to my dad at the emporium. I can't imagine my life without you in it. I don't care where we live I just want to spend the rest of my life with you. I've given you the ring, will you keep it and marry me?"

Tears filled her eyes, and she kissed him tenderly. "Yes. I love you, too."

"That's what I hoped you would say." His mouth claimed hers.

The kiss was everything she knew it could be, the seal on a promise of that happily ever after she'd never hoped to have. He ended the kiss and gazed down at her, his eyes filled with the love he'd declared.

"Fortune can be a great place to live, Red," he used the nickname he'd borrowed from Ryan and she smiled.

As a teen, she'd hated it, but now, when he or Ryan used it, it reminded her that people in her life cared about her.

Cole held her close. "Horace is awake and his offer of partnership still holds. If you give it a chance, I think we can be happy here, but if you want to stay in Santa Fe, we can make it work, too. I'll need to spend time here feeding my muse, but it's all up to you. As Ryan put it, I've joined the 'wherever thou goest, I'll follow' crew. I love you, Casey."

She licked her lips and smiled. "If that's the way you feel, it's settled then. I've come home to stay. I love you Cole Warner Junior, and I'll learn to love Fortune, too."

THE END

ABOUT THE AUTHOR

Amazon bestselling author Susanne Matthews was born and raised in Cornwall, Ontario, Canada. She is of French-Canadian descent. She's always been an avid reader of all types of books, but with a penchant for happily ever after romances. A retired educator, Susanne spends her time writing and creating adventures for her readers. She loves the ins and outs of romance, and the complex journey it takes to get from the first word to the last period of a novel. As she writes, her characters take on a life of their own, and she shares their fears and agonies on the road to self-discovery and love.

Not content with one subgenre, Susanne writes romance that ranges from contemporary to sci-fi and everything in between. She is a PAN member of the Romance Writers of America. When she isn't writing, she's reading, or traveling to interesting places she can use as settings in her future books. In summer she enjoys camping with her grandchildren and attending various outdoor concerts and fairs. In winter, she likes to cuddle by the fire and watch television.

Would you like to contact or follow Susanne?
http://www.mhsusannematthews.ca/

SUSANNE MATTHEWS

www.ingramcontent.com/pod-product-compliance
Lightning Source LLC
Chambersburg PA
CBHW051056030726
47504CB00006B/1652